Praise for
Darden North

"One of the best things about *The Five Manners of Death*—and there are many—is that none of the characters are who they appear to be. If you like plot twists and surprises, you'll love North's fifth novel, a fast-moving story of crime and deception in the modern South."

—John M. Floyd
Edgar Award nominee and three-time Derringer Award winner

"Darden North's *The Five Manners of Death* starts at Ole Miss in 1966 and takes us on a fast-paced ride to present-day Jackson, a ride so filled with twists and turns that it leaves us breathless. North gives us just the right details to make every scene happen at a place we recognize and make every character a person we have known at some time. He makes us want to know what happens next, and that just keeps those pages turning."

—Martin Hegwood, Author
Jackpot Bay

"Any reader will be spell-bound and fascinated."

—Gayden Metcalfe, New York Times bestselling co-Author
Being Dead is No Excuse

"… a suspenseful ride striking up feelings of fear, sadness, joy, and shock."

—Denise Grones
Delta Magazine

"Extraordinary and accurate descriptions … make the medical thriller realistic … the 'truth' of medical fiction."

—Lucius Lampton, MD, Editor
Journal of the Mississippi State Medical Association

"*House Call* is a murder mystery from the 'get-go.' Darden North, MD, may become to the medical mystery genre what Grisham is to the legal thriller."

—Mary Emrick
Bluffs and Bayous Magazine

D1328593

"*Points of Origin*('s)... heart-stopping, spellbinding ending ... haunted me for days after closing the cover.'
—*Reader Views*

"*Fresh Frozen* should come with a warning label: Insomnia and repetitive motion disorder caused by rapid page turning may result."
—Kathy Spurlock, Executive Editor
The News-Star

"Darden North has delivered with his latest. *Fresh Frozen* is no quick-and-easy 'beach' read, but instead makes the reader pause, look deep inside, and question his own ethical and moral standards. North is a talented writer."
—Susan O'Bryan
The Clarion-Ledger

"North's visually acute, action-packed style ... is likely headed for the silver screen ..."
—George Halas
New York Journal of Books

"A rollercoaster ride of murder, intrigue, and plot twists. *Wiggle Room* keeps you turning the pages to the final, climactic finish."
—Robert Dugoni, New York Times best-selling Author
The Jury Master

"*Wiggle Room* [is] a cleverly plotted, strongly written medical thriller [that] will pull you into a story world filled with danger, excitement, and conflict at every turn."
—D.P. Lyle, Macavity Award-winning Author
Run to Ground

"Darden North is one of those writers who pays meticulous attention to getting the detail right in the course of his riveting thrillers and *Wiggle Room* is no exception."
—Mason's Bookshelf
MBR Bookwatch

"*Wiggle Room* is a suspense-chocked, mature, medical/military mystery with smarts to boot. The end was a surprising – but exceptionally satisfying – conclusion to a shivering ride of deception and murder.
—*BookFetish*

THE
5
MANNERS
of
DEATH

Previous Novels by
Darden North

House Call
Points of Origin
Fresh Frozen
Wiggle Room

THE 5 MANNERS of DEATH

A novel of suspense

DARDEN NORTH

WordCrafts

The 5 Manners of Death is a work of fiction. All references to persons, places or events are fictitious or used fictitiously.

"Out of suffering have emerged the strongest souls; the most massive characters are seared with scars."

Kahil Gibran

TO MY MOTHER, EVELYN HAYS NORTH

ACKNOWLEDGMENTS

I would like to thank the following for their assistance in research for this novel: D.P. Lyle, Dick Wilson, Ed Hooker, Saeed Bajestani, Evelyn North, Tad Barham, Toni Upton, Mart Lamar, Bill Sneed, Marsha Cannon, Karen Cole, Amanda Johansson, Louis Wilkinson, Winn Walcott, Robin Ervin, Sally North, Anderson North, and William North. I reference D.P. Lyle, MD's column "Forensic Files" in the January 2008 issue of the *3 rd Degree*, the official newsletter of the Mystery Writers of America.

My advance manuscript readers included: Karen Cole, Evelyn North, Edra Kimmel, Ted Barham, and JoJo Payne. I am indebted to all of them. Hubert Worley is credited for the author photo on the cover. Many thanks to publisher Mike Parker and the staff at WordCrafts Press for taking me on.

I am also grateful to John Hough, Jr, not only for his literary wisdom and editing skills but also for his tremendous encouragement.

The character name *Phoebe* was sponsored in a silent auction benefitting the work of Peyton's House, a ministry supporting inner city youth—417 West Ash Street; Jackson, Mississippi 39203.

PROLOGUE

*W*ho calls a 45-year-old man a sissy?

Bob shook his head and climbed onto the bulldozer.

The assistant project manager saw him through the window of the job trailer and dropped his paperwork. He jumped from the cluttered metal desk and ran outside. "Hey, I was gonna take care of that," Carlos yelled up to the cab.

"Nope, it's my turn," Bob said. He closed the door, shutting out his assistant and the rest of the world, and jerked the machine deep into the work site. Rain delays had pushed the project on the University of Mississippi campus six weeks out. "I didn't operate a dozer for 27 years for nothing."

The bulldozer rolled up a small knoll, flattening a line of wiry vegetation that might have been a row of wild blackberries, then descended into a shallow creek bed camouflaged by tall ferns and vines. A few small rabbits ran for cover. Bob once admitted to his wife that he cried over crushing a rabbit's nest. That had earned the *sissy* comment. She laughed when he grimaced over the gory tangle of bloody grey fur discovered behind a rear wheel. Now she was his ex-wife, and he saw her in the path ahead. *If only that were real*, he thought.

Bob shoved onward with the power and forgot her. He admired this virgin patch of landscape around him, untouched by paved roads, dormitories, and parking lots. The surrounding terrain of oaks and poplars burst into a white blanket of early spring dogwoods, broken by a lone pink variety peeking through. Bob dropped into a creek bed, probably a ravine drained bone dry by the growing town and university. To the side, he envisioned scores of kids, maybe Indians, maybe hundreds of years ago, leaping from the large smooth rocks now partially covered by oak leaf hydrangeas.

Then the machinery lurched upward, rising onto smoother topography covered in scrubby vegetation, mostly overgrown brush and scattered trees. Bob looked to the left and right. *Maybe a walking path or narrow road ran through here?*

"Hey, Granola Boy." Carlos' voice boomed from the radio into the cab. "My job was to fill in that sink hole. Since you hijacked the dozer, push down everything real smooth. Me and Jerome be right behind you with fill dirt."

Bob turned the bulldozer inside the narrow clearing. He took a deep breath and rolled toward an earthen mound just outside the edge of the dry ravine. "This will make 'em all happy," he said.

His fingers squeezed the life from the hydraulic controls, blanching around the black shaft until his joints stung. The blade rose upward, then forward, pounding against the mound. Even though enclosed in the cab, he was enveloped in the cool rot of leaves interlaced in the fertile soil before him. The moist rich compost rolled nicely into the bin of the shovel like spools of carpet. He dropped the load into the void of the dry ravine, coming back for more. With each pass the mound seemed to melt under the power of the machine. Bob remembered what drew him to this, long before he went soft. He dug deeper.

There was nothing left to take down but the more mature trees growing haphazardly along the creek bed. He changed direction and tried to ignore the bright green leaf buds. "These oaks look at least fifty years old."

Bob pulled again on the control shaft and heaved the soil and roots into the center of the shovel, then dumped the load. The sheets of earth and vegetation fell in dismal slow motion. He felt numb.

Carlos was on the radio again, agitated. "Right behind you, Bobby Boy. You're the boss, but we all want to get back to Arkansas. Pick up the pace."

"Stuff it, Carlos," Bob answered. "Not much left to clear. I got this." The vegetation destroyed and most of the topsoil scooped away, he repositioned the bulldozer for the next section and checked the last load from the bin. The consistency of the fallen material appeared different—maybe just litter from oak tree roots or branches. One piece stood out as a slim, short, broken branch. He jerked the controls to finish emptying the bin. A similar piece fell, the same length and diameter as the first. *No way that's a piece of a tree.*

Stumbling from the cab, Bob fell into a soft pile of layered pine straw and twigs left crushed by the machine. He grappled for the two-way radio and snapped it from his belt.

"Carlos, get on out here and take over."

Another object dropped from the debris left in the shovel, the form different from the branches, almost rounded in shape. It struck a firmer section of ground and bounced to settle at his feet. The empty sockets of a human skull stared up at him. Bob realized that the splintered branches from the destroyed oak trees were human bones, femurs.

He screamed and kicked the skull toward the creek. It wobbled over the layers of dry leaves, striking the pair of bones, then rolled against a dense stand of ferns to stop upright. The hollow eyes glared at him. One of them winked.

Bob ran at the skull again. The soil left wedged in the mouth flew away on impact, the skull falling into an uncovered area of the once deep ravine, a tangle of roots twisting it back and forth as it fell. He was sure it winked at him a second time, and he screamed again—this time louder and with more of a shrill—a woman's scream.

His two-way radio—the transmission light was on. "Damn! They heard me. Those asses heard me!"

Bob jerked the radio off his belt and threw it after the skull. The radio missed and smashed against a large rock, a tombstone of sorts, splintering into pieces.

CHAPTER 1

Phoebe struggled against the sheets, pushing up with her arms. The glass of water on the silver tray rocked back and forth on the bed.

"Is the funeral home here?" she asked and settled against the pillow.

"No, because you're not dead," Diana said. "At least not yet."

Diana blotted the sweat from her aunt's forehead—skin hot enough to singe fingertips. She jerked away from the rattling cough that followed. Diana could not be sick too.

Phoebe managed to cling to the bed sheets instead of rolling to the floor. She shook her head when the hacking passed. "I told you to use one of the linen handkerchiefs, the ones with my initials."

"Forget the Emily Post," Diana said. "Here, take a sip of this." She put the fresh Waterford tumbler from the nightstand to Phoebe's lips. The red mane swung free of the pillow, strands of hair matted on Phoebe's forehead. Diana bent and tried to fluff the pillow back into shape. The satin felt moist, almost gummy. She gave up and flipped the pillow over to the unused side.

"For heaven's sake, please fill that glass with something besides water," Phoebe said, swallowing hard. She almost floated back against the padding. Despite the cigarettes abandoned a few years ago, cocktails every afternoon, and a two-day fever racking her delicate frame, Diana Bratton's aunt remained beautiful. No one judged her a day over 40, much less over sixty.

"Vodka and soda is in the rosewood cabinet inside my dressing room," she said, handing the glass of water back to Diana. "Get it, please, and refresh the philodendron in the corner with this."

"You should have listened to me about that flu shot," Diana said.

Phoebe took the monogrammed linen handkerchief from her. "This is a family heirloom—my family. It belonged to my mother." She blotted her forehead, then tossed the handkerchief atop the used pile near the lamp.

"I've never been much for free advice, even from you, Dr. Bratton," Phoebe said. She reached for a fresh piece of linen from the Chinese porcelain tray near the bedside table, one of the pieces of china left uncrated for the move.

"I should have sneaked that syringe of flu vaccine out of the office and popped you with it myself—a real freebie." Diana shielded her face just as more coughing and hacking racked Phoebe's body. "It's never too late for the pneumonia vaccine, but I give up."

Diana opened the drawer in the bedside table and unwrapped the small package underneath the magazines, ink pens, and note pads. "Will you at least take a breathing treatment?"

Phoebe grabbed the nebulizer, inhaled twice and sputtered. "You mentioned your office—makes me think of your surgery partner. A woman I play bridge with calls men like that arm candy."

"Brad's been real busy. We just had our seven-year anniversary."

"Should have been a wedding anniversary, my dear." She grabbed an extra puff on the nebulizer. "Not long ago, you and your Doctor Brad Cummins were all but married—except for the ring."

"I'll ignore that," Diana said. "Here's a fresh handkerchief." She dodged the path of the next coughing spell.

"*Arm candy*," Phoebe gasped. "Just thinking about that Dr. Brad Cummins makes an old lady feel better."

"This thing isn't doing you much good, even if overused," Diana said. She tossed the nebulizer at the oxygen tank. It landed near the head of Phoebe's four-poster mahogany bed and slid along the floor to behind the drapes.

"You sound worse." She dug a digital thermometer and stethoscope out of her purse. "Inhale and exhale, deep," she ordered.

Phoebe obeyed with deep breaths and release. "Where's that other thing going?"

"In that know-it-all mouth of yours," Diana answered. She put the stethoscope aside and placed the thermometer under Phoebe's tongue. "Your lungs sound horrible—like a tornado—not to mention that your temp is still up."

"I probably have pneumonia."

"That's another vote for the vaccine; and instead of a hearse, I'm calling Metropolitan for an ambulance."

"Please, please, Diana, don't. This is such a close-knit neighborhood, lots of busy-bodies. Sirens will cause such a stir."

"You're moving out of this place. You don't care what the old neighbors say," Diana said.

"Thank goodness we closed on the new house before I got sick, and I'm glad that I bought a place in town."

"Regardless, I should have insisted you go to the hospital sooner," Diana said. "Except for Kelsey, you're the closest thing I have to blood kin."

"I give up. Maybe you're right." Phoebe reached for the thick white cotton robe at the foot of the bed. The new silk one from Neiman Marcus remained boxed in her closet. "Here, help me with this thing and then get me to your car. Seeing your beautiful daughter once I'm settled into my room would really cheer me up."

Diana wrapped the robe around the sheer pajamas, moist from sweat. Phoebe's skin felt clammy. "Covering up is probably wise. This slinky outfit may get you arrested when we roll through admissions," Diana said. She eased Phoebe into the silk slippers waiting on the Oriental rug. "Better yet, maybe we should change you into something less provocative. I'll check your closet."

A long row of cocktail dresses and tailored suits on hangers lined the walls to the left and right of the master bedroom closet. A built-in bank of drawers was located at the end of the space. Diana searched and found a pink fleece set neatly folded in the bottom drawer.

"I'm glad everything is not already boxed up," Diana said. "Let's slip you into this."

"No, no. I'm much too weak to change clothes." Phoebe stood, unsteady at first, then grabbed her purse from the dresser, clutching it to her chest. She coughed and sputtered as they moved down the hall toward the living room. "Doctors and nurses make note of expensive pajamas. I won't part with these," she said.

Diana caught Phoebe before she stumbled over the stuffed boxes and cartons piled in the entrance hall. "OK, you win. We'll go as you are, but once I turn you over to the hospitalist, I'll come back and pack a bag for you," Diana said. "You won't need much. The gift shop will have toiletries."

She took Phoebe by the elbow and guided her out through the front door, past the white columns that anchored a wraparound porch extending across the front and along the sides of the house. Down the steps, at the foot of the narrow driveway, a dumpy, red-faced man in his sixties stopped to fumble with a plastic Wal-Mart shopping bag.

"Wouldn't you know it," Phoebe whispered under her handkerchief, "that fool, Carvel Eaves."

"Afternoon, ladies. Lots of tidbits on my afternoon stroll," he said. Like a pendulum, he swung the bag stuffed with empty soft drink and beer cans, crumpled fast food bags, and gum wrappers in Phoebe's direction.

She frowned and opened the door to Diana's car. "Interesting hobby you have, Carvel—keeping our Belhaven neighborhood free of litter during your walks. But I don't have time for ..." (The comment was stalled by another round of coughing, topped off with a protracted wheeze.) "... time for your nonsense today." She slid inside the car into the passenger seat.

Carvel Eaves leaned toward Phoebe. "Never know what people will toss out into the streets," he said. "Most of the time it's teenagers throwing beer cans out the window before mom and dad see or discards flying out the back of their pickups. Sometimes it's just careless trash collectors." Carvel took a second look at Phoebe. "Looks like you're a little under the weather, Miss Phoebe."

"You're not listening, Carvel," she said. "My niece and I are in a terrible rush."

"A rush? Just like during last Saturday's bridge tournament?"

"That wasn't me with the mistakes. Your game was off," she answered. "When I trumped you and closed you out, I was just trying to end the misery for us all." Phoebe tilted her head past him through the window for an even longer, deeper coughing episode—this time punctuated with two wheezes.

Diana opened the driver's door and tossed her white jacket out of the way to the back seat. She patted Phoebe on the back until the coughing and wheezing ceased. "Tell Mr. Eaves goodbye. We need to get to the hospital," Diana said.

"You do sound rough, Phoebe," Carvel said. "Guess you'll miss this weekend's bridge tournament and your master points?"

"Seems I will. My niece thinks I'm on death's door and insists on the hospital. She's a doctor, you know ... a surgeon."

"Everybody knows that, Phoebe. She fixed my golf buddy's hernia." Eaves reached low for the plastic cup lid and drinking straw spotted near the curb and stuffed his bag. He smiled. "No complaints since."

"Carvel, we have to go. Start the car, Diana."

Diana pushed the ignition switch.

"Funny you said something about death's door," he said. Carvel leaned closer, then seemed to think better of it. He smoothed the piece of paper. "Let's see ... The paper is old. It's some type of list ... The printing is a little smeared and definitely faded, but at the top it says *The Five Manners of Death*." Carvel tipped his Ole Miss baseball cap. "Better be careful at that hospital, Phoebe. Seems there are several ways to go."

"My God, Carvel. Those were notes from a college English composition class, creative writing. I found that when packing for the move and threw that ancient garbage away," Phoebe said. "Even now, I can't seem to get rid of those papers—thanks to busybodies like you."

He spotted a weathered, rolled-up newspaper flattened against the curb across the street. "I better get that. Newspaper decomposes quick." Carvel stuffed the sheet of paper back into his makeshift trash bag and headed across the street.

"Unique little man, that Mr. Eaves," Diana said and closed her door. Forgetting the car was already running, she again pushed the ignition, then placed her cell in a compartment on the console.

"Never mind that old fool. He tried to convince my bridge partner to go to the golf party at the country club last Christmas, practically begged her to date him." Phoebe fished a fresh disposable tissue from her purse, which nearly disintegrated under more coughing and hacking. Then there were sneezes. "Her husband hadn't been dead a month."

"Maybe you should just rest quietly," Diana said. "Let your seat back with that button between the seat and the door."

Diana reached for her cell but remembered the Bluetooth. "I better give a heads-up to the hospitalist at Metropolitan," she said. "He won't mind; he gets paid per admission." Diana pushed *CALL* on the steering wheel and spoke the name.

A voice blared from the stereo speakers. "Dr. Bahrain here." Startled, Diana swerved to miss the edge of a brick pillar marking the entrance to a driveway.

"Diana!" Phoebe screamed. "Is it too late for that ambulance?"

Diana straightened the vehicle and slowed at the four-way stop to turn the corner. She took a deep breath and answered the hospitalist. "Ahmed, this is Diana Bratton. Can you take a look at my aunt? She's not any better. I think pneumonia has complicated her asthma."

"Sure, Dr. Bratton. Bring her on in. I'll expedite the admission and fix her up in no time."

"Thank you. We're 15 minutes away." They ended the call just before Phoebe started to wheeze and cough. Diana reached behind to rummage through the pockets of her lab coat in the back seat. "I think there might be an extra inhaler in here," she said, "a sample from the office medicine closet."

"Diana!" Phoebe grabbed Diana's shoulder. "Something's ahead in the street."

Diana dropped her lab coat and swerved to miss the crumpled mound lying on the pavement. She slammed the brakes, the shoulder straps jerking them against their seats. Diana checked the rearview mirror, unbuckled her seatbelt, and sprang from the car.

Several aluminum cans, a rolled newspaper, and a plastic sack were nearby. It was Carvel Eaves. The note in Phoebe's handwriting lay next to him.

CHAPTER 2

"I thought I quit smoking in time to prevent all of this." Phoebe pulled at the plastic oxygen tube clipped inside her nostrils, picked up the knife on her hospital tray, and stabbed the butter pack. It burst open. She carved the butter onto her toast, spreading a thin, even layer.

Diana stepped back from the bed. "At least your voice is returning and so is your strength, it seems," she said. "You're lucky, Aunt Phoebe."

"Lucky? And why is that?" Again commanding the butter knife, she pierced each packet of jelly, the grape spread on one piece and the strawberry on the other.

"Yes, lucky. You scraped by with only bacterial pneumonia, and your chest x-ray is clearing. I slipped into radiology and took a look."

A man spoke from the opened door. "She's not the only lucky one, Diana."

"Dr. Cummins!" Phoebe fanned herself with her napkin. "Somebody better check my temperature," she said. "But sorry, Doctor, I don't need surgery this time."

"Good to know, Miz Phoebe, but Diana is the one I'm looking for."

"Brad, I'm not due at the office until 10:00."

"It's not about that. I talked to the medical examiner. Eaves' death was ruled natural causes. He had an acute MI."

"MI? That means heart attack, I believe." Phoebe took a generous, noisy bite of her toast and chewed. "When Carvel interrupted us in the driveway, the ol' busy body seemed the picture of health," she said before swallowing. "I don't think he has any family, but we should still send flowers."

Brad moved closer to Diana. "Can you help on that colon resection later today? It was posted before all this went down."

"No problem. I'm still on for your case," she said. "You know, I barely missed running over Mr. Eaves' body."

Phoebe paused between swallows of the fresh fruit cup on her tray, pushed aside what was left of the toast, and started on the crumbly scrambled eggs. "Whatever happened to Carvel Eaves, it was an act of God."

"Act or no act," Diana said, "he seemed well just a few minutes before. I'll check on you later this afternoon after clinic and surgery."

Brad smiled goodbye to Phoebe and followed Diana out of the room. They walked the short distance down the hall to a cubbyhole behind the nurses' station filled with computers.

"Guess who's scheduled to see me this morning in the office—Alex's new wife," Diana said. "He's bringing her in himself. And please don't say a word about it to the Queen of the Neighborhood back there."

"Wow, I'm not sure I'd tackle that," he said. "Treating an ex's new thing? Are you sure?"

"Why not? Alex and I are civil. We have a child together. Besides, he had another wife between Blythe and me."

"You're a better man than I, Diana Bratton," Brad said as he took one of the chairs at the computer bank and logged into the electronic medical records system. "What's going on with this third Mrs. Alex Bratton?" he asked.

"Severe abdominal pain, Alex says—onset of pain after she eats."

"My guess: gallbladder," he said.

"Congrats. *A-plus* to the med student here." Diana sat at the next cubicle. "I suggested she follow-up with her reproductive endocrinologist in New Orleans, the one giving the hormone treatments. But Alex wouldn't have it. He wanted Blythe to stay in town and see me, so I put her down for an abdominal ultrasound."

"She taking hormones? How old is this chick?"

"Only twenty-eight, but still not pregnant. Alex shared his sperm count with me—much more information than I wanted to know." Diana entered an incorrect password, was denied computer access, and started over with her log-in.

"I could have seen her for you," Brad said, "particularly if you feel uncomfortable taking her on."

"I suggested that, but it seems that Alex doesn't like you. Can't imagine why." On the third try, Diana's list of hospital patients populated the screen.

"Feeling is mutual, but you knew that already," Brad said. He clicked out of the computer screen as he stood. "I'll see you in the OR this afternoon ... and good luck with the bastard and Mrs. Ex."

Brad walked around the corner into the nurses' station. He thumbed through a rack of patient charts arranged by room number and slid out several. Before heading toward the patient ward, he stuck his head into the physician computer area. "Give my best to Alex and my condolences to the new bride," he said.

"Alex will be so glad to hear from you," Diana muttered. She entered her notes from morning rounds into the computer. When finished typing, she searched for Phoebe's file. Although her aunt by marriage was not technically her patient, Diana had made the referral to the hospitalist and initiated this admission. "I'm not breaking any rules, if I take a peek," she said.

She scanned the updated information including the day's entry: *Condition Stable, modest improvement.* "I bet what he wanted to say was *Mean as ever.*"

Diana logged out of the hospital portal and accessed the remote link to her office patient list. *Blythe M. Bratton* remained on the schedule: the last morning appointment.

"I'm surprised they didn't cancel. Since when did Alex follow through with anything?" she asked aloud. "Dealing with Mr. and Mrs. Bratton will probably cost me lunch."

"Tell me when the pain started."

Blythe Bratton lay supine on the examination table, her pale complexion and delicate, fragile features a sharp contrast to Alex's tanned skin and muscular build. He sat in the small corner chair at the head of the table and practically filled it, close enough to stroke his new wife's blonde hair. Blythe was without make-up and looked ashen, but they were still a beautiful couple.

Diana's medical assistant, Grace, a pudgy African-American woman in her early forties, entered the room carrying another pillow.

"When did I start hurting?" Blythe said. "A couple of nights ago. At first, I didn't think much about it. Can I have that extra pillow now?"

Alex asked, "It started under your ribs, on the right side, didn't it, Babe? Pretty bad ... wasn't it?"

"And it's worse after I eat." Grace motioned for Blythe to lift her head, then gently slid the pillow into place. "Thank you," Blythe said.

"Blythe's not a complainer, and she's not a big eater, either—real healthy lifestyle," Alex said.

Diana smiled. "I think that's obvious," she said and checked her notes. "It's clear you're not feeling well, Blythe. Don't worry. We'll figure out what's going on."

Blythe put her right hand behind her head against the two pillows. "I think I would feel better if my head was raised up even more. Alex, would you toss me that cushion from the other chair?"

"She exercises 24-7," Alex said, grabbing the thin cushion from the straight back chair across the room at the computer desk. He eased it behind his wife's head. "Guess what that quack infertility specialist recommended? He wanted her to gain 10 pounds, or maybe it was 15. That's some shit, huh? Blythe's never seen a fat day in her life."

Diana did not flinch. "Does it hurt here?" She pressed just under the last rib on the right. "You're not the type to have gallbladder problems. Most women with gallstones are overweight."

"It's not her appendix?" Alex asked. He tried to fluff the pillow. It would not give.

"No," Diana answered without looking over to him. "The appendix is in the right lower quadrant of the abdomen, not in the upper area where Blythe is hurting."

"Let her be the doctor, Alex," Blythe said. "Why don't you go back to your trainer at the club and the tanning bed." She reached for the basin on the nearby metal tray and gagged.

Diana removed a clean hand towel from a drawer and moistened it under the faucet. She blotted Blythe's face and looked over at Alex. Her ex-husband was smiling at his new wife, encouraging, and gently stroked her arm. His swollen, bronzed biceps stretched the sleeves of his polo. Between hours at the gym and having sex with Blythe, Diana wondered how things were working out at Alex's new law firm.

"I've warned you about all the tanning between workouts," Diana said.

Alex looked even more handsome than the day they divorced. She felt the same when he dropped Kelsey off after soccer last Sunday and walked their daughter to the door instead of the usual abandonment at the curb. Alex had been that attentive to her when they first started dating during residency. He even did the shopping when she had to study or work at the hospital.

"Remember, Dr. Bratton," Blythe said. "I'm the patient here."

Diana chuckled. "Fair enough. Okay, we'll start with a CBC and check your urine for a UTI and make sure you're not pregnant, although I'm just about 99% sure that it's gallbladder. We'll see what shows on ultrasound down in radiology."

Grace left and promptly returned with a wheelchair. "We'll need to go by the lab first for the blood work," she said, smiling.

"Blythe, I'll meet you downstairs," Diana said, "and check the sonogram findings myself."

"Don't I need to go with her?" Alex asked.

"Most guys would," Diana answered. "You know, like to hold the wife's hand?"

"Dr. Bratton, you think I'm a wuss, but I can handle it," Blythe said. "Besides, Alex hates places like labs and small, dark rooms." Blythe managed a smile and smoothed her hair. The assistant helped her into the wheelchair, and Blythe grabbed a tissue from the box near the dressing area as they rolled by. "This nice lady can keep me company."

"Maybe your wife is right, Alex. You nearly fainted when they drew blood for our marriage license," Diana said.

Alex laughed. "Nailed by two women—two wives. Guess I'll skip the blood spurting into a glass tube and a dark, cramped room with lights flickering on and off." He rolled the magazine he had been reading into a tight cylinder and blew into the end.

"Like I said, don't worry about me." Blythe took control of the chair, and Grace trotted after her. "Look, I'm feeling better already."

A chill permeated the room. Diana and Alex were left in an uneasy silence.

"You haven't changed," Diana said, staring at him. "Not one bit."

"And you're surprised?" he said.

Diana stepped to the desk, pushed aside the chair, and looked down to the laptop. She reached to run her fingers across the keyboard but never pressed *SAVE*. "I have other patients waiting."

"I'm sure you do." Alex walked to the door, the magazine even tighter. "Any guys waiting? Still hooked up with Brad Cummins?"

"Hooked up professionally." She tapped the keys even faster. "The practice is doing well, really well." More keys. "I put more on the books than he does."

"Glad to hear it. That's good for Kelsey."

Diana turned to the door. "Kelsey will be fine, but you're still on for child support—even if you are trying to replace her."

"I guess I was out of bounds bringing Blythe here. No matter what we've been through, no matter what I've done, I've always respected you as a doctor, Diana. Damn, you always do the right thing."

"Cut the crap, Alex." Diana walked into the hall for a paper file stuffed in the rack just outside the door. She lifted the patient information and spoke back into the room. "Wait, Alex, if you dropped the crap, there wouldn't be much left of you."

Alex followed, putting his hand against the wall to her right, his arm brushing against her. His body blocked movement in the other direction. "Believe it or not, I made law partner last year," he said. "I'm trying to spread my wings, move on. Maybe you should too."

Diana flipped through the papers like a deck of cards. She suddenly remembered Carvel Eaves, the crumpled paper, and his trash bag. "I need to go down to radiology."

"Getting pregnant was Blythe's idea," Alex said. "When it didn't happen after six months of hooking up almost every night, sometimes twice a day, she panicked and went to that doctor for hormone treatments." He grinned. "Can't say I haven't enjoyed the effort."

"We'll find you in the lobby after the ultrasound," Diana said. "Maybe you can bill an hour or two of legal work while you wait. Scrap paper is in that drawer back in the room if you need to make some notes."

"Or I've got games on my iPhone." Alex waved the phone in front of her, then tapped her shoulder with it. "Diana, would you help me if something happens to Blythe?"

"Nothing's going to happen to Blythe. If the ultrasound shows gallbladder, the surgery is routine, simple."

"We'll just have to trust you, I guess. You're the doc." Alex slipped past her.

Diana studied her ex-husband as he walked down the hall toward the waiting area. *What kind of help was he talking about?*

The desk phone rang. It was the first-floor radiology department. "Need you down here, Dr. Bratton. STAT!"

"Bridget? What's wrong?" The ultrasound technician was not one to panic.

"It's the lady you just sent down for a gallbladder sono. She stretched out on the table and then stopped breathing."

CHAPTER 3

Phoebe sat in a straight-back chair in front of the large window in her hospital suite, holding a china coffee cup and saucer—her personal pattern. Despite the upgraded room and the higher floor, the view was nothing but a busy construction site across a crowded parking lot.

"Why didn't you choose that more comfortable club chair or the loveseat?" Diana asked, entering the room.

"No need. It's time to go home," Phoebe answered. She balanced the cup and saucer in her left hand and fingered the pearl necklace and jeweled collar pin with the right. "I know the diamond earrings are costume, but on me everyone assumes they're real."

"Looks like I followed directions," Diana said. "You look ready to greet the outside world." The tailored ensemble accented Phoebe's white complexion and green eyes. She looked renewed and healthy.

"Oh, yes," Phoebe said. "Thank you for dropping off this suit and the jewelry."

"Sure," Diana sighed. "No one would ever guess that Jackson Metropolitan Hospital has kept you captive for a week. I wish I had your genes."

"You'll have to settle for genes-by-marriage," Phoebe said. She lifted the coffee cup. "I tipped the nurse's aide a dollar to bring me the newspaper and a refill." Phoebe's slurp surprised Diana. "Damn, only lukewarm. I wasted that buck."

The morning newspaper lay open on a small table beside her. "I've been checking the obituaries. Never miss a day, first thing." Phoebe said

"Anything about Blythe Bratton?" Diana asked.

"Nothing. Just a couple of old school teachers and a bank president," Phoebe answered.

"I guess it'll be in there tomorrow," Diana said.

Another slurp. "The write-up for Carvel Eaves a few days ago was so exaggerated—golf trophies, bridge tournaments won—but not many mourners listed. I guess he wrote it himself," Phoebe said. She stood, set her cup and saucer on the table, and moved closer to the window. "When are they going to let me out of this tomb? We certainly aren't waiting for a bellman."

Diana did not look her way. "Alex will probably sue me over Blythe's death," she said. "That's what he does best."

Phoebe reached into her purse for the inhaler. "He's still Kelsey's father. He'd never do anything like that." She inhaled deeply. "That foreign hospital doctor ordered this twice a day. I'll never be able to pronounce his name."

"We did CPR, used the AED unit, did everything we could to resuscitate Blythe until the paramedics arrived."

"Didn't you say the poor girl had seen some other doctor before you?"

"Alex and Blythe were trying to have a baby, but nothing had happened. She started having abdominal pain—stomach pain—a day or two before she came to my office."

"She wasn't pregnant?"

"No, but I'm telling you too much."

"Promise I won't breathe a word at bridge next week." She grabbed the inhaler again and coughed after two more puffs.

"Dr. Bahrain confided that you've got five days of antibiotics left to take at home. That should be about 15 capsules."

"I'll think about it."

The door opened to a moving wheelchair, pushed by the certified nursing assistant. "I see you've got another visitor. Oh, it's you, Dr. Bratton," the CNA said.

"Hi, Annie," Diana said.

"We hate to see you leave us so soon, Miz Phoebe," Annie said. She positioned the wheelchair near Phoebe. "But you gotta go sooner-or-later. You ready to be set free?"

"Go ahead with Annie. You'll need to sign yourself out. I'll get the rest of your things."

"Need some help?" They turned to the voice in the doorway.

"What's up?" Diana asked.

"Just came by to pick up Blythe's autopsy report," Alex answered. "Thanks for getting a rush put on it."

"Sure. But the ME's report will be in hospital administration on the first floor. You're nowhere close."

"I heard that Aunt Phoebe was ill, and I was concerned. That's another reason I came by."

"Alex, the divorce included me too," Phoebe said, "so you can drop

Aunt." The nursing aide helped her into the wheelchair. "Are you coming, Diana?"

"You go ahead. Like I was saying, I'll get a cart from the nurses' station for your flowers and bag."

Phoebe smiled at Annie and frowned at Alex. "We can wait for Diana. Can't we, dear?"

"Need some help?" Brad Cummins rolled a heavy aluminum cart equipped with empty shelving into the room. "Found this down the hall."

"On second thought, Diana," Phoebe chuckled, "I'm saying good-bye and putting you in charge of this little soap opera."

Diana wished she could find the humor. "We're good here. Meet you at discharge. The clerk will need a few minutes with you to sign papers."

"Should Annie call security before we leave?" The CNA pushed Phoebe down the hall, Phoebe's laughter fading toward the elevator.

Alex lifted a couple of flower pots and stacked them on the cart. "My real reason for coming by is to get some advice, Diana." He eyed Brad. "Didn't expect to get a double whammy: two experts."

"What's the problem, Bratton?" Brad brushed by him to reach the arrangements nearer the window. He pulled the cart away from Alex and loaded it. "Diana told me years ago that you weren't much for asking advice, much less taking it."

"Cummins, I'm not interested in anything you and Diana have discussed. I came here for some help."

"Please, both of you, just knock it off," Diana said.

Alex walked deeper into the room toward the window. "How come that infertility specialist didn't find what was wrong or even suspect a problem? he asked. "My wife had been using her for months ... all kinds of expensive drugs and tests and x-rays."

"It's normal for you to have questions, to want to know why." Diana said. "Have you talked to the doctor?"

"I guess we saw this coming," Brad said. "The blame game." He shook his head, lowered it, and backed away.

"Of course, I met with her. All she did was pull the file, shove all the treatment consents in my face ... showed me where Blythe signed for every surgery and medication. Her initials were all over that shit. What's worse, that crazy bitch charged me over $30,000."

"If you want to point fingers, you might as well hold me responsible."

"Diana, that's crazy," Brad said. "Blythe Bratton was your patient for only a few minutes."

"Hang on," Alex said. "Are you acting as Diana's business partner or ex-boyfriend?" He continued the stare out the window.

Brad kicked the door shut, rushed to Alex and threw him away from the window against the wall. Alex shook it off and lunged at Brad. Locked chest-to-chest, the two men stumbled together against the table with the china and newspaper. The cup and saucer crashed to the floor with Brad and Alex falling atop the splintered pieces.

Pushing up first, Brad dusted off his scrub suit. "You're the lawyer, Bratton. You figure it out," he said.

Alex sat up on the floor and brushed clean the lapel and sleeves of his tailored suit before standing to face opposite Brad.

Diana did nothing during the seconds-long wrestling match but admire the brawn of each man: a six foot two or three physique, similar narrow waists that rose to broad level shoulders, and hard, muscular legs. Each man still had a full head of hair.

She could not deny what had been her initial attraction.

"Asshole, you'd better add personal assault to your list of hospital privileges," Alex said. "Maybe you can take some weekend training course or something. Even get the hospital to pay you for it."

"Get outta here, Bratton," Brad said.

"Let it go, Brad," Diana said.

Brad shook his head slowly, but stepped away, his gaze locked on Alex Bratton.

"You've always been a top-notch physician, Diana," Alex said. "I'm not looking to sue you. Like you said, I just want somebody to sort this out for me. I need some answers."

Diana considered the suggestion that the three of them take a seat but thought better of it. "Maybe this will help, Alex," she said. "The final autopsy findings had not been released when I checked yesterday afternoon, only the initial report. Blythe's abdominal pain was from ovarian hyperstimulation syndrome, and that condition can lead to heart failure. Her shortness of breath was the first clue, but I decided she was reacting to the pain of a rotten gallbladder."

"That's all you need to hear, Bratton. The infertility specialist explained all the pros and cons of the treatment. You just admitted that."

"What Brad means is that what happened to Blythe is a recognized, but rare, complication of advanced infertility drugs," Diana said.

Alex removed a thick brown folder from his coat pocket, sealed at both ends and handed it to Diana. "Well, I have the completed autopsy report," he said.

"I'll look over this tonight, ask some questions of the ME and Blythe's doctor, and let you know," she said. "But if her physicians sense that you're looking for trouble, they won't be so open to talk off the record."

"Thanks in advance for the effort, Diana," Alex said, brushing away the wrinkles in his suit and straightening his collar. "And another thing. You don't need some dickhead doctor like Brad Cummins to take up for you. You never have."

Grateful for his silence, Diana felt Brad's daggers for Alex as he left. She slid the folder of autopsy results between two potted plants on the cart and a tightly wrapped basket of fruit, a gift from one of Phoebe's bridge clubs. The tag read: *Get well soon. We need our master player back!*

"The grieving widower," Brad said as the door snapped shut behind Alex. "I'm touched."

Diana remembered one of the last nights with Alex before she filed for divorce. She ran her fingers over the lower edge of her blouse, the place where his belt snapped across her chest. Her rib felt sore. "The grieving widower," she said.

CHAPTER 4

Key Martin wedged his coffee cup between several Styrofoam empties, the Jackson Police Department insignia peeking through the collection. Case files still under investigation covered most of the remaining desk surface. He crushed each empty cup and used his arm to rake the bits of Styrofoam into the trash can beside his desk.

"Just tidying up a bit," he said. "Come on in, Dr. Bratton. It's been a while." Martin stood as his secretary escorted Diana into the office. He studied the remaining mess on his desk and pushed several photos into a haphazard stack. The effort made the clutter worse.

Diana remembered Detective Key Martin as taller and younger. It had been over six years, and he was now chief of police. She accepted the seat across from his desk.

"I've been busy … raising my daughter and working, building my surgical practice."

"It's always a busy place around here, Doc, and these cases don't always go by the book." He picked up one of the files and turned it toward Diana. An 8 X 10 color photograph was clipped to the front. "Coroner thinks this one's self-inflicted."

"And you say no?" Diana asked.

"The bullet took off most of her forehead," he said. "Women don't usually disfigure themselves in suicide cases. Most kill themselves with pills or maybe poison."

Diana studied the photograph, gruesome even to a trauma surgeon. "Types of death that follow the rules or a list, or maybe don't quite make the list. That's sort of what I wanted to talk about."

"Well, here's another." Martin produced a photograph of another young woman, Caucasian. Her hair color matched Diana's shade of brunette, only cut shorter. She still wore jewelry. "I agree with the ME on this one—suicide."

"What's her story?" Diana studied her features and the earrings. "What kind of work did she do … or was she a student?" she asked.

"Pharmacist," Martin answered. "One of the chain stores snapped her up right after she graduated. Top in her class."

"That's it—the earrings. She always wore some style of butterfly earrings. This is the girl who worked nights at the drug store on Lakeland."

Martin smiled. "Good work, Dr. Bratton."

"A pharmacist has easy access to poison, to pills, handy for committing suicide, so not a worry when inventory comes up missing," Diana said.

"Family says the girl didn't even drink, but toxicology was positive for barbiturates."

"No one suspected she was depressed?"

"Sort of reminds me of that case in 2006—the crazy, dead nurse," Martin said, "the one that involved your boyfriend."

"Dr. Cummins and I have moved on."

"But you two are still associates. Partners, I should say, working partners, that is. I check your clinic website from time to time, and you've cut on some of my friends."

Diana stood and walked to the bookcase on the other side of the office. The dust looked the same as in 2006, just more of it. She overcame the urge to run her forefinger through the thick layer. Some binders were turned to the back, exposing edges of bound documents. Some books rested face forward. Some had landed askew when stacked on the shelving. Skinny paperback journals were piled on the top shelf, the corners of the pages sharp. They had never been read.

"What can I do for you today, Doc?" Martin asked.

"A lot of people around me are dying, Detective. She remembered the promotion and his desk placard. My apologies, I should say, *Chief* Martin. I came down here curious about two deaths in my circle of things; however, this makes three—if you widen the circle and count the poor pharmacist."

"So? Some patients live and some don't make it. Isn't that part of what you do, Doc?"

Diana slipped a nervous laugh. "Up until a couple of days ago, I had seen my share of people die. Some hemorrhage or code in the operating room; some roll into the ER all shot up or cut up; some drift away in their hospital beds. But something just doesn't seem …"

A loud echo of high heels came from the hall. "Excuse me, Chief Martin," a woman said from the doorway. "The Northeast precinct commander wants to brief you on that robbery in the church parking lot. She's made an arrest. TV reporters are all over it."

The woman's attempt at well-dressed was a dark suit rescued from the final sales rack at Chico's, Diana supposed, her heels and platform shoes too high and too clunky.

"Jade, give me a sec. Tell them *no comment* until I finish up with this."

Diana started for the door, walking past the secretary. Martin followed.

"Sorry to take up your time," Diana said. "Not really sure why I came down here."

"Have the commander wait for me in the conference room. Pretty please."

Jade nodded and left, again in a trail of echoes—even more commanding than before.

Diana remained just inside the doorway.

"You said you were curious about some deaths." Martin tossed the photo of the dead pharmacist to his desk and rummaged through the other files. From the rear, his soft, growing beer belly was hidden, the three-inch wide bald spot at his crown now the focus. Even with that, Diana did not find him unattractive.

"Are you talking about outside the hospital, people that are not your patients?"

"Well, sort of. First, a man drops dead on a street near my aunt's house. I almost ran over the body."

"A Mister ... Eaves." He produced a folder and looked inside. "Carvel Eaves, that's right. Not much gets by me, Dr. Bratton. You've been on my radar more than just keeping tabs on your website from time-to-time."

"Why am I not surprised?" she asked.

Martin returned the file to the desktop. He slid it and other documents around the surface as though making another attempt at organization. He finally tossed the file to the top of the pile.

Diana frowned. "Then the next thing that happened—my ex-husband's new wife died in my clinic."

"I didn't hear about that one, but I'm surprised you would go there."

"I surprised myself." Diana turned toward him. "Alex, my ex-husband, brought her by my office for a second opinion. All I did was order a couple of tests."

"So, the lady's death ... not your fault? Not really?"

"Not my fault. Really. Even the ex admits that. She suffered complications of medical treatment; she just happened to be in my office when she died. At first, I didn't think so much about it—the fact that I'm the common denominator in these deaths."

"These deaths—Eaves, Mrs. Bratton, and now your pharmacist—all different circumstances, and most likely all coincidence," Martin said.

Shoes clacking again in the hall ended with the secretary popping her head around the door. Jade grinned at Diana. "Sorry, Chief, but the commander says the press conference can't wait. The grandmother of those two young men booked for the church robbery is demanding to have her own press conference. She even called local TV herself."

"Looks like I gotta go, Doc. Don't let all this get to you." Martin grabbed his jacket from behind the door while Jade waited. "Bottom line: I think your ex is getting under your skin. I never have let mine get to me—none of 'em."

"Miss," the secretary said, "I'll escort you to front reception."

Diana followed her to the elevator, checking her iPhone for new messages. She was free—no one, not even Kelsey or Phoebe needed her, at least not at the moment. Phoebe was busy following up with her internist, and if his schedule was anything like a surgeon's, the appointments were running behind. Diana took the short ride to the lobby and walked to the street. This was a cool spring day, low in humidity, no hint of the upcoming hot Mississippi summer. A few minutes were left on the parking meter.

Traffic was light as Diana pulled out onto East Pascagoula and drove toward State Street and the exit to Interstate 55 North. *Martin's probably right*, she thought. *My imagination's gotten the best of me.*

Time remained for her to run by the office and catch up on medical records before driving back to pick up her aunt. They planned to attend Blythe Bratton's funeral visitation later in the afternoon. Alex would be in his element: standing in a black, lawyer-type suit; dark hair gelled perfectly in place in whatever he considered the hottest style; people lined up, a long line, anxious to see him.

✠

"I might as well get used to waiting in enclosed spaces," Phoebe said. "I'll be locked in a coffin soon."

"Most doctors' waiting rooms are a lot smaller," the man seated next to her said. "And I've seen my share. Besides, this one has that big window behind us, looking out into the garden and fountain."

"This clinic keeps patients waiting forever," Phoebe said, tossing her magazine to the lamp table. "You were here when I checked in over an hour ago."

In the row of chairs along the opposite wall a young mother breast fed her baby under a nursing cover. Beside her sat an elderly woman sporting a jeweled walking cane. She was in deep conversation with the silver-haired man next to her. A middle-aged couple near the check-in window struggled with the patient registration forms attached to clipboards.

Phoebe glanced over her shoulder through the window. Two women in surgical scrub suits took a seat on the stone bench under the ornamental magnolia. One of them lit a cigarette. The other plucked potato chips out of the bag, then slowly unscrewed the cap to a bottle of Coke. "See, look at that. No one seems in a hurry."

"It's worth the wait," the man said. He turned the page of his sports magazine. "I'm here with my wife. She came down with cancer a year ago. This doctor definitely knows his stuff. The chemo has beat it."

"So far, that's good," Phoebe said. She turned away as two young men in white uniforms tossed a football in the greenspace adjacent to the garden. She adjusted herself in her seat. "Don't get me wrong. That news does sound encouraging, very hopeful."

"And you?" he asked. "How have you been?"

"I know I should be grateful that I'm not in that same predicament." Phoebe caught herself. "I mean, I should be grateful that my pneumonia is better, that I only have pneumonia. I was in the hospital recently. Lots of those horrid IVs."

"My sweet wife knows all about those."

Phoebe said, "I thought you divorced her years ago."

A tall, emaciated woman appeared standing above them. She looked ashen.

"Darling!" The man stood, dropping his magazine to the chair cushion. "You're finished with the doctor. I didn't see the nurse bring you out."

"He's ordered another PET scan." The wife spoke in weak monotone. "The results of my blood work trouble him. His chemotherapy nurse is also worried."

The man took his wife's arm and walked her in the direction of the reception and check-out window. "I'm sure everything will be fine," he said. "Let's see when the doctor wants you back."

Phoebe sat forward in her chair, studying them, her copy of *Delta Magazine* held tightly against her chest.

"Miss Phoebe?" a nurse with a clipboard of papers called from the open door to the exam area. "You ready to see us?"

"What an odd thing to ask." Phoebe's answer carried across the room. "You kept me waiting long enough to take a nap. Problem was—the couches were taken." Phoebe stood and tossed the new magazine to the sofa table. Her voice and the thud of the magazine striking the surface startled the wife. She turned toward Phoebe in tears.

Phoebe strolled toward the nurse. "Question is," she said, "Are you ready for me?"

CHAPTER 5

Diana's cell rang, interrupting the monotonous flow of cars and trucks on the interstate leading downtown. Despite the clear weather, traffic moved slowly. The new ring tone had been a surprise from Kelsey, a downloaded clip from the latest Justin Timberlake song. Diana groaned and answered.

"I'm sorry, Dr. Bratton, but Miss Phoebe asked me to call you again," the receptionist at the internal medicine clinic said. "She's outside pacing."

"Thanks, but I'm trying to get there. Five o'clock traffic starts earlier and earlier."

A white sedan was pulled off to the right. The rear tire was flat. A woman and two children stood on the shoulder of the highway, leaning against the railing. A busy grocery store parking lot surrounded them on one side of the thoroughfare and a gas station serving fried chicken on the other. A police car had come to their aid, and the other vehicles moved past like a triple line of snails. Fifteen minutes later a road construction project on Fortification and State Street slowed Diana even more.

Diana spotted Phoebe in front of the office building and pulled close to the curb. She leaned toward the passenger door and lowered the window. "Sorry, traffic was a nightmare."

"I was tired of waiting inside, so I decided to meet you here," Phoebe said.

"And so I heard."

Phoebe tossed her purse onto the seat through the window, snapped the door open toward her, and fastened her seat belt inside the car. "I didn't want you to have to bother parking."

"Thanks," Diana said. "So how did it go?"

"Doctor said the reaper would get me sooner or later, but not from my lung problems."

"Good to know," Diana said.

"And he told me to give up cigarettes for good."

They drove north on State Street. Traffic began to mimic the highway. "We better hurry," Phoebe said. "I wanted to be home in plenty of time to redress for the visitation. But you know … on second thought, let's stop in Fondren for a drink to celebrate my return to good health."

"No way. I've got to take call tonight for Brad. He's got some meeting to go to. And I shouldn't miss the visitation."

"Then you can just have a tonic or soda water or a Coke Zero. Besides, my doctor might have the wrong diagnosis. I could be living on borrowed time."

"We're already been through that. Your internist is very thorough. And if he says you're OK, then I think you'll live long enough to see Kelsey graduate from med school."

"Diana, you've got to live a little."

"Still no," Diana said. "And you look fine. We're going straight to the visitation."

"I should have moved from Dallas years ago to help you, when I still had my health. Maybe you could have cultivated more of a social life and learned how to chill."

"My life … my social life … is fine, just fine, and I don't need …"

"OK, OK. I give up on the advice," Phoebe said, pointing. "But if we can't stop for cocktails, at least pull into that convenience store and let me get a beer or maybe a wine cooler."

"That Coke Zero did sound good." Diana turned into the parking area of the convenience store, driving past the passenger side of an empty black Lexus sedan parked alone at the fuel pumps. No cars lined the storefront.

Phoebe's seatbelt had crinkled the collar of her suit. She tried to smooth it. "I really do need to freshen-up a bit."

"You wait here. I'll get the drinks," Diana said.

Phoebe unbuckled and continued to straighten her clothes. "No, I need to go in. This is a clean place. Nice ladies' room."

"Then we'll both go."

Both women retrieved their purses and walked toward the front door. The quiet outside struck Diana odd. "No one else stopping for gas or coffee after work?" she muttered.

"Too anxious to get home, I guess."

Phoebe was first through the entrance. A girl stood frozen behind checkout, the man from the internist's office before her as though preparing to pay. A bottle of water and what looked like a pack of gum waited on the counter. "It's you again," Phoebe said to the man. "Are you with your wife?"

"Left her at home," the man said. He was tall and distinguished, nice-looking for his age—somewhere in his late sixties.

A young male in a dark leather jacket with ashy colored skin stood pressed against the man's back, his lips quivering. A baseball cap and sunglasses hid the upper half of his face, and a rhinestone stud earring covered more than half the left lobe. He seemed nervous, edgy.

Otherwise, the store appeared empty, quiet.

"Then you and your wife must live near here," Phoebe said. "But I've never seen you in the Belhaven neighborhood."

"We live in Madison."

The young male pressed even closer to the man.

"Let me introduce you to my niece, Dr. Diana Bratton." Phoebe offered her hand to the man. "And I'm Phoebe …"

"Shut up, old lady!" The young male stepped back. His teeth were yellowed and broken. The barrel of a revolver slid out from under his jacket. He waved it at Phoebe and Diana. "See this, bitches? Get down on the floor, face down, hands behind your head. And toss those purses on the floor, over here by me."

"I don't think I can do that, young man," Phoebe said. "It's my knees. I won't be able to get up."

"Lady, if I shoot your brains out, you won't need to get up!" He pointed the gun squarely at Phoebe. The girl behind the register screamed.

"Aunt Phoebe, let's do as he says. I'll help you." Diana looked hurriedly around the store and out the front door. They were alone, still no other cars outside except the Lexus. Diana threw her eyes at the clerk. *Isn't there something you can do?*

The terrified girl remained frozen, then a weak female voice floated from behind the cracker and chip aisle, near the rack of Doritos and SunChips. "Winston, I'm feeling a little better now after the restroom. I splashed some cool water on my face." A sickly woman appeared holding what was left of a bottle of Gatorade. "You need to pay for this, and could we go on home? I don't want to run any more errands."

The young man glanced at Winston, then fired his gun in the direction of the woman. The sound exploded in the compact store. Winston's wife fell against a stack of empty boxes and plastic bags, disturbing only a few of them. A deep red stain rose in the center of her chest, spreading through the thin fabric of her jumpsuit.

The next sound was a shrill, chilling scream from the girl behind the counter. The shooter pushed Winston toward her, scattering a box of chocolates near the credit card terminal and ran toward the door.

"No, you don't!" From her position on the floor, Phoebe swung her purse in his direction. The young man deflected the bag with a kick, firing again, shattering the glass storefront.

The clerk screamed again as the shooter disappeared across the parking lot. "I just activated the police alarm. It's silent," she said.

Diana pushed up from the floor and ran to the man's wife. "Phoebe, call *9-1-1!*" she yelled. Diana checked the carotid pulse—nothing. The blood stain continued to grow across the woman's chest.

"You're a doctor," Winston said. "Why can't you do something?"

Diana applied pressure between the breasts with her right hand and turned the woman onto her side, supporting her head and elevating it with a box of Wheat Thins. "I'll do what I can, but could use some help until an ambulance gets here," she said.

"Help you do what?"

"CPR." Diana started chest compressions.

"I'm afraid I don't know CPR," he said.

"Then stay out of my way," Diana said and switched to the single rescue technique.

Sweat erupted on Diana's forehead. She checked the pulse again. "Damn. Nothing," she grumbled, then realized that Winston had heard her.

"Doctor, should I call someone else to help?" he asked. He pulled the smart phone from his pocket and held it near his face, almost to hide it. Diana thought she caught a wave of relief in his expression.

Phoebe pushed past him. She was panting. "Diana, the operator said an ambulance was coming. They're sending one from the hospital down the street."

Diana wanted to wipe her hands clean on her slacks but decided against it. They were covered in blood. She spotted the roll of paper towels at the coffee bar but started another series of compressions, almost in reflex. There was no respiratory effort, no cardiac response from the victim.

"Might as well call 'em back," Diana said. "Tell them no need to hurry."

The girl flew from underneath the counter to dodge the broken glass and run into the parking lot. Two patrol cards sped toward her. Diana remained facing Phoebe with Winston behind her. She wondered why he had not knelt over his dead wife and wept or at least called her name.

CHAPTER 6

"With your recent track record, you should hole-up in the OR for the next few days," Brad said. "You're a lot safer holding your own weapon."

Diana was positioned to the patient's left, Brad to the right. Mallory, their surgical tech, stood beside Brad, nearer the foot. She hummed to the music playing in the background of the surgical suite. The anesthesiologist had downloaded Adele's latest hit and remained engrossed in Solitaire on his iPad.

"A surgical scalpel hasn't been the problem." Diana clamped a bleeder, then tied it off. The suture slid smoothly between her fingers. "I'm glad the black cloud hasn't followed me into the hospital."

"If you're looking for a black cloud, Dr. Bratton, I'd like you meet my first husband," Mallory said.

The three laughed. The anesthesiologist did not look up.

"A few years ago the black cloud was Detective Martin," Brad said, "barging into and out of our office, almost every day—a real pest."

"I gave my statement to the police officers on the scene in the convenience store," Diana said. "I don't think Martin will be hounding me like he's done before. Besides, he's chief now."

"Great. I like the idea of keeping the killings away from the clinic and the hospital, and especially my condo." Brad lifted the edge of the incision with a retractor and Diana systematically palpated the interior of the patient's abdomen. She inspected each segment of intestine to run the bowel. Brad thought about the murders of his brother and fiancée in 2006. Until the cases were finally solved, Martin repeatedly questioned Brad and Diana, treated them as though suspects.

Diana said, "Over the last few days, I've witnessed the unexpected death of three people, and I know of a fourth."

"Wow, this talk is a little much for me," Mallory said.

"Remember, what's said in the OR stays in the OR," Brad said.

"Got it, Dr. Cummins. Always."

"Let's see, Diana," he said. "There was that Mr. Eaves and his MI, your ex's wife and the complications of her infertility treatment, and the attempted robbery at the convenience store. I don't know of the fourth death."

Diana asked, "Do you use any of the pharmacies on Lakeland Drive?"

"No, I try not to be sick."

"Chief Martin showed me pictures of this young pharmacist, a suspected suicide. They found her in her apartment or condo. She filled prescriptions for me."

"Suicide. That's a shame."

"I knew her, Brad. Not personally. But it's another death that's crossed my path, sort of. Damn, what's next?"

"I'd keep my nose in an incision if I were you," he said. "Stay off the street."

"The five manners of death," Diana said.

"The five what?" Brad put two clamps across the splenic artery and then divided it with surgical scissors. "You gonna help with this dissection or am I solo?"

"Just hear me out." Diana leaned across the surgical field, her surgical mask at Brad's ear. "Mr. Eaves, my aunt's neighbor, the first body—Mr. Eaves showed us a note he picked out of the street trash. The paper looked old, dingy. It was a list of the typical causes or events that lead to death."

Mallory handed forward the Metzenbaum scissors from her instrument tray. She waved it between the two surgeons, waiting for a taker. Brad took the scissors and proceeded to release the spleen. He delivered it and passed it off to the back table. "Send that over to pathology for a gross," he said.

"Wait a minute. Whose case is this, anyway?" Diana said.

"The surgeon with the scissors or the knife, that's who," Brad answered. He irrigated the surgical site with warm saline and checked for any bleeders. "The fella that showed you and Phoebe the note? Thank goodness the poor guy was post-mortem when you nearly ran over him." He chuckled.

"You're not taking any of this seriously," Diana said between her teeth, pulling away from Brad's face. "And quit giving me hell about Mr. Eaves."

She relieved Mallory of a second pair of scissors and pushed Brad's hands out of the surgical field. "Anyway, his death was by natural causes, and natural causes is one of the five on the list."

Brad blotted the site of blood, improving exposure so Diana could continue the procedure. "Then Alex's wife—was her death also natural?"

"Maybe accidental," Diana said. "At first, you could have called it undetermined or unclassified."

"I know how to classify Alex Bratton," Brad said. He shifted his feet and cauterized a bleeding vessel using a bovie. The small metal clamp securing the vein sparked under the electric current. "I haven't seen him snooping around since he came by your aunt's hospital room."

"Neither have I."

"To me, a guy who's recently lost a wife would be a little more upset," Brad said. "That day with Phoebe, Alex seemed to be more about answers than grief. A nice tidy package—ready to move on."

Diana said, "Alex was born self-centered." She motioned for suture to close the incision. Mallory produced a zero loop PDS loaded on a needle driver, and Diana drove the needle into the tissue. "I'm sure Blythe saw that quality once she got to know him, just like I did. But I guess she didn't care."

"Then why'd you marry him?" Brad asked.

"For the same reason Blythe did." Diana blushed behind her mask.

Mallory giggled. "I like this kinda conversation a lot better."

"And that big reason gets old after a while. Doesn't it, Mal?"

More giggling. For a few seconds, Mallory stepped away from the surgical field to her instrument table.

"I'll see Alex again at parent-teacher conference this Friday. I'll get enough of him then, but not in that way." Diana tossed a bloody gauze at Mallory when she stepped closer to the patient. "Come on, girl. You act so innocent!"

Brad began to fire the skin staples in the incision as Diana applied tension to approximate the skin edges closely. "Problem for Kelsey at school?" he asked.

"Her grades have slipped a bit. It's probably her age and the hormones."

"If some of those tween guys are messing her up, just let me know," Brad said.

"Sure." Diana waited for Brad to place the last staple. "Over the last year Alex has taken more of an interest in Kelsey—even been on time with child support. Kind of reminds me that he used to be a good guy."

"All of a sudden the perfect dad," Brad said.

"Still a long way from that," she said.

"You want a pressure dressing, Dr. Bratton?" Mallory asked. "I noted a little oozing at the end."

"Knock yourself out," both physicians said, almost simultaneously.

Brad shed his surgical gloves. He tossed them to the waste receptacle. Diana followed. They broke loose their disposable surgical gowns.

"Maybe your ex is just trying to make up for lost time," Brad said, "especially since starting a family with a new wife wasn't working out."

"It didn't work out with the first new wife either, and why are you suddenly his best friend, making rationalizations?" Diana asked.

"Alex Bratton messed up a long time ago," Brad said. "Let's just leave it at that."

Diana and Alex walked down the hall toward Mr. Marzel's fifth grade homeroom, the last door on the left at the end of the corridor, just past the water fountain. Alex had attended this same private school in Jackson and had never quarreled about Kelsey's tuition. He always paid his share. His problem was with the other expenses.

"This place hasn't changed much," he said. "Except the hallways look smaller."

"I expected you to be late. Just like the other day."

"Email said three-thirty, Diana, so here I am. The other day … hummm … like when I brought Blythe to your office?"

"I'm sorry, Alex. That sounded insensitive. I really didn't mean to …"

"Sure you didn't," he said.

"Hello, hello." A wiry voice coming from inside the doorway startled Diana as she reached into her purse to check the parent-teacher schedule. This was the correct room number for Kelsey's English class. She motioned for Alex to follow.

They peered around the corner and moved slowly into the front of the room. A bald head was buried in a stack of papers on the desk, a bony hand tearing through them with a red felt pen. The head looked up and the hand stilled.

"I heard you shuffling out in the hall. You two must be Mr. and Mrs. Bratton?"

"Actually, we're divorced," Alex answered. "But we're Kelsey's parents … and it's Mr. and Dr. Bratton."

"All right, then. I'm Mr. Dewey Marzel." Mr. Marzel led them to a rear corner of the room and a bank of six wooden stools spaced evenly along a wall counter. Blinds covered the windows. "Please take a seat," he said and waited for each to take a stool while he remained standing.

"A wonderful place to start this conversation is with the student's work. We do our writing in groups—compositions, essays, term papers—

maximum of six students working at a time, as you can see." He motioned to the rest of the stools. A thin-screened, desk-top computer matched each of the six.

"Amazing. Truly amazing how our educational tools have changed over the last several years," he said. "Progress, some say. Now these contraptions are in every classroom. I still prefer pen and paper."

"I remember only a large computer in the school library," Diana said. "It was a novelty and very slow."

"This grouping proves to be a marvelous way to exchange ideas," Mr. Marzel said. "Bounce things off other brains, you might say. Everyone gets smarter and more creative." He stepped closer to Diana, and she pushed her stool a few inches away toward Alex.

Mr. Marzel brought up Kelsey's student file on the nearest computer and started to scroll through the information. "And what type of physician are you, Dr. Bratton? I don't remember seeing that in your daughter's file."

"Surgeon. I'm a general surgeon, sometimes a trauma surgeon."

"Too bad for Blythe that trauma surgeons don't know anything about fluid and electrolyte imbalances," Alex said.

Diana whispered, "We've been through that. I couldn't do anything to save Blythe."

"Pardon? Did you say something, Mrs. Bratton? Oh, yes. Sorry. *Doctor* Bratton."

"Nothing important, nothing to do with why we're here," Diana answered.

"I do have other appointments," Marzel said, "so we should move right along. Right along to Kelsey's work." He clicked through several pages on the computer.

Alex leaned into Diana. "That's right. I forgot," he whispered. "Dr. Perfect."

Diana stared back. *Knock it off, or leave.*

"Is that Kelsey's desk?" Alex asked. He pointed to the nearest row, a desk closer to the eraser board.

Marzel answered, "I believe so. But how did you know?"

"She told me she sat near a window, and close to the front of the room. She could see the flag pole outside from her seat." Alex left his stool for the desk. He pulled a notebook from under the seat and opened it.

"Alex, you shouldn't be messing in Kelsey's things," Diana said.

Several sheets of paper flew from the notebook to the floor. Marzel moved to retrieve them.

"As I was saying," he said, "I hold dear many traditional teaching methods. One of them is requiring that half of the essays be written by hand in class. That way, I see a sampling of their work without computer spell check or grammar review." He flipped through the sheets of notebook paper. "Just as I thought, this looks like your daughter's rough draft of the current assignment."

Marzel read through the first page. "Students are full of such surprises. Note the subject matter and outline she plans to submit for my approval. Intriguing title: *The Five Manners of Death*."

Diana slid off her stool "May I see that?"

"Certainly. The assignment was to write about an interesting relative, someone seen by the student as unique and creative."

Alex asked, "Who is Kelsey writing about? You, Diana?" He returned to stand at the computers.

Diana shook her head slowly. "Sorry to disappoint you. She's writing about our Aunt Phoebe."

"Smart girl," he said. "The red-headed swamp witch would make great material."

"I hope your daughter uses other ways to describe this aunt," Marzel said. "By this 'Manners of Death' ... is the poor woman deceased?"

"No, Phoebe is very much alive," Diana said. "Her English major at Ole Miss and a writing class came up recently in talking with a neighbor. I guess Phoebe shared that discussion with Kelsey."

"We encourage mentoring. Maybe Kelsey can absorb something from this aunt."

"She never used the degree. Left Ole Miss, moved to Dallas and married my uncle."

Diana skimmed the rest of her daughter's essay. "And that's all in here." Diana turned to the next page. "Even the part about growing up in the Mississippi Delta. A year or so ago she moved from Texas to Jackson as a widow. Recently she got sick, but before that she was tremendous help with carpool, babysitting, and picking up things at the grocery store—a real grandmother figure."

"Too bad Phoebe wasn't around when Kelsey was small, when her mother was scarce," Alex said.

Diana frowned. "Like you were the perfect father?"

"You did say that the two of you were divorced? I must say, I see that."

Diana grew pale at Mr. Marzel's comment and was surprised to see Alex appear scolded.

"However, I'm sure young Kelsey has the benefit of a healthy home environment," Marzel said, eyebrows raised. He took the student notebook from Diana, reinserted the missing pages, and returned it to the desk. He pivoted between the two to cut the tension, nearly losing his step.

"I look forward to learning more about this fascinating aunt with the completion of the essay. Now, about Kelsey's grades."

CHAPTER 7

Diana pulled behind a black Lexus parked at the curb in front of Phoebe's new house. She walked to the outside of the driver's door and read the plaque: *Ivy Residential Properties*. Diana ran her forefinger along the smooth, shiny surface of the vehicle. *I wonder how many sales commissions bought this baby.*

Phoebe's place already looked settled, at least from the exterior. The two-story stone and brick home spanned its share of street frontage, though not quite to the extreme of the neighbor on either side. More landscaping had been installed, including English ivy—the old variety, the type with the big, heavy, dark-green, almost bronze-looking leaves— planted to creep up the exterior masonry and entwine in the intricate black ironwork that dressed the front entrance. Lush Kimberly Queen ferns grew in antique urns on each side of the front steps. The blooming spring flower beds lining the walk were manicured, the mulch fresh.

"My savior! What a wonderful surprise!" Phoebe answered the door in a white linen pants suit. A powder blue shell peeked above the neck of the jacket. A diamond cross hung from a silver necklace, draping the top of the blue fabric.

"I dropped by to see if you were continuing your nebulizer and antibiotics," Diana said. "I guess so, because you look great, and so does your garden. Someone's been working out here day and night, but from the looks of that outfit, it hasn't been you."

"Of course not," Phoebe said. "But I am feeling better, stronger, and glad to be out of that rental house. And as far as the flower beds and grounds, I just hope my gardener can keep up."

The front door opened into an airy foyer than ran parallel to the home's front façade. The flooring was octagonal, whitish grey marble with an antique rug strewn in the center. A few pieces of packing material remained along the fringe of the floor covering. Near the foot of the circular staircase, an eighteenth-century chest stood against the wall.

Diana again admired the antique iron French chandelier lit inside the dining room. The whole place smelled of fresh paint.

A man sat in the living room, his back to the foyer. He sipped from a china coffee cup.

"Mr. Ivy surprised me this afternoon. We were just having some tea. Join us."

Diana walked into the living room. Both unpacked and sealed boxes lined one of the walls. The man stretched his neck to turn his head toward Diana and then stood. "Yes, green tea. One lump. It was also my late wife's favorite."

"You're the man from the convenience store," Diana said. "Aunt Phoebe? I don't understand."

The man stood and bent to set the tea cup and saucer beside the chair. He extended his right hand toward Diana. Phoebe darted forward with a linen napkin, sliding it under the saucer to protect the mahogany side table.

"We did not receive a proper introduction the other afternoon," the man said. "I'm Winston Ivy, the real estate broker."

Diana met him halfway. "Sorry for your loss, Mr. Ivy. One of your junior agents sold me my house. It's nice to put the name with the face, I suppose."

"You and I did meet under such vile circumstances ... that slimy thug. My wife was such a wonderful woman," Ivy said. "So far, the police have come up empty. I should probably hire a private detective. But where are my manners? Thank you for trying to save her."

Diana remembered the look on Ivy's face when she halted resuscitative efforts for his wife.

"As far as her illness, Mrs. Ivy and I had an understanding, an open relationship."

"Open?" Diana said. "That usually means ..."

"My late wife made her desires very clear. She wanted no heroic measures. She had faced the finality of her illness."

"Seems that the finality came sooner than expected," Diana said.

"You two are much too serious, almost morbid," Phoebe said. "Why don't you join us for tea, Diana? Won't take a sec to brew another pot of Earl Grey. I'll get you a cup."

Diana took a seat opposite Ivy in the living room. Phoebe lifted the small Wedgewood china pot from the service tray and walked toward the back hall. "It's a shame, Winston, that my help has the day off," she said and disappeared into the kitchen.

"My aunt turns over a new maid about every three or four months," Diana said.

"Your aunt is strong-willed."

"How would you know that, Mr. Ivy?"

"Something was familiar about Phoebe when I first saw her in the doctor's office. Then when the two of you walked into the convenience store, when that thug had the gun in my back, I remembered."

"Remembered what?"

"I remembered her from creative writing class at Ole Miss. On the contrary, Phoebe would never remember me, not after all these years, even if I had sat on the front row by the door."

Diana studied the attractive face: strong, sharp jaw with little sagging at the neck, raised cheekbones. The few facial wrinkles looked as though drawn intentionally. Ivy had a full head of hair, a textured gray. She assumed he was in his late sixties—Phoebe's age. "I doubt that you went unnoticed, Mr. Ivy," Diana said.

"Miss Phoebe was quite a looker in college, Dr. Bratton. Spectacular—still is, as you know. I would have recognized her anywhere."

"She moved to Jackson about a year ago. I'm surprised your paths haven't crossed before now."

Phoebe appeared with the tea and matching cup. "Winston's firm has been fabulous. They handled all the fine points of the move since I was ill. All that's left is some unpacking."

A silver tray filled with miniature petit fours balanced in the palm of her left hand, individual strawberry and butter cream arranged in perfect rows, the white ones crowned with a small fresh strawberry to tie it all together. "No doubt Diana regrets that I didn't relocate to Jackson years ago. I could have helped out with Kelsey before she was old enough for school."

Phoebe set the tea pot and tray atop the serving table. "Diana, you sit by me here on the sofa and let me serve you," she said. "Winston, are you comfortable? Let's all sit and reminisce," she said.

"Reminisce?" Diana asked. "Mr. Ivy said you didn't really know each other in college."

Phoebe laughed. "Winston was in the class two years ahead of me. No need for the exact year of graduation, but we all knew who the good-looking upperclassmen were."

Diana refused the petit fours but opted for one of the amber-colored sugar stirrers. She dipped one into her tea. A whiff of steam rose from the cup.

Phoebe laughed again, really more of a giggle. "Shortly before you arrived, Diana, Winston reminded me that I stood up one of the other KAs on a blind date. It was my freshman year, early during football season. Believe it not, I was shy, very demure, back then."

"Actually, Phoebe, I was substituted at the last minute for your no-show. My fraternity brother couldn't make it; and since it was a blind date, you wouldn't have known the difference. So I guess the joke was on both of us!"

"Sorority girls don't joke about such things," Phoebe said.

Diana stirred her tea again. The stick of sugar began to dissolve.

"I fibbed to my pledge trainer that I never got the message about the arrangements for the date," Phoebe said.

Diana took a deep breath. "Dating 50 years ago ... so formal, so arranged. So, Mr. Ivy, you're here to reschedule the night out?" she asked. "Isn't it a little soon—I mean—considering your wife's recent death?"

"Diana." Phoebe admonished.

"Not to worry, Phoebe. And, Dr. Bratton, my intentions are nothing but honorable. I only stopped by to express my appreciation on two counts: for the purchase of this wonderful home and for the rescue in the convenience store. If you hadn't dropped in when you did and distracted the gunman, he might have killed all of us, including that young girl behind the counter."

Unfortunately, your late wife missed out on the distraction, Diana thought.

"Hat's off to you, Dr. Bratton, for trying to save my wife." He toasted with tea cup and sipped.

Were you that disappointed, Mr. Ivy?

"My sick wife wasn't going to be with us much longer, but ..."

"But, what a tragedy," Phoebe interrupted. "And no arrest? No leads?"

Ivy answered, "I've heard little from the police since that miserable day in the tiny store. Obviously they're busy with other crimes."

"I have a friend in the police department. I'm sure they'll get the guy," Diana said. She lifted her cup but did not drink. Phoebe freshened Winston's. He eyed the confections but did not choose.

"I need to be careful," he said. "Metabolism isn't what it used to be."

"Like I said, Mr. Ivy, I have a friend at JPD. I'll do a little checking around for you—to ease your mind, to speed things up, maybe."

"Interesting," Ivy said. "A prominent surgeon with police connections."

"Actually, your wife's murder is not the first death to cross my path in the last few weeks," Diana said.

"I hope your other patients don't know about that," he said.

"Diana is an excellent doctor. She doesn't lose patients." Phoebe stirred her tea with a sterling spoon. "She's referring to this silly list that showed up in the trash. Notes about ways to die."

Ivy set his cup on the side table. "I don't understand."

"Coroners need to know the manner of death," Diana said. "And there are five: homicide, suicide, accidental, natural, and unclassified."

"Diana is obsessing over this, Winston. Carvel Eaves, a neighbor from my old neighborhood, died a few minutes after finding the note in the street."

"Mr. Eaves' death was of natural causes," Diana said. "Although I almost ran over his body."

"What an odd turn of events," Winston said. "I've never thought of death in this way."

Diana said, "Another death was accidental, a medical complication, and then my pharmacist at the local chain store committed suicide."

"So you're placing my wife's death into this twist of fate, into some checklist?"

"Diana, aren't you being insensitive? Winston is a grieving widower."

Diana stirred her tea. The crystallized sugar was spent, the stick slick inside a tiny whirlpool. She took a sip and studied Winton Ivy. He was leaning toward Phoebe and smiling.

"Mr. Ivy, I have to be honest with you," Diana said. "I've already followed up with my friend at the police department. He shared some of the details about your wife's illness, basically that she was dying of cancer and that the oncologist could only offer palliation."

"The police requested a timeline of our last 24 hours," Winston said, "and that included the doctor's visit. I told the police what the doctors told me. All treatment options were exhausted, nothing left but keeping my wonderful wife comfortable." He took another sip of tea. "I think that's what you mean by palliation, Dr. Bratton."

"The coroner would have ruled her death natural causes except for …"

"Except for the fact that my late wife died of a gunshot wound to the chest—despite your heroic efforts. Her limited time on earth was cut even shorter."

"So the cause was homicide."

"Diana, please." Phoebe set her tea cup hard into the saucer.

"Not a problem, Phoebe," Winston said. "I'm a big boy. The conversation just sort of tilted that way."

Diana checked the time on her iPhone. "Kelsey's due home from gymnastics. A friend's mother is running carpool."

Phoebe said, "And you'll owe her the same next week. Maybe I can fill in."

"Pure fate dropped you here today, Dr. Bratton," Ivy said, "so we could get more acquainted. Just like fate arranged our rendezvous in the convenience store and allowed me to run into Phoebe again."

"I hadn't thought of your wife's tragedy as fate, but if that's the way you're dealing with your grief—that's your business." Diana stood.

Ivy moved next to Phoebe to replace Diana on the couch. "Providence led me to rediscover this beautiful girl from college," he said, "and now I have a second chance at wooing her over."

Phoebe pushed up from the sofa before Winston could stretch his arm around to squeeze her shoulder. She gripped the handles of the tea tray and lifted it from the table.

Winston frowned playfully at the rebuff.

"Diana, another idea," Phoebe said. "Why don't you pay those other mothers to sub for you in carpool?"

"It doesn't work that way." Diana said, walking to the front door as Winston Ivy followed. "Doctors aren't the only busy people."

"Phoebe, your niece is just trying to be a good mom."

Diana bristled and reached for the door knob. She turned to stare up at Winston Ivy and backed away from him. "It was nice formally meeting you, Mr. Ivy," she said. "Perhaps I'll run into you again sometime."

Phoebe called out from the living room. "I was thinking of having a little dinner party before the end of the month if I can get completely settled—invite Winston and a few others. Would you like to join us, Diana?"

"Sorry … have to miss … on call again." Diana walked onto the porch and pulled hard against the door behind her, stopping just shy of slamming it shut.

CHAPTER 8

Chief Martin yanked the thumbtacks from the other photographs on the evidence board, exposing the deceased pharmacist's face buried between the home invasion on Northwest Street and the burned-out blues bar on Farish Street. Someone had decided to put a fiery end to the financially struggling establishment in the once thriving, historically black-owned business district downtown.

He rearranged the photos so that the girl returned to dead center, then flipped through the pharmacist's case file, still lying on his desk in front of the board. Earlier Jade had inserted the results of the final toxicology screen under the designated tab: all opiates, breakdown products of barbiturates.

Jade reentered his office with the same clacking of high heel shoes. "Chief, here's the printout of the pharmacist's résumé you asked for." The secretary waved a thin file under his nose and lingered at the desk. "One of the deputies downloaded it off her laptop and printed it out for you," Jade said. "Of course, most everyone else in the department deals in email. Will you ever take the plunge?"

She moved behind his chair and began to massage his shoulders. "But if you only email me, I'll miss the visits to your charming office and seeing your charming face so many times during the day."

"Plenty of women have already seen this 'charming face.' Spare yourself."

"Whatever you wish, Chief." Jade released her manicured fingers from the firm grip of his trapezius muscles. Martin's shoulders recoiled. She slid out from behind his desk chair and looked over to him. "Just buzz if you want me to come back and finish the job."

Jade spun around and left down the hall for her own desk, more noise in her wake.

"She's a little too much sometimes," Martin said under his breath and opened the file. The late pharmacist had first enrolled at Delta State

University in Cleveland, Mississippi, where she joined a sorority and went out for cheerleader, then completed her pharmacy degree in Texas. Her employment history was brief. She interned with the same pharmacy chain that hired her to work in Jackson. That was it.

He reread the transcript of the store manager's statement. The girl punched the time clock nearly to the same minute every shift. Nothing was ever out of line behind the pharmacy counter until her death. She joked with the other employees and was well liked. Since she never called in sick or missed a day of work, the manager did not at first question her no-show but expected her to call the store later in the day to explain.

The JPD investigator's notes were on the next page. Her landlord let the pest man in as usual, first Thursday of every month. No one was supposed to be at home. The pharmacist was found dead on her bed, no sign of a struggle. No suicide note. A pharmacy pill bottle lay open, empty, on the floor near her, almost hidden under the edge of the bedspread.

Martin went to the filing cabinets lining a wall of his office and ran his fingers along the edges until he reached year 2006. The dark dust stained his fingertips. He wiped them clean on his pant leg. Inside was the file on the Cummins and Coachys murders and, as he remembered, a sticky note scribbled with Dr. Bratton's cell number.

It was 12:30. Maybe even doctors took lunch. He slid his new cell from his suit jacket and punched in the number.

Three rings later she answered.

"Most women wouldn't answer a strange cell number, Doctor."

"Your number's not strange, Chief Martin. I kept you in my contacts. I'm between surgery cases, so I can talk."

"Hope you grabbed a sandwich or something. They probably feed you free at the hospital."

"You didn't call to check on my nutritional status. What's up?"

"I know. I know. I used to come up to your office, interrupt your day, get your assistant all hot-under-the-collar at me. But I guess I've gotten too old, too soft. A phone call just seemed so easy."

Silence followed, then muffled voices in the background.

"Need to make this quick, Martin. OR has my next patient in holding."

"This time I'm calling to help you, Doctor Bratton." The muffled background voices made it difficult for Martin to hear.

"Get him to sign the consent before he gets the Valium," Diana said to someone in the room. "And, Christine, don't forget to mark which one we're taking off."

Shit, Martin thought. *I'm glad I'm safe in my office.*

"Help me?" Diana said, her voice much clearer, louder.

"You were worried about all the folks dropping dead around you," Martin said. "Looking for some kind of pattern."

"Right now I'm more worried about this diabetic's gangrene—one of the worst leg infections I've ever seen."

Martin had seen a lot of messy crime scenes, but gangrene seemed worse. The twinge of nausea surprised him.

"I'm not so sure that the pharmacy gal was a suicide—more like undetermined or unclassified."

"Has something else turned up?" Diana said.

"Maybe so," he said. Martin did not push his old argument of asking the doctor to call him Key.

"Suture needs to be a 5-0?" a clearer background voice asked—some nurse or tech in the OR. *Bratton must be holding her cell loose against her face.*

"Martin, I'll get back with you later," she said and ended the call.

He slipped the cell back into his jacket and returned to the evidence board. It spanned nearly the entire wall behind his desk.

"Doctors ... the only ones who are ever busy," he said. He studied again the pharmacist's photo at the center. He thumbed again through the file for the autopsy report: no bruising, no concussion, no skin marks, and no one's DNA except hers.

The investigator's report followed, including a standard photo of the death scene. The girl lay on her right side, turned in the direction of the door to the hall. One leg was bent at the knee, and an elbow remained pressed into the bedspread. The investigator had captioned: "Body found sprawled across the bed." But to him it appeared as though she might have been planning to push off the bed for the bathroom or to answer the door. Except for the pressed elbow, she looked peaceful, simply asleep on top of the bedspread. The bed looked fully made, the covering still tight and smooth.

Nice outfit. Expensive-looking one piece ... like for a cocktail party ... pearls and maybe diamond earrings. Can pharmacists afford that? "None of my ex-wives could ever dress that good," Martin said.

There were close-ups of the empty pill bottle on the floor and the bedspread. Another empty pill bottle lay beside the pharmacist, the cap missing, just like the other bottle. Martin imagined the plastic containers tossed to bounce off the body onto the bedspread and floor, not dropped after the pharmacist gulped the contents. He flipped to the larger photo that took in the bedside table—no glass of water, no soft drink can, no beer bottle, no wine glass. There were no liquid stains on the carpet or bedspread. *Was this small young girl so miserable, so desperate, that she could swallow two bottles of pills dry?*

Martin turned to his computer, locating the same file electronically and maneuvering his mouse to enlarge the image of the spent pill containers. He decided that he could handle this computer stuff after all and fought back a smile. From several angles the pill containers were unlabeled, not even a partial, but then the girl wouldn't take time to generate printed labels for stolen drugs. She would have known how many it would take to kill her, but most likely included extra—filled each plastic bottle to the brim from a bulk wholesale container.

Martin reread the notes from the questioning of the drug store manager—not a single opiate missing from inventory. He lifted the receiver of the desk phone. "Jade, I'm gonna take a little drive over to the dead pharmacist's place."

✠

"Yellow tape would look really out of place here," Diana said, stepping from Martin's car parked outside the pharmacist's two-story condominium. A late model Mercedes was across the narrow street next to a Jaguar convertible with the top down. Freshly trimmed boxwoods lined the shaded, asphalt parking spaces, and sculptured thin evergreens marked the entrance to each unit. The Georgian facades were all detailed reddish-brown brick, and the roof lines and front window styles and dimensions varied little. White impatiens and early spring begonias filled the flower boxes. A couple in their late forties, wearing baseball caps, tee shirts, and shorts, rode by on bicycles and waved politely.

"Yellow tape? Nobody ever thought this was a crime scene," Martin said, leading Diana along the short brick walkway to the front door. "The ME might have missed something."

"I'm not trained in forensics, and you want me to check behind the medical examiner?" Diana asked.

"You save lives, Dr. Bratton. But you seem to have an interest in death too. Remember, you called on me."

Martin put on latex gloves and tossed Diana a pair. "I believe you're familiar with these? No allergy I hope. I'm gonna send my guys back up here for fingerprints." He unlocked the door to the condominium. "The manager of the complex was easy with the key, a sucker for a nice-looking cop."

Diana followed Martin into the living room. Unlike the light, breezy air outside, the interior was stale and still with a faint scent of souring garbage. "A unit in the newer section of Eastbrooke is pricey. Didn't know pharmacists made this much," Diana said. She wrinkled her nose in the direction of the kitchen. "Too bad the ME and your guys didn't take out the trash."

"The manager told me the lease was paid up through July," Martin said. "It was in the girl's name but her bank account doesn't show the payments."

Diana inspected the room, walking around the sofa and between the upholstered chairs, careful not to touch anything despite the gloves. A wide, flat screen monitor crowned the far wall of the living area. Oil paintings, oriented vertically, flanked the television. Diana ran the tip of her shoe over the antique rug between the sofa and the TV.

"Any idea who was bankrolling this place?" she asked, moving under an archway lined atop with thick crown molding to enter a short hall. "A sugar daddy, no doubt about it," she answered. "Or maybe a momma?"

"The few co-workers who knew her said she lived alone," Martin answered. He turned behind her into the hall. "The file diagram of the living spaces puts the master bedroom down this way. That's where the pest man found the body. Two more bedrooms are upstairs." He looked inside his large envelope and handed two photographs to Diana: one a print of the pharmacist on the bed and then another once the body was removed. "Her clothes and jewelry looked expensive to me, just like this place."

"This is sorta creepy," she said and studied both. An impression of the body remained in the tight bedspread.

Martin flipped through the file and produced two other photographs. One angle captured the closet outside the door to the bathroom. It was closed.

"Notice something's different?"

"That closet over there is cracked open. The door is closed in this picture," Diana said. "Has anyone had access to the condo or would the investigators have left it open? Do we know?"

"You docs know how to make the *A*'s, don't you?" Martin said. "Already scored in Detective 101." He inspected the interior of the closet, filled with more women's clothing. "JPD hasn't been back and we already know that the housekeeper has avoided the place."

Diana checked the dust on the bureau. "Yeah, like the plague," she said. "From the looks of that closet and the photo, the poor girl was undefeated for best-dressed at the pharmacy." She stepped into the bathroom. "She's probably got another closet full in here."

A set of double closet doors lined the wall of the dressing area across from the lavatory. "Is it OK to open these?"

"Go ahead." Martin called from the bedroom, then stood quickly behind Diana. She held a man's black leather belt with a thin silver buckle.

"This was rolled up on a shelf," Diana said. "Guess sugar daddy left in a hurry after the last hookup." She stretched the leather belt end to end, felt the texture, the width, the slightly worn edge at the tip, then put her nose to the familiar material.

"What's so fascinating, Doc?"

"Except for the new buckle, I think I've seen this belt before," Diana answered. She felt just below her last rib. The sting in her chest remained. *And I've felt this belt before,* she thought. "The belt I knew had a monogrammed silver buckle. The initials were *AB*."

"*AB*?" Martin asked.

Diana had ducked and avoided her drunken husband's second and third strikes that night, the belt instead hitting a doorframe. She recognized the scratch left on the inside grain of the leather. "The deceased pharmacist and I may have had something—or someone—in common," Diana said.

"Who?"

"My ex, my one-and-only. But Alex Bratton has a string of them."

"So that belt belongs to your ex-husband?"

"If I'm correct, then it seems that Alex Bratton is not only the grieving widower, but he's also lost a girlfriend."

Martin produced a red plastic bag from inside his jacket, gently took the leather belt and buckle from Diana, and tucked it inside. He sealed the top. "I could make a crack about notches on his belt, but I won't," he said.

He returned to the bedroom and once again compared the area to the scene in the photograph—the lamp, the bedside table, the curtains, the rug, and the bedspread—the same as when the body was reported, only dusty. The lamp shade remained straight, the alarm clock still turned at a right angle facing the bed, the paperback novel and bookmark.

"Maybe I should track down Mr. Bratton," Martin said. "I hope you don't still have some kind of thing for him."

"That thing is long gone." Diana eyed the red bag and rubbed her chest again. "Let's see who gets to him first," she said.

CHAPTER 9

Alex pulled just out of the street into the circular driveway, stopping further from the house than usual.

"See you next time, Dad. Really enjoyed the game and the weekend." Kelsey bounded from his car toward the front door. It was turning dusk but not dark enough for streetlights. Her old overnight bag had started to look dingy and worn, but this new one was constructed of bright pink cloth, branded with a lime green flower design and matching handles. Strapped to her back was her dingy school bag, the contents untouched since Friday and a sharp contrast to the new gift from her father.

Diana sat at her computer in the keeping room off the kitchen, paying bills on line as Kelsey entered the house. "Your dad didn't walk you to the door like usual?"

"Don't be so hard on him, Mom. He's been really busy." Kelsey's voice trailed from the kitchen.

"I don't doubt that," Diana mumbled and submitted the payment for the electric utility bill.

"Do we have any more of that blackberry cobbler? Dad said we didn't have time for dessert."

Kelsey yanked open the refrigerator and pushed aside the leftover roast and package of torn lettuce. "Here it is."

She set the half-eaten Pyrex dish of cobbler on the kitchen island, popped open the cabinet next to the refrigerator for a cereal bowl, and began to scoop out the remains. "I'm glad Aunt Phoebe made this for us."

"Phoebe never made a cobbler in her life. A takeout place is not far from her house. She had it sent over."

"Whatever," Kelsey said with a mouthful, still standing in the kitchen.

Diana closed out of her bank account and shut down the laptop. She joined Kelsey at the island just as she finished her bowl of cobbler and scraped clean the Pyrex dish.

"Why'd you bother using a bowl?" Diana asked.

"You're just pissed that Dad kept me a little later this weekend."

"I'm not pissed at you. And speaking of your great-aunt, she wouldn't appreciate such language—and neither do I."

Kelsey stepped over to the freezer. "How come we never keep any ice cream around here?" she asked. "Dad said you never liked to keep sweets around when y'all were married ... always watching your weight."

"That's bull sh…"

"Mom! My ears!"

"My surgical residency was too demanding, no way to gain weight. And no time for the grocery store. And I don't remember your father ever volunteering to do the shopping."

Kelsey dumped the empty bowl and dish into the sink; the spoon clattered and flipped out to the drain. She asked, "Do you think next time Aunt Phoebe could send over peach?"

Diana walked from Phoebe's new kitchen, pinching the flesh above her waist and holding a mug of coffee in the other hand. The Pyrex dish had been washed clean and stored in a cabinet until a caterer could fill it with something else.

"You need to stop sending food over to my house, particularly desserts," she said. Without the camouflage of a baggy surgical scrub suit, her middle felt thicker. "I'm barely holding my own, but Kelsey doesn't burn it off like I do."

"Maybe she needs more afterschool activities," Phoebe said. "What about adding softball or drill team?" She sat at her antique desk, wedged between unpacked and sealed moving boxes, addressing invitations to her bridge club.

"Problem is somebody has to be around to run her to all those activities," Diana said, sitting in the upholstered chair next to Phoebe's desk.

"In my younger years, I could have been tremendous help."

"I appreciate the concern, but Kelsey isn't your responsibility, never has been. I picked the wrong father. She missed out on one who is worth a damn."

The desk nearly shook under her pen strokes as Phoebe finished the next invitation. She licked and sealed the envelope, then squeezed the back with a sterling embosser complete with her new return address. The thick paper was almost crushed in the process.

"Your daughter's lucky to have her father around, even part-time."

"I've never tried to keep Alex and Kelsey apart. If you overlook the skipped child support payments, he's been a decent father—except when Kelsey was a baby. But Alex continues with his distractions."

Phoebe neared the end of the invitation list. "Distractions?"

"When I met Alex's his new wife, I thought he might have settled down a bit."

"But you don't think so," Phoebe said.

Diana reconsidered the belt in the dead pharmacist's closet. Martin had instructed her not to mention it. *Confidential police business,* he had said.

"Alex hasn't settled down," Diana said. "Not one bit."

"Your ex-husband comes from good stock, beautiful people. I remember his family from your wedding—the father's high cheekbones, handed directly down to Alex, his mother's flawless skin. And no way could anyone miss her ring."

"Beautiful family or not, once Alex graduated from law school, they cut the cord."

"Maybe the Brattons thought he had a cushion. After all, he married a doctor."

"Alex has never been interested in my career. He is one of the most self-centered ass…"

"Foul language, Diana? Don't cheapen yourself."

"Never was a debutante, Auntie. Never had time for it. Still don't."

Phoebe opened the lower desk drawer and removed another stack of envelopes. She stared at a name farther down on the list and retrieved a fresh pen from the desk blotter. "I don't know why I continue to include that bitch. If she weren't a Life Master …"

"Foul language is OK if you use it?"

"It's not foul if it's true."

"What's true is that Alex is an asshole," Diana said. She took a sip of her coffee and leaned toward to the desk. "You want me to lick the stamps?"

"No need, printed with self-adhesive," Phoebe answered. She applied the postage stamp with the swipe of a manicured forefinger. "I can't say it often enough. I should have moved to Jackson years ago. You need help with your life."

"Babysitting, running carpool … subbing as grandmother … or mother … none of that would have saved my marriage with your beautiful Alex Bratton."

"Maybe we … you … should give Alex another chance. You need to be married, Diana. And like I said the other day, there's still Dr. Cummins." Phoebe pressed deep with her pen into the parchment of the invitation to the Life Master bitch. "Dr. Cummins ... ummm ... talk about beautiful."

"Alex's track record with women isn't good and isn't getting any better."

"Stop babbling, Diana. What are you trying to say?"

Diana took a long sip of her coffee.

Phoebe said, "Your ex-husband just lost his wife. He couldn't help that." She moved to the next name on the list. Her pen strokes were even more deliberate. "As for you, a divorcee, even if you never remarry, then you won't die an old maid."

Phoebe flipped through the finished invitations without counting. A few unused stamps were scattered around the blotter. "If I skipped someone, she can return the favor."

Diana reached for the stack and shuffled them into a rectangular stack. "I can drop these at the post office on my way back to the clinic."

"Perfect. Last mail pick-up is at two, so you have time for a bite of lunch first. The everyday is unpacked, and I have chicken salad from Newk's."

"Raincheck, please. Need to get back to work, so I can leave on time this afternoon for the gym. The coffee has revived me, and I need to neutralize that cobbler."

Phoebe pushed the Sheridan style chair back from her desk and stood to hand Diana two more invitations completed earlier and stuffed in a drawer. "Your figure's just fine, Sweetie—with or without the baggy doctor clothes."

"I'll take that as a compliment, but I could really use that workout this afternoon. It's a dance exercise class."

"Good to see that you have time to do things that normal people do, that normal girls do."

"Your beautiful Dr. Cummins has hired another surgeon to help out. That makes four of us."

"Then less call and more time for clothes shopping. Maybe now you'll have time for some cuter outfits, maybe even something sexy. Reinvention of yourself wouldn't be a bad thing, Diana."

Diana tucked the invitations in her purse and swung the strap across her shoulder. "Whatever. But remember, no more dessert gifts, at least not to my house."

Phoebe followed Diana to the front door and watched through the front window until her car disappeared. She heard Alex walk from the first room down the hall to stand behind her. "Maybe you should try asking her out," she said. "Sounds like Diana wants a life."

"Sounds like Diana still thinks I'm an ass," Alex said. He returned with Phoebe to the library and stepped around the boxes remaining unpacked. She resumed her place at the desk.

"Diana's certainly opinionated," Phoebe said. "However, it's up to you to charm her back to her senses."

Alex Bratton rested his hand on Phoebe's shoulder. "I had hoped that taking Blythe to her as a patient would make Diana see me as a family man again."

"I'm afraid my niece-by-marriage failed to see it that way. She even suspected a setup for a medical malpractice suit. Besides, Mr. Family Man, you were already married."

"But that situation can always change."

"And so it did." Phoebe placed her pen and note stationery in the drawer, retrieved what was left of an iced tea, and stood facing in the direction of the kitchen. "Was Diana aware that you gave your late wife her injections?" Phoebe asked.

She pushed past Alex into the kitchen and emptied the tea into the sink, setting the glass at the bottom for the morning housekeeper. "Time for my nap. Addressing those invitations and thinking about all the nasty women on that list has drained me. I hope you'll excuse me."

"Sure. I'll go watch TV."

"Oh, and for a moment, Alex, I thought Diana might have suspected you were here. Don't see how, just had a feeling."

"I was careful, parked again in your garage out back."

"What ever happened to your arrangements with that young girl? I think that's another thing that Diana suspected. She was all about your distractions." Phoebe shuddered.

"That ended."

"The girl worked in a drug store, or something like that?"

"She was a pharmacist. I'm not seeing her anymore," Alex said.

"Regardless, you can't stay here much longer. People notice things. Even with someone like Carvel Eaves not roaming the streets, people still find things out. They talk."

"I appreciate the help since Blythe's parents changed the locks," Alex said. "They aren't exactly happy with me now, and they own the house. I'll be very discreet while I'm here."

"Be careful. Even if you park in the rear garage, one of my neighbors will eventually notice the same car turning into my drive."

"Like I said, Aunt Phoebe, I'll watch myself."

CHAPTER 10

Instead of the expected instructor for the exercise class, a new name appeared on the bulletin board. Pinned just below her credentials, a note explained that the regular teacher had flu. Built in the seventies, the entrance to the gym remained a vertical stripped blue alternating with what was originally a bright green. The wall color in the main lobby area had morphed into a dingy version of the original bright sunshine-yellow, the surface intact except for scuff marks and chipped paint from white plastic chairs pushed against the sheetrock.

"A sub from New Orleans. Taught Spin for over 10 years," Diana read. "Thank God she's getting the class organized and started on time."

Diana joined the men and women in the registration line, most of whom thought themselves too fat, too soft, or too tense, then followed her classmates into the dance studio adjacent to the basketball court. The female instructor's voice filled the room, amplified by two stereo speakers in the rear that were also vintage seventies. She was about five-two, thin, with bleached hair stretched into a short ponytail and heavy black mascara that made her head seem too large.

"OK, ladies and you gents, we'll get started in just a sec. Sorry, but I left my iPod back home. I need to check that music disc." The instructor pointed to the empty spots near the end of the second row and in the middle of the third. "Go ahead, please, and fill in those rows, and we'll get started."

Diana squeezed in between a woman in pink stretch pants and another in tight camouflage-design shorts well above the knee. She scanned the room, inspecting the others, her habit during warmup. Most were wearing Skechers.

She preferred a much younger group, but this day of the week and time fit both her schedule and Kelsey's afterschool activities, and the facility was on the way home from work. The under thirty crowd must attend earlier in the week, saving Thursday and Friday nights for bar scene hook-ups. Monday and Tuesday workouts were for detox. Maybe some of the more attractive, younger girls went elsewhere to other types of exercise classes, such as Pure Barre.

One of the sixty-year-old men in the last row continued to struggle through his stretches until the music finally erupted, something from a Donna Summer CD: *Hot Stuff.* Without the coat and tie and toupee, Diana almost did not recognize Kelsey's English teacher, Mr. Marzel.

"Enough rhythm to stir up a sweat, but let's shake things up a bit," the teacher from New Orleans yelled, pointing a remote at the stereo to lower the volume temporarily. "How about hopping off those fake bicycles and let's do a little dance and a little aerobics!"

No one slowed their bicycle.

"Today I've stirred in a little hip-hop, some samba and salsa, and more seventies disco: Bee Gees, Chic, the Village People. I want to surprise and inspire you. Squats and lunges … and some martial arts as a bonus. Let's do it!"

The music ramped back to blasting level and Miss New Orleans was hard at it: more yelling than coaxing, and lots of counting. Everyone obeyed her. In the first few minutes, Diana worried that the female beer belly to her right would pop out of the short-shorts, much less survive any high kicks or air punches.

Mr. Marzel was already ringing wet, the comb-over under the missing hairpiece no more than a stringy mess. Midway through the 30-minute session Diana saw him slip away toward the rear of the building near the restrooms. When the session ended and the group dragged to the front exit, Diana heard grumblings from several classmates: *I paid for Zumba and I want Zumba … I'm calling the manager …God, Stella's gotta get well soon.*

Diana rubbed the last of the sweat from her neck with her damp towel and stopped at the registration desk for a water. She put a dollar in the honor jar beside the counter-top refrigerator and withdrew a fresh towel from her gym bag to wipe her face. Fruity-colored drinks in plastic bottles floated among disappearing ice cubes in an opened cooler next to the refrigerator. A tray of peanut butter cookies waited on the counter.

"Cookies aren't that bad," Mr. Marzel said, brushing crumbs from the side of his mouth. "I suppose the sub brought these. Stella never treats us." He took another cookie. "You're Mrs. Bratton, right?"

"Yes, Diana Bratton, Kelsey's mom." Diana extended her hand to Mr. Marzel. It was soft, warm, and slimy and the size of hers. After the shake, she wiped her hand with the new towel and hoped Dewey Marzel didn't notice.

"Outside the classroom, please call me Dewey. And I am enjoying your daughter in my class—trust she feels the same. Fascinating young woman, fascinating."

"I'd like to see some fascinating grades soon," Diana said. She opened her bottled water and took a long sip.

Mr. Marzel turned to the bulletin board and ran his forefinger down the posted schedule. "Looks like our regular coach is down for the count next week too," he said. "Hope she's well by then and not contagious. This new gal today," he shook his head, "not much younger than Stella, but too much for an old man like me."

Marzel stepped into the men's dressing area near the front and reappeared with a faded cloth bag. He walked toward the rear exit. "Nice to see you again, Mrs. Bratton," he said.

"Sure, you too." Diana scanned the upcoming Zumba class schedule for herself and drank half the water bottle. She decided to try the Monday class and that younger crowd—sans the likes of Dewey Marzel—but unless things went better she would go somewhere else. She wiped her face and neck dry then stuffed the towel into the bag. Most of the class had cleared the building, and the substitute instructor was nowhere in sight.

Diana was on the sidewalk when she remembered her car was in the rear parking lot. Turning the corner, she heard a woman yell, "Somebody call 9-1-1. Somebody!"

A small crowd of people from the class was sandwiched between her car and a dusty black Taurus. Near the rear tire of her vehicle a man's leg stuck out stiffly from the edge of the group. The orange tennis shoes looked familiar.

The woman again: "Anybody know CPR? Somebody's got to know CPR."

Diana raised her workout bag and used it to push through. A man lay face down on the pavement.

"Everybody push back. We need to turn him over. You—get the feet."

The guy nearest dropped his water bottle and stooped to lift the man's feet.

"And, you, get the middle," Diana said to the woman who had done all the yelling.

She stared at Diana. "I … I …don't know what to …"

"Just grab the waist while I support the head and neck to turn him over."

"Don't think I can do that," the woman said, shielding her chest with her hands crossed palms open.

"Then get the hell out of the way!" Diana jerked her head to the guy at the feet and shook her head in disgust. "Come on, people. Someone else, give a hand."

"Will I do?" Brad Cummins eased the woman out of the way. The team of three eased Marzel's stiff body face-up, his cool, ashen complexion a stark contrast to the black pavement. "I spotted all the commotion from the hardware store across the street and called *9-1-1*, then alerted the ER," he said.

"Mr. Marzel," Diana cried. "Dewey! Can you hear me?"

There was no breath, no movement from Kelsey's teacher. Diana felt his neck for a carotid pulse. Nothing.

Brad started chest compressions, and Diana changed to the head, pushing aside one of the gawkers.

"Don't suppose you have a mouthpiece with you?" she asked.

"Sorry. I don't," Brad answered. "And I don't carry an AED defibrillator in my back pocket either."

After another series of chest compressions, Brad tried Marzel's neck. "Got a pulse now."

Diana hesitated a second, but started mouth-to-mouth. The first five breaths did nothing to expand his chest. "I think he's obstructed," she said.

"Anybody got a ballpoint pen?" Brad shouted. "His only chance is an emergency trach."

The woman who couldn't help before pushed back through. "Here's one." She handed Brad a slender, cheap giveaway.

"I'll do it." Diana took the ball point pen and felt just above the top of Marzel's thyroid cartilage. The instrument was flimsy but managed to pierce the center of the cricothyroid membrane. The woman behind her screamed, the sound familiar to everyone. Marzel sputtered and coughed, but remained unresponsive, cyanotic blue. Diana double-checked the positioning of the ink pen.

Still no ambulance or police siren. "I think I hear wheezing," Diana said. "We've got to enlarge the airway. The pen's not thick enough."

"One day in exercise class, he said something about asthma," someone in the crowd said.

"Will this do?" The woman handed Brad a 10-inch segment of green garden hose. "This was tied around that new tree over by the fence. They planted it last week—nearly fell to the ground when I loosened it," she said.

Brad examined both ends, brushed off the cleaner of the two and passed the hose to Diana. "Go for it."

To more sputtering and wheezing, Diana withdrew the first makeshift tracheotomy tube from Marzel's neck and wedged the garden hose into the opening. His breathing steadied somewhat, and a hint of pink spread through his skin.

Diana smiled an uneasy grin at Brad. She wondered if the blare of the approaching ambulance reminded him of the night his brother died.

"I'll ride with the EMTs to Metro," Brad said. "Kelsey's probably waiting at home for you."

Diana shed her exercise jacket, puffed it into pillow shape, and tucked it between Marzel's head and the pavement. "Thank you, Brad. I think I'll take you up on that."

✠

"Nothing gets by me when you're involved," Martin said, sitting across from Diana's office desk.

"This time nobody died," she said. Diana studied her appointment schedule on the computer screen. "You didn't waste any time with this episode."

"I've told my people to let me know when your name shows up in a report, even an ambulance run."

Diana darted her eyes at Martin. "Big Brother then, I guess? But like I said ... nobody died this time." She clicked forward to the next screen. "Is bugging my office and home next?"

"Detective Martin?" Brad stuck his head into Diana's office. "Not busy enough down at your own place?"

Diana pulled up the electronic record of her first patient for the afternoon. "Brad, I told you—it's Chief Martin."

Martin kept his seat. "Got no problem with you, Dr. Cummins. No problem with your partner either."

Brad stood between Martin and Diana, his back to the policeman. "I checked on our guy from the parking lot, Diana. Medicine says he'll make it, but won't be teaching for a few weeks."

"Kelsey told me last night that most of the kids cheered when the substitute English teacher showed up."

"But not Kelsey, the angel?" Brad said.

"I hope not," Diana said. "If Mr. Marzel is out of ICU tomorrow, I'm going to drag her up to the hospital after school to see him."

"Marzel's been pumped with so many steroids, she probably won't even recognize him. His face is bruised, all scraped up from the asphalt when he seized and fell—a scary sight even for junior high."

"Not sure why anyone would munch on peanut butter cookies after a work-out, particularly with a peanut allergy."

"Somebody want to fill me in?" Martin asked.

"Severe bronchospasm—the teacher's trachea, his windpipe, closed off—kept us from ventilating him during CPR," Diana answered. "We didn't know about his peanut allergy."

"He didn't wear a medical alert bracelet or carry an EpiPen in the pocket of his exercise pants," Brad said.

"Guess the EMTs showed up to save the day for that teacher," Martin said.

Diana made several strokes on the keyboard. "Gee, that's a real vote of confidence."

"Dr. Bratton was the real hero outside that gym, Martin," Brad said. "Her quick action with the airway made the difference. That poor fella was victim to his own bad luck."

"Otherwise, another dead body added to the pile," Diana said.

"Doc, hope you're not getting cold-hearted on us," Martin said.

"Had Dewey Marzel died, I guess his death would have been natural, or maybe accidental," she said.

Brad reached into his coat pocket for his phone and checked a text. "Nurse has the next patient ready. Gotta go."

"Brad, you're on the schedule to assist with that Whipple in the morning," Diana called out as he walked into the hall.

"Can't wait. Really looking forward to it." He stopped to check another text before going to his side of the building.

"What's a Whipple?" Martin slid a manila envelope from inside his jacket pocket.

"It's a procedure for pancreatic cancer—takes two surgeons, at least a couple of hours. Fortunately, it doesn't come up but three or four times a year."

"Fortunate for whom?"

Diana closed out the computer program and brushed by him toward the hall. "Sorry to say, Chief Martin, but just like Dr. Cummins, I've got patients waiting."

Martin held the envelope to his temple. "So it's OK for you to drop in on me at my office downtown, but I'm not welcome at yours?"

Diana stopped in the doorway. "OK, what's in the envelope?"

"Thanks to you, I took a photograph of the pharmacist's closet," he said. "Wouldn't have thought much about that belt if you hadn't come along for a look through the condo. Your ex-husband's prints were all over it. Got 'em from an old DUI booking."

"I already told you that the belt belonged to Alex."

"How would you know that? You two spending time together?"

"We have a child together—no way to avoid him," Diana said. The sting across her chest, the tearing sensation under her breast, returned. "That belt was an expensive gift, the last Christmas we were married. Alex was obviously having an affair. I'm surprised he left it behind."

"No one at the drugstore knew anything about a boyfriend," Martin said. He walked past her toward the exit. "I need to see what Mr. Alex Bratton has to say. You wanna join me?"

"Rain check," Diana answered. "But let me know if Alex started seeing the pharmacist before or after his wife died. I think we already know the answer."

CHAPTER 11

Martin's interruption put Diana nearly an hour behind with her office schedule. She made up the time when the last two patients were no-shows. With no carpool today to transport Kelsey, Diana had just over 20 minutes to make the 35-minute drive to the soccer fields located deep off Old Canton Road. This meant navigating around the Pearl River in more five o'clock traffic. Somehow she made it.

"How was Coach today?" Diana asked.

Kelsey was still wearing her cleats and shin pads. Her loose black shorts fell to the mid-thigh and the yellow shirt branded with the surgery clinic's logo was grass-stained. She tossed her bag into the back seat. "Same as always—a total ass."

"Young lady, I don't like that."

"Everybody knows Coach prides himself on being a bad-ass, at least in the eyes of 10- to 12-year-old girls."

Diana missed the abrupt slowing of the Tahoe ahead. When the red lights broke through, she slammed her brakes and punished the horn.

"Oh my God, Mom. Be careful!" Kelsey pulled against the shoulder strap that tightened with her seat belt.

The Tahoe pulled away. Diana thought its driver made a gesture in the rearview mirror. "I don't like your language, Kelsey. No mom would."

"Sorry. Dads do."

"I'll discuss that with your father … when I see him … after we go over some other things." Diana passed the Meadowbrook Road exit and continued south on Interstate 55 to Lakeland Drive. Traffic was heavy. New commercial construction including a hotel, a several-story office building, and restaurants had recently claimed the mature oaks and pine trees to the east. In contrast, the acreage to the right remained dense with foliage, a buffer to the Woodland Hills and Fondren residential areas beyond.

"We taking the long way home?" Kelsey asked.

"We're going to stop by the hospital and say hello to Mr. Marzel."

"Shit, Mom. You're kidding." Kelsey kicked the floor mat, twice.

"Careful with those cleats. And save those moves for the soccer field and the dirt bag language for your father, young lady." Diana changed lanes. "Seeing your attitude today, I feel even better about what we're doing."

"What are you talking about?" Kelsey postured to kick again, then thought better of it. She folded her arms tightly. "Why do we have to go see that nerd? And what's with this 'young lady' crap—I mean stuff?"

Diana shook her head. They were hitting every red light. "Mr. Marzel needs to see a little thoughtfulness, some concern, from his students. Besides, from your behavior in the last few minutes it's obvious you need to show some respect for others ... and maybe act like a young lady."

"You just feel bad about Mr. Marzel," Kelsey said. She knocked the soccer ball between her feet and against the sides of the floorboard space. Her arms were still crossed. "You couldn't help him when he got sick, and you want me to make up for it."

"Kelsey, you're wrong—wrong on both counts. I mean, you're right about my concern, but Dr. Cummins and I did what we could for Mr. Marzel."

"I don't like that ... that geek. No one in school does."

"That's exactly why we're doing this." The drive leading to Jackson Metropolitan Hospital was lined in a leafed canopy of Bradford pear trees, dense with white spring flowers. A man standing with an IV pole near the outside edge of the porte-cochere lit a cigarette under the *No Smoking* notice. Diana turned into the parking lot in front of the multi-story structure that was in no way a high rise.

"Hey, the doctors' lot is over that way," Kelsey said.

"We're visitors today," Diana said.

"Like I'm supposed to walk through the hospital dressed like this and all sweaty?" Kelsey tossed the soccer ball into the back seat. She exchanged the soccer shoes and cleats for the tennis shoes in her bag. "This whole thing is lame, Mom. Four-year-olds run around town in their soccer outfits."

"'Four-year-old'... exactly." Diana skirted them through the main entrance and lobby, passing several employees and a patient or two. Without her white jacket and dressed in street clothes, Diana was surprised that few noticed her, just another harried-looking mom. Instead, they smiled at the scruffy, brunette eleven-year-old girl in the grass-stained soccer outfit.

"This elevator is smelly, Mom," Kelsey said.

Diana pushed the button to Mr. Marzel's floor. "I think it's you," she said.

Earlier that afternoon Marzel had earned a discharge from the medical ICU and transfer to a private room. A nurse was checking his vital signs when Diana and Kelsey tapped on the open door and slowly entered the room. Diana noticed the thick white gauze covering the lower part of his neck. The room was devoid of flowers, not even a carnation in a vase. There was no display of get-well cards and not a single basket of fruit.

"How long do we have to stay?" Kelsey whispered.

The nurse made a note of the blood pressure reading and looked up. "Dr. Bratton? I almost didn't recognize you."

"My daughter and I are here to visit for a minute, if that's OK. Mr. Marzel is her English teacher. I know we're a little late for visiting hours."

"No problem, Dr. Bratton," the nurse said. "Mr. Marzel is doing fine, just fine. Up for a little company, sir?" She winked at him and wheeled the blood pressure machine toward the door, then stopped. "But only for a few minutes, please. His doctor wants him to get some rest."

"Sure," Kelsey said, "gladly." She stood stiffly at the foot of the hospital bed. "My mom said we wouldn't be staying long."

"Hello, Kelsey." Marzel's raspy voice sounded weak, but friendly. He made an effort to raise his head from the pillow. "And, Mrs. Bratton, I remember you from parents' night at the school and from exercise class."

With her mother's nudge, Kelsey stepped around toward the head of the bed. "Hope you're feeling better. We miss you at school." She looked up at her mother for approval—her words recited exactly as practiced in the elevator. "Mr. Marzel, you know my mom's a doctor; don't you?"

Diana shook her head: *No need for that, Kelsey.*

Kelsey shrugged *whatever* and moved over to the window.

"They told me that your mother tried to help me outside the workout center," Mr. Marzel said. "I don't remember much from that afternoon."

"My partner at the surgical clinic, Dr. Brad Cummins, was also there. If we had known about your peanut allergy, we could have done more."

Marzel bent his right elbow into the mattress, barely enough pressure to dent the bedding but enough to raise his skinny, pale frame. He reached for his water glass and swallowed a long sip.

"That's just it. I'm not allergic to any kind of nuts, much less peanuts."

Diana stepped back, unsure that she had heard correctly. "Are you sure?" she asked.

"I know my medical history: no allergy to peanuts."

"But I checked with the internist," Diana said. Based on your test results and your response to the epinephrine, there was no question that you suffered an overwhelming allergic reaction, Mr. Marzel, something we call anaphylactic shock. And the rest of the cookie was lying beside you on the pavement."

"I know I'm an English teacher, Mrs. Bratton, but ..."

"It's *Doctor* Bratton," Kelsey said. She looked through the window blinds. "Mom, can we go now?"

"I'm sorry, Mr. Marzel. She's tired from soccer practice." Kelsey's shoulders jerked in reflex to Diana's murderous stare. She slumped a bit and sank into the plastic and metal chair at the window.

"What I was trying to say is that I'm not a scientist or a doctor," he attempted a smile in Kelsey's direction, "but I know my allergies, and peanuts is not on the list. Bee venom: that is my only true allergy."

"Mr. Marzel," Kelsey called out, "what kind of meds are you on? Are you freaking out?"

"Kelsey, what's gotten into you?" Diana envisioned the miserable grade in English for this six-week period, maybe even for the semester.

"Not to worry, Mrs. Bratton. It's no wonder Kelsey finds that odd. I raise bees and often discuss the hobby in class." Marzel took another drink of water and swallowed slowly. He coughed. "I try to inspire my students to work harder, but I'm afraid they will never equal the ethic of worker bees."

Kelsey did not look up from the chair. She held her cell phone in both hands, both thumbs popping up and down against the screen. "Yes. Got it. Another score," she mumbled.

"When I first became a beekeeper, the stings did not bother me, but the allergic reactions have developed gradually over time. My doctor says that I have become sensitized to even very small amounts of venom."

"Yes, that happens," Diana said.

Kelsey stretched her neck around from her chair to peer again through the slits between the blinds. "Sounds like a bee got to you in that parking lot. What do you think about that, Mr. Marzel?" she asked.

Diana frowned again, but realized the question was not far off. Chief Martin would be proud of the detective work.

"A garbage can is just outside the rear of the gym, near the parking," Mr. Marzel answered. "The odor is always atrocious, but there were no bees. I would have remembered."

"Do you sell the honey to make money?"

Diana wanted to ask the same thing.

"It's only a hobby and, fortunately for me, a safe one. I have learned to use a bee smoker when entering my own hives." He struggled to sit up, propping a folded pillow behind his back.

Diana looked toward the door, wishing for the nurse to assist him. She thought about using the call button, but fought a grimace and stepped closer to help.

"Smoke settles the little things down," Marzel continued. "Makes them feed on the honey and not the intruder. Their full stomachs prevent them from flexing their stingers."

"Mr. Marzel," Kelsey looked up from her video game, "that sounds like something you would tell us in class, sort of off the wall—then put it on one of our tests for bonus points."

"Maybe he will, Kelsey," Diana said, laughing softly. "You certainly need the points."

"So even if the bees aren't lethargic from the smoke, they have trouble attacking anyone entering the hive," he said. "That summary might be worth at least two points."

Diana hoped Marzel missed her daughter's eye roll. "Kelsey and I will have to come by sometime and take a tour of your beekeeping operation," she said. "Sounds fascinating."

"And I'll give you a jar of Marzel Honey. I don't sell it. I give it away to the homeless at the Stew Pot downtown."

The nurse returned with a tiny clear cup containing medication and set it on the tray next to the plastic pitcher of water and ice. The pitcher was branded with the hospital logo. She activated the electric controls to raise the head of the bed and adjusted Mr. Marzel's pillow. "Sir, your doctor has you down for discharge tomorrow if you continue to get better."

The nurse handed him the pitcher and bent the jumbo straw at the top toward his mouth, then passed him the clear cup. "Take these two little pills with a sip of water. I'm sure your doctor will keep you on this for another week." She stepped back and mouthed to Diana, out of sight to Marzel: "It's a steroid, Prednisone. I hope he'll follow instructions."

Kelsey was already at the door. "Glad you're improving. Mr. Marzel. See you in class."

Diana frowned.

Another mouthing: "OMG, Mom. Can we go now? Please?"

"We better let you get some rest," Diana said. "I'll share with Dr. Cummins that you're OK. He'll be so thankful. We all are."

"Thank you, Mrs. Bratton." Marzel stretched to sit up straighter, his voice still so weak that it barely carried across the room. "And, Kelsey, see you back in fourth period and in homeroom."

Kelsey stepped back into the room. "Sure, Mr. Marzel. We all miss you."

Diana started to smile.

Chapter 11

"Looking forward to teaching you again."
"Yeah, whatever," Kelsey said.

CHAPTER 12

"I'm not sure what's gotten into her. I guess I wasn't meant to be a mother," Diana said.

Phoebe stood at the kitchen counter of her new house and slit open the next box. She scooped the Styrofoam pieces from around the small antique figurine and dropped the handfuls into a plastic-lined garbage can. It nearly overflowed. "I asked the movers not to use this popcorn stuff," she said and plucked the other piece from deep within the cardboard container. "That's what I get for being sick and not there to supervise. Such a mess, such a royal mess."

"I think you handled all of this really well and in great style," Diana said.

"And you handle Kelsey so well," Phoebe said. "You are a wonderful mother."

"She would argue. I came close to grounding her last night … bad argument at home after visiting her teacher in the hospital. I'm surprised the Department of Human Services didn't show up."

"Maybe the neighbors couldn't hear," Phoebe said. She slit open another box.

"You have such precision with that box cutter," Diana said. "Maybe you're the one who should have been the surgeon in the family."

"Then I could have used that career as a substitute for kids," Phoebe said, "instead of having no excuse at all."

"It doesn't work that way anymore for us girls," Diana said. "You have to do it all: professional, wonderful wife, and unstoppable mom. Besides, didn't you and Uncle Terry try for kids?"

"Your uncle Terrance would have been a miserable father. Our children would have been miserable."

Diana said, "I remember him as a nice man."

"A nice man? Umm … indeed. But how much could a four-year-old remember?"

"Good point. But let me try." Diana caught herself staring into Phoebe's keeping room located off the kitchen, checking for a photograph of Uncle Terry in the bookcase, then realized she had never noticed one in the rental house. "Someone tall? Laughed a lot, grey hair, receding hairline."

Phoebe chuckled and tossed the empty box to the corner near the door to the garage. "Your mother always kept you looking so adorable, even at Terry's graveside service. Your little dress was solid navy, sharp lines, perfectly pressed, such a deep blue that it passed for black."

"I don't remember anything about that funeral, much less what I was wearing."

Phoebe carefully lifted the two figurines from the counter and stepped to the bookcase, arranging them near the center between two rows of books. She stepped back to admire the placement and returned to the kitchen counter. "But I suppose you do remember your parents' funeral?"

"I suppose I do, just don't like to think about it."

Diana carried her cup of coffee into the keeping room and studied the wall covering. "I see that grass cloth is back," she called over her shoulder. "At least the previous owner thought so."

She stood before the built-in bookcase that spanned the wall. Rows of contemporary novels with pristine, colorful book jackets, mixed with leather-bound antique volumes, were tightly packed into the shelf spaces surrounding other pieces of porcelain. The book arrangement mimicked ocean waves or oscillating radio wavelengths from a science book, staggering heights to the volumes, some set farther back than others, the bindings each unique.

The shelves were filled except for one section far to the right.

"You've made a lot of progress unpacking and arranging all these books since the move," Diana said. "I'm impressed. Would have taken me days ... or weeks."

"My decorator's already been over." Phoebe walked into the room, still holding the box cutter. "He brought some of his assistants. Took them no time, no time at all to get most of those books set and the empty cardboard boxes to the trash. And by the way, we're going to rip away that grass cloth—tomorrow, first thing. So dated."

Two boxes rested below the empty space, both remained sealed. The packaging was discolored, almost faded, and of a different cardboard texture than the few empties left behind by the interior decorator's staff. "Looks like they didn't quite finish," Diana said.

"They were to have come back right after lunch to finish, but, as you can see, a no-show," Phoebe said.

"I think I could handle finishing this up if you'd like for me to help out."

"Be my guest!"

Diana extended her hand for the box cutter. Phoebe ignored her and stepped past to open the boxes herself, each in one swift stroke.

"I don't think I ever unpacked these when I first moved to Jackson," she said. "Call me when you finish, so I can admire the work."

You mean approve the work, Diana thought.

She lifted the top three volumes from the first box, more antique leather bindings: *The History of the World, Part I* in three installments. *Part II* filled the rest of the box. Diana meticulously arranged the set on the first empty shelf, placing every other book two inches deeper than the rest, the rich brown binding set off the impressive gold lettering. "Maybe I should have skipped medical school for interior design."

Diana stepped back a few feet and judged the completed shelves against Phoebe's commissioned work. "Very nice job. Really nice," she said.

"Did you say something, Diana?" Phoebe's voice came from the kitchen.

"Almost got it. Only one box left. Your decorator better watch his back." Diana pulled open the freed cardboard leaves of the remaining box. The cover of the *1966 Ole Miss* stared up at her.

"College yearbook? I don't think I ever picked mine up from the student union." Diana lifted it from the box. There was no dust. The color and print on the binder and cover had dulled with time, and Diana found the pages nearly fused when she thumbed through it. There was a hint of stale new paper smell within the covers. "I guess Aunt Phoebe never looked through this before it was packed away," she said to herself.

She flipped back through the black-and-white photos, interspersed with an occasional color—a memorial to the 1965-66 academic and athletic year at the University of Mississippi. On display were lots of cheerleaders and football players; fraternity boys with neatly cropped hair, some still long enough to comb into perfect, greasy-looking piles; and pretty white girls smiling in groups and drinking cokes. Diana laughed. Some of Kelsey's friends dressed the same last Halloween. Candid interior shots of the library or classrooms were rare, and the male professors were formally photographed in dark suits with skinny ties.

"Here she is!" A young, beaming Aunt Phoebe was frozen for eternity, standing in the grandstand, surrounded by fans waving rebel flags and arm-in-arm with a tall, great-looking guy. Diana called into the kitchen. "Hey, Phoeb, who's the stud? Don't think it's Uncle Terrance."

She looked inside the front cover before sliding the yearbook into the remaining empty shelf. An inscription written in faded blue ink was scrawled across the center: "Wow, what a year! Glad you and I made it through to the bitter end. Love, Winston."

Diana flipped back to the football game photo. The tall, great-looking guy was a young Winston Ivy.

Diana stood motionless. She realized she wasn't breathing.

"Nice job, Diana," Phoebe said. "Seems you really do have a flare for finery."

Diana snapped the yearbook shut and set it on the shelf. "I didn't hear you come back in here." She clumsily pulled the other volumes from the carton and shoved them into the remaining spaces—the alignment haphazard at best. Her fingers trembled as she fumbled to straighten the books.

Phoebe stepped closer and set an unpacked Staffordshire hunting dog opposite its match. "These two puppies somehow were packed separately. I was afraid I had lost the other." Between the two pieces of antique painted porcelain, she rearranged several of the old leather books, placing them upright, the Staffordshire to serve as bookends. "Your fingers are trembling, Diana. Everything OK?"

Diana looked down at her hands, surprised. She slid them into the pockets of her slacks. "It must be the coffee. It's not that strong at the hospital, and I never make it at home."

Phoebe adjusted the dog on the left a half inch or so back.

"I'm a little puzzled, Aunt Phoebe. The other day ... when I walked in on your tea party with Winston Ivy, you said that you barely knew him in college, and you didn't even recognize him during the robbery at the convenience store."

Phoebe hesitated a moment, admiring her arrangement, tilting her head, changing the angle of view a few degrees to the right and left, and then in reverse. She pulled a few more books and added them to the collection between the porcelain pieces. "That's right. He said he remembered me from class, had spotted me on the front row ... made such a lasting impression on him ... or something like that."

"That's what I thought," Diana said.

"Thanks for emptying those last two cartons." Phoebe brushed by Diana and broke down the empty boxes scattered on the stone floor, sparing the one that had contained the yearbooks. She stacked the crushed boxes atop a short corner pile of earlier discards and flattened them a second time with her foot. The noise was loud.

Diana left for the living room, and Phoebe followed. "I should be going. I just dropped by in case you needed any help, but it looks like you're almost settled. It took me six months to make my place look livable, and it still needs work."

"I'm sorry, Diana. I didn't mean to dredge up the past with all that gibberish about funerals and all. I'm afraid I've upset you with old memories, bad memories. Please, come back into my kitchen. I've got a bottle of chardonnay in the fridge."

Realizing that her purse remained on one of the Ultrasuede kitchen bar stools, Diana followed, expecting Phoebe to address what she had just seen in the college yearbook.

"It's time to celebrate my move into this new place," Phoebe said instead. Two glasses appeared from a side cabinet, and she loosened the stopper to pour. "Join me?"

Diana's eyes widened and she shook her head slightly. "Your new place is wonderful, but some other time. Kelsey will be home soon." Diana retrieved her purse and walked again toward the front entrance.

Phoebe swirled the wine, sniffed, and tasted. "Almost waited too long to finish this one," she said and stepped after her.

"This weekend I'll bring Kelsey by to see the new place," Diana said over her shoulder. "I think a couple of her classmates live down the street."

"Diana, please. Slow down just a moment. I want to talk things over."

If there was anything to discuss, it was Winston's inscription in the old yearbook, but Diana was silent. She stood in the foyer, facing the door, late afternoon sunlight streaming through the transom to flood her eyes.

Phoebe was directly behind her, holding her wine glass and the bottle. "About your parents … you lost them much too soon. But I think you owe your drive and your ambition to them —indirectly, I suppose," she said.

Diana asked slowly, "What do you mean?" She remembered the silver-framed photo of her parents' last night, displayed in Phoebe's old library but missing from the new bookcase. She had never followed through with having the picture professionally copied.

Her mother and father were smiling at the country club photographer, streamers flying frozen mid-air above their heads. A *HAPPY NEW YEAR* headband held her mom's thick dark hair in place. The same inscription in glitter glowed in the flash across the face of her dad's black top hat.

"What do I mean?" Phoebe poured a full glass of the wine. "After your parents passed away, you took charge of yourself, made your own way, even in pre-school. From the start, you totally amazed your teachers."

"I don't remember much about pre-school," Diana said. But the memory of the photograph was clear: a beautiful couple in their late twenties, both smiling, radiant, happy. Her mother held an almost empty champagne glass, her father a bottle of Coke.

"Thank heavens your father was driving," Phoebe said. She took a long sip of the wine and held it a few minutes before swallowing. "Anyway, the other car hit them first."

Diana said, "It's been hard for me to thank heavens for anything since except for Kelsey."

"The insurance money helped and the trust took care of you," Phoebe said. "All I did was make sure you got to school on time. Please, Diana, come back to the kitchen for just a few more minutes. This move has been such an ordeal."

Diana remained at the door until Phoebe was gone. When she reentered the kitchen, Phoebe returned from the garage with another box labeled FRAGILE. She set it on the counter next to her wine glass, straightened her posture, and rubbed her lower back.

"That financial settlement would have stretched if I hadn't met Alex," Diana said, searching for a way to shift the discussion to Phoebe's history with Winston Ivy.

"I hope this is my Baccarat." Phoebe struck again with the box cutter and then reached deep inside, drinking wine with the other hand and draining the glass to only a third left. She stopped to give her back another massage. "The crystal goes in the mahogany cabinet in the dining room if you'd like to help."

Diana set her purse back on the stool and lifted the first stem of expensive crystal between the thumb and forefinger of her right hand and handled another with the left. She nearly slipped on the shiny, marble floor leading to the dining room. "I see the maid's already been here," she said. "Guess she waxed the marble."

Scattered boxes cluttered the dining room, nearly all half-empty, some pushed underneath the mahogany inlaid table on the oriental carpet. Working her way toward the china and crystal cabinet, Diana maneuvered between the carved antique chairs surrounding the table—some pushed under, others pulled away. Her foot caught one of the chair legs, but she managed to steady herself and maintain her grip on the Baccarat. She eased the glasses to the table, then turned the key to the cabinet. The door sprang open, and she slid both pieces to the rear of the second shelf.

Stepping back, her eyes fell on another unsealed cardboard box shoved against the foot of the cabinet. Diana recognized Phoebe's handwriting.

Unlike the printed label atop the box of crystal, **LIBRARY** was printed in large black letters on the sides and on the top.

Diana pulled apart the flaps of the thick cardboard. She pushed aside a few strands of packing material, allowing several pieces to scatter to the floor. Her parents' faces stared at her, the framed photograph resting on a bed of magazines, partially covering an *Entertainment Weekly*. She glanced toward the kitchen—no sign of Phoebe. Diana slid the framed photograph under her blouse, moving it around to her rear waist band. The glass in the frame and the sterling silver felt cold against her skin.

Phoebe called from the entrance to the dining room. "I see you found a nice spot for the Baccarat."

Diana stiffened, pinching her skin a bit against the frame.

"Actually, I remember having the crystal on the first shelf and on the left," Phoebe said. "But that's fine for now."

"Good," Diana said. "And, Aunt Phoebe, I sensed a *no comment* a minute ago when I brought up Alex. I made him my problem, but maybe if I had had someone around to talk to—a mom, or a sister, or even a dad—someone who might have seen through a bastard like Alex." She placed her hand behind her and felt the frame, the only physical remnant of blood family other than Kelsey. "If I had had some support, then things might have been different."

"My dear, you could have run it by me." Phoebe came into the dining room, crossing the oriental rug toward an unopened box. She had traded the box cutter for a kitchen knife.

"Oh, yes. Here it is," Phoebe said. She read aloud the small print stretched across the top and sides of the box. "*HANDLE WITH CARE.* I can do that." She broke the seal and worked her fingers between the edges. "You landed a bad boy, a bad boy with money, Diana. My grandmother would have said you landed your butt in butter."

"He wasn't bad until three years into the marriage," Diana said. "Until his money disappeared, he seemed thoughtful, kind, truly generous—even emotionally."

"Money always makes things better. Don't you think?" Phoebe popped open the box.

"By the time the money was gone," Diana answered, "I was well over his good looks … his great looks… and everything that went with that body."

"Infatuation is fleeting," Phoebe said. "Oh, my God! They broke a stem." Phoebe held the crippled piece to the light streaming from the front yard then reached back into the box.

"Those jackasses. Here's another one." With one hand, she held both decapitated wine glasses to the light. "I paid good money for that move and still got incompetence."

"Maybe insurance will help with that too," Diana said.

"Those idiot movers will pay big, really big, for this. These are my precious, precious things."

Just before Phoebe turned away, Diana caught a tear streak from the corner of her eye, marring the perfectly applied make-up and smooth complexion. She decided not to mention Winston Ivy.

"Sorry I can't stay to help more, but like I said … I need to get home," Diana called to her and walked back toward the front entrance.

"Then please do go, Diana." Phoebe tossed the broken pieces into the metal trash can under the kitchen sink. The shatter reverberated across the walled cabinetry. "No one, even your fabulous-looking ex-husband, has ever stopped you from doing want you want to do."

Diana shrugged her shoulders, opened the door, and left.

Phoebe quickly left the kitchen for the keeping room. She listened. The house was quiet. She removed the college yearbooks arranged by Diana in the cabinetry and repacked them in the cardboard carton left uncrushed. She then firmly pressed her fingers against the adhesive remaining at the edges of the split packing tape and resealed the box.

CHAPTER 13

"Did you little guys miss me?" Dewey Marzel stood just outside the row of beehives that occupied the far corner of his deep backyard, his voice muffled by protective headgear. He fumbled with a cigarette lighter to ignite his torch of brittle pine straw wedged into a straight section of PVC pipe.

"There you go." Smoke filled the first hive and billowed to the end of the row. His prized collection of bees sank into dormancy. "That's the way to do it. Nice and calm. Make daddy's job easier."

Marzel patted his front pants pocket for his EpiPen and stepped to the first hive. The deep super near the top brimmed with honey. "Ahh, you fellas stayed busy while I was sick."

He had fallen in love with beekeeping after watching *Animal Planet*. His mistake was beginning the hobby with this first hive, constructed with the deep super near the top and a strain to lift when harvesting the honey—an even greater challenge after his hospitalization. His newer hives were equipped with the medium or shallow supers which weighed less.

"Let's get this one taken care of first. The rest will be much easier." Marzel worked his fists and took a deep breath before pulling up against the weight. He braced his right foot against the earth surrounding the hive, slipping on an unseen patch of moist moss. In the struggle not to fall, he ripped open a worn section of waist band material in his protective pants. A sliver of pale skin peeped through.

Marzel lowered the deep super to collect the honey, his underdeveloped shoulder and back muscles screaming under the weight. The painful process was slow, and Marzel grew weaker. He missed the faint breeze that had drifted across the backyard and brushed away much of the smoke.

He moved to the next hive and raised the shallow honey super underneath. Despite the lighter weight of the outer and inner covers, the same white piece of skin appeared at the separation in the waist band. A straggler worker bee lifted her stinger and flew at Marzel.

"Shit!" His own outburst shocked him. Marzel dropped the tray, knocked the bee to the ground and crushed it under his boot. He groped the front pocket of his jacket. The house key felt cold against his finger tips.

"Not that!" He threw the key to the ground.

The carrying case of the EpiPen waited deeper in his pocket. Marzel's fingers ached, went numb, then icy before he reached it. He struggled with the cap seal at the top of the case and fought the freezing joints of his fingers. A feeble, clumsy effort finally released the cartridge of epinephrine from its vault to land near the crumpled worker bee.

Marzel clutched the invisible rope that tightened around his neck, struggling to breathe as he fell to his knees for the EpiPen. He managed a series of gasps while the light faded around him. The transparent section of the medication label glared up from the dust—the contents of the cartridge discolored, the medication expired. Marzel tried to shake the image away—back to the last day he had serviced the hive, the day before he went to the hospital, the day he had tossed that expired cartridge into the kitchen trash. He thought he remembered dropping a fresh one into his pocket.

Marzel forced a deeper breath and extended his arm and fingers to grab the cartridge. He plunged the needle deep into his right thigh. The liquid stung through his thin muscle. There was nothing in response. The steel noose around Marzel's neck grew tighter and tighter until a vise flattened his chest. The row of hives went dark.

More stranglers found Marzel an easy target once slumped on the ground. Even against his weak frame, the bees looked tiny—crawling across the teacher's jacket and pants—jumpy—darting back and forth, by nature both defensive and offensive—searching for exposed skin. Then bingo: another sliver of pale flesh at Marzel's neck. They squirmed under the clothing to disappear down Marzel's back. He never flinched. There were no chest movements, no respiration.

On the street below, the afternoon baby shower was breaking up. Dense, overgrown greenery and trees bordering the rear of Marzel's backyard obscured the hives from the group. Women's voices and laughter, mixed with the sound of car and SUV doors opening and closing, rose through the branches and leaves.

"Dessert was fabulous! Caterer outdid herself this week."

"Yeah, I know. Yoga won't be enough tomorrow."

"It's power fitness class for me this afternoon."

"Not for me. I've still got to see clients at the office."

The ladies were preoccupied. No one was looking up toward the hives. No one would see, and come tomorrow the middle school principal would again be missing an English teacher.

No doubt the principal would first call Marzel's cell, then check with the hospital to see if he had been readmitted. When patient information turned up empty, she would send someone to this house, probably the assistant principal. A knock at the door would go unanswered. The assistant would not snoop around, not think to check the backyard, or might call out the name but not go to the extreme of walking all the way out to the beehives.

However, in a few days a neighbor's dog might sniff around the edge of the fence and bark at the body or at the smell.

CHAPTER 14

Oxford, Mississippi
Fall 1965

"I'll see you five and raise you ten. That roll in your pocket should cover it," Phoebe said.

The makeshift card table consisted of a tight blanket and mattress atop Winston Ivy's single bed, repositioned from the wall more toward the center of his dorm room. Turned sideways, Winston's leather recliner worked well for poker as long as he leaned across the arm. Phoebe and Dewey occupied the two desk chairs pushed up to the bed while Carvel had brought his chair from down the hall.

"Dream on. That roll in my pocket doesn't exist—what that a-hole last semester in English lit called 'fiction'," Carvel Eaves said. "I fold. Besides, don't you have curfew?" He slid his hand from the five cards just planted face-down and caressed the front pocket of his baggy pants. Hidden inside was a roll of bills, thickened to $1700 after last weekend and tightly bound with two rubber bands.

"Quit feeling yourself up, Eaves. If you want a hand job ..." Dewey Marzel tilted his head toward the only female member of the poker game.

Phoebe hurled a new Kennedy half-dollar at Marzel. It hit his forehead dead center. The coin fell to the bedspread and bounced twice. Phoebe retrieved it midair and returned it to her pile.

"Shit!" Marzel rubbed his forehead. "What about your curfew? Nine, isn't it?"

"None of you creeps should ever count on my curfew," Phoebe said. "Besides, if I worried about something as silly as curfew, do you think I'd be up in a boys' dorm room in the first place?"

"You're only on the second floor," Winston said and checked his gold wristwatch. "You got ten minutes to get back to Stewart Hall." He shuffled the deck and slid it to the right for Marzel to cut.

"Can you sprint back to Stewart in ten minutes?"

"I don't sprint, Winston." Phoebe answered. She counted the rest of her change and stacked it into piles of quarters and half-dollars. The dollar bills and fives were separated into neat stacks to complete the picture. "Besides, I tipped the dorm mother another ten. She cost me my bottle from Johnny's the last time I slipped out."

Winston started the deal to the left: Phoebe, Carvel, Dewey. With the second card, he said, "Johnny's doesn't get much whiskey, Babe. Too bad you wasted it."

"Just deal, Ivy," she said. "Deal."

The remaining cards whirled to the four positions around the bed.

"And I heard that roomie is squirreled away in the infirmary," Dewey said, still rubbing the red blotch on his forehead. "So what'd you do this time? Poison her?"

Winston's deal was completed. Phoebe inspected her cards. She spread the five into a perfect fan.

"Be careful, Marzel. She's liable to stuff one of those twenties down your throat," Eaves said. "Or up your ass."

"I think ass," Phoebe said. "But I'd rather take your milk money than trash mine."

The dealer said, "Ante up the usual two bucks, gents. That includes you, Phoeb."

Marzel was the last to toss in the ante. He produced a two-dollar bill. "I want to hear a little more about how a girl can escape curfew. Might come in handy this weekend."

"Doubt that you'd ever need it, Marzel," Phoebe said. "But for me, no reason to waste a roommate's stomach virus: all alone in the dorm and nowhere to go."

"So you really didn't poison her?" Winston asked as he studied his five cards.

"Think she got it with a bad burger at Lambert's," Phoebe answered. "Cramps hit her on the way back from Marks, and it wasn't her time of the month."

"Gross," Carvel grunted. "You could have skipped that." He studied his hand. "Go ahead and bet, Phoebe. After that last one, I'm down a hundred."

"Cash flow is never a problem for you, Eaves," Winston said. "Like she just said, you've got the market cornered."

Carvel switched his cards to his left hand and again stroked the thick roll in his pocket. "Anybody up for Kiamie's after we're done here?" he said.

"Hungry, Eaves?" Phoebe peered over the top of her cards. "I heard that stuff Dewey sells you works up an appetite."

"That's not it. I was late to supper—cafeteria already closed." He rearranged his hand. "I don't have a sorority house and guys standing around to serve me five courses."

Two light knocks at the door were followed by three loud thuds. Then the series was repeated. "OK, OK, Rusty, we'll let you in." Winston unlocked the door and slipped back to his seat in one smooth motion.

"I heard something about Kiamie's through the door," Rusty said in the doorway. "Sounds like a winner to me. I'm starved." He walked back into the hall and returned with his own desk chair. He closed the door behind him. Winston's room was getting crowded.

Phoebe said, "This game was supposed to be private. How's a girl going to maintain her reputation?"

"We ought to turn you over to Chief Tatum—lock you up and cut out the competition," Dewey said.

"UPD loves sorority girls, don't you know—almost as much as they love cookies ... fresh sugar cookies or chocolate-chip, warm and gooey," Phoebe said. "I pay the cook at the house to bake a dozen for me the first weekend of every month, and I drop them off. So, every officer at the campus police department knows me by name. They worship me."

"Don't we all," Winston said.

Rusty pulled his chair closer to the foot of the bed and straddled it. "Somebody loan me a dime. I'll call in the order from the hall phone."

"Pizza sounds good," Winston said. "Pepperoni. Add sausage, lots of it." He smiled at his hand.

"Go ahead and put it on my tab," Dewey said as Rusty left for the phone. "Tell 'em to charge an extra ten. I need a little cash back."

"We'll finish this hand while Rusty orders. I'll start at five bucks."

"Five, Phoebe?" Winston said. "Just five? You must not have much this time. I call your five and raise you ten."

Marzel studied his hand and scratched his head. "Let me see." The comb over had already started.

"Come on, Dewey," Phoebe said. "You can handle it. Your customers will cover you."

"OK, I'm in. Here's fifteen."

"Memphis is a pretty good market for you then, Dewey. That right?" Winston asked. He folded. "I hope delivery brings napkins this time. I don't have any toilet rolls to spare."

"We'll manage, Mr. Host." Phoebe counted out ten more ones and stacked them neatly in the center of the bed.

"Shit." Carvel rubbed his roll of bills. It seemed to be shrinking. He threw in a ten from the money in front of him on the bed.

"Keep your hands out of your lap, Carvel, for gosh sake," Phoebe said. "Watcha got, Dewey?"

Dewey showed his pair of tens and pair of jacks.

"I've got three kings." She spread her cards face up across Winston's cotton bedspread. She appreciated the finely woven cotton. "You, Carvel?"

Carvel Eaves tossed in his losing hand and rubbed the bankroll again. He silently pulled loose a twenty from his pocket and replenished the shrinking stack of bills before him.

"Maybe I can expand operations," Dewey said.

"You'll recover, Dewey." Phoebe raked the cash toward her and sorted the winnings into denomination. "Might be able to go to sorority ball after all," she said. "My dress is in the window at Neilsen's, on hold. I'll worry about a date later."

"It'll take more than a few pots on a window sill to make up for your lousy cards, Dew Boy," Winston chuckled.

"Pots for the pot," Phoebe said. "Very clever, Winston. Very clever." She collected the deck and shuffled. "Get serious and cut."

Winston chose only to tap the top of the deck with his forefinger.

Phoebe took back the deck and started to deal. The five knocks came again at the door. "Dewey, you're closest. Let Rusty in."

"All right, guys and gal. Two pizzas, and on your account, Marzel. Runner will have the extra ten for you."

"Thanks." Marzel pulled in the three cards and followed Phoebe's hands until the deal was completed.

"Y'all deal me in next hand?" Rusty asked, taking his chair.

"You at least got ante?" Phoebe said, trying to hide her grin.

"Just got my $25 for the month. Need to double it."

"Ahh ... you must have big plans," she said.

"My club's party is in Memphis this weekend—a cheap hotel downtown. We booked four frat guys to a room, but also gotta pay for the dates' room."

Carvel Eaves said, "Why don't all eight cram in and bunk together, Rusty? Might make for a hell of an intermission."

"Don't be crude, Carvel," Phoebe said. "A lady is present. And concentrate on the game. Start the bet."

"Lady present?" Carvel asked. "How does a lady climb a tree into the window of a boy's dorm room?" He was the last one to put in two dollars. He followed it with a ten-dollar bet.

"The tree worked for getting Phoebe up here last Monday. But tonight, this new guy was filling in as dorm monitor. He left check-in unattended for a few minutes, taking a piss or something." He studied his cards. "Sorry for the language, Phoebe," Winston said.

Dewey had folded, but Winston called the ten.

"See the ten, raise twenty," Phoebe followed. "The baseball cap, the jeans, Winston's jacket—didn't need any disguise this time. Just walked through the door."

Carvel reached into his pocket and peeled away an extra twenty. He dropped the crumpled bill into the pile. "I'll see you."

"Are you sure you don't have your own crop of weed stashed somewhere?" Dewey asked. "I'm out." He tossed his cards faced down on the bed, then stared out the window.

"Me too." Winston said.

Carvel spread his cards face up in a perfect fan, resembling a train of peacock feathers. "How about this straight, you suckers." He jumped for the cash.

"Don't be so quick, Carvel. Isn't that what your dates tell you?" Phoebe said, her spread of all hearts trouncing Carvel's peacock dance. "A flush for me, boys. Read 'em and weep."

She grabbed the money in her left hand and slid it toward her. "Guess I should start my own pocket bankroll. Or maybe a 'wad' of bills sounds more impressive."

"Too much for me," Carvel Eaves said, checking his pocket again. "I'm outta here." He brushed by Rusty on the way to the door. "Move over to my seat. Maybe I warmed it up for you."

The door slammed shut behind him.

Winston said, "Yeah, take Eaves' place over here by me, Rusty. And are you gonna get back to the game, Marzel. Or is it just three now?"

"I'm in," he said, still transfixed at the window. "Need to recoup some funds from this newbie." He spun around and flicked his forefinger and thumb at Rusty. "Really looking forward to it."

"Found a book on poker in the library," Rusty said. "Think I've got it figured out."

Rusty's hair had recovered from the freshman shave, enough to comb and part, and Phoebe compared him to handsome Dobie Gillis from TV. She liked the thick blond hair, a contrast to Winston's tight, auburn crown. College was agreeing with Rusty; he looked more handsome by the minute. She fought back a smile.

"We'll just have to see. Won't we, Rusty?" Phoebe shuffled the deck and slid it to him. "It was the quitter's deal, so you go ahead, or did you skip that chapter in your library book?"

"Memorized it," Rusty said.

Rusty's deal was fast. Before Phoebe could retrieve her cards, he was holding his and tossing in his ante. "Dewey?" he asked. "You gonna pass?"

"Don't take too much for granted, freshman," Dewey said. "Sound too eager and you give yourself away."

Dewey tossed the five into the center. He could not lose any more money. In fact, he hated to rely solely on his marijuana crop, but adding pots was an option. Traffic remained light on the short, dead-end street off College Hill Road where he rented, and sunlight was good there. More than likely adding marijuana plants on his front porch would go unnoticed.

"Marzel?" Phoebe and Winston said in unison.

He studied the cards and looked at the others. He winked at Phoebe and licked his lips.

"Disgusting, Dewey," she said. "Put up or shut up." He added the loan from Kiamie's to his first five-dollar bill.

"See your 15. Raise you 15," Winston said, stone-faced.

Phoebe: "See 30, raise 30."

Rusty: "See that 60, raise … 60."

Dewey envisioned the planted clay pots lining the waist high brick wall in the backyard, withering since it had not rained in days. He would have to water tomorrow. There was really no time to expand the business, what with packaging the dope, deliveries, and remaining undercover.

"Marzel?" All three spoke this time and much louder.

"I'm in." Dewey Marzel shook his head. He now had three bucks left to his name.

Winston looked at Phoebe's bank—much thicker than his.

Rusty spread his cards. "Three aces, two queens."

"Shit" sounded from around the makeshift poker table—the cursing repeated as three hands of cards were tossed at Rusty's outstretched arms and clenched fists held high in victory. He bent and dragged the cash to his chest.

"Shit," Dewey said again. "I'm out for good." He pushed away from his chair, sending it crashing to the floor, and pulled open the door to meet the startled pizza delivery man on the other side. The ordered pizzas were balanced on the guy's left arm, the right hand as though ready to knock. "I'll take that box on top," Dewey said. "Collect from them."

Winston called out, "Hey, you ass. You're buyin' next time."

Rusty paid the guy from Kiamie's and offered Phoebe the first piece of pizza from the remaining box.

Winston collected the scattered deck and shuffled. "Eat up, buds," he said. "Getting late. Lights out in the dorm in thirty."

To block any light seeping through the window, Phoebe drew the drapes over the closed blinds. The drape fabric felt expensive, custom constructed, too nice by dorm standards. "Your mom fix this room up for you?"

"What do you think?" Winston said. He shuffled another time. "We can get by with the desk lamp. Get the extension cord out of the drawer and move it over here to the bed."

"I'm not the maid, Winston," Phoebe said. "Too bad your mom didn't send one with you."

"You wanna help out and make enough money for that dress, or not?" Winston asked. "Just asking for a little teamwork."

Rusty was quiet. He stared down at his pile of money, mesmerized, as though he wanted to count it—over and over.

Winston shuffled again. "Stop gloating, Rusty."

"That dorm monitor downstairs is likely to walk the halls soon," Phoebe said. "He'll see light under the door. We gonna play in the dark?"

"You're the pledge, Rusty. Get off your butt and move the rug to cover the crack at the bottom of the door. Stuff it in there real good. Tape it to the door and floor if you have to. Tape's in my desk drawer."

"Good idea, Winston," Phoebe said. "But when your momma bought that throw from her decorator, I don't think she meant it as a way to fool the hall monitor."

"It's worked before," he said. "And what do you know about my momma?"

Rusty folded the rug slightly and propped one end up against the door with Marzel's chair, blocking the light from the hall. He stepped back to the game and cut the deck. "Besides towels, underwear, and one set of sheets, the only thing my mother sent up with me was a transistor radio," Rusty said.

"No shabby transistor radio in here." Phoebe looked at her first two cards and then pointed to the small stereo sitting on the unused second desk. Winston's family paid extra for no roommate. "A private room, custom drapes, woven rugs, matching towels and washcloths—plush Egyptian cotton sheets? Yes, I know a lot about your momma, Winston. She shipped you off to Ole Miss in style."

"It takes more than money to be in style," Winston said.

"But a lot of money is a great place to start," she said. "I wouldn't be in your room for any other reason."

Winston hid his smile. "Are you going to bet, or not?"

"Keep your voice down. I think I hear the monitor walking outside. Last thing I need is to get busted again." She rubbed her right thumb across the face of each card as though to count. "Nothing this time."

"And you, Rusty?" Winston asked.

"Twenty-five." Rusty dropped the five dollar bills into the center of play from high above the bed. They almost floated in place. His bank barely looked touched.

Winston smiled, but hesitated a little too long. "See yours. And raise you 25."

"See the 25 and raise 50."

Winston's artificial smile disappeared. "Fifty it is." He felt for the thin wallet in his back pocket. He still needed to eat.

Today's letter from his parents turned down the request for an advance. *"Finish out the semester with what we've already given you."* Winston was confident that his father overruled his mother and typed the letter himself.

"Three aces," Rusty said.

Winston rolled his eyes and scattered his cards across the bedspread. "Fuck. Three kings."

"I'm afraid, Baby Rusty, that Winston is a poor loser, very poor," Phoebe said.

CHAPTER 15

"I'm a little hungry. Don't suppose you have enough cash for a hotdog?" From low in the student section, Phoebe looked blankly down at the football field, empty except for the cheerleaders and the photographers standing on the track.

"Afraid not," Winston said. He brushed a wrinkle out of his blue blazer. It was early afternoon, the first fall day in Oxford cool enough for a jacket. "And if our student tickets weren't free, we wouldn't be here at all."

"My life's story," Phoebe said. "Guy invites me to a free football game and can't even buy lunch."

Another sweep at the jacket, beginning at each shoulder, crossing first with his right and then left hand, before Winston said, "Same goes for our dinner date at Grundy's."

A long black Cadillac rolled down the track from the north end of the stadium, parting the cheerleaders and photographers while the team burst onto the field. The car eased to a stop at the box seat on the 50-yard line. A diminutive elderly woman stepped from the rear seat and extended her hand to the chauffer. Phoebe admired the woman's tailored suit, the alligator pumps, the jeweled lapel pen, the floppy silk hat—not for a girl her age but a definite if she were 50 years older.

As she eased into her seat, the woman threw a tight wave and smile at the cheering football spectators around her, the chauffeur holding the seat in place as though it might spring from its base any second.

Phoebe said, "That lady's got it made."

"Something to work toward, I suppose," Winston said. "You can be that, Phoebe."

They both drank straight Coca Cola from their stadium cups.

"Maybe, but for now I'm thinking about dinner," she said. "What about driving up to Holly Springs instead of Grundy's? The Harbor Grill?"

"Last thing I remember eating there was a pickled egg."

"The place is cheap. Isn't that what you're after?" Phoebe asked.

"If it weren't for Rusty, I wouldn't be in this predicament."

"Me either." Phoebe smiled and waved weakly at one of her sorority sisters. She hated her. The breasts couldn't be real. No one should look that good in a sweater.

Winston asked, "Whose idea was it to let that cheater Rusty into the card game?"

"Yours, Winston. I'm sure of it."

"That's not what I remember," he said, shaking his head but unable to resist returning a smile from one of the cheerleaders. "Doesn't matter anyway. The money's gone."

"And it looks like I won't be getting that party dress after all," Phoebe said. She took the final swallow of her soda. "Consolation prize is an offer from my roommate's big sister. It's from a couple of seasons ago, but fits—barely. Too bad it smells like moth balls."

The Rebels ran the kickoff back to the forty. Phoebe and Winston stood with the crowd and joined the screams and clapping. Both worked up a smile. "Dixie" boomed from the band in the next section.

"Phoebe, we can't let that happen again. My parents don't give me a blank check. This morning when I called home for more money, my mother said she was gonna drive up from Forest and haul my ass home."

"I doubt that's what she said, Winston." An interception lost 10 yards. The crowd and the sea of miniature Confederate flags deflated. Winston and Phoebe had shown no interest in waving theirs.

"Are you sure you don't have enough money at least for another Coke?" Phoebe asked.

"My mom really said that. They might make me come home because of the cash," Winston said. "And besides, isn't a water fountain down in the girls' room?"

"Your mother is as polite and well-bred as that lady down there in the Cadillac. She'd never let her baby go hungry, and that water fountain smells, black algae growing all along the rim. Just nasty."

"I'll let you update your opinion of my mother later." Winston lit a cigarette. Wind caught the smoke and blew it in Phoebe's face. "Sorry," he said and turned away.

"We should have stopped the game with Rusty after that first night. Shit-ass Eaves and that dope-head Marzel … even they had sense enough to stop playing with him."

"Phoebe, that pristine mother of mine calls such crappy language 'potty mouth.'"

"I'm not surprised." Phoebe took a drag from Winston's cigarette, then stuck it back between his lips. She exhaled with the breeze, her face angled toward him.

Winston coughed and waved the smoke away.

They turned to see the defensive halfback intercept a pass and run for a goal line. "Go, Tommy, Go!" Phoebe screamed with the other co-eds around her. Seconds later Tommy James made the touchdown. The girls jumped up and down, their skirts flopping in unison as though choreographed. Phoebe continued to force another scream or two of exhilaration, but stopped short of squealing with the others.

Winston said, "You know that roll Carvel used to carry around in his pocket? The guys used to think he was playing with himself when he would finger it. He was trying to count the bills without letting anybody see."

"Rusty took care of that problem, finished him off at the last game," Phoebe said. "No more roll to finger. I heard that Carvel couldn't even pay his rent last month."

"He'll be lucky to make it to Thanksgiving, much less next semester."

Ole Miss kicked the extra point. The first half was over. More cheering, screaming, and flag waving. The band erupted with "Dixie." Phoebe stayed put.

Both teams ran toward the locker rooms. The marching band parted out of the way, but not before a stout girl brandishing a flute and a much trimmer Rebelette in sequined uniform were nearly knocked down.

"I wonder if Rusty carries his winnings around with him like Carvel did," Phoebe said. "I'll have to check his front pocket for a bulge."

"You do that. Let me know what you find."

"I will. Count on it."

And now ladies and gentleman ... presenting the Ole Miss Marching Band ... the Pride of the South bellowed from the loudspeakers. The Rebelette had recovered and joined the others in line. A majorette tossed her baton to catch it twirling to earth. The girl with the flute was lost among some trombone players.

"Carvel was always ready for a card game. Always churning that roll," Phoebe said. "Let's hope Rusty's the same."

The Rebelettes were performing to "Leader of the Pack." The band was spread across the center of the field in what was supposed to be the shape of a motorcycle wheel, while the majorette twirled in the center of the spokes.

"I'm going to hit the men's room." Winston said. He flashed open the inside of his blazer. The cap of a small flask peeked out from the pocket.

He fingered the sterling silver cap. "This is the last of it. Guess we could indulge a bit."

"Ladies don't drink bourbon straight, especially from a bottle, even a fancy one like that."

"You and your standards." Winston let the flask drop deeper into the pocket and buttoned the jacket. The brass buttons were imprinted with a Roman soldier's profile. "I think I can scrounge up enough money for another Coke, even a big cup," he said. "I'll stop by the concession stand on the way back."

Winston worked his way into the dense crowd as it spilled slowly down the concrete ramp to the concession area under stadium seating. He was halfway there when Phoebe slid her arm around his waist.

"I need the ladies' room," she said. "And I need to make sure you don't come up with money for that hot dog and eat it all yourself."

"You think I'm that stingy? Maybe I was trying to surprise you."

A throng of noisy hungry and thirsty football fans surrounded Winston and Phoebe. The lines to the concession counters were already eight to ten deep, puffs of cigarette smoke beginning to collect in a cloud overhead. The confines of the concrete stadium overhead and the supporting pillars trapped the clamor into an almost deafening roar. The line leading to the ladies' room stretched around a corner. "I better take my place before it gets any longer," Phoebe said.

"Then I'll meet you back at our seats ... if that's OK. Halftime's almost over."

"Sure ... but save me a bite of that dog."

Winston smiled as Phoebe disappeared around a concrete post toward the restroom. He looked up to the board posted on the wall behind the counter: *Coke or Sprite—Small—10 cents, Stadium Souvenir Cup 25 cents. Small Coke – Hot Dog Combo 49 cents.*

Several members of a scout troop were manning the counter. Toward the rear of the booth an overweight lady dressed also in cub-scout blue dropped weiners onto electric rotisseries. She barked orders to the boys at the front.

"May I help you, sir?" asked one of the taller ones. He was sweaty, looked to be about eight or nine, dark hair poking from under his hat.

A voice from the line to the popcorn machine yelled above the crowd. "Put it on my tab, young fella. Whatever my associate wants: popcorn, hot dog, slice of pizza, whatever."

Winston glared at Rusty, then wished he had ignored him.

"Just a large Coke, the big red cup," he said and felt the flask inside his jacket.

Rusty called out, sticking his head clear of the others in line and cupping his hands. "Little Cubby, go ahead and load that fella up—whatever he can carry up to his date. It's all on me."

The Cub Scout's nearest partner, a shorter kid who was beginning to get pimples, handed off the large plastic cup filled with ice and topped with Coca-Cola. He looked up at Winston. "Want anything else, sir? I'm sorry, but you're holding up sales."

"Just the Coke." Winston paid and escaped from the line behind him. He maneuvered toward the student section.

Rusty pushed through the line to block Winston's path. He was loaded down with a cardboard tray of food. "I hope there're no hard feelings from the other night," Rusty said. "Man, those were some shitty cards you got. Couldn't help but clean you out." He lifted the tray under Winston's face. "I thought I might lend a hand, so to speak."

"Don't need charity, Reynolds. What I need is to play cards with someone on the up-and-up." He brushed by Rusty. "You better look for yourself a different game. You're not welcome in mine anymore."

Rusty trailed Winston up the ramp to the seating, within easy earshot despite the stadium noise exploding with kickoff. "Nobody would teach me the game, hot shot, so I studied up. Sometimes if you're smart it's easy …"

"Look, you ass, if you were really smart you would stay clear of me." Winston was just a few rows away from his seat. "And like I said, find somebody else's game and keep your shitty food."

Rusty shrugged and stepped over to the trash can with the tray, then seemed to think better of it. "Shouldn't be a problem, your highness. Heard your trust fund's blown for the semester, so your seat at the table is empty. Seems like you'll be looking for some other pastime."

Winston raised the cup to slosh the Coke and ice in Rusty's face. Rusty recoiled, then Winston remembered that was his last quarter and lowered his arm.

"You guys having a little chitchat?" Phoebe moved between them up the ramp and considered Rusty's tray. People were brushing against them from all sides. "Looks delightful."

Rusty said, "Take whatever you want."

The three were shoved along with the crowd back to the aisle between the rows of bench seating. Phoebe waved her forefinger over the cardboard tray with a little twirl and reached for the peanuts. "These should be the easiest on the waistline," she said.

Winston grunted, "No, Phoebe. We're gonna pass."

Her hand froze in mid-air over the small bag. "The popcorn instead?"

"Nothing. This asshole bought all that shit with blood money, my money. See you around, Reynolds." Winston grabbed Phoebe's hand suspended over the food and escorted her into the row of fans, barely missing several feet.

Looking back at the snacks in admiration, Phoebe tripped over the three people closest to the aisle. Winston's long legs stretched over them as Phoebe continued to stumble behind.

"Excuse me. So very sorry. Not sure why he's in such a hurry. Hope that toe's OK," she greeted each person. Seated she asked, "Winston, was that necessary? Why the hurry?"

"I needed to get away from Rusty before I leveled him. Don't need campus security on my back. My parents are already threatening to bring me home, and I don't see myself working in a chicken plant."

"I don't either, but the real question is why turn down the handout? We're both hungry."

"Still have my pride, don't you?" Winston said. The Ole Miss Rebel defense prevented a touchdown. Waving Rebel flags again sprung around them. Screams of the "Hotty Toddy" chant deafened Winston and Phoebe.

"Whatever money Rusty Reynolds is carrying around … a good chunk of it belongs to me," Winston said. He found his own flag at his feet and waved it limply, the jubilance lost on him. Then he remembered the bourbon and the Coke. This was the right time. He learned forward toward his feet, head down, and removed the flask from his jacket, then poured.

Phoebe said, "He's cleaned us all out: Carvel, Dewey, and me. At least you've got a bankroll at home to prop you up."

Winston had ripped apart the last letter from his father, an angry answer to his request for another advance. His father's profanity surprised him. "I'm afraid the well might be running dry," he said. He leaned into Phoebe's ear to whisper, impossible because of the noise around them.

"Grandfather Ivy's stingy trust fund spits it out on a strict schedule, and Dad's stopped filling in the gaps. He's still pissed that he never got total control over my inheritance."

"I've never had that problem," Phoebe said. A fumble and bad call from the officials brought boos and a smorgasbord of profanity around them.

"I've gotta take some of that back from Rusty Reynolds," Winston said. He took a long drink from his cup. The bourbon burned his throat.

"You said you weren't going to play with him anymore."

"Who said I was going to get it back playing poker?" The screaming fans began to collapse in their seats. Winston put the cup again to his lips, but Phoebe eased it away from him, took more than a taste and swallowed hard.

"One more of those on my empty stomach and I'll be shit-faced in no time," she coughed, her throat burning. "But before you finish that, let me have another sip … a quick one."

Winston glanced down into the cup, already half empty. He looked around for any easy target for a small loan to buy more and spotted Rusty Reynolds 10 rows up—laughing, talking, eating, drinking—looking happy and rich. Rusty eased his arm around the girl next to him. *Reynolds has a date?* The girl was cute, some coed Winston had never seen before, probably some freshman that slipped by.

In his anger down in concessions, Winston had missed Rusty's blue blazer. Even from where he and Phoebe sat, the jacket looked perfectly pressed and much better tailored than his—probably from Duvall's on the Square or an expensive men's store in Memphis—like Oak Hall. Even the starched khakis and white button-down looked new. The tie—the new tie—might be silk. Winston Ivy was a good judge of expensive, and he could spot an expensive tie even from 15 rows away. Grandfather Ivy's money had dressed that bastard and dressed him well.

Rusty pulled his date closer and kissed her. "The asshole just winked at me," Winston said under his breath.

"You say something?" Phoebe said, her eyes on the football field.

Winston's drink was almost gone. A money patsy was nowhere in sight. He thought again about his shrinking trust fund. There was no way to replace it. That afternoon on the long, wide lawn when his grandfather had told him: "You'll be taken care of when I'm gone, Win," his response was: "Come on, play ball, Granddad."

The smooth green grass of his grandfather's house had been perfect for baseball, especially if the team had only two members. The house on Highway 90 in Pass Christian, Mississippi, looked as though it were transplanted from Natchez or Columbus, Mississippi, or somewhere in the Delta. Winston's parents dragged him to such places on weekend road trips, any place within easy driving distance from Forest. He forced himself awake during the tours of stuffy rooms, defined by heavy furniture and thick carpets and docents rambling on and on about what used to be.

Grandfather Ivy's house was different. Winston loved to visit. It looked lived-in, but remained bright and cheery, Grandmother's influence lingering after her stroke and death. Then a few summers later, after that final baseball game on the front lawn, his grandfather died alone in that big, old house—a heart attack or a stroke or maybe both. Winston never understood which.

Within a few days, his father announced: "Your grandfather has left you some money for college, Win. Enough to send you to an in-state school, Ole Miss, if you're wise. That's what Dad would have wanted."

The promise of a trust fund meant little to twelve-year-old Winston Ivy, but it meant the world to him now.

"That's your only chance for college, Winston, unless you work your way through, like my father made me. Just stay focused and study. Your grandfather's given you the cushion I never had."

A Rebel interception on the 22-yard line brought everyone to their feet, including Phoebe, and brought Winston out of his trance. He sneaked a look back at Rusty and his date. They were the only two persons not glued to the football field. He turned back around to the game just as the pair unlocked their faces and their lips. The losing fans on the opposite of the field were streaming out of the stadium. Winston wanted to join them.

"Dixie" again exploded from the band, the music nearly drowned by the screams of *Hotty Toddy, Gosh Almighty* erupting around Winston.

"Come on, Winston. A little yelling will make you feel better," Phoebe said into Winston's ear, her voice hoarse. "My throat's gone from whiskey sore to yelling sore."

Who in the hell are we? Flim flam, bim bam. Ole Miss …

Again Winston glanced in Rusty's direction. Waving Rebel flags blocked the view this time.

"By damn," he muttered in synchrony with the last of the cheering crowd and stared in anger at the jubilant pandemonium down below.

A young male student wearing a red bowtie and working as school photographer aimed his camera at Winston and Phoebe. She nudged Winston in the side and slid her arm around his waist. "Snap out of it for gosh sakes—and smile."

One benefit of little money to spend on Saturday night beer and liquor is little hangover on Sunday. After the game, Phoebe's spare change sprang for a hamburger and fries to split at the Beacon as long as Winston bought the Cokes. He did not argue when the split looked more like 60-40, her way.

In the ensuing weeks and for the first time in months, he squirreled himself away in the library, knowing that without a financial windfall, graduation was doubtful, much less paying his fraternity bill. But perhaps better grades to end the fall semester might bring some sympathy from the chicken farm. He doubted that even a Taylor medal in his major would help much.

Winston slammed the textbook shut and earned a loud "shush" from the desk around the corner and another from behind the bank of periodicals. In retaliation, he pushed his chair hard away from the cubicle, scraping the metal legs against the floor. He left for the small snack bar in the student union, an easy walk from the library but a rather long one with no money to spend. If a girl was working the counter, there was sometimes free coffee from the dregs of a pot or maybe a sliver of pie from the last of a pan. Ice water was always free, and Winston still had his looks. Unfortunately, a guy was working the counter tonight. He wore a white cook's cap and apron.

The snack bar was empty except for Carvel Eaves and Dewey Marzel sitting across from each other in the first booth and a couple snuggling in the far corner one. Brenda Lee sang "Too Many Rivers" from the juke box. The black-and-white tile floor looked freshly swept.

"Mind if I join you?" Winston hovered until Carvel moved over to the wall. "And pass those fries, Marzel," he said.

Dewey picked two long French fries from the basket, dipped them into the ketchup at one end, and waved the flimsy red basket at Winston without passing it to him.

"Thanks for the hospitality." Winston reached for the plastic edge of the basket and eased the food toward him.

"Go easy on those, Ivy," Carvel Eaves said. "That's my supper."

"Mine too," Marzel said.

"You think I'm sitting with you guys because I like you?" Winston said, his mouth open to the first shredded French fry, the ketchup making the mash look bloody. He studied the second fry and debated the merits of chewing more slowly.

"Heard that Rusty wiped you out the last game," Carvel said. "You should have got out when you were ahead."

"I don't think you came out much better, Eaves." Winston swallowed and drank from the glass of water. "You either, Marzel."

Dewey Marzel shrugged. "Rusty's one lucky fuck." He took a long sip from his cherry Coke.

"Well he sure fucked me over," Winston said. "Nobody has that much luck."

"He's got nothing but luck," Carvel said. "There's nothing upstairs, no way for any poker strategy."

"Under the table strategy," Winston said. He tossed the last of the second French fry into his mouth, then reached toward the basket.

"Only two more, Ivy," Carvel and Dewey said together, loud enough for the guy behind the counter to frown.

Gripping his last two fries between thumb and forefinger, Winston straightened his middle finger in gesture and dragged his hand across the Formica surface. He looked back to the counter area near the door and spotted several loose packets of saltines. "Both of you are assholes. But I guess you know that already," he said and stepped away to get the packets.

"Hungry assholes," they called from the booth.

"Blame Rusty," Winston answered.

"We do."

"Blame Rusty for what?" Rusty Reynolds pushed through the door. The coed to his right was blonde, the one on his left arm was a shade near redhead. The two girls were about the same height but each had about an inch on Rusty. Winston studied them from behind as they moved by.

A third followed, another blonde, the loudest of the three, to join the other girls and Rusty at the counter. They all took stools. "I want a milkshake. Dieted all day, so I deserve it!" the third girl laughed.

"Joanne, you need more than one day," said the redhead. None of the three girls was Rusty's football game date. Winston recognized one of them as a Tri-Delt, a junior. One of the others was a KD, but he wasn't sure about the sorority for the third girl. He ripped open one of the packets of crackers and returned to the booth.

"Let her get what she wants," said the other blonde, bobbing her head with each word, the flip at the back of her stiff hair keeping tempo. "It's fries for me since I've been good all week. No problem squeezing into my dress for the formal."

"Three, Rusty? Three chicks?" Winston said loud enough for Rusty to hear. "No way you can handle three chicks." Carvel and Dewey lowered their heads, shook them and laughed. Winston followed.

The couple snuggling earlier in the corner left the snack bar.

"Ignore those jokers, girls. Like I said over in the library, order whatever you want," Rusty said. "It's on me."

"You're the greatest, Rusty," the girls squealed.

The redhead said, "Take us to Memphis next time, maybe for the weekend. I want more than a milkshake." She ran her fingernails up and down the back of Rusty's shirt.

Winston felt nauseated. He would have vomited, but the pounding in his chest overpowered the acid boiling in his stomach and spurting up his throat—and he did not want to lose the French fries. He watched Rusty struggle to pry the stuffed wallet from the back pocket of his starched, pressed khakis, and he hated him. He felt the thin empty leather in the pocket of his own wrinkled pants.

Winston had not been to a men's clothing store or dry cleaner in months.

Rusty finally produced his wallet and spread several bills on the counter. The girls squirmed on their stools. "Like I said, order whatever you want. It's on me."

Winston found his eyes glued to the floor, like a hungry pet dog waiting for a morsel of food dropped in the dining room.

Rusty placed a second order: another shake, more fries drowning in ketchup, even a cheeseburger—two patties.

"Hey, guys. When's the next game?" he called with a mouth full from his perch. Rusty spotted another French fry on the thick ceramic plate and smeared it across the ketchup, then popped it into his mouth.

"Screw you, Reynolds," Winston said loudly.

The girls giggled.

"Rusty, I need to head back to the dorm," the freshman said, the KD. "It's almost curfew."

"I'll walk you back," he said. "You, too, Terry and Belinda. Just give me a minute more with this burger."

The girls took one last drag from their straws. "We can make it home by ourselves, Rusty," Belinda said. The others nodded. "But thanks for the snack," all three said in unison and walked toward the exit.

"Reynolds, it takes more than a couple of milkshakes to get some," Dewey yelled across the dining area. Rusty continued working on his food.

The guy behind the counter looked up from loading paper napkins into dispensers. He frowned. "Hey, keep it down, or I'll call campus security."

Carvel reached across the booth and thumped Dewey's shoulder with his thumb and middle finger. "What would a virgin know about getting some, Marzel?" he said.

Halting at the door with the commotion, the girls looked Winston's way and giggled. Rusty shot the guys the finger and mouthed, "Fuck you."

Another giggle. "Thanks, again, Rusty. But like we said, we gotta get back to the dorm." As though rehearsed, the girls swung their heads almost as one and left.

Rusty slurped the remainder of his cherry coke and slammed the thick glass to the counter. Several cubes of ice shot from the glass to hit the floor behind the counter, barely missing the server. He was flipping hamburgers for a new group that walked in during the banter—more lucky ones with money to burn.

"Hey, guy. Watch it!" the server grumbled and flattened slices of American cheese atop the paddies. "One more thing, and I'll throw y'all outta here myself."

Rusty tossed a quarter tip and stormed out, the door shutting hard behind him.

Winston said, "I can't take much more of this."

Rusty descended the concrete steps from the student union and crossed the walkway to turn left onto Student Union Drive. The buildings facing the student union from across the street were positioned in close proximity to the sidewalk, creating a tight space for outdoor pep rallies and other student gatherings. His dorm was one of the compact, red-brick ones located not far up the street, just past the cafeteria. The night was dark: no moon and the street lighting scant. The area seemed deserted.

Rusty thought about the prettiest two of the three girls and felt the swell in his pants. The night had turned out a total disappointment. He would try the younger one later—by herself. She might be easier. Maybe he could smuggle her into his dorm like Winston had done Phoebe.

"Dammit! My mail," he said and stopped at the curb. The key to his mail box was in his front pocket.

He turned back to the student union steps and up to the compact lobby then left to the flight of stairs. It was quiet, even for a Wednesday, as still and empty as the street. If things were heating up down a level in the snack bar, you couldn't hear it from the second floor.

The doors to a few of the post-office boxes were carelessly left ajar, student election flyers and other throw-away circulars littering the floor. Rusty's box was in the far rear corner, obscured by a support column typically covered with posted announcements and more campus political propaganda. The janitor had ignored the mess on the floor created by fallen papers from the makeshift bulletin board, the plaster on the column wiped clean except for Scotch tape stains and scattered nicks in the paint.

Rusty bent to peer through the tiny window into the mail box. It was crammed full of tightly rolled paper. "All junk mail, I'm sure," he said. "Boy, was this a wasted trip."

Before he could turn to the faint footsteps behind him, he felt a hand on his shoulder then something tight around his neck, choking him.

CHAPTER 16

Present Day

Her house would be empty. Kelsey was at a Friday night sleepover with one of the girls in her gym class. The other mother was to pick up both of them after school—no need to rush home.

Diana sat in her parking lot and typed *Winston Ivy* into the browser of her iPhone. Multiple listings popped up, most belonging to Ivy Real Estate, although some were social media links to professional organizations.

"He's on Facebook?" she said and scrolled through the real estate listings, looking for the business address. Most of the sales listings were expensive homes surrounding the Jackson Country Club or located in the Eastover or Bridgewater subdivisions. A few were estates in Madison or Rankin counties; two were larger houses in Phoebe's old Belhaven neighborhood. None were priced under $300,000. Most were over one million.

Diana had once heard someone refer to the "quiet wealth" of Jackson, Mississippi. She smiled at the idea, since nothing was quiet about the Ivy Real Estate offerings. Ivy's sprawling estates and columned mansions easily dwarfed her own red-brick house, which was out-of-reach for the average American. She highlighted several of the properties and browsed through the virtual tours, wishing for a larger screen.

Diana settled on a sprawling one-story with a pool and tennis court. "By the time I can afford this baby, I'll be a grandmother." She closed that window and scrolled to the home page of the real estate firm. The graphics offered audible directions to the business. Diana tapped the icon and was soon in route to Ivy Real Estate.

The entrance to the one story dark brick building was flanked by ornamental magnolias and cedar trees. There were no more than eight or so visitor parking spaces, all empty. The receptionist and secretary at the front desk smiled through the ringing phone on her desk. "You're in luck. Mr. Ivy just returned from showing an estate outside of Madison. The valet is parking his car now." She grabbed the receiver and put the caller on hold. "Mr. Ivy is freshening up a bit. He can be with you in just a sec, Dr. Bratton."

She offered the leather chair, but Diana remained standing, fighting a look of impatience and a desire to pace in front of the reception desk. The secretary handled two more calls.

"Mr. Ivy will want you to complete a client questionnaire so we'll just go ahead and start filling out the form."

After several strokes on her keyboard, she handed a black tablet to Diana. "All of this is electronic, you know. Please take a seat, and we'll get started."

"I'm not looking for a house. I'm here to …"

"OK. Then you must want to list a property for sale. That's a different form. I'm sure what you own is fabulous." The receptionist tapped a few additional keys on her keyboard. "Sorry for the confusion. Now, what is the address of your listing?"

"I'm not here to buy or sale anything. I just want a few moments with Mr. Ivy."

The woman paled. "He's very, very busy. I don't think …"

"A few moments?" Winston Ivy appeared in the door behind the desk.

Ivy was a bit taller than Diana remembered. His posture was regal, straight, height about six-two, maybe three including his full, dark grey hair. There was not a strand out of place. The navy suit was tailored, a snug fit more likely to be worn by a younger man. She had seen Alex try that and pull it off well, just like Winston Ivy. A silk tie in a perfectly symmetrical Windsor knot and a crisp white shirt finished the ensemble. He turned slightly to hand a file to the receptionist without looking at her and reached to sign a few paper forms on the desk. Diana caught a glimpse of diamond cufflinks and French cuffed sleeves.

"Yes, Dr. Bratton," Winston slipped the pen back into his jacket. "Can I help you with something? I do hope that Miss Phoebe is doing well."

"My aunt is splendid, as she would say. I was just over at her new house, sort of helping her unpack."

"That house was quite a steal, I might add. The previous owner was over his head, and his bank is still weeping. All parties lost on that deal, all parties except your aunt."

"And Winston Ivy Real Estate," Diana said. She took another look around the reception and lobby area. Although the quarters were tight, plush upholstered furniture lined the walls, and a pair of petite antique-looking side tables flanked the tall picture window.

Winston noticed her studying the silk window treatments. "I'm proud to say that Winston Ivy Real Estate has been number one in sales in Mississippi during the last twenty years," he said. "Our new offices on the Gulf Coast and in Oxford are busting local sales records, and once the legalities are worked out, I'm going to expand into Tennessee, starting in Memphis."

"Then I expect you'll need a bigger office," Diana said with another look around the space.

"Unlikely. Our agents are out in the field, not hanging around these four walls. Besides, so much is done electronically these days." He turned back to the reception desk. "Miranda, email that contract over to Darla Bender in Larkspur. I imagine she's already spent her commission."

Diana checked the time on her phone. "You seem busy. I'll make an appointment and come back."

"Nonsense," Ivy said. "No time like the present. Your aunt's move no doubt planted the seed. Now you're ready to move up to a really important property."

Winston led Diana through a pair of louvered doors to a media room of sorts. Inside were three cushioned leather chairs arranged around a wall-sized flat screen monitor. He motioned for her to sit, retrieved another electronic tablet from a lacquered cabinet, and then fumbled with reading glasses from his jacket pocket. After tapping a few times on the pad, photos of properties offered by Ivy Real Estate floated across the screen.

The first few frames captured the front of a three-story residence featuring a smooth, dark masonry façade and circular windows across the top floor. Diana had once seen pictures of it in a magazine. She still thought the windows looked like protruding frog eyes caught at night by a flashlight.

"I never know what kind of background music to play with these presentations," Winston said. "My assistant usually takes care of these things. The geek that put all this together for me calls it 'audio.'"

"Mr. Ivy, that's not why I'm here. I'm perfectly happy with my home."

"Bet I can change your mind." Winston Ivy punched the tablet again and an aerial view flooded the screen of tennis courts and a swimming pool with waterfall. A rectangular green space was sandwiched in between. Diana guessed a croquet court.

"The house is just under 8,000 square feet and features a four-car garage," he said.

"I think my aunt used to play croquet when she lived in Dallas—at least when she wasn't at a bridge table. You should have unloaded this palace on her."

"I must confess, Dr. Bratton, we tried."

Diana swiveled her leather chair away from the screen toward him, the collage of expensive homes and lake houses behind her. "Actually, I came by to discuss Aunt Phoebe."

"She's not happy with the place on Lacewood? My agents showed her everything on the market, some places not yet available. However, with a potential cash buyer, everyone has their price."

"I'm not here to discuss Phoebe's housing situation—old or new. And I'm not sure that I really need to be here at all," Diana said. "But I have questions."

"Questions?" Winston fumbled with the tablet until he powered off the slide show. He took the far chair across from Diana. "What are your questions, Dr. Bratton?"

"In the convenience store with your wife, you and Phoebe acted like you didn't know each other. Then when I surprised both of you at the afternoon tea party in her home, you said something about admiring her from afar in a creative writing class at Ole Miss 50 years ago."

"Yes, I believe so—something like that."

"Something like that? 'Something' doesn't make sense. I was helping my aunt unpack and came across a picture of the two of you, arm in arm at a college football game."

"Oh, yes. I think I remember that casual photo from one of the yearbooks."

"From the smiles and arms around the waist … didn't look casual to me, Mr. Ivy."

"Did you ask Phoebe about the picture?"

"No, I didn't." Diana did not have an explanation of why not, except for the shock of realizing Phoebe had lied to her—and for no apparent reason. "It … was too emotional for me at the time. I also stumbled across an unpacked picture of my parents the night they were killed."

Winston Ivy's expression did not change—as though he had not heard her. "Phoebe wanted it that way, Dr. Bratton, that afternoon in her living room. A lot needed to be forgotten about our time at Ole Miss."

"Forgotten?"

"You should talk to her."

Miranda stepped into the presentation room. "Mr. Ivy, hope I'm not interrupting, but a contract on that commercial property in Biloxi just came over the fax. You wanted to be notified."

"You'll have to excuse me, Dr. Bratton." Miranda held the papers clipped inside an opened leather portfolio, a Montblanc pen in the opposite hand.

"I'll use this one again if you don't mind, my dear." Winston retrieved the slim gold pen from inside his suit and took the papers and binder. "This moment deserves much more—a red-carpet roll-out—a gilded, mahogany desk and chair to match." He remained seated and signed the document in broad, slow, flamboyant strokes.

Acid rose in her throat. Diana swallowed hard. *Winston Ivy isn't that long a name*, she thought.

He seemed to catch her stare and the questioning tilt of her head. "Like I said before, Dr. Bratton, Winston Ivy Real Estate is branching out—spreading its wings."

A steady stream of traffic at the end of the real estate firm's driveway delayed Diana's departure. Just when she spotted a break in the traffic and eased forward, iron gates glided shut behind her with a snap, barely missing her bumper. She had not noticed them left open when she entered the parking lot forty-five minutes before.

So much for 'warm and inviting', Diana thought.

The traffic abruptly stopped, and Diana strained to see the traffic light at the intersection up the street—red again. There remained no break in sight. She checked her phone: no messages, no missed calls. She noticed the time and remembered Kelsey's Friday night sleepover. The other mother was to pick her up after dance team practice, but Diana's responsibility was transportation to the sleepover. *I forgot. It's all she's talked about for weeks.*

The traffic crept forward. Diana slowly released the brake, edging closer to the curb. The dusty Volkswagen perpendicular to her moved forward, creating just enough space for her Nissan to squeeze between it and a Minivan. The slow-moving minivan and its driver on a cell phone never looked over to Diana. She took one last look to the right before releasing the brake and easing into traffic.

Suddenly the iron gates swung open and a black Lexus sped around her to follow the Volkswagen, then changed lanes to pass it. Diana slammed the brakes. The familiar *Winston Ivy* placard on the side of the vehicle was a blur.

"Quitting time—what's the big rush, Winston?" Diana lowered the visor to shield her face and pushed ahead to beat the Tahoe coming up the four-lane road, swerving into the same lane as Winston and closing distance rapidly.

"What am I doing?" she laughed at herself and flicked the visor back out of her eyes. She and Winston were almost bumper-to-bumper. He was using his cell phone. Diana felt through her purse for hers. She tried the voice activation feature—*Call Phoebe*—but the programming in the phone did not respond. She tapped the name from her favorites' list. The call went to voice mail. Diana tried again—same thing.

Winston signaled for a right at the next block, the exit to Interstate 55 approaching. His head and the cell phone to his ear moved up and down as though he were laughing, and his car inched near the next lane.

Kelsey's text caught Diana's attention: "At Angie's house. Her mom treating movie and popcorn."

Diana balanced the phone against the steering wheel with her left hand and started to type a response: "Her mom dropping off at theatre before sleepover? Curfew? Meeting boys? Tell me!" but remembered the last MVA she treated in the ER, a result of texting and driving, and instead slipped in: "OK."

An SUV followed by a rusted pick-up wedged between Diana and Winston. They were now headed south on I-55. The moving air picked off loose clumps of pine straw from bales stacked in the back of the truck. A couple of paper cups and what looked like a potato chip bag joined the pine straw to skip along the hood of Diana's car. The trash rolled onto the windshield into her line of vision and then flew over the roof. She swerved into the other southbound lane, spotted her target, and passed the two vehicles again to ease behind him.

Winston Ivy remained on his cell. *Probably dealing property—two more mansions sold while I almost wrecked*, Diana thought.

Without signaling, Winston slid right, taking the exit to Northside Drive. Diana followed, but held back several feet at the upcoming red light. She ducked when he checked the rearview mirror. Still in conversation, he turned left past Maywood Mart and Whole Foods. Grateful for the upcoming green light and moving traffic, Diana was certain he rechecked the rearview mirror.

Suddenly he seemed to have both hands on the steering wheel, and her cell rang.

"Winston Ivy thinks you're following him, Diana."

Diana abruptly turned the opposite direction unto Ridgewood Road. "Why would he think that, Phoebe? Anyway, why would I be following Winston Ivy?"

"Let me check this text," Phoebe said. There was a pause. "He says that you just turned north on Ridgewood."

"Dusty black Nissans are all over Jackson. Could have been anybody."

The speedometer beamed *52*. She took her foot off the accelerator, and the vehicle slowed into the upcoming intersection. The traffic was light, no cops at the corners. "Like I said, it could have been anybody."

"Successful men like Winston Ivy don't miss much," Phoebe said. "He's sure it was you."

"He's just got me on his mind—wants to sell me a house, a bigger one."

"I'm sure he does," Phoebe said.

Diana checked behind her. Winston was not following her. "I'm almost home. Kelsey has spend-the-night plans."

"That young lady is always so busy."

Diana made the next corner, driving back toward Phoebe's.

"It never stops. Gotta go." Diana ended the call. She maneuvered up and down every short, out of the way street, winding her way back into Phoebe's neighborhood. She drove well below the speed limit, to avoid attention, expecting Mr. Winston Ivy to dart out at her from every driveway or hit her head-on from around every curve. Diana could see the photograph from the college yearbook: Winston and Phoebe, standing together at a football game, smiling. She thought about what her aunt had said: *"Mr. Ivy and I haven't gotten a chance to know each other better."*

She slowed over the next hill into the shaded parking bay at the corner across from Phoebe's house, parking designed to accommodate the neighbor's party guests, and there had been many. Winston Ivy's Lincoln was parked in Phoebe's drive, not far from the front entrance. Diana saw him climb the steps and enter through the double doors.

The photograph in the *Ole Miss* yearbook, the smiles, the youth, stared Diana in the face.

"I need to get back into that house and find out what those two are up to," she said.

CHAPTER 17

On his second cup of coffee, Key Martin spotted the follow-up article in the Sunday edition of *The Clarion-Ledger*. Placing it below the fold and near the back of the first section, the Jackson newspaper had run an earlier piece concerning the discovery of a shallow grave in Oxford. The human remains were uncovered at a construction site on campus. The police continued to investigate.

Diana answered just before her voice mail. "Anyone you know missing up in north Mississippi?" he asked.

"Can't help you with that one, but I've got a hot gallbladder from the ER I need to take out in a few," Diana answered. She wedged her phone between her face and shoulder and continued to enter notes in the computer outside the patient's room. "Things are really busy in the hospital right now, but I think I should take Kelsey to Mr. Marzel's memorial. You don't see many funerals on Sunday."

"There's an article in the paper about a construction worker digging up human remains," Martin said. "But it's up in Oxford—so you're probably in the clear with this one."

"Details?" Diana asked. She looked over some printed documents and handled them back to the nurse preparing the gallbladder patient for surgery.

Martin answered, "Don't know much about the campus. Says somewhere on the west side, close to Fraternity Row."

"Must be near Guyton Hall. The old med school was there before they moved it to Jackson. Maybe the remains of a stray cadaver."

"You think so? Sounds like it's a complete skeleton. Don't you guys saw off parts in a lab and carry them off to study certain sections, like maybe right before a test?"

Diana kept typing. "They put us in groups of three or four and assigned each a complete body to dissect. But right before each test, the professors put out extra sections of the anatomy for us to study—spread

102

arms, legs, feet all around on different counters and benches."

"I think I'll stick to what I do," Martin said. He picked up his coffee, decided it smelled bad and looked dirty. He felt a little queasy and put it down. "I called a buddy I know at OPD. Forensics picked up fragments of clothing, a few buttons and remnants of a zipper. So it looks like it's not a tossed specimen from the old med school."

"I can't help with this one, Martin, and I'm glad there's no connection. Anyway, my specialty is fresh corpses, I mean, stumbling upon fresh corpses. And I don't plan on a fresh one after surgery this morning." Nearing completion of the patient's medical record, she did not stop to check for any typos and misspellings missed by the computer software. She could not remember the last time she had put a pen to paper in a medical record. "Hate to rush off, Chief. I'm kinda busy and last night on call was a real ..."

"I know—always busy. Never enough time for me," he said. "But that bulldozer may have unearthed some history. Someone thought they were off the hook, maybe completed the perfect crime."

A member of the patient transport team approached Diana. "Doctor Bratton, we're taking the patient to the OR. Anesthesia has already seen him, so it wouldn't be long."

Diana pulled the phone away from her ear. "Just a little shave and prep," she told the nurse. "Thanks much."

"The OR will call you when the patient's ready," the nurse said.

Diana returned to her phone. "That 'perfect crime' stuff—sort of melodramatic, don't you think?"

"Sometimes simple is better, Doc."

Martin heard something in the background about *bleeding out in the other room* as the call ended. He poured out the dregs of the replacement cup of coffee and refilled, then walked to the little room off the small kitchen. His last ex-wife had claimed this spot as her home office. She didn't hang around long enough to spruce it up, so the chipped, off-white Formica counter survived. Martin completed the look with a white plastic scoop chair with scratched metal legs, slipped out the back door from the police department break room. No one seemed to miss it.

Mrs. Martin left him this desktop computer although she took his iPad—claiming an anniversary gift for year two. She didn't want to wait around for three.

Martin's home Internet connection was much slower than the department's, but soon enough his browser responded: *Public Records: missing persons Lafayette County, Mississippi.* He scrolled through a too-long report about a woman missing for a week after not showing up to check on a sick aunt in Memphis and another about a couple located yesterday after hiding from creditors in a motel near Holly Springs. Nothing went back more than ten years.

"They said you could hear the scream all the way up to Highway 7," Corey said into the land line on his desk.

A minute into the conversation, Detective Corey Myers pulled up Chief Key Martin's personnel photograph on his desktop, then tried to suck in his belly. He had already scooted his desk chair forward to straighten his posture in attention, the respect deserving of a superior—although long distance. Chief Martin was white and looked about twenty-five or thirty years older than he, but from other pictures on the JPD website Martin looked much more fit and trim.

"Don't know about your place, Chief," Corey said, "but OPD doesn't get many calls like that." One thing that drew him to police work in a small university town like Oxford, Mississippi, was that you could keep it simple, down to earth. Whenever he got tied up with people down in Jackson or up in Memphis, it just seemed to get more complicated.

"Yes, sir, the call came in through emergency dispatch. Like the news reported, a construction crew unearthed the human remains. The guy's voice was shaking, said a skull was staring him in the face and that there were other bones. You could hear voices laughing in the background."

Martin said, "Most of the time, the bone is just a thick old stick—an old, moldy stick."

Corey scrolled through the Jackson Police Department website. Other archived photos showed an even thinner and younger Key Martin. Corey again looked down at his own paunch. The attempt at a straighter posture did no good. "You know, Chief Martin," he chuckled, "the guy pushing the 'dozer kept denying that he had screamed when he found the bones, but he's the one that brought that up."

Martin asked, "So how's the investigation going?"

"So far, my chief has turned it over to me. We've got a few Indian burial sites in north Mississippi, but no record of one at that location."

"Congratulations," Martin said. He'd already known about the assignment from the Oxford Chief when he called for Detective Myers.

"The state crime lab directed me to email all the photos from the scene to the forensic pathologist. They've also got all the remains for close exam carbon dating. Should have the sex and age of the victim soon."

"Assuming homicide," Martin said. "Less likely suicide or natural causes."

"We don't have a lot of cold cases or open files on missing persons up here," Corey said.

Martin decided not to mention his own research into missing person cases in North Mississippi. "So, no leads?" he asked.

"Not yet, sir." Officer Corey Myers figured the veteran Jackson police chief had checked the HR files and could see through his lack of experience, particularly in murder investigations. Corey had less than two years on the force, and while the law-abiding citizens of Oxford and Lafayette County were not immune to crime, the local homicide rate could not touch that belonging to Jackson.

"Wasn't trying to step on anybody's toes, Officer Myers, but I already checked with my friends down here in forensics. Looks like your bones belonged to a young male, died about 50 years ago. It's amazing what those guys and gals in the lab can figure out these days."

Corey thought back to the Oxford, Mississippi, of the mid-sixties. His parents were toddlers. His grandparents never went to college but used to talk about the civil rights movement: James Meredith, the first black student enrolled at Ole Miss; the riots; the National Guard on campus; the guns; the tear gas. Every citizen in the town had been nervous—black or white. Lots of white parents worried about the safety of their sorority daughters. His grandparents worried that with all the upheaval the white merchants and employers would come to resent them and others like them.

Corey asked, "Did they say anything about racial origin?"

"White male, late teens, maybe early twenties."

"White. That's good," Corey said softly.

"What's that, Officer Myers?"

"Think you can get those forensic guys to speed up an official report, maybe email me something? I'm the one on the front lines here, and it's a long way to the top."

Martin answered, "Sure, see what I can do."

Corey thanked Chief Martin and hung up. He stood unsteadily from his desk—almost a wobble—but there was no one around the cluster of desks in the precinct to notice. Everyone was either on patrol or at lunch except for the switchboard operator at the far end of the building.

"White male, college-aged. Body found on the edge of campus," he said and reached for the rest of his Mountain Dew, by now room temperature and flat. Through the window, he studied the vehicles passing up and down Molly Barr Road, back and forth between campus and the new apartment complexes, condos, and zero-lot line homes springing up the hill toward South Lamar. Lots of students and weekend

Rebel sports fans lived there and very few sped in front of the police station. "A student dropout, maybe? Didn't show up for class or back at the dorm or frat house, and nobody cared?"

Corey took another sip, frowned, and tossed the nearly empty into the trash. The can sprayed light green liquid across the wadded sheets of paper and used coffee cups. He walked to the receptacle and stared down into the mess. He thought about the registrar's archives. "Computers weren't around in the sixties. I guess I'll be going through a lot of paper."

The phone line on Corey's desk lit. "Guess Natasha's back from lunch a little early," he said, patting his stomach, empty except for the Mountain Dew. His conversation with Chief Martin had blown most of his own break. He hit the speaker button. "Yeah, Natasha. Whatchu want?"

The receptionist's voice was hushed. "A lady's here to see you. I told her to take a seat out in the lobby. Says she saw the article in the newspaper, you know, the one about the bulldozer and gravesite. Read that you were the investigating officer."

"She's probably just the first of a lot of crazies."

"This lady don't look crazy to me. Just kinda nervous."

"Black or white?"

"White," Natasha answered. Corey ran his right hand down the front of the shirt to his belt. All the buttons were buttoned, even the one just before the top of the belt, the one that had the tendency to open after he'd sat too long at his desk. He breathed deeply and pulled in the paunch as best he could. He felt the pistol strapped at his waist.

Everything was in place.

Natasha had skipped the woman's age or looks. Corey gave another try at a straightened posture and rubbed his forefinger back and forth over his front teeth.

Several vending machines crammed the wall of the short walk to the reception area. The break room had been taken up by storage. Corey made it past the Coke machine but slowed in front of the snack dispenser. That same bag of Doritos still called him from selection *B-6*. The large Snickers bar at *C-12* remained a close second. He tipped his head at Natasha, who was on her cell, texting that boyfriend again, he decided. The OPD switchboard looked quiet.

Natasha looked up and tilted her head toward the far corner of the waiting area. A woman sat in the plastic chair nearest the window, staring out at traffic, her thin legs crossed. Deeply tanned skin peeked out below her slacks, a dramatic contrast to the yellow and orange sandals. Her face, neck, hands, and arms were wrinkled and leathery from too much tanning although her biceps looked firm and well-defined. She worked out.

Slender fingers gripped a rolled newspaper and tapped it nervously against a knee.

"Ma'am, I'm Officer Myers. Something I can do for you?"

The woman hopped up, reaching about five-two, very agile for someone who looked about fifty. Her thick blonde hair was pulled into a tight ponytail that rubbed against the nape of her neck, the color too yellow to be natural. Her light blue, one-piece casual outfit could double for an expensive workout suit.

"I believe you can help me." She tapped the newspaper into the palm of her left hand. "And maybe I can help you."

Corey was familiar with many of the white women who lived in and around Oxford and frequented the Square, and this woman was an outsider. He had pulled over a good many of the female citizens in traffic, usually for incomplete stops at stop signs, a few for crossing over into the next lane, and a couple that were near misses for DUI. He never had the heart to ticket any of them, and enjoyed the way the white ladies smiled and talked their way out of an arrest. Besides, he wanted to be liked around town and saved the bulk of his citations and arrests for weekend football traffic.

"Your name, ma'am?"

"Is there someplace we can talk, like in private?" She glanced at the receptionist. Natasha had lost interest in her boyfriend and was looking their way.

"My desk is back there," Corey said. "It's not a private office, but it's all they give me." The woman followed him down the hall to the precinct work area and the crowded desks. On the way, he again scanned the offerings in the vending machine. Someone had slipped in through the back to grab that last bag of Doritos, but the Snickers and its bulging wrapper waited for him.

"Ma'am, if you'll take a seat right here." Corey motioned to the wooden chair at the side of his desk. He waited for her to sit down and pulled a note pad from the top drawer. A couple of other officers had returned from their lunch break, both busy with toothpicks and milling about their own spots. One opened a file and spread papers across her desk, then shuffled them, standing to read. The other plopped noisily into his desk chair, flicked the toothpick into the nearest waste can, popped open the Doritos and scrolled through the desk top computer. Neither looked toward Corey and the woman.

"My name is Sylvia DeLoach. I live in Louisiana ... New Orleans." The rolled newspaper dropped from her hands onto the desk. She reached into her purse and produced a Louisiana Driver's License. Corey copied the address and number at the top of his notepad and drew a rectangle around the information. "My maiden name is Reynolds."

He noted that too.

Sylvia Reynolds DeLoach said, "I've been in Jackson, subbing for another exercise class instructor. That's when I first saw the article." She retrieved the newspaper with her right hand as though she had almost lost it and unraveled it. "Here," she pointed at the black and white photograph of a pile of leaves, sticks, and dirt with a bulldozer in the background. "I've been looking for my older brother all my adult life, and you people have found him."

CHAPTER 18

Corey fought the urge to put down the pen and call Chief Martin back. His grandmother had always told him to pray for answers. But this white woman's revelation had been free—no need to pray anymore. "What makes you think the remains are your brother?"

"I was eight when my brother Rusty went to college. He got a scholarship to Ole Miss, really a grant of some sort to low income farm families. The weather had been hard on my father's crops, just like everyone else around Sunflower, Mississippi. The only difference was Rusty had smarts—made good grades in high school, played football. He was small but still good in football. And he was handsome." The woman's eyes began to water.

"I'm sorry, ma'am, but I'm fresh out of Kleenex. But I can get you a tissue from the men's room." He glanced around the precinct. Maybe Natasha would have something.

"Don't worry about it." She wiped her eyes and cheeks with the back of her hand.

Officer Kimmel, two desks over, looked up. *What's the deal with that chick?* He shrugged and returned to his phone call.

"Like I said, I was in the second grade. Rusty had been in Oxford, at Ole Miss, for almost a full semester, the fall semester. He came home the first couple of weekends, said something about not having any money, then stopped. I didn't think anything about it at the time. What eighteen-year-old guy would be interested in his eight-year-old sister and the dead air in Sunflower."

"Miz," he referred to his notes, "DeLoach, I don't see the connection here."

"Can I see the picture of what they found, about what they talked about in this article? There wasn't much detail."

He reached for the top drawer of his desk, then thought better of it. A copy of the precinct photographer's work was stored there in a large, sealed brown envelope. He envisioned the soil- and water-stained human bones tangled in a mixture of rotted leaves and tree roots. "No, ma'am. I'm sorry. All of that's evidence. Sealed up. Locked away."

"'Sealed up' for what?" she asked. "What's going on here?"

"There's an ongoing investigation into …"

"Investigation into what, Officer Myers? I'll tell you what needs to be investigated." The full lunch crowd was back at their desks, filling the other four spaces. All eyes turned toward Corey. Most lingered only a few seconds. Most looked annoyed at the visitor's outburst.

She lowered her voice. "When Rusty didn't even come home at Christmas, my parents told me that he had sent them a note—said he was flunking out of college, that he was ashamed to disappoint them. Said he had fallen in love with some girl he met in class from somewhere up North—Illinois, I think. The girl's father was going to find him a job up there."

More tears.

"I was just learning about sex," she said. "I used to lie in my room at night and think about Rusty probably getting the girl pregnant—a piece of sorority trash, fake pretty with long, blonde hair and big boobs—and that my parents were too embarrassed to tell me the whole story."

Corey hesitated, "I have other cases to work here, Miz DeLoach. I just don't have any other information to give you right now …"

"Don't you see? Rusty was a really handsome boy. I looked up to him—missed him when he left home to come up here. It was easy to imagine some sweet thing trapping him in the backseat of a car with her skirt hiked up above the waist, but not the part about him flunking out. The Rusty Reynolds I remember was too smart for that."

Natasha walked from the front with a long, brown envelope. She dropped it onto Corey's desk.

"What's this?" he said.

"You asked me to keep a look out." The receptionist smiled, flashing a gold-capped tooth with a miniature white heart in the center. "UPS truck just made a delivery. It's the report from the state forensics lab."

Sylvia DeLoach reached first for the envelope. Her voice quivered, pleading. "Does that have something to do with this case?"

Corey eased the envelope away from her, tore open the seal, and slid out the papers. He scanned the information, realizing that Martin had already seen it. This woman seemed sincere. Maybe he should give her a tidbit. Corey read aloud: "Young male, early to late twenties. Bone structure—the skull—points to Caucasian."

"I hadn't seen my brother in over 50 years, but I began to think it might be Rusty."

"Why?"

"That pathologist from Jackson … said in the newspapers that some sort of mummification process may have preserved the bones, especially if the … body … didn't have a lot of fat and was partially burned."

"We don't have any evidence that fire or arson had anything to do with the cause of death," Corey said.

"I know," Sylvia said. "I haven't seen anything about that in the news, but Rusty was always fit, in good shape."

"Ma'am, I can tell you that forensics will still be at work."

"They used to talk about dental records on those TV crime shows …"

"Now it's all about DNA. Don't suppose you've got any DNA hanging around from your missing brother?"

"How would I have any DNA from my brother?"

"Old clothes at home? Maybe a toothbrush? Maybe he had a baby with that sorority girl. Of course, if you're his blood relative, then we could use yours."

"I don't think that story about getting married and moving to Illinois was true, and the house out in the country burned to the ground a couple of years ago—the one where we lived when Rusty was in high school."

"The same house you grew up in?" Corey asked. He studied the largest of the photographs. A technician had loosely reassembled the once scattered human bones into a skeletal pattern, displayed on a series of blue surgical towels.

Sylvia fumbled through her purse and found a small pack of tissue and popped one loose. "We moved from that house a couple of years after Rusty was gone. I was in the tenth, maybe eleventh grade. My parents built a new house … a nicer, bigger place in town in Indianola … even though I was the only child left at home." She dabbed the corner of an eye with the tissue. "I guess my mother wanted something closer to neighbors to help her deal with empty nest."

"Your parents retired at the time?" Corey asked. He shuffled through the next series of prints, magnified views with three or four photographs to the page. He stopped at the numbered ribs and vertebrae and the various angles of the skull, the edges and discoloration highlighted with a yellow marker and photographed under higher intensity lighting. From the side view, the back of the skull did not seem as smooth as the frontal bone.

"They're deceased now," Sylvia answered.

"Who's deceased?"

"My parents. You were asking about my parents."

Corey turned to the next print and grabbed a magnifying glass from the top drawer. There was a yellow arrow at a tiny indention over the fifth rib and another labeling the sixth a few more millimeters from the spine.

"You said something about your parents and a nicer house, a bigger house?"

"Yes, but I don't see what ..."

"Do you know if they had any life insurance on your brother?" Corey studied the rendering of the parietal views of the skull—no indention on the sides of the skull. He checked the back of the skull—he remembered that as the occipital area—not nearly as smooth.

"I don't think so. I doubt if they had money for premiums." Sylvia hesitated. "Officer, I'm not here about collecting any life insurance."

"Insurance ... just a routine question, ma'am, in these types of investigations," Corey said. "What'd your dad do for a living?"

"Repaired appliances, when he wasn't farming."

"Mom work?"

"School teacher, Sylvia answered. "Elementary. But she retired a year or so after my father."

"Your brother had disappeared. Your parents were building this big, new house. If there had been a life insurance policy on your brother, they sure could have used it."

"I would remember records of a policy in their lock box at the bank after they died. There was nothing."

"You said your brother was supposed to be in Illinois somewhere."

"Mom and Dad never talked about Rusty. They sort of wrote him off, but they knew he was alive ... at least they told me he was."

Corey shuffled the pages of photographs together and tapped the edges against his desk until the bottom of the short stack aligned.

"Where is this going, officer?"

"Sounds like your parents had a modest income, probably little savings if they were like most folks, and then all of a sudden they're building this new house."

"I'm not here to talk about my parents ... rest their souls." Sylvia grabbed her bag and stood, scraping her chair hard against the concrete flooring. No one looked up in the busy room. "I'm not here to accuse my parents of anything."

"So all that time they thought their son was alive and well and shacked up with this girl he met at Ole Miss. Right?"

"*Married* to the girl from Ole Miss," Sylvia said, "and working for her father. At least that's what they told me."

Corey took a second look into the large brown envelope. He slid two fingers inside and removed the smaller white envelope that accompanied the prints. He unfolded the report it contained.

"Tell me a little bit more about your brother," he said. "Like what he looked like. Height. Build." Corey read the report.

"Average height: five-nine, I guess," she said. "Maybe five-ten."

Caucasian male, late teens to early twenties. Height: 68 to 72 inches. Corey did the math. "Yes, five-nine or -ten will work," he said.

"Miz DeLoach, did you find anything of interest in your parents' safety deposit box?"

She hesitated. "I did find some letters from the University about Rusty, fastened together with a paper clip. Only the top one had been torn open."

"His grades from that last semester?"

"No, and I read them all—all the same—letters from the registrar about Rusty's absences. The dates ... way before Christmas ... long before I was told me he left school to get married."

She fought back more tears.

"I know now that my parents lied. Now I understand why I never heard from my brother again, not even when I graduated from high school." Sylvia DeLoach laid her palm on the stack of photographs. "Those are pictures of my brother, Rusty Reynolds."

"I think you may be right," Corey said. "Here's more." He added the photographs of the campus burial scene stowed away in his drawer.

CHAPTER 19

Corey worked south on North Lamar away from the gas station and hotel and tried to think of anything but the remains found on the Ole Miss campus, the body that could belong to one Rusty Reynolds. The information shared yesterday by Sylvia DeLoach was the only lead on the case, and a sketchy one at that.

He took a deep breath. Holding in the stomach was fruitless. Nonetheless, today was his day to think parking tickets and to contribute his fair share to the city coiffures. His take so far: two. Corey shook his head. The poor souls were only thirty minutes delinquent, but somebody had to pay for the upgrade to digital parking meters. Of course, sales tax revenue from the clothes and jewelry shoppers and diners choking the parking spaces on the Oxford Square trumped the parking fines.

Here was number three. The owner of the Ford with the Shelby County tag in the expired space had stayed too long in the jewelry store. Corey marked the tire with his chalk stick, copied the license plate information and entered it. "Not a bad haul so far. Time for a break."

He put away the chalk stick and eyed the frozen yogurt shop at the corner. Walking toward it he decided on cookie dough flavor, his favorite. Through the shop window Corey saw the short, dark-skinned girl rinsing out some of the dispensers and was glad she was working today. He moved closer and peered at the colorful labels on the yogurt dispensers. "What the heck? Damn, no cookie dough," he said.

Corey pushed through the front door. "Is this marble chocolate stuff as good as the cookie dough?"

"I can give you a little taste," the girl said.

"Why don't you do that?"

Corey looked down her blouse as she walked past him toward the machine, holding up a teeny, crinkled white paper cup like a miniature crown. The frozen yogurt dropped in a thick strand, filling the cup, terminating in a long, brown taper. Corey waited for her to straighten it with her finger, wishing she would let him taste. But she didn't.

She passed the sample cup to him, and he squeezed it empty into his mouth.

"Awesome," he said. "Give me your largest cup. But tell your manager he's gonna lose customers without that cookie dough."

She walked over to the stack and handed him a quart size cup and a spoon. "Here you go. You do look like a large guy," she said.

Corey thought about his paunch. "I guess I better stick with the regular size."

She smiled. "OK, just get what you want from the machine, and I'll be glad to weigh it for you."

Corey returned the smile, paid with the bills in his front pocket, and yanked a few napkins from the dispenser near the window. He walked onto the Square. His first full spoonful of frozen yogurt shocked a sensitive rear molar. "Shit!" he said, rubbing his cheek and balancing the overflowing cup in the opposite hand. "I missed my last dental appointment."

The white lady walking past him with a Sheltie on leash paused and stared, then gave an embarrassed smile. Corey nodded and watched her cross the intersection, pass the bank, the dress shop in the old Duvall's building, and the interior decorating store to disappear into the parking lot around the corner.

A black Lexus approached the intersection ahead, but slowed to a stop for the uniformed policeman to enter the crosswalk. Corey saluted with the cup of frozen yogurt and walked in the same direction as the lady with the dog. Reaching the corner, he turned opposite to cross Jackson Street past the red phone booth toward the bronzed statue of William Faulkner. Faulkner sat on a bench just off the sidewalk behind a short iron fence, smoking a pipe.

"Hi, Bill, mind if I join you?" Corey asked.

By now the chocolate was about half consumed, beginning to drip down the sides. Corey studied it carefully and caught the brown liquid with his spoon. "No way near as good—no way." He ran his tongue around his lips to be sure. "Manager better restock my favorite or I ain't going back," he said, licking away the sticky drops that coated his fingers and surveying the smooth traffic out of the corner of his eye.

Today shoppers and visitors to downtown Oxford seemed to slip in and out of parking spaces with ease—unlike the situation on football weekends. Corey thought about crossing his legs and turning his body at the exact angle as Faulkner to see if a tourist would snap a photo, but decided against it.

"Sorry, Bud, break over." He winked at the statue. "I'll leave you to your smoke." Corey imagined a pint of whiskey in a brown paper bag, leaning against the statue's crossed legs. He looked across the old courthouse lawn toward the traffic on South Lamar then realized he had not checked the meters in over an hour. Parking there was at a premium around Square Books and the shops on the other corner.

Corey scanned the meters as he walked in front of Neilson's Department Store: no violations, no lawbreakers. He took a final swipe at the rim of the cup and sucked the spoon clean. There was a trash can ahead, secured to the sidewalk and constructed of thin, green metal strips—easy to see through. Corey flipped the empty cup and spoon into the can. The cup and spoon slid down the outside of an empty pizza box to land deeper in the receptacle on a crumpled mess of orange and yellow fabric.

Yellow and orange fabric, what his mother would call gaudy, the same color as the sandals. Corey remembered that Mrs. DeLoach had a purse to match.

He fished the purse out of the trash can, using the last of his napkin to wipe away a strand of pizza sauce that soiled the wide orange stripe in the center.

"Officer, could you give me directions to the Lyric? Someone said it was in walking distance."

Corey pulled open the purse. Keys, a wallet, the package of tissues, an old Danielle Steel paperback were all inside. He looked down at the two young girls standing near him.

"We're from Oklahoma—just visiting a friend. We don't know our way around."

"Oh, sure." He pointed down the street. "You're headed the right way. Just down on the left."

"Thanks, officer." The two smiled and walked into the intersection down Van Buren.

"You, ladies, watch out for traffic." The one a little taller and maybe a little older threw her right hand up in a wave. A Jaguar and a Prius driving east slowed to miss them and then continued through the loop around the Old Courthouse. Corey watched the two cars; they were going too fast and headed toward Jackson Avenue. He thought about calling ahead to get them picked up but gave them a pass. He needed more parking tickets to his own name, and certainly there were tires on South Lamar that needed to be marked. He slid a fresh piece into the chalk stick, stepped into Neilson's to borrow a shopping bag to store the purse, and proceeded to the first vehicle violation.

"Why can't the department upgrade?" He finished with the first vehicle and streaked his white chalk across a shiny black tire of the next car, a red Ferrari, just missing the chrome rim. "The city oughta spring for those handheld citation writers, those electronic jobs, like those guys in California."

"I'm sorry, officer. Did you say something?" A man dressed in an expensive-looking dark suit and carrying a leather briefcase approached from behind. The driver's door snapped unlocked by remote. Happy hour started early at the popular bar a few spaces down, and Corey figured the guy had spotted him from the outdoor patio—therefore, the big hurry. The man frowned at the marked tire and tossed the briefcase to the passenger side of the convertible.

"What gives, Chief? I just had this thing washed before I left New Orleans." Before sliding into the driver's seat, he grinned at Corey's colorful shopping bag. "Pick up something a little special for yourself?"

Corry caught the license plate number as the Ferrari yielded at the intersection of Van Buren to enter the Loop and disappear around the Old Courthouse. The citation would not be expensive, no more than a cheap business lunch or two drinks, maybe three. He considered fudging a bit on the times to ramp up the parking fine. "Jerk deserves this ticket, but I should have stopped him for a sobriety test," Corey said. He reached for the radio control to call ahead to Jackson Avenue for a pick up on suspected DUI. "That'll be something special for him."

Before he could depress the control, a loud buzz came from his radio and a pronouncement: "Officer Myers?"

"Yeah, Natasha, what's up and why so formal?"

"UPD just called in a 10-54."

"A DB? Where? One of the dorms?" Corey stuffed the ticket pad into his front pocket, picked up the bag from the sidewalk, and moved swiftly toward his cruiser.

"Caucasian older adult, female. No dorm."

"Suicide, maybe?"

"Hey, who knows?" Natasha said. "I'm just the sexy dispatcher." Corey heard a potato chip or maybe a bagel chip snap. "UPD probably wants you or the ME to decide that."

"Paramedics on the scene?" Corey asked, almost out of breath.

"If they are, doubt they're busy. Body's face down in that new pond on Sorority Row." The next crackle was louder. Definitely bagel chips. She was the only one who bought them out of the machine.

Corey shut the door of his cruiser. He breathed deeply. In seconds the blue lights illuminated at the turn west onto Jackson. He added the red lights—the lighting drama not as much fun compared to evening. Corey liked the way the lights draped buildings and street signs and pedestrians after dark—the curious look on their faces. The woman from Natasha's call was already deceased, but he sped around several cars anyway, passing the Episcopal Church, Lafayette County Jail, and new townhome construction.

At Sorority Row a slender crowd armed with cell phones leaned close into the barriers circling one end of Silver Pond. From the backpacks, tee-shirts, shorts, and torn jeans most of them looked to be students, maybe a teacher or two, and most interrupted their conversations to snap photos or videos of the scene. A male and female officer from the University Police Department stood awkwardly near a small flat-bottomed boat, partially pulled onto the bank of the pond not far from an ambulance. The female held a clipboard and seemed to be filling out a form.

A skinny male in his early twenties with stringy hair, dressed in blue jeans and tee shirt, pointed a professional-looking camera at the paramedics and ambulance, then snapped the crowd of onlookers and the floating yellow markers near the center of the pond. Corey noted the laminated badge hanging twisted from the guy's neck and recognized him as a reporter from the Oxford newspaper. A girl, even younger, tagged behind him with a similar camera. Corey guessed someone from the *Daily Mississippian*, the student newspaper. He assumed someone from one of the Memphis TV stations would arrive soon, maybe even up from Jackson.

He pulled his cruiser against the curb, blue lights still flashing, and walked toward the paramedics. A stretcher carried a body bag. "Any ID?" Corey asked.

"No, officer. Nothing."

"Note?"

"What kind of note and where? Like pinned to her blouse?" one of the paramedics answered. "Ink would have been all smeared, paper all wet."

Corey ignored the chuckle from the two paramedics and a couple of the bystanders behind the yellow tape.

"Unzip that bag," he said. "Let me take a look."

"OK, but ME hasn't been here yet. She told me she would check things out when we got the body to Baptist."

"This won't slow down your trip to the morgue." Corey lifted the zipper and slowly opened the bag. Bleached blonde hair tangled in the metal strip. He reached to free it.

"Here, officer. Better use these." The nearest paramedic tossed him a pair of medical examination gloves.

Corey fumbled with the wad of silky plastic until he unraveled the sleeves for the fingers. He found the thumb and worked the glove to fit his right hand. The left was easier. Corey sensed the grins behind him and eased his hand to the butt of his weapon. The gun and holster felt smooth through the thin plastic gloves. He felt the evaporation of the smiles.

Triumphant, Corey took the zipper and continued to open the bag. The matted hair covered the right eyebrow and eye. He glanced down at the foot end of the bag and peeled further. The nose was next and then the chin. Despite the facial swelling, there was an easy familiarity.

Corey muttered, "Sylvia DeLoach."

"Sir?" The paramedic standing nearest leaned forward. "You say something? You know this vic, this lady?"

CHAPTER 20

"**I** would rather have made it up for a baseball game," Key Martin said, standing at Officer Corey Myers' desk in the Oxford Police Department.

"I submitted the purse I retrieved from the trashcan downtown to evidence," Corey said. "It was just where she left it."

"I'm not so sure she's the person who left it there," Martin said, still standing.

There was an awkward moment, at least Corey thought so. It was his desk, but he decided that maybe Martin's seniority back in Jackson trumped his ownership of the desk chair. To his relief, Chief Martin took the chair to the side, the same as Sylvia DeLoach. "I thought I owed you a call about this case, since you called me about the other one," Corey said.

"All this up here is in you guys' jurisdiction, not mine," Martin said, "but there's no harm in collaborating—and in my doing a little research."

Corey opened the Mountain Dew he'd bought from the vending machines. "Here you go, Chief Martin. They don't stock Coke Zero in the machine, so I got you a Diet Coke."

Martin took a long drink as he studied the room from his seat. "You're a young guy on the force," he said. "You train at the academy in Pearl?"

"Yes, sir. They trained me very well, I think, like all the other guys around here. Even like her." Corey nodded toward the officer in the center of the work area. Martin looked in that direction. "She's the only one they don't look to for a bunch of parking tickets or DUIs," Corey said.

The female officer sat at her desk, bent over a keyboard and monitor. Her full, brunette hair was pinned up at the nape of her neck so that it fit into the crown of her cap. Her makeup pushed the limits of the dress code, her uniform about a half-size too tight. She seemed to be copying information from the computer screen onto a clipboard.

"We don't get many nice-looking girls on our force, not like that one."

Martin grinned. "Your chief got an eye for her?"

"Maybe. I try not to ask too much. Except for her, there's no favoritism. Everybody's on their own around here."

The officer slammed the clipboard to her desk and began to erase several of her pencil marks. After "Shit" she looked their way, embarrassed.

"You oughta see her after hours," Corey said, "out of that black polyester and after a couple of beers at that place out off the highway."

Martin pulled the chair closer to Corey and took another drink of the Diet Coke. "Since this isn't my precinct, I could get to know that officer with the clipboard a little bit better—no HR issues."

Corey smiled. "Yes, sir. I guess you could."

Martin said, "But for now, I'm here to lend some outside help, maybe help you move up the ladder with this John Doe case."

"Yes, sir. I could use the help. Ten years ago they used to give a young black guy the minority upper hand. Not anymore … now there're women and Latinos to compete with."

"To be honest, Officer Myers, curiosity brought me here."

Corey touched his forehead, almost absent-mindedly. The sweat surprised him. "If I don't come up with something quick on the John Doe case, my chief will assign it to someone else," he said. He wiped the sweat with the back of his hand and glanced over at the other officers in the room. "I've got reporters from Memphis and Jackson crawling up my ass. Don't have nothing for 'em."

"There's plenty to tie me up at home without meddling with what's goin' on up here. But for the life of me, I've got this feeling there's a connection between your case and …"

"Key Martin, what the hell! What are you doin' slummin' it up here with us?"

Martin stood, pushing his chair away from Corey's desk. The sound of the unguarded metal footings against the concrete reminded Corey of Sylvia DeLoach.

"Chief Richardson …" Corey stood to face his boss. "I didn't see you walk in from the hall." The chief of the Oxford Police Department had already lost the battle. His belly permanently hid the belt buckle. Again, Corey attempted to suck in and straighten his posture enough to show his. On a good day he could stand a good inch above the chief, but not today.

"Good to see you again too, Ron," Martin said. "Long time since the academy."

"You don't have enough to keep you busy down in Jackson?"

Richardson pushed past Corey to the photographs spread across his desk. "Officer Myers here doesn't have time for a bunch of chitchat."

"If I remember right, Ron, you were the one with all the 'chitchat.' Figured that's why you liked it up here in Oxford. Lots of night life."

"Corey, type me up a report real quick on this case. The department needs to issue an updated statement."

"Put a hold on that a minute, Ron." Martin said. "Your young officer here is onto something. This woman." Martin pointed to the ME's photograph. "She may be connected to a series of deaths or near misses in Jackson."

"How so, Key?"

"She was working as a fill-in, sort of a traveling substitute exercise teacher, the day of one of the near misses. The victim recovered, then was found dead later."

"So?"

Corey shifted nervously from one from one foot to the other as Chief Martin referred to Sylvia DeLoach. He strained to straighten his shoulders taller, then realized he was staring at Chief Richardson's bald spot. He looked away.

Martin continued. "After one of the lady's students died unexpectedly, she claims that the bones of her long-lost brother have shown–up. Now she's dead." He pointed to that file on Corey's desk. "Call it coincidence, but you and I've both been doing this long enough not to fall for that."

Richardson tossed the photographs back to the desk—destroying Corey's neat stack. "The mayor of Oxford and the chancellor over at the university don't appreciate crime, Chief Key Martin. Oxford's not like Jackson. Folks up here aren't used to a dead body showing up for the whole world to see. All this commotion gets in the way of the tourists looking for some culture, going for a nice dinner or patronizing the bars after a game. And for the corpse to float to the top on Sorority Row? Mommas don't want their little girls exposed to that crap."

"I expect the students and the faculty don't like the attention either, Ron."

Chief Ron Richardson flicked the top photograph with his middle finger. The shot featuring the dirty human skull had landed atop the others. "I want this over, Corey. Hell, even CNN just tried to call me." He used the same finger of the other hand to do the same.

"That report, Corey? You've got the weekend."

Richardson ambled over to the desk where the female officer with the tight uniform was working. She had kept her head down until he hovered over her. Richardson patted her on the shoulder.

122

Chapter 20

Martin shook his head. "Nothing's changed."

Richardson patted her shoulder another time, but let his hand linger a few seconds longer.

"I'd help you now even if you hadn't asked," Martin said. He started toward the reception area and Corey followed.

"We found nothing in the woman's car," Corey said quietly. "Found it parked off Highway 7 toward Water Valley. No witnesses. No traffic cam. No credit card charges. Nothing on her cell. And no prints."

Martin said, "Then why don't you take a little visit to Jackson—team up with me for a few days. I bet we find some answers. And why don't you bring along a copy of those photos your chief made such a mess with."

CHAPTER 21

One of those photos was of the body of Sylvia DeLoach. Martin pinned it to the evidence board behind his desk. "This woman must have planned to stay in Mississippi for some time," he said to himself. "She had rented an apartment in Belhaven."

Martin laughed softly and sipped more coffee. "If Ron Richardson is the same Ron Richardson from years past, and I think he is, he would have contacted me about this stuff sooner or later. That young kid just saved him the trouble."

"Pardon?" Diana checked her cell phone in the corner of Martin's office, near the window. "Damn, the ICU again, and it's Nurse Fortenberry. Always Fortenberry."

"Gotta give it to him, though," Martin said. "Always knew how to get someone else to do his work."

"I was expecting those results," Diana said into her cell. "Consult's already been put into Infectious Disease. I had to run downtown to an appointment, but I'll be in my office this afternoon if you need me." She looked back at Martin, still standing at the evidence board, and studied the posted photographs from a distance. Some were of the pond scene, some made with the body still afloat.

With his forefinger he traced the outline of the ashen, somewhat bloated face of the deceased. There were bruises at her neck. "Suicide? No way," he said.

Before Diana could end the call, the RN in ICU interrupted and Diana frowned. She cupped her hand around her cell phone. "Yeah … yeah, Fortenberry," she said. "Mr. Riley can have a regular diet. Whatever the family wants to bring in—burger, fried chicken, fries … whatever."

Martin gestured again to the bruises on the neck, before positioning his right and left hand over the enlargement of the color photograph, his thumbs at the woman's trachea to mimic strangling.

"Perfect fit, almost—don't you think?" he asked.

Diana frowned again. "Got anything else before we hang up?"

No answer.

"Good, then I gotta go." She walked back to the photographs and leaned into the evidence board. In the movement, she brushed against Martin's back and shoulder and missed his grin.

"You said something about her renting a house in Belhaven?" Diana remembered the music from the late afternoon exercise class, a New Orleans jazz CD that the substitute provided. "This is her." She touched the bloated cheeks and forehead.

"You sure?"

"I only went to her class once, but she was definitely the sub the afternoon Mr. Marzel collapsed in the parking lot."

"You've been looking for a clear murder case to complete your list, so there you have it. Not sure why they first presumed suicide. Even the Lafayette County coroner confirmed death by strangulation." Martin pointed again to the bruises and repeated the strangulation gesture. "Easy call."

"I got it," Diana said.

"Somehow I knew this lady would have some connection to your string of bodies, Dr. Bratton. That's why I posted her up here with the other folks in your collection: your husband's ... ex-husband's ... new wife, a medical mishap, so that's accidental, sort of; that deceased man you almost ran over ... Mr. Eaves ... natural causes; your pharmacist, committed suicide ... we think ... maybe that should still be undetermined. Oh, and here's that lady shot in the convenience store, who was already dying of cancer—another natural causes with homicide mixed in. So ... I guess we really have two deaths as the result of homicide."

"OK, OK," Diana said. "I get it." She sank into the chair in front of Martin's desk. He took his seat.

"ID-ing this victim as Sylvia DeLoach wouldn't have been so simple if she hadn't been snooping around, asking questions about that body— or what was left of it—the one the construction worker dug up at Ole Miss a couple of weeks ago. She figured it was her long lost, older brother disowned by their parents when he dropped out of college and ran off with some sorority girl."

"But suddenly she thought different? And years later?"

"Found some papers or something that raised suspicion," Martin answered. "She talked with this young officer handling the case up in Oxford. He snooped around the university registrar's office the afternoon after she left, and guess what?"

Diana checked her cell phone. Another text from Fortenberry.

"The information was buried in the archives, but he persisted until some notes turned up. The parents had lied to Sylvia DeLoach about what happened to her brother. They withdrew him from school due to illness. A scribbled doctor's note was in the file."

"So the school didn't question his absence from classes."

"Right. Now Rusty Reynolds turns up buried in the woods on the outskirts of campus. Or at least outskirts back then. And the DNA is a match to this woman."

"When was back then?"

"Mid-sixties."

"I wonder if Aunt Phoebe knew him?" Diana looked down at her phone again and shook her head. "Looks like I'm going to have to go in."

"If your aunt was a co-ed when Rusty Reynolds registered for classes in 1965, I expect she did know the guy. Student body wasn't nearly as big as it is now, almost all white kids, probably a pretty close knit group."

"So this woman, Sylvia, sees something in the paper, thinks it might be her brother, and suddenly she's floating face down in a pond. Doesn't seem like a coincidence to me."

Martin smiled. "Gee, and you skipped police academy."

Diana began to enter letters into her smart phone. "I've noted the name: *Rusty Reynolds*." She slid the phone back into the case attached to the waist of her surgical scrub suit and stood to leave. "Better get back to the hospital; then they'll need me at the clinic."

She stopped briefly in the doorway. "But I'll ask Aunt Phoebe about the name when I see her."

"Yeah, Dr. Bratton. You do that. Ask Aunt Phoebe."

CHAPTER 22

Phoebe tossed another crumpled sheet of newspaper at the trash can pulled out from under the kitchen sink. "That damn Elba. She wrapped my mother's set instead. Careless, just careless."

She crushed the next sheet into a tighter ball so that it sailed easily into the trash. The heavy cardboard box now stood empty of fine china. "Thank goodness I checked behind that idiot. The Goodwill truck will be here in an hour."

The antique Lenox china waited stacked by the sink, black newspaper smudges across the inside of nearly every cup. Phoebe used her thumb to sweep away the wide, black streak obscuring the face of a peacock inside a dinner plate. "Elba never listens to anything I say. Momma would have died if she had seen this."

She yanked open a drawer and chose a soft, white dishcloth. In seconds two of the Lenox teacups were gleaming. "Waste of my time." Phoebe cleaned two more. "Serves her right. Now Elba will have to wash all of this by hand." Two more. "Last time she tried to put these priceless pieces in the dishwasher. Caught her on that too."

Phoebe slid the stacks of china closer to the sink, as far from the dishwasher as possible without allowing them to teeter. The heel of her left shoe speared a loosely crumpled wad of paper, and she kicked it lose. The right heel nabbed another, almost dropping her to the stone floor. She opened the cabinet under the sink to find other crumpled sheets of newspaper that had missed the trash. "I ought to leave all this for that worthless maid."

Freeing the right shoe, Phoebe grabbed the paper and stuffed the pieces into the receptacle. She thought about the mess left in the walkway between the kitchen and dining room from unpacking—more newspaper and shredded pieces of white Styrofoam. "Elba will say there's no time to bag up all that crap. I can just hear her now: 'You know, I've got to press those tablecloths and hand wash that china, Miz Phoebe, and all by myself. And I can't stay late after work no more.'"

Phoebe shook her head. There was no time to interview new maids. Besides, she was to host a bridge game in two weeks. She envisioned four square bridge tables, seating for 16, placed around the antique dining table and smiled at the beauty of the decor. The leaded glass doors opening into the spacious dining room stretched nearly to the ceiling and glistened in the light from the crystal chandelier and window.

"Oh, my goodness. The drapes!" She spotted the left side of the tailored silk drapery, falling well off center in front of the over-sized windowpanes, the beaded tasseled border of the fabric pulled inward to accentuate the asymmetry. "What a mess. My decorator should have known better."

The movement outside caught Phoebe's eye; several children were playing in her garden. The boy with kinky light brown hair from next door, who looked to be about eight, kicked a ball along the slag stone path. He barely missed the blanket of white blossoms crowning her New Guinea Impatiens. "Might as well have those clumsy kids inside cleaning house, instead of that damn Elba."

Phoebe flitted toward the window to straighten the carelessly hung drapery. In her haste, the heel of her right pump snagged the fringe of the fabric covering a serving table, jerking her leg back and to the side. Pain shot through the calf muscles, exploding in her thigh. As Phoebe fell, the clasp of her pearl bracelet snagged the border of the Stark rug, ripping the bracelet apart. Beads bounced along the wide planks of the oak floor.

She could see the face of her gynecologist at her last appointment, the warning about thin bones and what happens to women her age with broken hips. She imagined what came next: surgery, a blood clot in the lung, a wheelchair, death.

"My God," she groaned, rubbing her wrist. She twisted it in circles: no pain, no limitation of movement, no crackling of bones. No swelling, not yet. Still face down, she worked herself up by the elbows and from that angle caught a layer of dust covering the bare areas of the wood floor. "I need a new maid. Elba's history."

Phoebe rolled onto her side, coming almost eye-to-eye with a section of the Jackson newspaper used for packing and left unraveled when Elba half-emptied a box. The old headline stared at her, reminding her: "Remains Identified in Oxford."

She managed to push up from the floor with her hands to sit and reached for what was the second section. Concern over the sore wrist and the scare of a broken hip evaporated. Phoebe straightened the newsprint and again scanned the article, closely rereading the quotes from the police officer in charge of the case, a Corey Myers.

Forensics estimated the time of death about 50 years ago, a male—a young male—Caucasian. The body had been wrapped in material that in dry conditions had somewhat mummified the skeleton. Her hands shook. The wrist was not sore anymore.

"Winston never mentioned this. He must have seen it and read the other articles and seen the TV," she said and wiped away the sweat and smeared makeup from her forehead. "He and I need to talk."

Shrubbery obscured the side entrance and her car from the street. Wearing fresh slacks and a blouse, Phoebe worked her key into the lock and grinned at the security camera. Winston had assured her there were no cameras in the bedroom.

The house was quiet. "Winston, Winston!" Phoebe studied the kitchen—the empty sink, the spotless stone floor laid in perfect two-foot squares. She considered stooping to wipe a finger across the surface but then remembered her sore back and hip. The granite countertops gleamed under the pair of white-washed carriage lantern fixtures hanging overhead and the recessed lighting. "I really do need new help," Phoebe said softly. "I'll just steal his girl away from him—up her salary two or three dollars an hour. Winston'll get over it."

"Winston," she called out again. She checked the walk-through butler's pantry that connected the kitchen to the dining room. The room was dark, the table unset. "Winston wouldn't be in here anyway. There're no servants around."

"In here," Winston said, his voice slurred and coming from the opposite direction. "I thought I had set the alarm."

Phoebe joined him in the garden room. "If you had," she said, "I would have punched in the code. Unless you've changed it."

"I don't know how to do that. Never paid attention." Winston sat in the upholstered chaise lounge by the bank of floor to ceiling windows, twirling mostly melted ice and watered down bourbon in a Waterford tumbler. He was cocooned in a light wool throw. The empty bottle lay turned on its side atop several newspapers that littered the carpet.

Phoebe settled into the swivel chair at the side of the brick fireplace. Spring in Mississippi seldom lent enough chill to warrant a fire, and today was no exception. She ran her hands along the textured fabric covering the arms of her chair. "How many is that for you?" she asked.

"Lost count, but not enough," he answered and finished the drink. "For sure … not enough."

"Had enough of the newspapers or the liquor?" Phoebe said. "Which is it?"

"Newspapers," he said. "There's a new piece in the Memphis paper, even something in *The Times-Picayune*." The subsequent articles pertaining to the discovery of the skeletal remains in Oxford and the police investigation were spread across the coffee table between Phoebe and Winston's chair. The newspaper headlines and subheads glared at her from where she sat.

"I've been playing too much bridge, not paying attention to current events," she said. "Some of those women can't hold their cards, much less play the game—including my yesterday's partner. I don't care if she is a Life Master." She leaned over to study one of the articles, half of the page hanging over the edge of the table. "Most of the lost points were her fault."

"A bad bridge game isn't the main problem, Phoebe." Winston tossed loose the wool throw and knocked the newspaper away with the back of his fist. It fluttered upward and then fell to the carpet nearer her. She picked it up.

"This Oxford policeman—maybe we should talk to him," Phoebe said.

Winston grunted and wobbled up from his seat. He straightened his shirt and ran his hands down his legs, a fruitless attempt to smooth the wrinkled khakis. "Doubt that the newbie knows anything," Winston said, and stumbled into the bar that adjoined the butler's pantry. "By the way, I'm trying to sell your niece a new house."

"So Diana said. I'm not sure she makes quite enough to deal with the likes of you, Winston Ivy."

"Her banker will take care of it," he answered. The crash of an empty bottle came from the trash can in the bar.

"Diana's financial status is the least of your worries. And … no, thank you … I don't care for anything to drink," Phoebe said.

She returned to the pantry to stand under him. Winston stood on a short wooden footstool and reached into a cabinet near the ceiling. He stretched his neck into the space. "I was supposed to have another bottle of Woodmark."

"My niece is not the issue. What they found up in Oxford … that's the problem."

Winston wobbled a bit on the stool just before one end lifted from the floor. He stomped the top of the stool to steady it. Phoebe wrapped her arms around his upper thighs to help. "Now, that's more like it," he said.

Phoebe jerked her hands away. "I'm not interested in any more of that," she said.

Winston produced another bottle of whiskey and climbed off the stool. "Here it is. Sure you won't join me, Phoeb?"

"Rusty and I always sat next to each other in those horrid, uncomfortable chairs in Conner Hall, the only time I ever stepped out of Liberal Arts. It was supposed to be easy: 'Introduction to Business Ethics.' I scraped by with a *C*." She turned back toward the garden room. "But Rusty didn't finish the semester. You heard that he had gotten married … run off."

Winston unscrewed the top of the new bottle and followed her. "Yeah, I remember. Probably knocked somebody up."

"You guys laughed about it at the next card game in the dorm. Something about a virgin drives one home on the first try." Phoebe picked up the newspaper and scanned a follow-up article to the one that was crumpled on her floor. "This Oxford policeman seems to want to make a name for himself."

"How so? Wait a sec. I need more ice."

"Guess you haven't read the related story in yesterday's paper. Someone identifying herself as Rusty's sister showed up in Oxford asking questions."

Winston returned from the bar area with more ice. "He never mentioned a sister," he said.

"You never acknowledged that Rusty Reynolds existed except in a card game. Remember, I had class with him. He mentioned a younger sister, elementary age, or maybe early junior high school." Phoebe opened her Louis Vuitton bag and removed the morning paper. She had rolled it back unto more of a cylinder—better for tossing. "I guess you haven't seen the follow-up yet."

She flung the newspaper across the room and barely missed Winston's drink. It landed on the floor beside his chair.

"Phoebe, come on!"

"This is serious, Winston." She walked over to him.

"Yes, I saw that article about the sister. It was all over the local news this morning—Jackson newscasters up in Oxford interviewing one person after the other. The speculation about the body seemed more exciting for those jokers than beating LSU or Alabama in football."

Phoebe reached for Winston's glass and swallowed. "Does Winston Ivy Real Estate have listings outside of Jackson?" she asked.

"We have listings all over Mississippi—and some in Arkansas and Louisiana. You know that."

"When I called your office a couple of days ago, your secretary said that you were in Oxford on business."

"Like I said ..." He took the drink back. "We have clients and listings all over the South, and that includes North Mississippi and Oxford. So?"

"Diana called me this morning," Phoebe answered. She now stood near the fireplace, opposite Winston. "You would think she would have enough to do—single mother with a busy surgical practice—enough to do without worrying about mysterious deaths."

Winston picked up the newspaper and thumped the title of the article with his thumb and middle finger. "Mysterious, for sure."

"A few years ago Diana made friends with this Jackson detective. He's chief of police now, name's Martin, I think."

"Key Martin, yes."

"He called her about Rusty ... about the body they dug up at Ole Miss. He guessed she might be interested. He told her that tests had revealed a young male, likely died in the mid-sixties."

Winston swallowed then laughed, then took another swallow. "Sounds like it was too late for her to save him."

Phoebe ignored that. "She knows when and where I went to college," Phoebe said. "Diana asked me if I knew Rusty."

"And your answer?"

"I was so taken back, I said no."

"Not an unreasonable response. The school wasn't as large as it is now, but still we didn't know everybody. Not really."

"That's nonsense, Winston." She faked a kick at the bottom of his chair. "We knew everybody, even the one or two black students—hard to miss them. And I'm certain Rusty and I were in a few pictures together in the yearbook. We had more than one class together, in fact. There was this pitiful English teacher."

"Not sure why you're so worked up about this, Phoebe."

"Diana told me that Martin has started asking questions, gotten chummy with this Oxford policeman investigating the case, the one who's all over the papers." She waved her hand over the messy pile on the dark oak floor. "Martin has figured out that Rusty's sister stayed in Jackson for a few weeks before she got curious and drove to Oxford. And now she's dead."

"That she is," Winston said.

"And now the black officer from Oxford is coming to Jackson. He wants to know more about the sister's time here."

"I know a lot about real estate law, but I'm not sure about police jurisdiction across county lines." He reached over the side of his chair for the most recent newspaper article, straightened the sheet, and began to read.

"Winston, you were in Oxford a few days ago."

"Yes, like I just said, we have properties up there ... very hot market. Closed on a house just off the Square and a condo on Old Taylor. Next, I listed a redo near University Avenue. Exhausting day, but worthwhile." He toasted the air with his glass, still immersed in the newspaper. "Here's to the Ole Miss Rebels. Touchdowns, goals, and home runs move property."

"Diana's become some kind of super sleuth. She told Chief Martin that I was at Ole Miss about the time that Rusty died, that we both were. So she thinks that the police will want to talk to us."

"But you denied knowing Rusty," Winston said.

"I did, but they'll see through that. This young policeman is out to make a career over all this mess."

Winston's cell phone vibrated. He checked the number and finished the drink. "If you'll excuse me, Phoebe, I need to get this."

He left the room.

Phoebe picked up the article detailing Officer Corey Myers' ID of the body floating in the pond as Sylvia DeLoach, Rusty's sister. Winston's loud voice from the bedroom interrupted her. He always misjudged how his voice carried. She moved toward it, taking the newspaper with her.

The sound grew louder as she turned into the hall leading to the master suite. "I paid you already. Anyway, you were never to call me on this cell."

Winston tossed his phone onto the bed. It bounced twice on the tight coverlet and landed atop a pillow. He looked up at Phoebe, surprised. "You said you weren't interested in the bedroom anymore."

"I'm not." She chose the chaise lounge near the window that overlooked the pool and waterfall. She once accused Winston of having the semi-nude garden statue fashioned in his likeness. "Who was that poor caller?" she asked.

"Just one of my newer agents. The girl thinks I shorted her on a real estate commission ... the Summerford house. Dumb thing doesn't know how to punch figures into a calculator."

Phoebe stared into the paper. "Do you always handle your newbies like that? No wonder I'm always seeing some fresh face in your ads." She pointed to the half page ad for Winston Ivy Real Estate. "Look, here's an example, and this new agent is cute, young, or at least looks young. He'll do well with my crowd."

"I've asked them … my agents … not to call me so often after hours."

"And I'm sure that girl on the phone won't try it again," she said. Phoebe tossed the rest of the newspaper aside, holding only the section that detailed the case in Oxford. "Diana told me this Myers fellow, the police officer from up there, would be in Jackson tomorrow."

"So?" Winston said.

"I wonder which one of us he's coming after," she said.

Winston retrieved his cell phone from the bedspread. He stood in the window and opened the drapes, then started to text. "And, Phoebe, why would a cop from Oxford be coming after us? I don't have any outstanding parking tickets … as far as I know."

He continued punching keys on his cell.

"I'm not sure that you and I are on the same page, Winston, or maybe it's that you're not listening. I'm sure he'll want to talk to people who might remember Rusty Reynolds from Ole Miss."

"We're talking about 50 years ago. How would the cop know who Rusty hung around with in college?"

"I don't know," Phoebe answered. "Maybe the sister remembered. Maybe they talked."

Winston slid the phone into his front pants pocket and took the newspaper. "I read this article. I read it twice," he said. "The dead sister was in her early fifties. Rusty would have been only a couple of years younger than me. Considering the difference in ages, I doubt the two were close growing up."

"Police have their ways of finding out things," Phoebe said. "Don't you watch TV?"

CHAPTER 23

Martin maneuvered the dark blue sedan around the series of potholes on Riverside Drive, blamed on the picturesque live oaks and their roots lining the broad median. Corey sat in the front passenger seat, enjoying his latté from Cups in Fondren. After accepting Chief Martin's invitation to Jackson, they rendezvoused at the espresso café. Just as Corey removed the lid from the cup, his coffee caught the end of the next cluster of breaks in the asphalt.

Corey brushed the splatter from his lapel.

"Damn. Bought this suit at Neilson's last week. A whole week's salary."

Martin tossed him a clean handkerchief from inside his jacket. "Sorry, but they say we've got a lot of Yazoo Clay around here. The road crews can't keep up with repairs."

Corey continued wiping clean his suit jacket. "Lucky it missed my shirt, but almost took out the tie."

"You look nice," Martin said. "Belhaven is an old Jackson community, lots of eccentrics live here, like this lady who was renting to Sylvia DeLoach. She'll appreciate the effort."

Martin squeezed into the space in front of a grey stucco home, a thirties-style on a corner, located deep within Belhaven but a fairly new house by the district's standards. Beginning sometime in the early 1900s, the neighborhood stretched east of North State Street to border what would eventually be Interstate 55. Martin eyed the fashionably shabby apartment building on the opposite corner, not nearly as pristine as this particular two-story, but judging by the series of planted window boxes broken by air conditioner units, it appeared fully occupied.

Martin led them up the stone walkway to the front door, the façade of the house partially hidden by fig vine climbing to the copper rain gutters. A second story balcony extended in a half-moon shaped projection from the center, the railing crafted of thick iron molded to resemble flowers with large petals—enormous daises or maybe sunflowers.

A Boston terrier ran back and forth on the other side of the white picket fence separating this petite front lawn from the next. The incessant, ear-piercing yelps were disproportionate to the dog's size, but the noise made Corey jittery. He wanted to shoot his pistol over the animal's head for quiet.

"Hey, Officer Myers, ignore that mutt and look behind here." Martin had stepped off the walkway to the right side of the main house in the direction of the apartment building across the street. A cottage detached from the garage and cloaked in greenery stood at the rear of the property at the western boundary of the corner lot. White, pink, and purple flowers graced stalks of dense leaves that rose to cover the bottom edge of the only windowsill visible from this direction.

"Do you think that's where she was staying?" Corey called out to Martin.

"Yes? Can I help you?" A woman's voice above him easily muted the dog. Corey stepped back from the front door and from under the balcony to look up while Martin peered through the break in the window curtains of the tiny cottage. A tall, elderly woman in a billowing, floor-length, light-blue dress leaned over the balcony railing. Her collar reached high to the neck with sleeves completely covering the arms.

"Young man, why are you poking around my house? And where did that other fellow go?" The southern accent was thick, even by Mississippi standards—almost overdone, like that of an actress misguided by an ignorant dialect coach.

Staring at her, Corey covered the lower part of his face to hide his amusement. Even in the quaint neighborhoods back home, he had never seen anything like this.

"Are you laughing at me young man?" she asked. "If so, I ought to come down there and slap that black right off of your face!"

"Ma'am?" Corey wanted to believe that he had misunderstood her.

"Callers at my home, particularly gentleman callers, must always receive a proper invitation. Don't move. I'll be right back."

Chief Martin slipped up beside Corey. "And what's that all about?" he asked.

"Not sure, sir. Not sure that this lady isn't coming back with a shotgun."

A basket tied to a thick, long pink ribbon dropped over the railing from the second story balcony to descend toward the two men.

"Oh, I see the other gentleman is here. I only had a moment to scribble one invitation, so you'll have to share," the woman said.

Corey reached for the Easter basket woven in bright colors.

"Good. You've almost got it," she said. "I had just emptied the mail from my basket. Postman left about a half hour ago."

Corey removed the note from the basket. It was folded, the edges sealed with a wax embosser, and heavy with perfume. He decided the fragrance was roses and handed it to Chief Martin. He was about to give a slight tug on the ribbon to signal a return of the basket when it seemed to levitate back up to the woman on the balcony.

Martin said, "No, you do the honors. You're her boyfriend." He returned the note to Corey.

Careful not to tear the linen paper, Corey gently pried loose the flap. In flowing handwritten script the note read: *Please do come in.* The writing reminded Corey of signatures on the "Declaration of Independence" studied in junior high history. *I will receive you in the parlor to the left. Sincerely, Drusilla Minton.*

A buzzing sound followed by a click at the front door drew the attention of not only the two men but also the neighbor's dog, who resumed barking just as the carved mahogany door flung open. Drusilla Minton appeared in the doorway, lanky and boney despite the loosely fitting dress, a brightly lit chandelier hanging behind her.

"Gentleman, do come in," she said, pulling the heavy door open even wider.

Martin stepped past Corey and presented his credentials. Corey followed, fumbling with his badge case.

"Oh, my," she said, staring at both badges. "My family's always had too much money ... and too much leisure. But we have never, ever, been criminals." She returned the credentials and motioned them into the parlor. "I don't serve tea until 3:30, but you gentlemen are welcome to relax until then. Should I excuse myself and pack a bag for incarceration?"

The parlor furniture was rosewood, heavily carved in sweeping curves and raised scrolls similar to Minton's handwriting. The upholstery looked hard and uncomfortable, old faded fabric indented with oversized buttons spaced evenly across each piece. Corey remembered that his mother once brought home something similar from a Saturday rummage sale.

Martin shook his head *No* when the younger officer headed for the chair near the fireplace. "Miss, uh, Minton," he said. "Officer Myers and I are not here to arrest you. We just have some questions about ..."

"Please do call me Drusilla. Miss Minton has always sounded so formal." She walked to the mirror above the fireplace and ran her hand down the back of her head, fluffing the long grey hair a few times until it sprang back in place—exactly the way it looked before she touched it.

"You're Officer Myers. Is that right?" She turned her head toward Corey for a second, then resumed the study in the mirror, brushing her hair on and off her right shoulder with the flick of a hand. "I apologize for the slapping comment. When I was growing up, I used to play sometimes with the help's children—in the yard way back behind our house, of course. Our downstairs maid, her name was Fourtunia." She looked again at Corey, then swung back to the mirror. "Fourtunia used to yell that same expression to her oldest, a particular rambunctious boy. I found him kinda cute."

She fiddled with her hair again; this time it failed to fall back into place. Corey darted his eyes at Martin, who nodded for him to proceed.

"No problem, ma'am. No offense taken," Corey said. He stepped at little closer to the fireplace, hoping for eye to eye contact. "Like Chief Martin was saying, we're just here to get some information."

"Information?" Drusilla spun around to face Corey. She put her right palm to her chest, as though to cover her heart. "Information? Bout what?"

"That little cottage you have around back."

"Yes, I saw your partner from upstairs, this older gentleman here, snooping around the cottage, looking through the window—a regular Peeping Tom, I suppose. I could see him from my bathroom window."

Martin cleared his throat.

"Chief Martin is with the Jackson Police Department, but he has been kind enough to assist me in a death investigation. I've from the Oxford Police Department, sort of new, ma'am."

"Oxford?" she said. "I haven't been to Oxford since I was at Ole Miss. Never had a reason to go back."

Corey could see the impatience in Martin's eyes and stepped back when the chief interrupted.

"That rental cottage in the back of your property, the one you said I was snooping around? Officer Myers discovered your tenant floating face down in a pond on the campus."

Corey said, "Well, someone else actually found ..."

"Oh, my. Is Sylvia dead? I don't think she's paid next month's rent." Drusilla ran to the antique walnut secretary in the corner of the parlor and checked a small leather-bound journal. "Thank goodness. I was mistaken. Check cleared last week. Tenants pay a month in advance."

Corey returned a few steps in her direction. "Uh, Mrs. Minton ..."

"Please ... *Dru*. At least *Drusilla*."

"Mrs. Minton," Corey said, "we need some information about the deceased. Your cottage out back was her last known residence. Any way we can get inside?"

She tilted her head first at Officer Myers and then at Martin. "I suppose so since this doesn't seem to be much of a social call. I expect you gentlemen to behave yourselves. Follow me."

Drusilla led them back to the foyer and through the rear of the house to the patio. Constructed of uneven red and brown brick, the patio tapered at one end into a narrow walkway to the cottage. Both men nearly tripped on the rough surface.

"Gentlemen, do be careful. These bricks are salvage from homes built in the early 1800s, slave-made brick, I suppose. And the clay soil underneath shifts so, makes it treacherous even to walk a short distance."

They reached the door of the cottage. "A few years ago, I started renting this quaint little place by the month, furnished. Like I said, I always require rent in advance. Sometimes the Belhaven or Millsaps students aren't very dependable with payment. Occasionally I'll let in a medical student." Drusilla worked the key into the lock and shook the door until the mechanism engaged. "So an adult renter was entirely welcome.

"There," she said, as the door creaked open. She felt inside for the switch to the overhead light. Corey and Key Martin followed. "Sylvia had been here for only a few weeks."

The living area was no bigger than a garage storeroom, the floor space covered with a braided, multi-colored rug and opening into a much more compact kitchenette off to the right. The windows were shut, the air stuffy. Between the living area and the bedroom stood a small desk with lamp, the bedroom just spacious enough for a single bed and thin bedside table.

A bulletin board hung askew above the desk and abutted the lampshade. Pinned to the cork were eight-by-ten individual photographs of several young men and one woman, their college-age faces encircled in red ink. They were all white. Corey studied the photographs in the dim light as he reached to turn on the lamp. "I thought this kind of stuff was only on TV cop shows," he said.

"Who do you think these folks are?" Martin asked. He pulled a pen light from his coat pocket and examined the faces. "See this gal's hairstyle? It's pure sixties."

"Yeah, I've seen people like that in old James Bond movies," Corey answered.

Martin shifted his flashlight into the dim bedroom. "How much rent do you charge for this matchbox, Miz Minton?" he asked over his shoulder.

A suitcase lay on the floor at the foot of the bed. Undergarments peeked from under the top. "She wasn't planning to be gone long," Corey said from behind Martin.

"Yeah, but her time in Oxford turned out to be a one-way trip."

"Gentlemen, let's get a little more light in here." Drusilla flipped another switch, illuminating the bed and the entrance to the shower stall and toilet. Thick books with dingy pages lay opened and spread across the bedspread, some of the pages torn, shreds of paper trimmings scattered in between the volumes. She walked to stand by the bedroom window. She drew open the curtain and stared across the street to the apartment building.

Corey eyed the pair of scissors on the desk and picked up one of the books. The dust from the binding and cover stuck to his finger tips. There was a stale aroma of old ink on paper as he flipped through the pages. "*Ole Miss 1966*," he read from the title page and looked back down to the mess on the bedspread. "These are college yearbooks, Chief Martin."

He took the volume to the desk and switched on the lamp. The yearbook fell open to two pages, a picture cut from the page on the right, jagged edges remaining at the center. The left page was intact and featured a different young woman from that on the bulletin board, but the hairstyle and smile were the same, the same affected glamour. He removed the photograph from the bulletin board and returned it to the gaping hole on the right. The fit was perfect. Now both women smiled together, their faces turned slightly toward each other.

"*Phoebe.*" Corey read the bold black font composing the header of the page he had just reassembled. "*Most Beautiful.*"

Martin joined Corey at the desk. "I agree with the judges," he said. "That gal was real good lookin.'"

"Everybody at Ole Miss thought so," Drusilla said from the window.

"Did you know her, Chief?" Corey asked.

"Are you kidding? These types are out of my league, and besides, be careful about that age and appearances thing. I was in diapers in the sixties."

"Sorry, Chief."

They both studied the other black-and-white photographs on the bulletin board. One male had thick, tightly cropped hair brushed up off his forehead and wore a thin cardigan. He grinned at the camera, and judging from the others standing next to him he was tall.

"Officer Myers." Martin pointed to another photograph. "Here's your girlfriend in a snapshot with this same guy at a ball game."

"Let's see who this guy is." Corey flipped back through the yearbook until he found a page missing a photograph that matched the size of the group of men. He began to read the caption—something about a fraternity party.

Drusilla moved closer to peer over his shoulder. "That's Winston Ivy, of course," she said, as Corey compared the picture to the hole in the paper. "Every Ole Miss girl's crush, even the ones who had boyfriends. And Winston knew it."

"Winston Ivy," Martin repeated. "Winston Ivy."

"Know him?" Corey asked.

"He's the real estate guy," Martin answered. "Name's all over the place in Jackson."

"What about some of these other people?" Corey gestured to the bulletin board and the faded paper and black-and-white print. "All these guys were students. Know any more of 'em?"

Drusilla leaned closer to the bulletin board to study the photographs. She slid the tips of her nails under the edge of one of them.

"In 1965 to 1966 everybody knew everybody ... maybe didn't like everybody ... but still knew them."

Martin watched Corey continue to turn through the pages of the yearbook. "Officer Myers, can you find the pages where these other photos belong?"

There was another snapshot of Winston Ivy playing cards.

"I can save you a little time," Drusilla said, pointing a long, tapered nail, polished in thick layers of sea blue. "This boy here is Carvel Eaves. And my, my, here's Dewey Marzel. We had a history class together, I think, or was it art? I remember that Dewey was studying to be a teacher ... English. I always considered his last name odd."

Martin unpinned both pictures and slid them into an envelope. "I know someone who may be interested in these," he said.

"And that cutie still pinned at the top is the same Rusty Reynolds playing cards in that other photograph. He was a little younger than the other guys here—I think a freshman, maybe a sophomore." She ran her fingers through her hair and twisted the strands around a forefinger, then released the coil. It sprang back in place. She slid her fingernail again behind the photograph and popped it loose. Her eyes grew brighter. "A lot of girls were interested in him," Drusilla said. "He suddenly came into some money, threw a lot of it around. But never at me."

Corey took the photograph of Rusty from her, the last picture freed from the bulletin board. "Rusty Reynolds was your tenant's big brother. We found what was left of him up in Oxford."

"Those bones they dug up? I read about that," Drusilla said. "That was

Rusty? What a waste." She took back the picture and admired it, then smiled, surprised. "With the different last names, DeLoach and Reynolds, I never put it together."

Martin took photographs of the clippings of Phoebe and Winston still scattered on the bed, then scooped them up and added them to the envelope. He took what Corey and Drusilla held and added them to the collection. "Rusty Reynolds' sister wanted some answers."

"What I want is a paying tenant," Drusilla said. "I don't care how much my daddy left me. I need the rent money."

CHAPTER 24

Without looking up from her work, Diana's nurse waved Key Martin through the door into her boss's office. "I've already told Dr. Bratton that the receptionist let you back here, Chief Martin. She'll be with you in a sec. But please, no more than ten minutes. I can't stay late like last time. I've got to pick up my kids."

Alone in the office, Martin removed the photographs collected at Drusilla Minton's guest house and spread them across Diana's desk. The "Most Beautiful" picture was near the center. From a thicker envelope, he produced the remains of the yearbook and thumbed through it. He studied the "Class Memories" section and the snapshot of a young man with swollen lips and face, still holding a stadium cup and Rebel flag. The caption read: "Bees like a toddy too, Marzel. Check your drink before you sip. Forget your allergy?"

He sensed Diana enter the room as she walked to her desk. She spoke over his shoulder. "That girl looks like a young Aunt Phoebe," she said. "Where'd you get that?"

Martin held up the *1966 Ole Miss* yearbook. "You've mentioned your aunt, just like anybody does when they talk about an older parent." He held Phoebe's picture at the corners, bringing it to the light. "So this is Aunt Phoebe," he said. "Is she still this good looking?"

Diana sifted through the pictures Martin had strewn on the desk. "She's definitely held up well. Too bad there's no blood relation." Diana traced the crow's feet on the side of her face with her fingertips before moving on to the picture of "Winton Ivy, Colonel Rebel."

"These days, I think they call it 'Mr. Ole Miss.'" She placed Winston's picture next to the picture of him and Phoebe and studied all of it. She had a few more minutes today than she had in Phoebe's library.

"It's odd," Diana said. "Aunt Phoebe insists that she and Winston barely knew each other in college."

"How about those other folks?" Martin continued to flip through the book. "Anybody look familiar? Some of the same characters are pinned up on my board down at the precinct, but look about 50 years older."

Diana asked, "Where'd you get all this?"

"Compliments of this lady ... sort of." Martin pulled two, fresher-looking black-and-white prints from a large brown envelope—one the bloated face of an adult female, her swollen eyelids shut. A white sheet covered the body to the shoulders. The other was of the same woman, an enlargement of a Louisiana driver's license.

"The substitute exercise dance teacher," Diana said, "from the day Mr. Marzel collapsed in the parking lot."

Martin opened the *Ole Miss* yearbook to the pages of the class photo section. A dog-ear marked the page. "Look, here's your daughter's English teacher, back in '65 to '66, when he still had hair. I think they call it a candid shot. His face is all puffy."

Diana read aloud the caption about the bee allergy below the picture of Dewey Marzel with the stadium drink cup, his lips swollen.

"We also found handwritten notes on bee venom allergies in the desk drawer of where Sylvia DeLoach was renting," a man said from the doorway. "Looks like she had been doing research."

Diana turned. A heavyset, young black man in a navy suit stood in the doorway. The buttoned jacket strained around his paunch and the shirt collar stood tight against the neck. His tie was perfect, his hair shaved. He seemed about her height, five-eight. "Don't tell me you're a new patient that my nurse somehow squeezed into the schedule," she said.

"Dr. Bratton, Officer Myers," Martin said without looking up from DeLoach's autopsy photo. "Corey was the first investigator called to the scene when this body was discovered."

Corey extended his hand. "Corey Myers, Oxford PD."

"Sorry for the weak humor," Diana said, shaking Corey's hand. "It's getting more and more difficult to squeeze in a little medical practice in between my police work. But I am curious to know how you got mixed up with this guy."

"Doctor, I went back to the deceased's apartment this morning," Corey said. "There were printouts of Internet articles about the effects of bee venom on people with strong allergies. One site listed chemicals in foods that mimic that venom." Corey handed Diana another envelope.

Martin added, "The apartment owner didn't seem interested in a search warrant; so we didn't offer—creepy lady, real creepy, even by my standards. I had to promise to come back sometime for wine and cheese and a tour of the garden."

Diana removed the pages from the Corey's envelope and read the scribbled notes in the margins. "There were some homemade cookies—peanut butter—on the counter at the front of the workout center. I remember a note posted nearby: something about a healthy energy snack. Mr. Marzel ate some of them. I initially assumed he had a peanut allergy."

"I studied the case files down at Chief Martin's department," Corey said. "Strange that Mr. Dewey Marzel would be allergic to bees and be a bee keeper."

"We found an expired EpiPen on the scene with the body," Martin said. "The guy apparently knew his limitations, just screwed up."

Diana's nurse waved to her from the hall, then held up four fingers. "Four ready for you."

"Maybe Mr. Marzel didn't screw up. At parent-teacher conference he struck me as very meticulous, detail-oriented, sort of old-maidish."

"The guy lived by himself. If it hadn't been for the school, he wouldn't have been missed," Martin said.

"Doctor, any idea why Sylvia DeLoach would have wanted to harm Dewey Marzel?" Corey asked.

"How would I know that?" Diana answered.

Corey pointed to one of the yearbook pictures of Phoebe. "We identified one of your aunts from these old pictures. It looks like she was in the same circle of friends."

"I only have one aunt, and only by marriage. Why don't you talk to her about it?" Diana picked up the picture of Phoebe cut from the "Beauties" section. Martin was still thumbing through the remains of the yearbook. She again remembered the day in the library during Phoebe's move to the new house. *What did she do with her yearbooks?*

Diana said, "Maybe we should all talk to my aunt about this."

"Good idea," Martin said. "We also found this newspaper clipping in DeLoach's things."

It was the follow up story summarizing the autopsy findings in the death of Carvel Eaves, crediting Dr. Diana Bratton with finding the heart attack victim in the neighborhood near a relative's home. Diana scanned the article, again grateful for the ME's findings that resuscitation would have been unlikely—even if Diana had spotted him earlier.

"Your aunt was with you that day, wasn't she?" Martin asked.

"I was driving her to the hospital. She wasn't in much better shape than Mr. Eaves." Diana remembered the banter between the two regarding the trash in the streets and Phoebe's later comments about the bridge games with annoying Carvel Eaves.

Corey asked again, "Do you think she knew this fellow back then?"

"I don't see the two of them together in any of these photographs,"

Diana answered, "and she's never mentioned knowing him at Ole Miss. But she recently played bridge with him."

"Then they were in college together—at the same time, I mean," Martin said. "Right?"

Diana raised her right hand in recognition of the nurse, back in the doorway and now holding up all five fingers. "I'm coming, Grace," she said and pushed past Martin and Officer Myers.

"Suppose your aunt might be able to help us?" Martin called out after her.

"Maybe," Diana answered as she took the papers from her nurse. "Somebody sure needs to connect the dots."

"Doctor, do they teach you anything about bees in medical school?" Corey asked. He had trailed Diana to the door as she flipped through the paperwork.

"Bees? You're kidding."

"Why would that lady have been researching bee venom?" he said.

"Grace, give me just another couple of minutes," Diana said to a loud sigh.

"I guess I can take another bathroom break," the nurse said and went down the hall.

Corey handed another file to Diana. "We also found this in the woman's Belhaven residence. Looks like she was researching the mannerisms of honey bees and their habitats, including bee hives."

"Harvesting Bee Venom," Diana read from the Internet article. "A small amount of venom can be squeezed from a captured bee …"

"English teacher dead in his own bee hives," Martin said. "Useless EpiPen beside him. Who would have thought."

Diana read on, "Even a drop of venom mixed in food or absorbed into a piece of gum can induce anaphylaxis."

"It looks like Mr. Dewey Marzel played victim to his own little pets turning on him," Corey said.

Again Diana remembered finding the small crowd around an unconscious Marzel in respiratory arrest and Brad's and her effort to resuscitate him in the parking lot. "Mr. Marzel denied a peanut allergy, and I didn't believe him. There must have been venom in those cookies."

"This picture in the old book," Corey said. "The guy's bottom lip is as big as an orange."

Martin pointed again to the caption. The last sentence referred to someone spotting a bee fly out of his cup after he cursed. "If she could believe a college student publication, then DeLoach knew that Marzel was highly allergic to bee venom," he said.

"There was a note about the snack at the front near the exit," Diana said. "No one would have brought it but the teacher."

"Looks to me that DeLoach was at least targeting Marzel, but maybe she suspected all these folks of motive in harming her brother," Martin said, studying the photographs, the circled faces.

"They all look like best buds in these pics," Diana said.

"Maybe guilt by association?" Corey said.

"If DeLoach did flub up poisoning Dewey Marzel at the workout center," Martin said, "she may have lucked up later with his carelessness."

"Or maybe she helped the situation along that day in the hive," Corey said.

"We need to go check out his little bee hobby. Marzel's death doesn't seem so accidental," Martin said.

Aunt Phoebe, what the hell is going on? Diana thought. "Guys, you go ahead. Leave me to practice medicine before I lose all my patients." She handed the file of research articles once belonging to Sylvia DeLoach to Corey and stepped one foot into the hall. "OK, Grace, I'm headed to room 2 in just a sec."

The nurse held her hands up in relief.

Diana glanced back into her office at the two police officers. "And if DeLoach was out for vengeance, then somebody got to her first, don't you think? But like I said, you two are the professionals."

"We'll nail whoever murdered Sylvia DeLoach when we know why DeLoach was after these people," Martin said.

CHAPTER 25

Winston Ivy rarely arrived at his office before ten, sometimes closer to twelve unless a client demanded a house showing before noon. Miranda was due to open the building for business by 9:00 and start the first pot of coffee. Winston abhorred those single-cup, pod packet coffee makers. He preferred a full pot at his disposal, and any of his agents who beat him to the first cup of that first daily brew knew to start another fresh one by the time their broker arrived.

However, today the employee parking lot at the rear of the building was empty. Winston drove past twice to make sure. He had just signed two eager real estate agents, a husband and wife team new to the business with freshly granted licenses who had already garnered several expensive listings. The couple had a key to the office, but Winston doubted that even they would be at work as early as eight-thirty.

There were no scheduled morning appointments to see real estate broker Winston Ivy. Nothing jotted down last minute on the calendar. Winston had made sure of it. Short, grey-haired, and dumpy, Miranda had worked for him for thirty-five years, beginning shortly after he passed the real estate broker exam and earned his own license. Not only did she serve as secretary, receptionist, and office manager, she was also his personal assistant in charge of installing yard signs for his own listings and purchasing sale advertisements for the firm.

Despite their advanced ages, Miranda was quick to master navigation of the Internet—uploading new property listings along with well-written descriptions and quality digital photographs, most with clever captions. Her diligence made even the most ordinary house, condo, or commercial building stand out from the rest. Winston steadily increased Miranda's healthy monthly salary and quarterly bonuses. She never complained about the increasing workload or the number of fresh real estate agents forced under her wing.

There had never been any romance, no hint of the need, and, as far as

Winston could tell, she held everything in the strictest confidence.

Several years ago, after neighboring businesses were burglarized, Miranda suggested an office security system. Winston agreed to something simple, no more than three cameras. He'd balked on the more expensive option of live, off-site monitoring of the camera feed via the Internet, choosing instead a system of digital recording with a 30-day memory. The components were hidden in a closest behind Miranda's desk. The flat, compact box included a small black-and-white playback screen.

He remembered the camera mounted at the back door and its view of the employee parking lot, but of greater concern were the cameras covering the front entrance, the window and the lobby reception area. Winston unlocked the door to the closet with his master key and fumbled through a stack of manuals until he found the operating instructions for the security system. He recalled little of what the salesman had said although there was a way to replay recorded frames from specific dates and times.

Sylvia DeLoach had come by unannounced early during the week— Monday or was it a Tuesday? Miranda would know. Winston punched in a date and found the fast-forward, the images a blur as he watched several agents and a client or two come and go—no one that resembled Rusty's sister.

Next, he tried reverse.

Finally, he found her. He did not need Miranda.

Winston's pulse quickened when he spotted himself coming from the hall into the lobby to greet Sylvia DeLoach. Despite the low level black-and-white resolution, the surprise on his face was clear when she spoke. Even without audio, he could hear her. "Are you Winston Ivy? I'm Rusty Reynolds' sister. I think you knew him."

"Miranda, you stay at the desk," he had said. "I'll show this nice lady to my office." Winston hit *Delete*. Those frames disappeared.

Miranda's receipt of a Fed Ex delivery followed, and she laid the cardboard sleeve aside on her desk. Winston remembered the document inside, a multi-page contract for the sale of 1000 acres of prime hunting land near Pickens. He hit fast-forward through several answered phone calls. Next came the pass-through of one of his higher producing agents greeting a client in the lobby after waving to Miranda. The visit from the mail man followed. Then Miranda answered the intercom and left to run Winston's errand.

The meeting with Sylvia DeLoach in his private office had been brief, and Winston had mostly listened. She talked about seeing an old *Ole Miss* yearbook containing pictures of him with her brother Rusty. Her parents had told her Rusty ran off with a girl, although now she knew he died while in college. She wanted answers.

"I'm going to drive to Oxford tomorrow," she said. "I'm going to make someone in that police department tell me what happened."

He remembered the threat in her voice, the tremble in her hands.

"You said you were going to Oxford," Winston said. "Tomorrow."

"Yes, why?"

"All our properties in North Mississippi are handled out of our branch office in Oxford, very near the Square. I keep a skeletal staff; however, my assistant will be happy to help you during your visit."

"I'm not interested in buying any property in Mississippi. I need to find out what happened to my brother, then get back to Louisiana and my own exercise and dance students."

Winston stood behind his desk. "I'm sorry, but I don't know anything about your brother, Mrs. DeLoach."

She remained seated across from him and looked up. "I always hoped I would find Rusty. I guess I never wanted to accept the possibility that he might be dead. Since my husband died, Rusty was the only family I had left."

Winston easily forgot the moist eyes. He recalled walking around the corner to put a hand on the sister's shoulder. "I know this has been devastating for you, Mrs. DeLoach," he said, "and, of course, you want answers. Of course, you do."

He leaned back against the desk. "You misunderstood me earlier. My Oxford real estate assistant will be happy to direct you to the people you need to talk to. It is important that you find out what happened to your brother."

"I'm sure I can find the police station," she said. "The town can't be that big."

"It's not, but your loss has been so stressful and emotionally consuming. You need time to sort things out and a place to stay. We have furnished properties available."

DeLoach picked up her purse and stood. "I don't have money for anything like that, Mr. Ivy," she had said. "I've been renting a place in Jackson. It was cheaper than a hotel, but now I'm strapped for cash."

Winston said, "You misunderstand. You can stay free of charge. I would have done the same for you here in Jackson had I known the need." Winston slid a business card from inside his jacket and took the pen from his desk. He wrote on the back of the card. "Here's my assistant's cell. Just give him a call as soon as you get to Oxford. Name is Alex."

DeLoach started for the hall and the lobby.

"Wait, let me help you to the door," Winston said before walking ahead to the empty lobby and the receptionist's desk. Both of them were now in view of the security camera, and Winston made a note of the recorded time on the digital monitor. He watched DeLoach and himself reach the front door. He then opened it for her and checked outside. No clients were coming up the walkway, and the only car in the visitor parking bay was hers. They were still alone.

"Is that your Toyota?" he had asked.

"Yes, and I'm late on that too," DeLoach said. She brushed against the thick leaves of shrubbery on either side of the entrance as she headed to her car.

Winston called out, but not too loudly. "Be sure to check with my assistant. He'll take care of you. I'll let him know you're on the way."

He highlighted the video frames recorded from both the lobby and exterior cameras and touched the delete button. The evidence vanished. No one else would ever see Sylvia DeLoach in his office, and Miranda would never mention it.

"You could have picked a more secluded spot," Winston said. Standing at the granite counter top inside the bar, he poured enough whiskey to drown two ice cubes then returned the crystal decanter to the glass shelf. The bottle he opened yesterday during Phoebe's visit was long gone.

Winston's architect had designed the oak-paneled bar off the garden room area to work well at parties, and it did. Social expenses were an easy tax write-off, and Winston's accountant never argued. Two bartenders easily fit into the space, and his caterer was on retainer—stress-free party with little notice.

Alex answered from inside the garden room. "The woman was asking too many questions. She had just been to the police, couldn't even remember the name of the officer she talked to. I was trying to be nice. I tried a heavy dose of Southern hospitality to calm her nerves, unruffle her feathers."

From a distance Alex Bratton looked several inches taller, but standing next to him the difference was only an inch or so. Alex resembled a younger version of Winston's look alike brother, thus the importance of not being seen side by side.

"You did more than ruffle feathers." Winston laughed and poured another glass. "Splash of water for you, or is it soda?" he asked.

Alex met Winston halfway to the bar, took the drink and finished half. "I was surprised that she followed through and called me. Shit, what a basket case. Just like you warned."

"Such a mistake to let her leave Jackson," Winston said. "It's rare when my charm fails me."

He looked at his reflection in the glass cabinet. His hairline had held up, but he stopped coloring the gray about 10 years ago. And while his hair was not as thick as Alex's, he still had much more of it than many men his age. "At one time in my life, charm and these looks were all it took to stop questions and diffuse an issue."

Winston took another glance into the glass and finished the bourbon. "But not that time."

He poured another one but skipped the ice.

"That chick talked on and on about seeing pictures of you taken at Ole Miss with her brother," Alex said, stepping past Winston into the bar as Winston left for the game on television. "She first found the pics in her parents' things and then when snooping around her landlord's house in Jackson." Miniature recessed lights encircled the mirror that covered the wall area above the sink. The light burned through the thin layer of makeup applied to camouflage the scratches on his cheek. Alex ran his fingers down the bridge of his nose, still sore where she hit him before he pinned her down. "Bitch nearly broke this," he said.

Alex reached into the ice maker for the ice scoop.

"You say something about her parents?" Winston called out into the bar from in front of the TV. "It didn't take much to keep them quiet."

Alex held his hands closer to the light and looked under each finger nail. Such an unexpected struggle from a slender woman who looked 50-plus. His nails were clean—no blood or skin; his toothbrush had worked well in the shower. Besides, he wore gloves—the same kind Diana wore at work.

Alex walked back into the room. "You didn't take her seriously, Winston. The woman was angry." He gingerly touched his sore nose again. "She was sure you were covering up about her brother, and it didn't help that some guy at OPD didn't take her seriously."

"What a shame." Winston twirled the brown liquid in his glass. "But you couldn't leave it at that?"

"Like you suggested, I told her that Winston Ivy Realty would put her up while she looked into things some more. I showed her the place on the lake out by the country club."

Winston chuckled, "We needed to put that property to good use. What a white elephant, been on the market for over two years. Last contract fell through because Ole Miss lost a football game."

"She wouldn't bite on a comped three-month lease, out of courtesy to soften her loss," Alex said. "Even threw in a free club membership. There was enough in petty cash to cover it."

"That woman wasn't some lame jury, Alex," Winston said. "You must have come on a little too strong. That reeked of a bribe." He changed the channel. The Reds had won the baseball game.

Alex topped off his drink and checked his collar stays in the glass reflection of a framed wall print. The crease in his Peter Millar slacks was still fresh. "She wouldn't shut up."

"DeLoach say anything about heading back to Jackson to continue her little Nancy Drew mystery?"

"I knew you wouldn't want her back down here asking more questions," Alex answered.

"You're right about that, but dumping the body on campus was too dramatic, Alex." Winston walked to the window for a look out into the garden. He thought about Phoebe's earlier visit. "Not your usual degree of professionalism."

"Things just got out of hand. I put a hand on her shoulder when she turned for the door. Next thing I knew, a swinging purse pounded my face."

"And you cleaned up around the office? No trace?"

"I never leave a trace," Alex answered and rubbed his cheek.

"Won't bruise if you ice it," Winston said. "And no one ever accused you of omitting details, Alex."

"Speaking of details—that crackhead said you really looked surprised when he shot your wife." Alex swirled the ice and sipped his drink. "Kid won't be calling you again for quiet money."

"My wife was suffering, growing more emaciated every day," Winston said. "Some of our friends at Riverhills Club didn't even recognize her. But I wonder…"

"Wonder, what?" Alex finished his drink and pushed away from his chair and the television. "Don't be a hypocrite."

"The doctors were out of options," Winston said. He picked up the iPad, found the Savant icon for his wireless remote, and switched to ESPN Classic. The Cowboys had just scored. "My wife wasn't facing the truth. But who was I to argue. Her hair was falling out. The wigs looked more and more fake, no matter how expensive."

Alex returned with a full drink and dropped onto the cushion. He swung his feet onto the matching upholstered ottoman. "Your friends were right. Aunt Trudy looked horrible."

153

Winston stared down into his glass and saw two separate, but blurry, cocktails. Enough alcohol for him, at least for the afternoon. "Your empathy is touching—so very sincere," he said. "No wonder that Bratton girl divorced you."

"That *Bratton girl* is clueless," Alex said. "She'd never guess that we would even know each other, much less figure out that the convenience store was a setup."

"Your little pharmacy girlfriend provided more than enough to pay the shooter off. Should I thank her sometime?"

"No need. She started whining, feeling guilty about smuggling narcotics from the pharmacy. She wanted to come clean with the manager. I held back just enough from Javier's pay to put her down, and I was beginning to like her, especially in bed."

"Haven't heard anything about that one in the news, so I guess you were good with the details once again," Winston said. "However, leave your first ex-wife alone. She's not my concern, never has been. Dr. Diana Bratton is very dear to Phoebe."

Winston walked back to the window, steadying himself on an eighteenth century mahogany breakfront filled with china and pushed against the wall. He and Trudy Ivy had purchased it from Manheim in New Orleans years ago. "Phoebe is all wound up over what Rusty's sister was up to."

Winston held his empty Waterford tumbler to the window at the precise angle for the streaming light to strike the crystal in a prism. He treasured having a deep backyard, lots of privacy. "In fact, dear Phoebe came by the house yesterday," he said. "She may be the real problem."

CHAPTER 26

Chief Martin sat in his office chair, studying Diana while she scrolled through her phone. Maybe she was wearing more makeup than before. Officer Myers was busy looking through the file. "New iPhone, Doc?" Martin asked.

"Yeah, the latest upgrade—a business expense." Diana checked a text. "Kelsey forgot about Spanish club. She'll catch a ride home after school, so I have time to stay downtown."

Martin pointed to the picture of Sylvia DeLoach mounted on the corkboard. The picture to the far left was the morgue shot of Carvel Eaves, the second the young female pharmacist, the third Dewey Marzel, the fourth a photograph of the human remains unearthed in Oxford. DeLoach made number five. Diana slid her phone back into her jacket and moved closer. She studied the different-sized photographs, shook her head, and moved the pins around to align the top edges. She found the last two particularly uneven.

"Doc, if you like housekeeping, my desk is a mess," Martin said.

"Yeah, that's nothing new." Diana saw herself that day in front of Phoebe's previous home, leading her seriously ill aunt to the car. Mr. Eaves was holding the crumpled note. "Five Manners of Death," Diana said.

"What was that you said, Dr. Bratton?" Corey asked.

"So, we're back to that," Martin said.

"I'm a doctor. Of course, I see people die—but it's not supposed to be under mysterious circumstances. That's correct police jargon. Isn't it?"

"Officer Myers," Martin said, "Dr. Bratton found a note ..."

"It was a crumpled piece of paper with a list," Diana said, "actually found in the street by my Aunt Phoebe's neighbor—this guy." She pointed to the likeness of Carvel Eaves. "Mr. Eaves stopped to pick up loose trash in the neighborhood during his daily walk—carried a plastic bag with him. He was some kind of clean freak or maybe just a good citizen."

"That piece of trash set my buddy Dr. Bratton off on a wild goose chase of sorts," Martin said. "She suspects that your waterlogged lady from Oxford is on that list."

"How'd you get mixed up with this guy?" Diana looked over her shoulder to the young black officer. "It's not too late to run, Officer Myers."

Corey smiled. "I actually sought out Chief Martin, sort of needed a consult," he said.

"I'm sure that somewhere in your police manuals it says something about the five causes of death," Diana said. "My books call for natural, accidental, suicidal, homicidal, and unclassified."

Martin added, "Or undetermined."

"Yes, that's straight from the police academy," Corey said.

"This poor guy, Carvel Eaves, died of a heart attack—natural cause." Diana next pointed to the pharmacist.

"Coroner ruled suicide on that one," Martin said. "Dr. Bratton believes she shared her ex with this girl."

"Then, Mr. Dewey Marzel, my daughter's teacher. His was accidental."

"Maybe not," Martin said.

"His bee-keeping hobby got the best of him," Diana said. "And, Officer Myers, the human remains in Oxford?"

"Initial cause of death was unclassified or undetermined, but it looks like he met with foul play."

Diana pointed to the photo of the bloated face with bruises nearly encircling the woman's neck.

"Murder, homicide," Corey said. "That one's on me too."

"We don't need a medical degree or any police training to see that," she said.

"There was no ID on the body when they called me to the scene. I almost didn't recognize her from the day before, but she was wearing the same clothes."

"Truth is," Martin said, "if Sylvia DeLoach hadn't met with this rising star in the OPD, she would have been a Jane Doe, at least for a while, probably a good long while."

Diana was sure that Myers blushed or at least looked a little embarrassed.

"The paramedics already had her body on the stretcher when I was called. Maybe they shouldn't have disturbed the scene, but there were pictures. I had just recovered her purse and wallet, even her cell ... really just by accident."

"No accidents in police work," Martin said.

"We later matched dental records," Corey said. "There were no fingerprints in the bank. But once we had ID confirmed, we matched her DNA to the John Doe found on the university campus."

Martin directed them to the shots of the skeletal remains. "So, we believe that's Rusty Reynolds."

"The cell phone carrier led us to DeLoach's temporary address in Belhaven," Corey said.

A few seconds of hesitation passed on Martin's part, unusual for him. "Dr. Bratton, do you think there could be a connection between your aunt and DeLoach?" he asked.

"I don't think you would have shown me all of this if you didn't think so."

"DeLoach may be the common denominator here," Martin said.

Diana's cell phone vibrated a text message. She ignored it. Instead, she stared deeply into the woman's pale, bloated, expressionless face, trying to look past the strangulation marks on her neck. She looked carefully for any resemblance to the boy in the *Ole Miss* yearbook, the photographs captioned with the name Rusty Reynolds. Maybe they were indeed brother and sister. DNA does not lie.

And if so, somebody wanted this woman's brother to vanish, someone careless.

CHAPTER 27

Martin stood on tiptoe to retrieve the invitation from inside Drusilla Minton's basket as it dropped toward them.

"I assumed you were kidding about the basket," Diana said.

A low drawl cascaded from the balcony. "I see you gentlemen brought a young lady with you this time." Drusilla stretched over the railing and began to reel in the thick red ribbon. "Go ahead and open your invitation, Chief Martin, and everyone come inside the living room for tea. Our party seems to be expanding."

Martin called up to her. "We appreciate the invitation, Miss Minton, but we must respectfully decline." He checked Diana for approval of his genteel response and received a shrug. "Officer Myers and I have brought Dr. Diana Bratton and hope to take another visit to your backyard apartment."

The pale face framed in locks of long grey hair disappeared. In moments, Diana heard footsteps approaching the front door. It flew open.

"I'm so sorry, Chief Martin. There's not much there. You and your Officer Myers here took practically everything Sylvia left—as evidence of some sort, I guess?"

"Dr. Bratton's aunt was one of the college students in those photos that Miss DeLoach had pinned up on the bulletin board," Corey said.

Drusilla Minton stared at Diana and limply extended her right hand. "I really can't let you back into the garden apartment. It wouldn't be proper. You see, I've already rented it to someone following in your footsteps, Dr. Bratton—a very nice medical student and quite handsome."

Diana shook Minton's hand, the boney fingers ice cold. Diana thought of a fairy tale, the description of the witch character, but couldn't recall the title, not even an exact scene. *"Hansel and Gretel?"*

Minton held Diana's hand a couple of seconds too long and said, "I have a wonderful view of the cottage from my rear balcony. I can sit in a rocking chair behind the white posts and see everything that goes on."

Diana peeled her fingers free and slid her hands into the pockets of her jacket. She wished for a sanitizing wipe or hand spray.

Minton smiled and said, "I wasn't at all surprised when that handsome young man slipped a girl into the cottage this past weekend, then took her home and slipped in another for dessert. Did I mention that the young man is quite good-looking?"

Diana said, "You did, and he is an adult, paying rent, so what business is it of yours if ..."

"If your handsome new tenant is out at the moment, couldn't we take a quick tour?" Martin asked.

"You policemen have already seen the apartment," Minton said. "I guess it's really Dr. Bratton who needs to see the place, but like I said—what's left to see?"

Martin answered, "Officer Myers and I would like to take another look around."

Drusilla Minton seemed to study each of them and then check up and down the street for traffic. There was none.

"Since you're such a smooth talker, Chief Martin, I'll let you all in just this one more time."

"Thank you, Miss Minton," Corey said. "This could also help my investigation."

"My cottage rental comes with weekly maid service," Drusilla said. "And guess who the maid is?" She smiled. Her teeth were dingy, yet perfectly aligned. "Follow me. I have my key."

She led them along the uneven flagstone walk to the gate. Her full-length dress squeezed between the overgrown holly fern that lined the path. She held her hands at eye level and fanned the fingers in admiration. "Rubber gloves protect the maid's nails."

Diana watched the pleats of the dress sway from one side of the walk to the other. The leaves of each plant seemed to spring alive as she passed. "So you keep a close watch on your tenants, Miss Minton," Diana said, "both from your balcony and from the inside, when you're cleaning?"

Minton halted the parade and reversed direction toward Diana, nearly mowing down the two men directly behind her. "You're exactly right. It's my prerogative," she said. "Your aunt was in one of the larger photographs. I think it was pinned near the center of the bulletin board. "Miss Ole Miss" was printed in bold letters at the top of the page, but I remember her from college as a bitch."

Minton leaned closer, and Diana detected a hint of bourbon on her breath. "And I see the resemblance, Dr. Bratton," she whispered.

Diana forced a smile and pulled her head back. "Thank you, but I hope you mean in appearance."

Martin interrupted, "Miz Minton, we don't want to take too much of your time. The inside of the cottage?"

He and Corey stepped away so that Drusilla could finish leading them to the cottage. Without knocking, she slid her key into the lock, then opened the door. "Young Doctor Randle isn't at home; he has a long afternoon lab class today."

"You oughta know," Martin said, pushing into the apartment. Diana and Corey followed.

The furnishings were as Martin had described them; but instead of the shredded college yearbook and photo pages scattered around, there were medical texts and short stacks of typed pages and handwritten notes on the small desk. A laptop remained opened.

"Young Doctor Randle must be on a pathology rotation," Diana said, thumbing through the note cards. "From the looks of this, he studies pretty hard. I'm glad to see that everything's not all electronic—still a lot of hands-on."

"That's exactly the way he is when his girlfriends come over, but he's all books when they leave," Minton said.

Diana flipped through the pages of one of the medical textbooks.

"Your aunt has aged well," Minton said.

"How would you know that? Diana asked. She set the notes and book back on the desk.

"Dusting that desk when Sylvia rented, I would stare at Phoebe's photograph, so wonderful, so alluring. Back then, I would have given anything to look that good."

"But why would you say that the bitch had aged well?" Diana asked, eyebrows raised, eyes fixed on her.

"I recognized Phoebe as soon as I saw her get out of the car and walk up to the front door of the cottage. Sylvia looked surprised when she opened the door."

"My aunt was here?" Diana looked at Martin and Officer Myers.

Martin shrugged his shoulders. "Proceed on, Dr. Bratton. Looks like it's your investigation."

"How long did Phoebe stay, a couple of minutes, a half hour?" Diana asked. "What did they talk about?"

"I didn't check my watch, but I'd say only a few minutes, maybe five or six. And I don't have any idea what they talked about. The place isn't bugged."

Martin winked at Diana. She glared at him.

"All I know, Dr. Bratton, is that your aunt did not leave happy—still beautiful after all these years, but not happy."

Corey Myers was standing at the front window, looking toward the front lawn. "If you weren't able to hear the conversation, Miss Minton, how do you know she left unhappy?"

"Officer, do you see the stone planter by the drive, the one with the miniature swan figures at each corner, their wings extended as though ready to take flight?" She joined Corey at the window and pointed. "The woman sped out of the drive so fast that she nearly clipped the head of that nearest swan."

"My Aunt Phoebe can be quick and direct at times, but just because she left in a hurry doesn't mean that …"

"Those planters are valuable antiques. My grandmother had them shipped over from Europe. You can't fake that grey-green patina and detail."

"It's possible to see the planter from here, Miss Minton," Corey said. "But if I'm correctly judging the angle of sight from the rear of your upstairs, that corner of your property would be impossible to see."

Diana and Martin kept silent. Diana could hear Minton's breathing.

"Oh, I should have explained," Minton said. "I ran to the front, to the front balcony. I could see everything from there. I'll be happy to show you …"

"We've taken up enough of your time," Martin said. "Besides, your nice looking med student might be back from class any minute now. He could have one of those hot girlfriends with him."

Martin walked out first. Diana and Corey followed him to his vehicle.

Drusilla Minton called from behind. "It was lovely to have you all come by today. My same grandmother, the one who bought the planter in Europe, left me another treasure, a most wonderful recipe for pineapple petit fours. Just give me a day's notice, and we'll have coffee and petit fours in the rose garden."

Martin forced a polite wave and unlocked his car. Diana slid into the front passenger seat and shut the door. Corey sat behind her. "I think I know why that woman made up the story about seeing my aunt leave in such a hurry," she said.

As Martin pulled from the curb into Belhaven Street, Corey turned for another look at the Minton house through the rear window. "Even if she ran through the upstairs to the front balcony as your aunt left," he said, "I'm not so sure that she could have seen that corner of her precious antique planter."

"Me, either," Diana said and shook her head. "I wasn't much into studying literature in school, took only the requirements for med school and to pass the MCAT, but I feel like I've just seen a real-live character from a Faulkner or Hemingway novel."

Martin drove the unmarked squad car past the Presbyterian church on the corner and turned left onto North Street, heading downtown. "I'd say that those two literature guys could have made up a story a whole lot better than that nut case."

"I don't think she made it up," Corey said. "She probably does have the place bugged."

CHAPTER 28

Drusilla stood in her driveway, watching the police car pull out of her driveway, imagining how forced her smile must look—maybe like the Joker in *Batman* or like in that old Jack Nicholson movie. She kept her posture painfully straight and resisted the trite gesture of waving good-bye after she practically begged them to return sometime. What would those policemen and that pretty doctor think if they saw her panic and run back into her house?

She thought about the neighbors. One of them was surely watching, even now. They were always so interested in her. The neighborhood was quiet; it was nowhere near quitting time. The afternoon air felt safe—no one walking the streets—too early for the late afternoon power walkers and neighborhood strollers—no strangers, no undesirables. The geraniums in that same swan planter were headed toward wilting, but Drusilla decided to water later. Besides, she needed to mix some fertilizer in the water.

"I'm just a landlord," Drusilla said aloud, looking up and down the street to see if anyone could have heard. "I know I wasn't entirely forthright with those policemen, but then I've done nothing wrong. And that female doctor, why isn't she at the hospital curing somebody?"

She wanted to run, not stroll, to the front door. She could only hide so much anxiety. Drusilla felt the same as that horrid afternoon in Maison Weiss, when she felt an incredible urge to urinate just as the saleslady placed her things in a dressing room. She had helplessly grabbed her lower stomach and tried not to run to the ladies' room.

At this moment, after this second intrusion by those policemen, she felt the same sense of urgency, except her bladder was not about to rupture. For now, she needed to go to her library, the little room off her bedroom originally meant as a nursery and a marvelous hiding place.

Drusilla stiffened, again checked the street and sidewalks. She slid the house key from the front pocket of her skirt, then realized the front door of the main house remained unlocked. She turned the doorknob, and felt the security of the foyer: the antique rug, another hand-me-down, the weave thinned, but her property just the same; the twisted brass light fixtures, sconces, mounted just above eye level on the plaster wall on each side of the door; and the flowers filling the porcelain vase on the delicate entry table. She admired the reflection of the robin's-egg blue columbine that grew in her garden until yesterday and fanned the stems apart to make the arrangement appear fuller.

"There," she said. "That's nice. Much, much better. But I should have picked several more. I should call the two policemen and that doctor back to see." She decided they were probably all the way to the interstate by now.

Drusilla stepped back to the light switch and the sconces came to life. Beginning at the base of one of the antique fixtures, she stood on tiptoe to trace her forefinger along the entire length of the gilded arms.

"Just look at that horrid dust," she said, staring at her fingertip. She jerked loose the tail of her blouse from the dress. Nearly tearing the fabric, Drusilla used it to polish the gold metal until it beamed. The same worked for the opposite fixture.

"Monday I'll have to have a little talk with that new maid." She stuffed the blouse back into her dress without unfastening her belt. "That is, if I can pull her away from TV and the game show channel."

Drusilla pushed open the heavy wooden and lead glass leading into the library. Gone was the thick layer of dust that once coated the rich brown leather chair in the far corner. Even more surprising was the fireplace hearth, swept clean and filled with freshly cut magnolia leaves from the side yard. "Maybe I should wait another week before I fire her," she said.

Except for the faint wrinkles at the foot of the walnut secretary, the Oriental rug filling the room appeared smooth and freshly vacuumed. The early nineteenth century secretary stood bright in the light streaming from the window. She ran the same forefinger across the base of the upper glass and wooden section that housed the leather books and studied her fingertip—perfectly clean.

"Grandmother Minton would never forgive dust on her secretary. She had no patience with sorry help." She wedged her fingernail under the swollen door protecting the antique books from the Mississippi humidity and pried it open. "Thank God that Grandmother left this precious piece to me."

The lower section of the secretary remained locked and housed the writing surface, no wider than a shelf and complete with a padded, though firm, red leather center. The key was hidden behind the painted

Staffordshire dog on the fireplace mantel, the dog's black eyes peering at her between green highlights in the ears. Drusilla reached behind the animal's orange-brushed tail.

The small key rolled from her fingertips to land in the palm of her left hand. The dark metal felt cold against her thin, pale skin. She worked it back to her fingertips and slid the key into the lock. Though familiar, the opening snap still startled her as the front panel of the desk fell forward to reveal the interior. Drusilla reached for the small white porcelain knob on the center cabinet meant to store stationery or other writing supplies— but for Drusilla the perfect place to keep the old college yearbook if you turned it to just the right angle.

She slipped her hand inside the cabinet and jerked it away. She looked at her fingers, the polished nails, the undersurface of her nails—as though something had bitten her. *It can't be empty*, she thought. She felt the bottom of the cabinet, tracing the two sides and the top. She waved her hand through the center of the 9 by 12-inch space—*empty*.

"Someone's been inside my house. Someone beside the maid." Drusilla dropped into the arm chair. "That Phoebe woman didn't get inside my house. Did she?"

She remembered that it was an afternoon when the doctor's aunt first came by her house. The knock at the front door caught her off guard, downstairs cleaning up after the maid. Drusilla resented the intrusion, but even more so the missed opportunity to lower the invitation basket and impress with her ornate longhand.

Nevertheless, she opened the door. Phoebe was standing there.

"I'm looking for Rusty Reynolds' sister," Phoebe had said almost in panic. "You don't resemble Rusty. Are you another relative?"

"No, I'm Drusilla Minton." She gestured right and left with her arms spread wide. "This is my home, inherited from my parents years ago."

"Oh, then I must have the wrong address." The doctor's aunt checked the ceramic house numbers above the door and compared them to the note she held.

"You have the correct address," Drusilla laughed, "but there's no way she could live here, not in the main house. My God! She only rents the garden cottage."

"I'm sorry to inconvenience you," Phoebe said, "but could you show me where to go? I really need to see her."

Drusilla led the visitor from the front porch toward the cottage. Doubting if Phoebe would recognize her or even recall her name from college, she said, "You look familiar." Drusilla did not need the tenant's photographs pinned above the desk. She could never forget this woman.

Years ago, everyone at Ole Miss seemed to love her. They loved to call her name: Phoebe.

"Do I know you?" Phoebe asked. She seemed to study the backyard and garden and the exterior of the cottage. "Lovely area. Do you maintain all this yourself?"

In a few steps they were at the cottage.

"Why don't you try the door?" Drusilla said. She stroked her long gray hair to the split ends and admired Phoebe's. The color was the red she remembered, maybe a little darker now, but just as thick. Watching Phoebe at football games or strolling across campus between classes, Drusilla had always wondered how long she kept it up in rollers.

"What's in the other corner of the yard, on the other side of that oak?" Phoebe asked. She tapped a tight, pale fist against the door. The sound echoed through the tight interior without an answer.

"Guess no one's at home," Drusilla said.

Phoebe knocked again, this time more rapidly and much louder.

"My father dabbled in bee keeping. My mother hated it. She always fussed about seeing one of those 'damn bees' in her rose garden."

Another couple of knocks.

"Actually, her rose garden was on this spot where the guest house is now. One summer, fungus nearly wiped out the roses. What survived was gone the next year."

Phoebe cupped her hands to peer through a window that was only a couple of feet from the door. She stretched her neck to try the upper and lower sections of the glass, angling her head just so. Her jacket rose slightly above the waist and her slacks pulled a bit at the buttocks. "No reason she would hide from me," Phoebe said.

"I told my tenant all about it—about my mom hating the bee keeping and wanting to enjoy her rose garden. My great-grandmother left mom those rose bushes, even willed the yardman to remove them from over by the gazebo—or was it the back porch, the wrap-around porch—and put them in big tubs—or was it in barrels—and then …"

Phoebe jerked her head away from the window and pivoted to face a surprised Drusilla. "When do you think your tenant will be home?"

"How would I know? My tenants don't have to check in and out with me."

Phoebe rechecked the window and rang the doorbell again.

Drusilla said over the chimes, "My mother wouldn't speak to my father until he finally showed up with a bulldozer, a compact one borrowed from a man who had a farm down in Raymond. He even borrowed the trailer and the man's truck to bring it up here." Drusilla followed Phoebe around to the side of the cottage. A cramped bathroom occupied that end of the cottage, which backed up to the brick wall that defined the rear property line. The window shade was lowered.

"I was in junior high school, I think. I watched him level the rose garden or what was left of it with that machine," she said. "I know my great-grandmother was spinning in her grave. The next day men with lumber and pipes and wires arrived and had the guest cottage up in no time."

Phoebe interrupted. "I should come back later."

"Mother got busy decorating the new place since Dad said it was too small to hire out to a decorator. She even painted the walls herself. The original wallpaper and tile are still ..."

"Your tenant is obviously not here." Phoebe headed for her car, crossing the lawn.

Drusilla followed. "My tenant seemed so much into history and people," she said.

Phoebe pulled the keys to her BMW from her purse, then pushed the fob to unlock the door. "What do you mean: into history and people?"

"Very curious woman," Drusilla answered.

Phoebe stood in the driveway, her keys tight in her right hand. "Curious?"

"Yes, just like me." Drusilla turned toward her house. "What I truly love about my family home is that from my master bedroom there is a wonderful view of the backyard. You see, I have this wonderful upstairs porch to the rear. I can even see the cottage."

Phoebe remained motionless. "Curious. You said Sylvia DeLoach was curious."

"She had rented for only a few days. I was enjoying coffee on the porch and saw Sylvia walking through my backyard as though on tour."

Phoebe rummaged through her purse and scribbled a note card. "Here's my cell number. When you talk to your tenant again, please ask her to call me."

"Don't you want to know why she was snooping around my backyard garden?"

"I just want to talk to the woman," Phoebe answered. "I don't care a flip why she was snooping around your plants." Phoebe tossed her bag to the passenger seat and stepped into the BMW.

Drusilla held the top of the door. Phoebe pulled it a second time before putting both hands on the steering wheel.

"She found what was left of the bee keeping equipment."

Phoebe relaxed her grip. "Bee equipment? Who … who was the bee keeper?"

"My father kept all of it in the far corner at the rear of the property … the hives and the screens and the bees. He kept it hidden over behind the oak trees. My parents would fight about it. Mother thought all the stuff ruined the look of her garden."

Phoebe said, "I didn't notice anything like that in the back."

"I let that part of the garden go to the vines and volunteer trees. That's what Mother would have wanted. Even though Father bargained with her."

"Bargained?"

"He would get to keep the bee hobby since she got her guesthouse, the cottage," Drusilla answered. "That is, if you can call his yelling at her bargaining."

"Why was … your tenant … so interested in the old bee equipment?"

"My daddy would drag me down to the hardware store in Fondren to buy these little glass jars—said he needed help carrying them back home. Then he paid me a quarter each for washing them, drying included. Once clean, he filled them with his honey."

"Fascinating," Drusilla remembered Phoebe saying. "But why is your renter so interested in bee equipment?" Phoebe asked.

"Not sure. Maybe planning to take up the hobby or just inquisitive about how my father produced his honey."

"I've wasted enough time here." Phoebe started the ignition, jerked the door closed, and backed the car down the driveway to the street.

"Thanks for coming by!" She had waved after her. "Nice talking to you."

Drusilla then walked back to the guest cottage to peer through the outside window, trying to duplicate Phoebe's angle of sight. The pages printed from the Internet had been too far from the window to read clearly—the information about the deadly effects of bee venom on allergic individuals and the action of EpiPens to prevent death, only a blur.

CHAPTER 29

The eccentric woman's house had bones but was faded and washed out like its owner, Phoebe had decided as she drove away, Broadway tunes blaring from the satellite radio and Drusilla Minton waving goodbye in the rearview mirror. Her decorator could spruce the structure up a bit, and she could live there at least for a few years … or sell the property for profit. Nevertheless, that Drusilla Minton woman was a lost cause.

"I need to get into that cottage," Phoebe said. She circled the block to Pinehurst before turning back toward Peachtree and Drusilla's house. Staying just under the speed limit, Phoebe would do nothing to arouse suspicion from the neighborhood security patrol or noisy residents. Still, she kept the windows up and the radio on. "I can talk my way out of anything," she said, remembering a speeding ticket beaten with a bright smile and her best Texas drawl.

She spotted the same car in the driveway. "Surely that woman goes to the grocery store or gets a pedicure or gets her hair done," she said under her breath. "Definitely, never gets her hair done."

Success would come a week later on her third drive-by of the day and just before Sylvia's fatal trip to Oxford. The remaining sunlight of late afternoon provided a clear view of the driveway despite the eighty-year-old oak tree growing between the street and segments of concrete sidewalk displaced upward by its roots. Phoebe pulled under the the tree and tapped the volume control to quiet the radio. "Finally!" she said.

Drusilla Minton's yellow, early seventies model Mercedes no longer choked the narrow, open garage that faced the street. Instead, to the right of the cottage was an inexpensive-looking, dark-blue, four-door sedan, maybe a Ford, parked in the moss-covered brick section of driveway that served the guesthouse.

"I won't stay but just a minute," she said, pulling behind the Ford. Her impulse was to peer again through the window to the side of the door instead of knocking. Maybe she could see more with that crazy woman not breathing down her neck. Instead, she knocked. The sound echoed from the wall opposite the door and went unanswered.

She returned to the window. A lamp suddenly lit on the other side of the room and she stood back. A series of clicks came from inside the door and the knob turned. "Maybe this wasn't a good idea," Phoebe said softly.

"Yes? Who's there?"

Rusty's sister was much shorter than Phoebe had imagined and more wrinkled, but appeared athletic: no stooped shoulders, drooped bust, upper arm flabbiness, or oddly shaped stomach rising from the belt line and typical of some women in their mid-fifties. Grey roots showed from under a dyed blonde mane. The sister should be about eleven or twelve years younger than Winston and she. "Miss ... Mrs.?"

"It's Mrs. DeLoach, Sylvia DeLoach," Sylvia said from the doorway. "And you?"

But before Phoebe could answer: "Wait a minute ... you're the pretty girl that won all the pageants."

Phoebe caught a glimpse of the photographs posted on the bulletin board behind her before the sister stepped into the sunlight. "Well, they weren't all pageants," Phoebe said. "Some were student body elections, campus votes."

"You've aged well," Sylvia said. "No way to miss you. You're plastered all over that yearbook." She checked behind Phoebe for anyone else and Phoebe did the same. "Something I can do for you?"

Phoebe answered, "I was hoping to talk to you for a few moments—in private."

"I'm getting ready to go to Oxford. Then I'll come back here, straighten up, pack, and go back home to Louisiana."

"You're going to Oxford? Why?"

No answer.

Phoebe paused a second, shifted on her feet, almost bit her lip. She would try another angle: sincerity, the face of true compassion. She searched for *sad* or *tragic*, trying to emulate a recent television drama or at least an ad for one. "I'm here because I knew your late brother in college at Ole Miss."

Sylvia's expression did not change. "I know you knew him, and I know about some other people who ran around with Rusty," she said. "And it's not because he ever talked to me about his college life. No, we rarely talked at all. There was such a difference in our ages."

"That's what I want to discuss: Rusty's time at Ole Miss and the other people he knew, maybe his close friends," Phoebe said, forcing a kind smile. "It would help me deal with his passing."

"I already know their names," the sister said. "I've done my research. But I'm the one who has lost someone here."

Phoebe pushed forward a bit, craning her neck into the opened doorway toward the posted photographs. What looked like a reference book lay open on the desk. "Please let me come in out of this pollen. It's destroying my sinuses."

Sylvia moved away from the door. "OK, but I don't understand. Why are you so interested in Rusty's death?"

Phoebe stepped into the cottage. She stopped at the desk and the opened reference book, the pages a large color photograph of white azalea blossoms. Several bees hovered over the engorged pistils. Her eyes drifted up to the bulletin board and the captioned picture of a swollen-lipped Dewey Marzel and his bee sting allergy. Turning the pages, Phoebe said, "I see what you mean by your research, all these things you have pinned above the desk. You've been nearly as busy as the insects in this lovely photograph."

Sylvia said, "I was curious about Rusty and his friends. By this yearbook and these pictures, you and these other people were his best buddies at Ole Miss."

"Rusty was a couple of classes behind me and shouldn't have finished until well after I graduated." Phoebe saw the sister's eyes moisten. She remembered a pack of tissues in her purse. That would be a nice gesture.

Sylvia accepted the Kleenex. "When I saw that article in the newspaper back home, I somehow knew they had found my brother," she said, dabbing an eye. "I needed to drive to Oxford and find out for sure, but got cold feet—afraid of the truth, I guess. I decided to stay in Jackson and try to figure things out first."

Phoebe cringed each of the two times Sylvia dug into her nostrils with the tissue. She was horrified that the woman might blow her nose.

"Now I'm ready to go talk to the policeman in charge of the investigation into Rusty's remains. But I bet he won't know a damned thing. I need to see other people who knew Rusty."

"I want to know how you got this yearbook," Phoebe said, pushing it toward Sylvia's face.

Sylvia hesitated and stepped back. "Found it at a garage sale."

Phoebe wondered if a call to the reference section of the University of Mississippi library might turn up a missing volume.

"On second thought, maybe I should come clean about the yearbook," Sylvia said. "I had only lived here a few days, and that crazy woman who rents this place asked me to water her houseplants while she went to a weekend garden show in Mobile. Whose houseplants need watering in just a weekend's time?"

"So there wasn't a garage sale?"

"No, she left me a key to the main house, so I took a tour. I was curious; wouldn't you be? I found this inside an old desk." Sylvia pointed to the butchered yearbook and then to her collection of photographs. Funny thing," she said, "of the five people here, you and this Winston Ivy fella are the only two still alive."

"Did you also find that information at the imaginary garage sale?" Phoebe continued to flip through the pages of the reference book on bees. She stopped at the chapter devoted to the harvest of honey, then studied the photographs of bee keeping equipment.

"No, when I typed in the names on the Internet, recent obituaries were the first things to pop up," Sylvia answered.

Phoebe noted the closed laptop on the bed.

"This student died fairly recently." The sister pointed to a photo of Marzel. "His obituary said that they found him at home. It mentioned school teacher and an avid bee keeper—said that he died doing something he loved, but then this picture makes fun of his allergy. So, like I said, I started to dig a little."

"Yes, Dewey taught my great-niece in school. English, I think. Such a tragedy."

Sylvia pointed to the color pages of the reference book. "I read something in there about the dangers of bee stings, particularly if you're allergic—wheezing, can't breathe, dying. Sounded awful. It says that people with allergies to bees, wasps, or other bugs should carry medicine around with them for protection just in case."

"An EpiPen," Phoebe said.

"You know a lot about bee allergies?"

"Nothing at all." Phoebe ran her forefinger along the margins of the azalea blossoms and over the bodies and wings of the swarming bees. She again stared at Dewey Marzel's picture on the bulletin board, the swollen face at a football game, and read aloud the caption about his venom allergy. "I heard from my niece that poor Dewey didn't have anything with him for protection when he was stung by his own bees. Such a terrible tragedy; a waste."

"How would your niece know so much about how this guy died?" Sylvia asked.

"She's a doctor, a very prominent and busy surgeon here in Jackson." Phoebe lifted the corner of her "Most Beautiful" picture. "And Diana has friends at the police department." Phoebe left Marzel for the picture of her and Winston standing in the first row of the student section in the football stadium. "The Chief of Police, in fact."

The picture pinned below was Rusty surrounded by sorority girls. Phoebe remembered them as KDs. She turned to Sylvia and said, "I never knew any of these girls."

Sylvia stepped closer and touched the picture of Carvel Eaves.

Phoebe did not move. Sure, Sylvia was athletic, but petite. Phoebe could squash her.

"This guy standing next to Marzel," Sylvia said. "I also found his obituary on the web. Heart attack, I think."

Phoebe relived finding the crumpled, dead body of Carvel Eaves with Diana. "Mr. Eaves lived with his old maid sister down the street from where I used to rent—perfect match-up for the eccentric fool he was. I'm sure she wrote the piece."

"At least he had a respectable send off—something stolen from Rusty—and me," Sylvia said.

"You sound so very sad," Phoebe said.

"Sad? All I want is to find out what happened to my brother."

"A brother you hardly knew?"

Sylvia ignored the question. "What I do know is that three of these happy, young people here in these photographs are dead." Sylvia stepped closer to the desk and the bulletin board and waved her palms in front of the posts as though to conjure. "And why did my brother have to die so many years before you and your friends?"

Phoebe retrieved her purse from the desk chair and felt inside for her keys. "I'm deeply sorry for your loss," she said, pressing her finger first into the face of Carvel Eaves and then Dewey Marzel. "But the fact that three of the group is dead is just an odd coincidence. Don't you think? Besides, like you just said, Dewey and Carvel died later as adults."

Sylvia motioned Phoebe aside, almost to put her nose into the happy picture of 1960s Winston and Phoebe. "It's good that you stopped by today. You've saved me some time."

"And how is that?" Phoebe asked. She stepped back for the door latch.

Sylvia lifted a felt marker from the desk and circled Winston's face on the photograph. "Now all I have to do is talk with this fella."

CHAPTER 30

Today was Wednesday, Phoebe's late afternoon bridge club away from home and the maid's day off. Because of a couple of no-show appointments, Diana had forty-five minutes. With luck, she would still make the supper for Kelsey's softball team.

There were no neighbors out nearby, no one strolling down the sidewalk in front of Phoebe's house. She left her car at the curb, used her key to the front door, and slipped inside. This would only take a minute or two. The yearbooks were shelved in the keeping room.

Easing the door closed, Diana thought she caught Ivy's car drive by, but a quick peek out the living room window proved her wrong. She was also wrong about the yearbooks. "There're not here," she said, staring at the bookcase. The yearbooks she had unpacked and shelved were gone, replaced with an antique walnut lap desk, supporting a piece of black and white Herend porcelain on top, a large deer or an elk with antlers.

The basement, Diana thought. *I bet she moved them to the basement.*

She found the box under a dusty shelf in the corner.

Diana pulled into her driveway and waited for the garage door to lift. She pushed the control a second and third time before there was a slow grind upward. She could see through the bay window into the dark breakfast room and kitchen area. That meant Kelsey wasn't home from softball, at least not from the after-practice supper the moms served. Diana had paid another mom to sub for her just in case she missed, supply her portion of the meal, and drive Kelsey home. Easing onto the double garage, she looked at the empty space next to her car. *It won't be long until I have to get Kelsey some type of vehicle*, Diana thought, turning off the ignition. She remembered her first car, a four-year-old Honda purchased with money her young parents left her. *I hope Kelsey's life isn't nearly this complicated.*

"Diana, you've brought most of this on yourself," she said aloud, stepping out into the garage. She had chosen long years of education, picked worthless Alex for a spouse, and for some reason become consumed with this series of deaths and her aunt's secrecy.

I've got to put this behind me. But why did Phoebe hide all of her college memorabilia in the basement?

The sturdy shopping bag in the back seat was space enough to hide the yearbook, covered with leftover tissue from the sweater purchase at J Crew. As the garage door lowered behind her, Diana reached deep into the trunk for the handle, grabbing the thick nylon string and pulling the bag close to her chest. She realized that the package would attract Kelsey's curiosity and exchanged it for her overnight bag kept in the backseat. She slid the yearbook to the bottom under yesterday's scrubs, her wallet, her toiletry case, and the change of underclothing.

Kelsey's room was off the hall leading to Diana's bedroom. Maybe she was wrong about the softball practice and the time of the supper. "Kelsey?" she tapped on the door. "You home a little early?"

Several more knocks brought no answer and relief for the complete privacy to look through the yearbook. Kelsey could be so nosey.

"You'd think the child would be totally exhausted after batting and running after that little ball all around and up and down that godforsaken field," Phoebe had said once after babysitting. "And with all that nasty sweating."

Tonight was like any other night, and regardless of any after-practice snacks or light supper on the sidelines, Kelsey would barge into the house, rummage through the refrigerator, clank dishes in the cabinet, and yell for the leftover caramel cake or whatever confection brought by one of her mother's patients to the office—but long since consumed or thrown out.

In her bedroom, Diana removed the yearbook and tossed the overnight bag to her bed. Mr. Eaves, the heart attack victim, was the first picture. The editor of the yearbook said something silly about his being called "the professor."

"No doubt a smart man, probably the only person in town who could beat Aunt Phoebe in bridge," Diana muttered and turned the page. Dewey Marzel appeared a few pages later, a follow-up to snapshots of couples drinking milkshakes. "It was a small school then. These people all knew each other ... had to."

She thought again about interrupting Phoebe and Winston Ivy that afternoon during tea. "He reminded me about our writing class together our junior year," Phoebe had said.

Or was it their freshman year, sophomore year? Phoebe and Winston's picture was next, smiling, arm in arm—the page she had seen before Phoebe interrupted her. Diana took a photo with her cell phone. Phoebe needed to explain this, all of this. Diana flipped back to the other pages and photographed them too.

"Rusty Reynolds is bound to be in here somewhere." She stopped to admire the "Beauties" section. The "Freshman Class" section was near the end of the volume. One of the first photos scattered among the miniature individual black-and-white student portraits was a close-up of a handsome, light-haired boy surrounded by girls, all beaming. The student photographer had captured the tight spacing between the straight, white teeth and the detail of the Greek symbols hanging from the center of the girls' single-stranded necklaces.

"The epitome of sixties' co-eds." Diana whispered. "Not a good look for me."

Diana placed the yearbook on her desk. She opened her laptop and brought up the Internet browser. In seconds she pulled up the Oxford newspaper articles about the discovery of the remains, later identified as Rusty Reynolds, a student now missing from the 1960s. She flipped through the follow up stories. In more than one update there was the same smiling boy from the class day pictures, lifted and enlarged from the yearbook for the whole world to see.

She returned to that page in the *Ole Miss*. Rusty's hair was a little less perfect in the happy group picture. She imagined one of the girls running her fingers through it, mussing his hair. The caption below read: "Winston, just look at these beauties and their escort. Another game lost to Rusty?"

Diana heard the door to the kitchen slam shut. She hurriedly closed the yearbook and hid it in her desk drawer.

"Kelsey?"

"Mom?" Kelsey's head was deep in the refrigerator. "Where's that leftover chicken salad? You bought a whole quart at Newk's."

"And you ate the other half of it yesterday," Diana answered, grabbing her phone. "Remember the toasted wheat bread, the pickles, the Sun Chips?"

"Oh, yeah," Kelsey said and attacked the pantry. "Here's a bag of Zaps. This will do."

Diana heard the seal of the potato chip bag explode. "Better enjoy eating like that while you can," Diana said. "Won't take but a minute for me to warm up the chicken strips from the freezer. There's ketchup in the fridge and a bottle of Comeback sauce."

"That kind of junk will make me fat." Kelsey pulled the rest of the loaf of wheat bread from the shelf. She untwisted the end and reached for two of the slices. "I think I saw some sliced turkey in the bottom bin of the refrigerator. Two pieces will do."

Diana smiled as Kelsey looked at her reflection in the glass cover of the china cabinet.

"I guess you're right, Mom. I can't count on soccer and softball forever to burn all this off."

Diana was halfway into punching in Phoebe's cell number. "What happened to the after-practice meal, and why don't you skip the mayonnaise? Mustard would be a better choice."

The jar hit the kitchen counter with a thud. "Mom ... you know I don't like mustard!" Kelsey had the top off and a knife deep into the mayonnaise before the call went through.

"OK, just take it easy," Diana said, frowning at the thick white condiment layer covered by a handful of turkey, a tomato slice, and several pickles.

"Take it easy?" Phoebe's voice came from Diana's cell phone.

Diana forced a smile in Kelsey's direction and put the cell to her ear. She hurried from the kitchen into the garage. "Oh, I was just chatting with Kelsey. I was kinda surprised that you answered, thought you might have had late bridge this afternoon."

"We're usually finished by six on Wednesdays. You know that," Phoebe said.

Diana stood outside her car, thinking about Phoebe's yearbook, once out for the world to see and admire, memorializing an era when her aunt was worshiped by her peers—then strangely stashed away in a basement where you put stuff that you don't care about, that you'll never miss.

"Do you mind if I come by for a minute?" Diana asked. She touched the driver's door handle, wondering where this was going, wondering what answer she hoped to find.

CHAPTER 31

The morning after Diana looked through her yearbooks during unpacking, Phoebe had bribed Elba to take the carton and the books to where they belonged. "Miz Phoebe, I made it down to your basement, but that's the last time for sure," Elba said after. "I dropped that heavy box at the bottom of those shelves on the far wall. Nearly put my back out, for heaven's sake."

Phoebe could not remember when she had last thumbed through her yearbooks, maybe not since the school handed them out, maybe not even then. She regretted Diana's snooping. The movers were to have placed the packed carton directly in the basement, so Diana should never have seen them, particularly the *1966*.

"Most folks around here don't even have a basement, Miz Phoebe," Elba had said more than once. "If they have enough stuff to put down in a basement, then they need to throw more stuff away. Black folks, white folks, nobody likes to go down some narrow little stairs to a dark, moldy place underground. Spiders, rats, maybe even snakes. Nasty, just nasty."

However, an extra twenty on Elba's birthday bought two more trips down those narrow little stairs, hauling boxes of other things overlooked by the movers.

"Miz Phoebe, some of these boxes is almost too heavy for me," Elba said.

"Simply bend at the knees when you lift, Elba." Phoebe lowered her body a couple of inches to demonstrate. "That way you won't strain your back."

Phoebe met Elba at the top of the stairs after the first trip, a spider web dangling in her maid's coarse hair, strands of whitish-grey against pure black. Phoebe saw it, averted her eyes, and kept quiet. Elba had not changed her hair style since that first job interview: hair pressed tightly across the front of her scalp but left bushy at the sides. Phoebe thought she spotted a spider crawling from the hair covering Elba's ears, but decided maybe not.

"Take this and I'll have the $20 ready when you come back up."

"It's dark and moldy down there, Miz Phoebe. Really, really nasty."

"Twenty-five, then," Phoebe said.

A week later, even forty dollars would not buy another trip down the stairs.

"Why don't you call that moving company?" Elba had said. "Ask them to send one of those black guys back over here to put what else you want down there. Or get that sorry gardener you hired to haul down the rest. I bet you pay him more than me anyway."

"There's no need to go down there again," Phoebe said. "If something's not already in the basement or put up on a shelf or stored in a cabinet in the house, then it belongs in the trash on the curb. You said it yourself. I'll take care of this myself."

Today's trip down the driveway would be the last. The garbage man would be by tomorrow, and this empty box remaining from the move would be gone. Phoebe stepped back onto the sidewalk as she ended the call with Diana. "Of course, my dear. Come on over. My house is your house."

Phoebe began to walk through the front yard. Depending on traffic, Diana's house was 15 to 20 minutes away. Two days ago, she watched from the bay window as the gardener held by Elba in such contempt cut the grass using a push mower. It was amazing that the lawn still looked fresh. Maybe the Mexican—or was he Guatemalan? —wasn't so worthless after all. Maybe she should raise him the 10 bucks he requested last Saturday instead of tipping Elba to do the work she was already paid to do. And to the Mexican's credit, he didn't beg and did such pristine work even after the "no."

Then it leapt at Phoebe. A light-green weed with broad, jagged leaves marred the razor-sharp surface of zoysia turf. Reaching to trace the stem of the plant to its base, she yanked the weed loose by its roots, soil falling from the fibers. She rolled the leaves between her fingers as though rolling a cigarette.

True to form, another one of her help had disappointed her; the gardener committed an atrocity—and probably ignored other weeds—and wasn't worth an extra ten or twenty after all. Phoebe was headed to the rear lawn and the exterior entrance to the basement and cringed over how the landscaping could look. She needed to look through that yearbook again, and the backyard entrance to the basement would avoid what Elba called the "dangerous, creepy, cold stairway down."

From the street view, no one would imagine the house included a basement, made possible by the rear slope of the property toward the creek. The real estate agent listed the extra space as an amenity, a plus for storage and certified flood-proof. Winston later reassured Phoebe that she would never have to concern herself over that space. "The help takes care of places like that," Winston had said.

When Phoebe bought the property, the basement looked as though it had not been mopped, must less dusted since construction in the late 30s. Abandoned, partially used paint cans lined the floor under the shelving, the dried paint frozen in drippings from tops left opened, the brand labels long since painted over or stripped away. A wall of peg board cluttered with rusty, abandoned tools that hung from metal hooks hid the southwest corner. If one stared long enough, the wood saw and hammer seemed to swing.

Phoebe stood on the landing of Oklahoma limestone outside the exterior door to the basement. The slab of stone was covered by a thin layer of soil and patchy, dark green moss. The entrance was camouflaged by soft, creamy green shoots of elaeagnus growing wildly at all angles from the main body of the shrub and also ignored by the gardener.

"Who am I kidding," she said under her breath. "He's nothing more than lazy."

A discarded, moss-covered brick paver lay to the side of the door atop a dense layer of rotting leaves and old pine straw mulch. "I've never seen a snake out here," she said, wincing and lifting the brick for the key to the door. This was the only key hidden outside the house.

She looked over her shoulder and pushed the door open, the creaking sound not unexpected. The cool, moist air enveloped her, just as dank and musty as Elba fussed about. No one could know that she cared anything about the stored boxes, certainly not see her rifling through them.

She groped for the light switch inside the door. A fresh mat of spider web entangled her long nails. Whitish-grey clumps with stringy ends laced her fingers. "Damn," she screamed. "How disgusting!"

Phoebe flung her hands against the thighs of her slacks, at first to brush away the nasty, then the thought of spider matter on her clothes made her cringe. Instead, she wiped her hands against the brick wall. The rough masonry scraped her thinning skin, and drops of blood smeared the surface.

"For God's sake, Phoebe. What are you doing? The new manicure." She cursed and pressed her lips to the torn skin. A box of Band-Aids was upstairs in the kitchen cabinet.

"This is silly." She turned to stick her head out the door. No one was running toward her; the neighbors had missed her scream or at least ignored it. Other than the squirrels scampering across the lawn to the steps leading to the brick patio, the yard remained quiet. Phoebe tried again for the light switch, an old push-button panel original to the house. She expected the loud thud when she pressed it, but the sound nevertheless startled her.

Phoebe checked the light coming across her shoulder from the backyard—still, no one—and shut the door. The three light bulbs suspended from the ceiling cast shadows across the space. The stairs from the kitchen were on the far side of the basement, but the shelf that held her yearbooks was only a few steps away.

The heavy cardboard boxes strained the faded, two-by-four wooden shelving. The third box from the end remained unsealed, unlike the other cartons. Phoebe walked toward the bank of shelving, butting her foot against one of the stray, rusted paint cans with the dried drippings at the mouth. *What an unusual shade of green*, she thought. She looked around at the other refuse left by previous owners and her things scattered among it. *It's a wonder I talked Elba into hauling any of that crap down here.*

Phoebe stepped forward, and a mouse ran across the toe of her right shoe. She screamed again. It disappeared across the room behind the torn, faded oil canvas and frame leaning against the wall. The artist's scene was a patch of forest decorated with a dilapidated cabin in the corner, a weak stream of smoke creeping from the chimney. "That piece of junk belongs out by the street."

She walked carefully across the cracked concrete floor to the repacked box of yearbooks and split open the top with her house key. The 1966 edition was left buried toward the bottom.

She pried the box open with her nails, finding the worn paperback novels added at the last minute that should have been discarded. Phoebe tossed the first one toward the painting. It landed on the concrete below the split wood frame, sending the frightened mouse toward the staircase. *Another reason not to take the stairs*, Phoebe thought.

Repacked in chronological order, the history of her freshman year, the *1963 Ole Miss*, remained at the top. The *1964* would follow, then the *1965*. The *1965 Ole Miss* framed their junior year, the fall and spring that she began to date Winston. Startled, Phoebe looked back toward the rustling sound coming from behind the painting. There was no movement, but the mouse was back, had to be. As long as it stayed away from her, she wouldn't call the exterminator. Winston would know of a good one.

Phoebe reached for the *1965* volume, anticipating that the one from her senior year would be underneath. After Diana found the yearbooks while unpacking, Phoebe had later flipped through the *1966*, forgetting how often Rusty's picture was published with bee-hived co-eds she remembered as cheap, money-grabbers. There were many other poses: cute ones with him cheering among pretty, classier girls at pep rallies, shots with attractive friends outside the student union, big wide smiles in the crowds at football games. Even though her own likeness appeared on page after page, she knew that there would have been many more candids had Winston not despised Rusty so much, waving away the yearbook photographer if Rusty Reynolds was anywhere near. Phoebe considered Winston's statement from earlier in the afternoon that Rusty had become much more popular in college than she remembered.

She put aside the *1965* and stared into the box. It was empty. Phoebe was certain she had repacked the volumes with her freshman year at the top and the senior year at the bottom, the others in between. Maybe she had left the last one out, not repacked it. In the dim light she looked around the floor space for the yearbook that all but featured Rusty Reynolds. Nothing.

Pushing against the stiffness in her right knee, Phoebe reached the other boxes. She had not thought about a knife; she shouldn't have needed one. She spotted a bent, rusty nail near the bottom shelf and used it to split open the packing tape, stretching her fingers around the loose stack of picture frames filling the top. The collection was vintage 1980s: gilded wooden surfaces, heavy with colored stones—orange, leather-brown, opal, somewhere between dark and light green—mounted onto the wood with a thin layer of white glue visible under the stones in a few places.

She lifted the frames from the box, unable to keep the small collection together. The frames scattered to the damp concrete floor in a series of thuds and thumps, some breaking apart at the corners, others shattering. Her eyes fell on the one broken frame at the center and its faded photograph, and for a moment she forgot about the yearbooks, particularly the *1966 Ole Miss*.

Somehow I'll have to get Elba down here with a broom—and a dustpan. That'll be another bribe. I'm so very tired of the bribes. Phoebe picked at an upper corner of the black-and-white photograph and shook it free from the splintered wood and shards of glass. The seven-year-old boy smiled at the camera. Despite the faded image, the boy's eyes were bright in comparison to the dull cast of the woman standing next to him holding hands in front of a sidewalk gate, his head nearly to her shoulders, thick wavy hair neatly combed—the texture matching the woman's.

Phoebe studied the rendering of her younger self—tight skin under the chin, shoulders a little more square, only a hint of crow's feet. At least her hair had held up, although she wished she had worn it a bit shorter then. She patted the loose skin under her chin and regretted last year's decision to cancel the facelift.

"Enough of that," she said. "Where is that damn yearbook?" Phoebe stood to toss the loose photograph back into the box atop more picture frames. She groaned and massaged her lower back. "I should have brought a foot stool with me ... all this bending."

In the next cardboard box were items she remembered from the junk drawer in her Dallas laundry room: a dog leash (even though she hadn't owned a dog in ten years), stapled receipts from a hardware store, a few worn kitchen brushes, a small half-empty box of powdered detergent, two boxes of paper clips, and a wad of tangled rubber bands. She felt deep into this box as well, pushing around the contents until she reached the bottom. Nothing.

Phoebe split open and searched the other boxes, emptying the contents on the concrete, dreaming that Elba would return to tidy the mess. She studied her opened palms. Rust, grime, and damp dust stained the creases, even reaching to her fingers. She returned to the first carton to search through it again. The yearbook she wanted was gone.

Phoebe looked around. The light oozing from the backyard through the dingy window slats helped little to erase the murkiness as she moved toward the door. She hesitated at the foot of the flagstone steps leading up to the main level of her house, still wanting to avoid the interior stairs to the kitchen. She turned off the lights and closed the door.

Slick moss spread from the surrounding moist earth, partially obscuring the stones of the walkway, almost too slippery for the soles of her Feragama shoes. Phoebe brushed away the strands of cobweb clinging to her slacks and began the climb to the patio and back porch.

The chime of the doorbell penetrated the house to the outside. Phoebe looked up to find the door to the patio ajar and slipped, her knee barely missing the heavy stone surface before sinking into the surrounding sod.

"Damn!" she screamed and tried to brush away the brown stain on her slacks. Her knee cap was sore but in place.

"Aunt Phoebe?" Diana's voice followed the doorbell. "Are you at home?" Diana pushed open the door to the patio.

Phoebe still held the bent, rusty nail and dropped it into the pocket of her slacks. "Yes, I was just checking to see if my yardman was earning the exorbitant amount I pay him."

"I used my key. I hope you don't mind. The living room lights were on … so were the ones in the kitchen … and I had called ahead."

"You're always welcome here, Diana." Phoebe again felt the soiled area over her knee. The skin underneath was growing tender. *I guess I scraped it.*

"Are you okay?" Diana asked, walking across the patio.

"I'm fine, perfectly fine. Stay put. I'm coming up." Phoebe stepped carefully up the flagstone steps. She liked the green of the moss but it was treacherous.

Diana stood leaning against the wrought iron patio table nearest the steps. "I've never known you to do your own gardening. So, you were just taking a tour of your own place, you said?"

Diana looked past the boxwoods and raised flower boxes that lined the patio. Dense camellias and azaleas filled the shade under the oak trees in the far corner of the property.

"Did you remove anything from my basement, Diana?" Phoebe pulled a chair out from the table and wiped away the leaves in the seat missed by the yardman. "Diana?"

Diana took the chair opposite. "You have a basement? Who in Jackson, Mississippi, has a basement?"

"You are the only person who has an extra key to my house," Phoebe answered. "The only one I trust."

"I appreciate that. I've never been in your basement—don't care to."

Diana's facial expression did not change, no air of being on the defensive. She seemed to tell the truth. "Is something missing?"

She reached across the narrow glass table to pull a strand of spider silk from Phoebe's hair.

"Just some old pictures," Phoebe answered. "I had forgotten all about them but wanted to take another look."

Diana stared down into the glass, as though to study the intricate wrought iron design underneath. "Another look?" she asked.

"Never mind. Since you don't know anything about them, I guess I'm at a dead end."

Diana continued to study the twisted black iron. "It's been all about pictures for me today too," she said. "I just came from downtown, talking to a policeman about photographs and evidence."

"I remember a nosey policeman bothering you a few years ago, back when that doctor in the other practice was doing all those bad things. You considered the policeman a real pest."

"I did say that about him," Diana said. "But Key Martin is now JPD Chief of Police. I may have misjudged him."

"I've never heard the name," Phoebe said. "The ten o'clock TV news is too depressing, and I never read the paper—cancelled my subscription shortly after I moved."

"Chief Martin had this younger officer with him today, a guy from Oxford named Corey Myers."

Phoebe did not mention her familiarity with that name. She had nearly memorized the newspaper article about the discovery of Rusty's body.

"Today was sort of like what you see on a TV drama," Diana said.

"I don't watch that stuff either."

"You walk into the center of the police department. There's this line of photographs tacked to a bulletin board that they wanted me to look at—a row of dead people, victims or individuals they think are victims. I half expected actors from *Law and Order* or one of those *CSI* shows to walk by." Diana's forced smile evaporated. "However, you said you never watch much television."

"What was so interesting about the photographs they showed you?"

"Chief Martin was obsessed over the picture of the woman they found up in Oxford. You didn't need a forensic pathologist to know she was murdered."

"Murdered? How awful."

Phoebe put her hand to her neck, then remembered how filthy it was.

"Where did they find her?"

"Floating in a pond or tiny lake on Sorority Row," Diana answered.

"I don't remember any lake or pond on Sorority Row," Phoebe said. She sensed another strand of cobweb and ran fingers through her hair. "What else did they show you?"

"They were photographs from the morgue. The police are trying to connect that woman's death with the others."

"The others?" Phoebe stood and moved to the window looking into the den. She studied her pale reflection and lowered her eyes to the soiled slacks.

"The woman's photograph was displayed next to Mr. Eaves' picture and Dewey Marzel's picture and a female pharmacist. But it's not what they showed me about the woman's photograph—it's what they told me."

Phoebe smoothed her slacks, massaging her sore knee and spreading the smudge. She spoke over her shoulder. "And what did they tell you, Diana?"

"The woman's permanent residence was Louisiana. The police located the apartment she was renting in Belhaven ... somehow through cell phone records."

"Belhaven?"

"Yes, Belhaven. They mentioned the landlord's name, but I've never heard of her."

"Why on earth would the police care where the woman lived or what she was renting, that Mrs. DeLoach?" Phoebe asked.

"Just doing their jobs, I guess. Doing an investigation into her death."

"You said she was from Louisiana. Why didn't they go there and ask questions?"

"I'm just telling you what they told me today," Diana answered.

Phoebe stepped to the next window. The branches of the crepe myrtle broke the late afternoon sun, making her complexion in the window's reflection seem not so washed-out, although the color was nearly drained from her face.

"Why did you say they called you down to the police office? The 'JPD' as you call them?"

"The reason the police were in that woman's apartment in Belhaven is not what's important; it's what they found."

Phoebe chuckled. "Of course, they would find something. I doubt if the police ever spend the taxpayers' money to search someplace and come up empty-handed."

"Martin and Officer Myers told me the woman's bed was littered with black-and-white pictures she had cut from a yearbook from Ole Miss, and you were in a lot of them. I think that's why Chief Martin called me to his office today."

"Me?" Phoebe remained at the window.

"Because you're my aunt, he pulled me into it, sort of out of respect for me, I suppose." Diana stepped toward Phoebe.

"Out of respect?"

"The dead woman had been told a lie by her parents. She was asking questions of the police, trying to get answers about her only brother's death. Then she turns up dead."

Diana stood behind Phoebe, her voice now just above a whisper. "I've felt all alone most of my life," Diana said. "Kelsey's my only true flesh and blood. Then you moved here, and I trusted that you were here for me, for Kelsey and me."

"Certainly I'm here for you, Diana—you and Kelsey." Phoebe continued to study herself in the window. She wished that her only concern were the crow's-feet. The light, still filtered by the landscaping, showed Diana as a shadow behind her.

"Chief Martin and the other officer have a mess on their hands, pieces to a puzzle that needs solving."

"Diana, how overly dramatic."

"Those pieces are three deceased individuals who knew each other well in college."

"And those policemen are trying to figure where my piece fits into their little game?" Phoebe asked. "But why? I'm definitely not deceased."

"When I walked onto the patio a few minutes ago, you said that you had been checking your landscaper's work, but then you asked if I had been in your basement. My guess is that you wanted to see the same photographs in your copy of the *1966 Ole Miss* that the woman chopped out of hers."

"I'm not sure that I follow you, Diana."

Phoebe wished she were back in the basement where no one could find her. Her neck felt hot, and her dirty palms felt both icy and clammy at the same time.

"Martin's manner can be deceiving, Aunt Phoebe. His pattern of investigation is one of subtlety, almost innuendo." Diana stepped a few inches closer. "And I'm sure he assumed I would head right over here to see you after meeting him downtown."

"You're correct about the photographs." Phoebe's voice was steady. "I looked through the yearbook after you saw it, then moved it to the basement—out of sight. It's so musty and dank down there where all that old stuff is stored. But I needed to remind myself ..."

"Of what?" Diana asked.

"Of how familiar we all were, the little circle of friends. That's what it was—a circle. But we were all different."

"Different, how?"

"Winston was very wealthy. My parents gave me what I needed, but there was a bare bones allowance. And then there was that nuisance Carvel Eaves and pot-dealing Dewey. And, of course, Rusty."

"Aren't you tired, Phoebe? Don't you want to go inside? Sit down?"

"No, I'm fine here. The fresh air out on the patio is what I need."

"You just mentioned Winston," Diana said. "That afternoon when I dropped by your house, the two of you were in the living room, having tea. You lead me to believe that the two of you barely knew each other at Ole Miss. You said something about having a class or two together, a literature or writing class."

"And from all those yearbook photographs, you think that I was lying to you?"

"I can't think of a reason for you to lie to me," Diana said. She returned to sit at the patio table. Phoebe remained glued to her reflection in the window.

"You know, I'm tired," Diana said, "and this isn't going anywhere. I've got early surgery tomorrow and should get home. I pray Kelsey has started her homework."

Phoebe turned and stepped over to the table.

"When I looked back through that yearbook … I was flooded with memories."

Diana's stare was deep, dark. "But you didn't want those memories?"

"This afternoon I went back down to the basement. I wanted to look through that book again." Phoebe began to pace.

"You were walking back from there when I came through your house. Why didn't you take the basement stairs from inside the house near the kitchen?"

"You probably know my house better than anyone—including my maid. That's why I asked you about your key and any trips to my basement because the yearbook is gone."

"Are you sure? Maybe you put it in another spot, on another shelf, or maybe you forgot and brought it back into the house. Let's go inside and check the den."

"No, I don't want to trouble you," Phoebe said. "Besides, I'm sure I stored it in the basement. And I've searched everywhere—through all the boxes—nothing left but junky shelves, cobwebs, and a mouse."

"Has the maid been here? Could she have been in the basement straightening up? Thrown some things out?"

For the first time that day, Phoebe smiled. "Elba wouldn't be caught dead down there again," she said, then almost laughed. "It's an absurd idea that someone could have entered my basement, rummaged through stuff I saved from college, and taken one of the yearbooks—the one from 1966." Phoebe followed the smile with a laugh. "However, I need to know who that person is."

CHAPTER 32

Diana cinched the knot to the last suture as Brad removed the arterial clamp. "I need some help," she said. "Or do you want Mallory to sub for you?"

The surgical tech laughed. "No way. This place doesn't pay me enough."

The anesthesiologist grunted but did not look up from his computer tablet. The OR circulating nurse continued charting.

"Looks like you're in total control," Brad said. "That's one of the most meticulous liver resections I've seen since residency ... and that one was done by the departmental chairman."

Diana said, "That's not what I mean."

Brad slid the tip of the suction probe into a pocket of blood pooling in the patient's peritoneal cavity. In seconds it was gone. "I thought Alex had quit bothering you."

"That's not what I mean, either," Diana said, and handed the block of liver tissue to the transplant nurse. "They'll be glad to see you next door," she told him.

The nurse nodded and left the room for the recipient patient's procedure. Someone turned up the volume of the music in the surgery suite, Beatles.

"Let's get out of here," Diana said. The anesthesiologist nodded and adjusted the IV rate, then flattened the bed position.

"So what's up, Diana?" Brad took the needle driver and suture to close the abdominal incision. "The least I can do is finish up for you after this stellar performance."

"You taught me everything I know, Dr. Cummins." Diana held the Parker retractor to gain exposure for Brad as he drove the needle into the tissue. "You have done more than enough."

"You two are making me sweat," Mallory said, standing with them. "And it's not because the air isn't on."

189

"Get your own life, Mallory, and quit watching so much *Grey's Anatomy*," Brad said. He was already midway through closing the fascia.

Diana smiled underneath her surgical mask. "I'm not sure what to do about Phoebe, Aunt Phoebe," she said.

"What's she been doing? Playing too much bridge? Screwing that Winston guy too much?"

"You oughta write for TV, Dr. Cummins," Mallory mumbled. She shifted on her feet and leaned back a bit. "Somebody's gonna have to wipe the steam off my visor. I can't even see the surgical field. Way, way too hot in here."

"It's more like reality TV, Mal. Sexy old boyfriend, Winston Ivy, shows up, and my aunt says she barely remembers him."

"Alzheimer's?" Brad said. "That's it. Your aunt has Alzheimer's."

"No way," Diana said. She lowered her voice to a whisper meant only for Brad. "I think she's hiding something. Phoebe mentioned the name of that woman murdered in Oxford, but I'm sure the victim's name has not been released to the media."

Mallory moved in closer.

"My aunt is a liar."

"Dr. Bratton!" Mallory admonished. "I don't know your aunt, but …"

"Dr. Bratton is joking," Brad said. "Her aunt is a wonderful lady, beautiful, well-spoken. Hair long and thick like yours, Mallory … when it's not all rolled up in that surgical cap."

"Phoebe does no wrong because she flirts with you," Diana said. "Every chance she gets or every chance you let her." She took the scissors and cut the suture, the tag left too long.

Brad retrieved the scissors and trimmed it. "What's really going on, Diana?" he whispered.

"OK, who said something about sexy TV?" Mallory asked to chuckles from the circulating nurse and the anesthesiologist. "Do the rest of us need to leave?"

Diana laughed, "Stop the rumors right here, Mallory." Then into Brad's ear she returned the whisper. "First, I need to do something, and I need you to help me."

Brad inserted a k-cup-pod into the coffee maker in the doctors' lounge and waited for Diana to finish visiting the family in the waiting room. Since the procedure went well, the update on the patient's condition should be quick. While the coffee brewed, he checked the mirror in the men's room. His eyes were bloodshot. He needed another shower, and the five o'clock shadow was ahead of schedule. *I must not have shaved close enough this morning,* he thought.

Diana anticipated only a small number of people waiting for her among the donor's and recipient's families. The pre-operative matching blood types and DNA prerequisite to the liver transplant had been simple. She stepped around backpacks and overnight bags into the dimly lit space claimed as a temporary home in the waiting area. A waste-high trash can, near overflow in the corner, was surrounded at the base by used Styrofoam cups and paper bags and what was left of Chinese takeout. French fries streaked with coagulated ketchup, a mostly eaten hamburger, and some broken taco shells with scraps of lettuce added to the mess. Several sleeping children were draped across some of the chairs wedged together, gum and candy wrappers on the floor underneath. One boy had an iPad, slid partially under his seat, the screen frozen on a computer game.

Housekeeping must have run for cover, Diana decided.

The adults were immediately on their feet, gathering around her, the resemblance between the young woman nearest and the liver donor remarkable. "My brother, Doctor?" she asked. "Is he OK? I wanted to be the one to give some of my liver, but I just had a baby."

"Your brother went through the donor procedure just fine," Diana answered with her hand on the weeping girl's shoulder. "Plus, I'm told that your mother is stable. Her surgery should be over in a few hours." She looked into the faces of everyone surrounding her. "Someone from the other team of doctors will be by as soon as they're finished."

"Do we need to be worried, Doctor?" one of the other adults asked. The children in the room sat or squatted, motionless and silent.

"Your brother will need to heal from his part of the procedure," Diana answered. "We have to watch for the usual things—infection, bleeding, and blood clots—but he's young and healthy and should be out of the hospital soon. Of course, in your mom's case, we have to worry about rejection of the donor tissue, but we trust she will do well."

Diana repeated the promise of another update to come, delivered by her or someone else from the transplant team, and left the waiting room. She realized that she still wore her surgeon's cap and removed it, crumpled. Her scalp felt moist at the hairline, and she hoped that she had hidden her fatigue from the family that needed so much reassurance.

As she pushed the door open into the stairwell, her thoughts shifted to concerns outside the hospital. "What am I going to do about Phoebe?" she almost screamed. Her voice echoed from the masonry walls to fill the stairwell and mix with her footsteps. She rapidly descended the concrete stairs. "Brad's probably still in the doctors' lounge. I need some help with all of this."

The exit placed her outside the entrance to the lounge. She swiped her plastic hospital badge through the receptacle and the door clicked open. Brad was in a leather chair on his cell, the TV turned to a baseball game. Diana found a china coffee cup in the cabinet above the coffee maker and rinsed it in the sink near the refrigerator.

"I wish the snack bar offered healthy alternatives to the family and visitors." She selected the cinnamon-laced coffee, removed Brad's spent high-octane caffeinated choice, and pressed her pod into the machine. "On second thought, from the looks of those tired folks in the waiting room, I doubt if they would have gone for turkey and wheat or hummus and fruit."

Brad ended his call. "We gave that family their brother back and a lot of hope for their very sick mom. That's all they cared about."

Diana ignored Brad's long slurp of coffee and dropped into the deep leather chair next to him, planning to dictate her operative report later. She sipped her own cup and eyed the two other doctors who walked into the lounge. They took seats at the elongated table near the refrigerator. The table was actually three four-by-four foot square tables pushed end-to-end that rocked on pedestals unless someone put a sugar packet under a foot.

"Brad, I really do need you to help me with something," Diana said.

He changed the television channel with the remote. "I already helped you with something, that case of surgery. And why are you still whispering?"

"You didn't help me all that much with that case. Besides, Mallory and I could have done it ourselves," she answered. The television was noisy, and the several other physicians now gathered at the table were discussing a weekend golf game. "But that's not what I'm talking about. It's Aunt Phoebe."

"It's OK if she has a boyfriend, or is it that she's back in the hospital for some reason? I haven't been by the general medical unit in a couple of days. I guessed I missed her name."

"No, not that. I need you to help me take something back to her house. Something I took."

He shifted his attention away from the coffee and TV and looked into her face. "I know what you earned last year. You don't need to be stealing things from relatives."

"It's nothing of value, at least not to me," Diana said. "But to Phoebe? I'm not so sure."

CHAPTER 33

Kelsey peeked through her bedroom drapes as Diana pulled her car down the drive onto the street. Daylight Saving Time was in effect, and it would be light for two more hours. Brad stepped from his car parked at the curb into hers. He had agreed to meet her after work, and Diana thought she caught a thumbs-up between the panels of the curtain. Kelsey was so young when she and Brad dated, but Diana knew that Kelsey always approved.

Diana said, "I've got it in the trunk."

Brad said, "You surprise me, partner. I think you're making more out of this than it seems."

In the seconds waiting for him to shut the passenger door, secure his seatbelt, and adjust the air-conditioning vent and sun visor, there was a flashback to over six years ago and the shooting death of Brad's twin brother. Avoiding the word *naïve*, she responded, "You've always been so trusting, Brad."

"So we're going over to your aunt's house and break into her basement?"

"We're not going to break into anything," Diana said. "I have a key."

"And what's my part in this?"

"I need backup—someone to keep an eye on things when I go inside. Before, I didn't think much about going through her things—like checking out her basement. But now, after yesterday, I feel a little uneasy."

"Uneasy?" Brad said. "Can't imagine why. You're entering somebody's house without their knowledge—to return something that you took without their knowledge."

Diana pulled into the street and little traffic. A few doors down, she waved to the woman who was watering the flower planters at her front door. "I'm just trying to help Phoebe," she replied. "She's the only relative I have besides …"

"I know—besides Kelsey," Brad said. "You've worked that in before, several times. I'll help. Tell me what to do."

"I really took a chance the other day when I went through her things. I used the front door, but I don't think any of the neighbors saw me. I've entered her house with my key only a few other times when she wasn't at home, and that was when she lived in the other place—and never without giving her a heads-up."

"If her neighbors did see you, they probably wouldn't have thought a thing about it," Brad said. They were only a block from Phoebe's street. The neighborhood was quiet: no walkers, no joggers, very little traffic. A one-truck lawn service seemed to be finishing up on the corner.

Diana said, "I realize now that she has a backyard entrance to the basement. I found her coming up from there yesterday. I'm gambling that my key works that rear door or that there's another key hidden nearby."

"What's my part in this reverse heist?" Brad asked.

"Wait in the car with your cell and play lookout. Today's her weekly late afternoon and early evening bridge game, so text me if Phoebe drives up. I know where the yearbook goes—won't take but a sec."

They were almost to the house.

"Have you thought this through, Diana? First, Phoebe tells you that her college yearbook is missing, the one that you think holds all these secrets, and then suddenly the thing turns up? She'll put it all together. The woman is not stupid."

"I know my aunt. She stays very busy. If she goes looking for it again, she'll just believe she overlooked it before."

Diana drove by the house before stopping around the corner. In play was Phoebe's bad habit of failing to lower the garage door, proving her car was gone. "Brad, you can see the front from here. But I'm not using the main door and let the neighbors see me enter," she said. "Instead, I'm slipping around to the backyard from a few lots down. Then, if she comes home early and you give the signal, I can be clear of the basement and her property before she makes it to the kitchen."

"I still think that you're over-reacting. You know … *mountain out of a mole hill?*" Brad said.

"Then just humor me."

"Let me keep the car keys, in case of a shootout," he said. "I'll do a wheelie in front of the house, slow down just long enough for you to hop in through an open window, then burn rubber on the getaway."

Diana frowned, killed the engine, and tossed Brad the keys. "I should have taken John Haynes' offer and gone into practice with him instead of you even if he did go to prison."

"OK, OK. I'll be right here waiting," Brad said and climbed over into the driver's seat as Diana stepped out onto the sidewalk. She grabbed the heavy cloth shopping bag, the yearbook inside. A six-foot tall hedge bordered the neighbor's three-story brick home ahead and ran along the sides and rear edge of the property. She turned to follow the shrubbery toward the rear. Barking erupted from the opposite side of the prickly green wall. Another dog from a nearby yard answered him.

"What in the hell am I doing?" Diana's pulse quickened. She reached the rear border of the yard and stared into the narrow path between the hedge and the gully below. A pile of crushed, rusted soda cans littered an area of the concrete chips and poison ivy that lined the edge. Diana guessed that in a heavy rain the swollen ravine drained along to the Pearl River and carried its refuse with it.

She stepped over a short mound of decaying cigarettes, gripped the bag even tighter, and leaned away from the creek into the shrubbery fence. Only inches from the dog, she sensed the earth vibrate under her feet each time he pounded the lawn and rushed the dense leaves and branches. The barking grew louder, angrier—now a growl.

Maybe he'll get tired and give up, Diana thought as she moved forward. *Stay calm, follow the plan.* She took her eyes off the narrow path and looked ahead. From the change in the shrubbery, the property line separating the dog's yard from the next was only a few feet away. "Phoebe's place should be only one more lot over," she muttered.

Diana felt a swish of air near her left hand just as teeth bit through a narrow break in the shrubbery. Her right foot slipped from the edge of the walkway and caught the side of a large rock embedded in the side of the ravine. A jolt of fire ripped side-to-side through her ankle. Somehow she suppressed a scream and in seconds the pain subsided.

Diana shifted her weight to right herself, grabbing a branch with her free hand just above the reach of the animal. He lurched higher, striking and shaking the shrub with his teeth. She jerked her grip free, once again losing her balance. This time Diana slid to her knees in the middle of the path, dropping the bag and the book, the package sliding about a foot down the side of the ravine to wedge against another large rock peeking out from the vines.

Grateful that her package remained together, she reached over into the space for the bag, her knees firmly pressed against the black, dry earth. *Oh, great. That's poison ivy,* she thought.

Diana maneuvered her fingers over and past the leaves to wrap a fore- and middle finger around the strap of the bag. Heaving it up, away from the vines and back to the path, the yearbook dropped from the bag to land sideways on its binding. The pages fanned back and forth with the movement, exposing the inside back cover and a dingy white envelope tucked in the crease. Diana grabbed the envelope before it could fall into the gully.

Sealed, or maybe resealed from humidity, *To Phoebe* was scribbled in faded ink on the front. She worked the soreness out of her hands and fingers and slid the envelope into a back pocket of her slacks and then brushed her knees clean. "How could I have missed that?" Diana said softly.

A male voice called from the yard on the other side of the shrubbery. The sound felt only a few yards away but grew closer to just beyond the branches of the shrubbery. "Calm down, calm down, Rage. What's going on back here anyway, Boy?" Diana could hear the dog panting, calming in response. "That possum rootin' around in the bushes again?"

In just a few steps Diana would be away from the dog and the man. She held the bag and yearbook tight against her chest with both arms and picked up speed, watching the pathway even closer than before. Now all she needed to come across was a snake. The neighborhood lots were deep and wide, but she would reach Phoebe's property in only minutes. This whole thing had been a bad idea, a silly plan, just ridiculous. But at least no one but Brad would know.

The upcoming backyard had the same rear terrain as the side of Phoebe's property, sloping sharply away from the house toward the gully. A forest of tall cane blocked the sight of the house. She continued to follow the well-worn path, the work of peers of that insane dog and the neighborhood kids who slipped away from their parents to smoke and drink and do who knows what else. Forget snakes. She knew any minute she would step on a used condom or spot one tossed among the rocks and vines. Diana prayed that Kelsey would never do such.

Finally, at the rear of Phoebe's backyard, Diana pressed through the ornamental magnolia trees and camellia bushes onto the lawn. Next was an antique iron arbor and weathered stone bench surrounded by lilies with a birdhouse to the side. A martin, followed by another, flew away as she approached. Diana checked her watch: a few minutes past six. Bridge was not over until seven, and traffic would delay Phoebe. She still had plenty of time and didn't think about Brad waiting in her car.

Diana cleared pine needles from the surface of the bench and set the bag next to her. She withdrew the envelope from her pocket and stared again at the inscription: *To Phoebe*. The paper was old, almost light brown in color. Even when held to the fading sun, it was impossible to see through it, but so flimsy that Diana was unsure it held anything.

There was still no movement at the rear windows of the house. The neighborhood dog had quieted. Even though it remained daylight, lamps would shine through the den windows if Phoebe were home. Diana found a fingernail long and sharp enough to pry open the top flap of the envelope and unfolded the sheet of paper inside. She studied the masculine handwriting, read the short note, refolded it, and returned it to the envelope. She licked the seal, surprised that the flap stuck closed, and slid the envelope back into the yearbook.

Diana looked around the quiet yard. She wanted to throw the yearbook and note into the gully. "It wasn't the book Phoebe was worried about losing. It was what was in that envelope," Diana said, as another bird flew from the birdhouse.

Brad ended the call to the dictation line and pulled up the Internet site to his electronic medical records on his smartphone. He entered the password, and The Cummins – Bratton Surgical Center server appeared on the screen. Diana was taking longer than expected, enough time to complete all of his delinquent records, time once spent in a dark room filled with musty paper files.

"Finally," he said. He spotted movement in the curtain of a front room of Phoebe's house, what Brad figured to be the living room. "I guess Diana's checking to see if I hung around," he said and shook his head. "No trust. What a shame."

Brad started the car and pulled into the traffic lane toward the driveway.

"I'm ready to end this crazy errand," he said, closer to the house. Diana would come to her senses soon and leave through the front door like any sane person.

Unexpectedly, a hand parted the middle panels of the living room drapes. Alex Bratton appeared in the window.

"What the hell? What's that ass hole Bratton doing in there?" In seconds Brad was in the driveway and up the steps to the front door. He punished the doorbell until it stuck in the metal casing, the ring a steady drone. Brad checked the window. Bratton was gone. He pounded on the door, then shook it— "Diana!"

An eager Pomeranian with a fifties-something couple in tow walked down the sidewalk. The man and woman stopped. The dog relieved himself on a low branch of Phoebe's azaleas that looked like a blanket of snow earlier in the spring.

"Anything wrong, sir?" the man asked.

The woman pulled the dog away from the azaleas before he was finished. A wet trail appeared on the sidewalk. "Come on, Johnny," she said, loud enough for Brad. "Let's don't get involved."

The man tossed Brad a stern smirk and followed.

"Got locked out, folks. Lost my keys," he called after them, then pounded the door again. "Diana!"

Deciding against the overhead light, Diana activated the flashlight of her iPhone and stepped carefully across the concrete floor toward the shelves and the boxes underneath. She halted at what seemed like movement behind a piece of faded, framed artwork propped against the wall. When she heard nothing else, she swept the beam of light to the row of boxes. The sound of a doorbell drifted down the basement stairs.

Diana shook her head. "Phoebe wouldn't ring her own doorbell. I've still got time."

Diana remembered the location of the box, but it appeared different— seemed spaced a little more away from the one beside it and turned at a different angle—but then she could not be sure. Maybe Phoebe had moved it. No, this had to be the correct box, same packing tape, same broken seal, same markings in her aunt's handwriting across the top: *Books – Ole Miss stuff.*

The doorbell again, then knocking.

Diana said, "Probably UPS. Something else she's ordered." She was uncertain of the arrangement of the yearbooks, maybe chronological, but maybe in reverse. Nevertheless, she was sure that the 1966 yearbook had not been at the top of the stack. Diana tried several arrangements, settling on chronological-oldest to most recent.

She closed the box, pressing the flaps together. The adhesive was spent from the wide piece of packing tape and the edges of cardboard sprung back at her. Diana worked back to the door to the outside, stepping over an old broom and a rusted shovel. She reached for the doorknob. "Now I've got to face that damn dog again," she said.

A deep voice rolled down the stairs in Diana's direction. "That dog will just have to get by without you, my love. No need for you to use the back door again."

"Alex, what the hell!" She twisted around and nearly stumbled on a stray paint can. "What are you doing here?"

"Trying to keep your boyfriend from breaking down the front door," he answered. "I guess Dr. Cummins dropped by to pick you up. He seems to be tired of waiting."

Alex reached for the light switch at the top of the stairs. The light bulbs hanging from the ceiling cast sudden shadows across the concrete, broken by more scattered old paint cans and a dust-covered bicycle with flat tires that Diana had missed earlier.

Diana surprised herself. She felt unsettled. She hadn't talked to Alex in weeks, and at this moment his tone matched that of the final days of their marriage, authoritative and condescending, artificial—sometimes threatening.

"You still haven't told me what you're doing here," she said.

"You go first," Alex said.

More doorbell, the knocking at the front door had become pounding. "Maybe we should let Brad in," Diana said.

Alex laughed. "Your knight in shining armor—come to the rescue." His voice moved closer as he descended the stairs in the dim light.

"Stop playing games, Alex." She reached behind her for the door and turned the knob. It groaned open. The light of dusk filled only a few feet of that corner of the room. She decided she could get out into the yard and halfway up to the street before he caught her.

"OK, Diana. No games." Alex was far enough down the stairs that Diana could see his face in the shadows. "I'm going to go back to the living room, open the door, and let your boyfriend—I mean Dr. Cummins—into the house and put an end to all the commotion. I'll show Cummins to a comfortable chair in Phoebe's parlor and tell him you'll be right up."

Diana waited until Alex had climbed the stairs. The door creaked open. Alex left it open for her. She listened for the doorbell again or Brad's knocking at the front. There was nothing, until she heard muffled male voices coming from the first floor and followed the sound up the stairs.

CHAPTER 34

Brad and Alex stood face to face in the foyer. She had not seen the two men together since shortly before Phoebe's discharge from the hospital. She remembered thinking how similar they looked, nearly the same height and build. Alex must still work out.

Brad spoke first. "Mr. Bratton was telling me that he's been living here."

"Living here with Aunt Phoebe? That's impossible. And why?" Diana said. "I know you haven't been hiding in the basement."

"I didn't make partner again in the law firm, Diana," he answered. "Go ahead. Make me wallow in it."

He ambled into the living room and sat, his shoulders no longer tall and square. He picked what Diana considered the most comfortable chair—the overstuffed piece, upholstered in flowered linen fabric from an expensive Jackson decorator. She had placed the chair near the fireplace. Alex raised his legs slowly and dropped them on the matching ottoman.

"You being a lousy lawyer still doesn't explain why you're living here," Brad said, as he led Diana into the room. "Did you offer to sleep with Phoebe or something? Or maybe you didn't give her a choice, Bratton."

"Let's don't go there, Brad." Diana fought the image of Alex and her late sixties-year-old aunt in bed together. She remembered the things Alex had demanded of her.

"Come on. Give it up, Diana," Brad said. "You thought the same." He stood against the mantel over the fireplace. He checked the time on his phone and folded his arms across his chest.

Drained and too tired to stand, Diana sank into the couch, wondering if she looked as overwhelmed as she felt. This wasn't happening.

"Diana, I was as surprised as hell when Phoebe called me," Alex said. "I didn't even know she had my cell. But I'm sort of in between jobs, and my license to practice law is current. So ... I decided why not. Besides, I still have child support to pay."

At that moment, Diana no longer felt herself foolish. Maybe her actions were justified: the time spent away from her practice and from her daughter dealing with Key Martin and all of the deaths, the worrying about Phoebe, and the sneaking around her property. "Help my aunt with what, Alex?"

"She told me she didn't want to confide with anyone in my old firm downtown or with any other Jackson lawyer. Said she needed some help, a consultation, and was willing to pay me. And I wasn't in any shape to refuse anything."

"So, Bratton, ... if you didn't offer to sleep with her, then you're working for room and board?" Brad's question more of a sneer.

Without turning from Diana, Alex answered. "She's paying me by the hour, Cummins—for legal work—that's all it is. Everything's strictly professional, and for a discounted hourly rate, she agreed to let me stay in the guest room upstairs."

For Kelsey's sake, Diana had tried to forgive Alex, to fight her revulsion for him, which at times seemed easy because of his looks—appealing even when downcast. At times she had caught herself wanting to sleep with him again, to feel the way she did when he first touched her.

However, she realized the battle was lost. She could never have a normal, cordial relationship with her ex-husband. Alex Bratton was a liar. When he first told her that he loved her, he was a liar. At this moment, she never hated Alex more.

Diana shook her head clear. "Why in the world would Aunt Phoebe need an attorney?" she asked, dreading Alex's answer.

"Now you're the one with the bullshit, Diana," Alex said. "And maybe you, too, Cummins. You think that Phoebe's got something to do with that guy's death at Ole Miss in the sixties. Don't try to deny it."

Diana answered, "That's ridiculous. I love Phoebe. She wouldn't do anything like that."

"Screw this, Diana. Let's leave," Brad said. "Besides, won't Phoebe be home soon?"

"Stay out of this," Alex said, still seated. "Diana, if you didn't suspect that dear ole Aunt Phoebe was mixed up with the death of the guy, then why are you sneaking around her house?"

"I didn't want to ..."

"Phoebe told you that her college yearbook was missing," Alex said. "And you didn't want her to know for sure that you took it."

Diana paused, regretting the hesitation. "That's straight BS. Why would I take it?"

Brad pushed away from the mantel to stand over Diana, blocking her view of her ex-husband. "You need to be honest with yourself, partner. The first step is to get away from this guy. If he really is representing your aunt, then he's not going to break a confidence."

"The person you need to get away from is this rich, obnoxious asshole, know-it-all doctor," Alex said.

Brad swung to the side to grab Alex by the collar and pull him from the oversized chair. Alex flew toward him, pushing hard away from the chair. The force overturned the large piece of furniture to fall hard against the front window, shattering the central section and splintering the wooden mullions framing the glass. Diana didn't know which man's name to scream, which man would come to his senses first.

She gambled on Brad. "That's enough!"

Both men stared at her. Diana studied the beads of sweat erupting on Alex's forehead. Brad seemed cool, calm. "Brad, let's go," she said. "Kelsey will wonder what's taking so long. Besides, Phoebe will be here any minute."

Alex wiped his forehead with his shirt sleeve. The fabric conformed to the shape of his skull, not starched stiff like when they were married. She remembered the new Italian shirts he brought home nearly every other week, most woven of Egyptian cotton. Bills soon followed from the expensive men's clothing store on the hill, bills she struggled to pay from her resident's salary.

"I'll come up with some explanation about the window," Alex said, righting the chair and kicking away some of the splintered wood. Shards of glass were imbedded in the weave of the Stark rug. "But we've all got to talk this through."

Blue lights burst through the broken window, the strobe casting fingers across the rug and splattering Phoebe's furniture. The light bathed Diana and Brad as they walked into it, shielding their eyes. Alex backed into the foyer away from the light. He felt his front pants pocket for his car keys.

Diana said, "That couldn't be Key Martin outside. Why would he be here?" She squinted to see better and held her hand to her face, the light still flickering in her eyes. She studied the vehicle with the revolving light coming from the dashboard. "That's definitely his squad car."

"Don't tell me that joker is starting to stalk us again," Brad said.

"Then, I won't," she said. "And Martin's really not so bad." Diana looked toward the foyer, expecting to see Alex. He was gone.

"Who's the guy riding with him?" Brad asked.

Corey Myers exited the police car first, then Martin. The two men checked the house number marker posted in a flower bed before studying the broken window. Diana watched Martin shake his head. He stepped past Myers to take the path to the front steps.

"They're coming in," Diana said. "Guess the neighbors saw me creeping around out back and called the police … probably that neighbor with the rabid dog."

The chime of the doorbell ricocheted throughout the house. "So it does work," Brad said.

A rapid series of knocks beat him to the front door. Brad opened it. "Martin? What the hell are you doing here? And you brought reinforcements?"

"*Reinforcement*, you should say, Dr. Cummins." Martin moved past Brad into the foyer and tipped his hat to Diana. Corey Myers followed. "Officer Myers is more than that. He wants answers."

The two policemen walked into the living room, continuing their study of the broken window. Diana checked the dining room and the hall that lead to the rear of the house. "Brad, where's Alex?"

He shrugged a whisper, "Dunno." Then shrugged again, "Don't care."

"Did you say something, Dr. Cummins?" Martin picked up a piece of wood broken between two panes and put it to his nose. "You asked why we're here." He moved closer to the window, then back into the center of the room. "I saw the call come in. This nice couple was out strolling their little one, saw a commotion in the neighborhood—something about a chair coming through a window. Of course, I was curious, 'specially after the earlier call concerning a neighborhood disturbance at this same address. That couple described a man who resembles you, Dr. Cummins."

Diana asked, "Simple neighborhood disturbance deserves the attention of the chief of police?"

"When you and Dr. Cummins are involved, it's not so simple," Martin answered. He pulled a note pad from inside his suit and flipped through the pages. "But to tell you the truth, I'm really just tagging along to help out Officer Myers."

"Chief Martin's been working with me on an unsolved murder case in Oxford," Corey said, diverting his eyes away from Diana toward Brad. "When this address came across the emergency dispatch center, we took notice."

Diana remained expressionless, or at least hoped she did.

"What's this address got to do with a murder case in Oxford?" Brad asked, avoiding Diana.

"I'd like to know that myself." The four turned to the voice coming from the kitchen area. "I'd also like to know what happened to my bay window," Phoebe said.

"Ma'am, I'm Key Martin, Chief of Police of the City of Jackson and this is Officer Corey ..."

"That's all very good, gentleman," Phoebe said. "But the reason you're here?"

Martin answered, "We had planned to drop by soon for a little chat, but when the call came in about a commotion at your residence, the time table sort of got pushed forward. I'm surprised that Dr. Bratton hasn't filled you in."

"Filled me in about what?" Phoebe asked. She looked first to Diana, then to Brad, then back to Diana.

"That you have been on our radar, ma'am," Corey said, "so to speak." He glanced at Chief Martin.

The chief's expression read: "Go right ahead, as long as you think you can handle the woman."

"Diana, I demand to know what in the hell is going on," Phoebe said.

Diana remained silent, her mind filled with thoughts of the envelope and note that slipped from inside Phoebe's college yearbook from 1966.

Phoebe stepped toward Diana, taking her arm and turning her face to face. "Diana? Diana? Can you hear me?"

Diana reached into her pocket and ran her fingers along the edges of the envelope. She wished she had never found it, or at least not read the contents.

"Well, if you won't fill me in, maybe this young black man will help me," Phoebe said.

She studied the face, followed his neck down to the collar of the uniform, and settled at the name badge. The precisely pressed uniform fit him snuggly. Several cloth badges with official-looking insignia were sewn prominently into the lapels. Unlike the older white man, he wore a gun on his right hip.

"And who did you say you are?" she asked.

"Officer Corey Myers of the Oxford Police Department."

"Myers and I are working together on a case," Martin said. "He may have questions for you."

Phoebe raised her eyebrows. "Why would he have questions for me?"

"Ma'am, you visited a woman's residence here in Jackson, a day or two before she was murdered," Myers said.

"A woman murdered? How terrible." Phoebe darted her eyes to Diana, still expressionless.

204

"She was the sister of a missing university student," Myers said, "missing for 50 years. The remains were recently recovered in Oxford."

"Two murders? My, my," Phoebe said. "Was the murder of the Jackson woman in the ten o'clock news? I usually miss and don't always read the paper. If it's not talk at bridge then I don't know anything about …"

"Please be quiet and listen to what they have to say, Aunt Phoebe." Diana moved a few inches away, this time sliding her hand into her pocket as though the note could disappear. "I went with the officers to the cottage in Belhaven; it wasn't that far from where you used to live."

"This is getting to be a little too much, Diana. I feel as though my home has been invaded. I think you should all leave."

"We can come back with a search warrant, if you like, Ma'am," Martin said, "or take you down to the precinct now to discuss this."

Phoebe stepped back a few steps in the direction of the hall. A wisp of red hair fell onto her forehead.

Diana said, "I was at the house in Belhaven when Officers Martin and Myers talked to the owner, a Mrs. or Miss Minton."

"Drusilla Minton is a fool, an eccentric ol' fool. Everyone knows that," Phoebe said. "I've never met her, but at bridge they all talk about how 'off her rocker' she is."

"Eccentric or not, I think you have met her," Diana said. "Miss Minton told us that you dropped by her house, to the rental cottage out back. You wanted to talk to her renter."

"You seemed annoyed that she wasn't at home," Myers said.

Phoebe glared at the young black policeman for a few seconds until Diana continued speaking. Several more strands of hair fell.

"Minton wouldn't let you into the cottage since the renter wasn't at home, so you peered through the window at her things," Diana said. "Since the place is small, my guess is that you saw the same stuff through the outside window that the three of us saw inside."

"Why would I care about what some renter had in that miserable, cramped place." With a look of desperation, Phoebe shifted from Diana to Brad for support. He only shrugged.

Diana continued. "That 'some renter' had college photos of you and Winston Ivy and Mr. Marzel posted on the wall, even one of Mr. Eaves."

"There was also a photo of the Ole Miss student whose remains we discovered in Oxford," Corey said.

"And I'm sure he was in a lot better shape then," Brad said. Diana noticed the glance at his watch, and she checked the time on her phone.

"Phoebe, these guys want to know if you can piece this together for them," he said.

"Maybe if I knew the student's name," Phoebe said.

"Rusty Reynolds," Corey answered. "He was a freshman."

"I may have heard the name," Phoebe said, "but I didn't know him. And I certainly didn't know his sister."

Chief Martin closed his writing pad and slid it back into his jacket.

Diana suspected the page remained blank.

"We have probably overstayed our welcome," Martin said.

"You have," Phoebe said.

"But there is that other question," he said.

"What question?"

"What led you to that rental cottage to pay the sister a visit?" Martin asked.

With one stroke of the hand, Phoebe cleared her forehead of the fallen hair except for a couple of matted strands glued to sweaty skin. "Like I told you, it's just crazy Drusilla Minton's word against mine. I can't control the words of a demented woman." She folded her arms across her chest. "Gentleman, I'm sure you can show yourselves out."

Martin and Officer Myers both nodded. Corey retrieved his hat from the small table near him and had it in place before they reached the front door.

"And another thing, officers," Phoebe called out from across the living room. "Don't bother me again. Why would I know anything about some bones you dug up in Oxford, some fifty-year-old body with its neck and arm broken?"

CHAPTER 35

"How much did you tell them?"

Phoebe paced before the windows that looked out over the patio, where she and Diana first discussed the missing yearbook. The timer for the landscape lighting was on cue for dusk, and fireflies glowed in and out of the shrubbery and oversized planted clay pots. "I didn't tell them anything," she answered.

Alone after Diana and Brad pulled out of her driveway, she had drawn the living room drapes across the broken window, kicking clear with the toe of her heels the shards of glass and broken wood from the expensive drapery fabric. "And where were you the whole time?"

"Running errands," Alex answered.

"Errands? How did you miss Diana and Dr. Cummins?"

"I parked in the rear driveway. They never saw me," he said. "I circled through the neighborhood until the cars out front were gone."

"There were two policemen. They asked me about Rusty and his sister. One of them, not the older guy—not the one that has worried Diana to death—mentioned the body—the bones—the bones they discovered on campus."

"There were two cops?" Alex swung open the fridge of the mini-bar and took out a bottled beer. He checked the date on the bottom and twisted off the metal cap. "You rank two cops?"

"I denied knowing any of the people they were talking about. I played dumb to all of them, including Diana."

"Diana was still around?" Alex took a long drink of beer and chose the leather chair by the mini-bar. He held the bottle cap to the recessed ceiling light and rotated it between his thumb and forefinger as though to peer through the center. "No one has ever thought you dumb, Phoebe. If Diana was still in the room during your charade, she saw right through it."

"Diana didn't say much," Phoebe said. She stopped near the pair of

Staffordshire dogs and ran her finger across the top of the heads. She examined her fingertip and the dust. "Damn you, Elba."

He gripped the neck of the bottle and guzzled a third of it. "Forget Diana," Alex said. "Get real, Phoebe. You were a royal snob in college, had to be. You knew everyone, especially if they had money, and that included Rusty Reynolds."

"That's absurd. No one was friends with everybody." She finished with the Herend piece next to the Staffordshire and was at the shelf of antique leather books.

Alex watched her movements while he finished the beer and started a second. "The police aren't as dense as you think, Phoebe." He tossed both bottle caps into the sink.

"That's just it," Phoebe said. "Rusty Reynolds wasn't supposed to have money. And as far as Diana is concerned, she wasn't paying much attention to the conversation with the police; she kept checking the pocket of her slacks. I took care of the two guys—convinced those creeps how absurd their questions where."

"And how did you do that, Phoebe?" Alex got up from the leather chair and stood close behind her. He set the beer bottle on the counter by the sink.

"I turned the tables on the questioning. I asked them to explain how I could know anything about a bunch of bones some buffoon dug up in the woods, old bones with the right arm broken and the neck bones crushed."

Alex stepped even closer. Phoebe had reached a small, gilded vase that was even dirtier than the Herend piece. "The only money Rusty Reynolds had was what he beat out of you and Winston and your other buddies," he said.

"There's no way the police could know that, and Diana would have no idea."

"Maybe so. On the other hand, you weren't supposed to know that Reynolds' neck and arm were broken."

Alex unsnapped his leather belt and jerked it from around his waist. He looped it around Phoebe's neck and yanked her tight against him. The vase fell from her hand and crashed to the floor.

The kitchen light was on when Brad drove them into Diana's driveway. They had said little during the drive from Phoebe's house. Kelsey's curtain was pulled, but Diana could see movement in the light from the desk lamp and was certain she spotted the outline of an open laptop. "At least she's started on her homework," she said. "Somehow I've raised a responsible daughter."

Brad slid the gear into park. He softened the sound from the Jimmy Buffet station on the satellite radio. "Now that you've got your household together, maybe it's time for a dog," he said.

"Last thing I need," Diana said. She pulled the small envelope from her pocket. "I found this in that yearbook. I want you to read it, but ..."

"But, what?"

"Mom, mom!" A hard rapping against the raised passenger window stopped Diana's answer. Brad lowered the glass. "How long are you gonna stay out here with your boyfriend? I need help with that damn English paper."

"Kelsey! We were just ... just ... and watch that mouth!"

"I wasn't born yesterday, Mom, and what a place to go parking. Like they say: 'Get a room.'"

"I was only dropping your mom off after work. She needed a ride," Brad said. "By the way, how's school going?"

"School's fine, Dr. Brad, and y'all are in Mom's car. So you're busted."

"Kelsey!" Still holding the envelope, Diana opened the door and gently pushed her daughter clear. The envelope fell to the pavement and blew under the car in the light breeze.

"I'll get it." In seconds Kelsey was out from under the sedan, with both hands brushing her jeans clean, the note clinched between perfectly straight white teeth. "That was a tight squeeze even for me," she said.

"Thanks, show-off," Diana said. She pried the envelope from her daughter and used her blouse to wipe away the saliva-coated teeth marks. "Why don't you take that tight little body back into the kitchen and get that paper finished. I'll be there in a sec."

"Sure, Mom," she winked. "Sorry I interrupted. You and Dr. Brad go ahead and take as long as you like." Kelsey double winked and turned. "But don't forget, I can see the both of you through the window. I'll be watching!" she called back over her shoulder. "After all, I have a lot to learn!"

"When did she grow up?" Diana sighed.

"Save the mothering for later," Brad said. "What's with the envelope?"

"Here, open it." Diana tossed it to Brad. "Read it and we'll discuss it later. I need to go in and help my daughter with her homework."

Brad studied the writing scrawled across the front of the envelope. "Hold on, Diana. The address must be Phoebe's post office box at Ole Miss—old, faded stamps and everything."

Diana remained in the car, her door open, her long right leg extended from the passenger seat to the pavement. She looked out to the breakfast room window. Kelsey's head was deep into her laptop. "Brad, I don't feel good at all about Phoebe's involvement in this."

Brad held the envelope into the dome light. "Was the flap glued shut when you found it? You think Phoebe ever read this?"

"I think so," Diana answered. "Sometimes humidity will reseal an envelope."

"If whatever's in here is such a big secret, then she would have tossed it long ago," Brad said and again studied the name and address scrawled across the front of the envelope. "If I'm wrapped up in all this crap with you and your aunt, I need to go ahead and read this."

Brad slit the top with his house key. He shook loose the letter and let it drop into his lap. He cleared his throat and read with light added from his cell:

"*Dear Phoebe—I hope break goes by really fast. I'm going to miss you really bad. You've taught me so much and not just cards. We did it, didn't we? Showed that ass, Winston.* Writer means Winston Ivy, the real estate guy?"

"Yes, the real estate guy. Go on." Diana shifted her hips and stared forward as Brad resumed reading.

"*That's what you wanted, right? Money? Winston's got plenty of money, family money.*" Brad looked over to Diana and flipped to the second page. "It's not that this guy is long-winded, but you don't see big, cursive letters like this anymore.

"*Phoebe, I hope and pray that you'll write me back, but I know you won't. You're too afraid.*" Brad stopped reading. "Afraid of what?" he asked.

Diana said, "Let me have the note back. You're taking too long."

"No, no, no. You wanted me to read. Let me finish. This stuff is deep: *What we're doing can't be all in secret. We love each other too much. That's what's important. You're beautiful. You're mine. We can take Winston down.*"

"I still don't believe this, Brad. Give me back the letter." Diana took the pages and studied them.

"It's signed: *All my love, Rusty.* Wasn't *Rusty* one of those names y'all were asking your aunt about?" Brad asked.

"Rusty Reynolds is—was—the body they dug up at Ole Miss. My dear aunt said she never heard of him."

"Your lying aunt, that is," Brad said.

"And Winston Ivy, the real estate guy, is the longtime college friend that Phoebe said she'd forgotten."

"Then what's the next move?"

Diana looked toward the kitchen window. Kelsey was missing from the table. "I need to get inside," she answered. "It's time I got back to being a mother."

"You need to look for the common denominator in this situation with Phoebe," Brad said. "Something even that joker Martin and his sidekick have missed."

She stepped onto the driveway. "Maybe that's just what all this is," Diana said. "A joke."

She walked toward the house. Kelsey was back, seated at the kitchen table, buried in her laptop screen. She shoveled ice cream into her mouth from a deep bowl. "That's the big mixing bowl. Oh, the calories—thank God she's so athletic."

"That's your cell, Diana." Brad startled her, standing behind her. Her cell phone was ringing. "It shouldn't be the answering service," he said. "Neither of us is on call."

"Believe it or not, partner, I might have a life outside of our practice— maybe even a personal life. Some normal individual, some regular guy, could be calling."

"I've wished for normal for so long that I'm not certain it exists," Brad said.

The caller ID blared *Key Martin*. "Normal?" she said. "Never gonna happen."

A police siren screamed in the distance. "Hold on, just minute," she said and hit *MUTE*. "I'm going inside, Brad, and check on Kelsey. But I need to thank you first. I really appreciate all your help today."

Brad eyed the iPhone and stepped closer. "Key Martin again, right? Before I leave, go ahead and see what the hell he wants."

"I'll call him later. It's really late, and you've done enough, more than enough."

She stopped before giving Brad a peck on the cheek. The siren grew louder, closer. Again Diana felt the phone vibrate before the tone of a new call. She looked at the screen: Martin again.

"He must have hung up and called back. Let me take this inside. I'll see you in the OR tomorrow."

Brad frowned. "Whatever you say. See you at seven." He walked over to his car. "Call me if you need anything, even later tonight. Diana, I mean it," he said.

Diana was at the top of the steps to the kitchen door. "OK, Martin. What is it?"

"Hi to you to, Doc. You remember that busybody couple, the one walking the baby earlier today? Guess they got JPD on speed dial. They called again about your aunt's address since …"

"Even Phoebe's no miracle worker. There's been no time to get someone over to fix that mess at her house. However, I could be wrong. If anyone can order a yardman around at the last minute, Phoebe can."

Diana could hear the waning of the siren.

Martin said, "It's more than that. Officer Myers and I are on the way back to your aunt's house. One of our units should already be on the scene. This time the couple found the front door wide open, your aunt lying face-up on the front lawn, strangulation marks on her neck."

"My God!" Diana ended the call, almost dropping the phone as she rushed into the kitchen.

"Mom?" Kelsey looked up from the vanishing bowl of ice cream. She scraped the sides with the spoon and eyed the freezer. "What's up?"

Diana could imagine Phoebe sprawled across her own front lawn, her eyes fixed and glazed over, opened to the starry sky—a trail of ants, attracted to her thick makeup and hairspray, crawling across her forehead. Turning back toward the door, Diana answered, "I've got to go out again. Please go ahead and finish your homework, Kelsey. I know I promised, but you'll have to get that paper done without me."

Diana opened the door and depressed the lock button. "Make sure the other doors are locked and turn on the alarm. And, don't you dare leave this house until I get back."

Kelsey lowered the empty bowl to the table. Her mouth still open in question.

Diana ran to her car and pulled her cell from her jacket pocket. Brad had asked her to call him if anything changed, if she needed anything. Or was it more of an order? She dropped the phone back into her jacket. "Not following orders this time. You really didn't mean it anyway. Besides, one of us needs to be rested for that case tomorrow."

She pushed aside concern over the morning's surgical case and tried to focus on now. Phoebe brought all this shit on herself Diana decided during the drive to Phoebe's house. "I need to prepare myself for the worst."

Diana stopped at the red light and pulled out her phone. She needed to talk this whole thing through with somebody, anybody. No, not Brad or the police, and Kelsey was too young to burden. "I've got to spare her the nasty details, whatever they are, for as long as possible."

The cross street was clear of traffic—not a single pedestrian or stray dog. Diana rolled to the edge of the intersection, planning to run the red light, then the signal changed to green. The new chime from her cell phone startled her. After repeated texts from patients and the clinic, Diana had grown immune to the old tone. A few days ago her office manager selected a new sound, surprised her with "Spell," and the twinkling sound caught Diana's attention.

She swerved over to the curb and read the text. It was from Kelsey: "Mom? Supper? Nothing in fridge. CC on file at Pizza Hut. Ordered online—added tip."

Diana sighed, responded "K" and pulled back into the light traffic—chalk up another time Kelsey left at home alone and without plans for supper, even the typical takeout—another reason she would lose Mother-of-the-Year. "That makes thirteen years in a row."

The approaching red light was about two blocks from Phoebe's house. Diana checked her phone. Kelsey's return text "Will save you a piece" was followed by an emoticon of a pizza and a thumbs-up.

Happily, her young teenage daughter was content at the moment, but tomorrow could be another story. The light changed. Diana set her phone on the console between the seats and turned right onto the next street. Her other concern, more of a financial concern, was how this mounting personal distraction centered around Phoebe could affect her surgical and medical practice. Diana had been a single mom for over ten years, and her financial backup was a worthless, philandering ex-husband. She needed her income—Kelsey needed her income.

Little of her general surgeon's salary was squirreled away. Outstanding college and medical school loans as well as credit card and legal fee baggage lingering after the divorce had eaten up most of her expendable income. Just enough remained for Kelsey's private school, the mortgage, and a short vacation or two. "I guess we could go back to public school and downsize," Diana said to herself.

Reassurance had come from her office nurse and the administrator of the surgery clinic. The time spent in meeting with Key Martin had produced no negligible effect on her monetary production in the practice. The two women reminded her that the other surgeons, the male doctors, took afternoons off for golf, sometimes every week or maybe even every few days, and long weekend trips with wives or girlfriends, even at the last minute. They said she was just being paranoid, that she was still the best doctor in the practice, overall the most productive and the nicest. They only laughed when she accused them of female prejudice.

One afternoon her clinic nurse had pulled Diana aside and whispered, "Dr. Diana, don't worry about the time you spend on your personal issues. You got a life to live. We all do." Then in a soothing, comforting tone, she handed Diana several charts and said, "But for now, our favorite, prettiest, and best-est doctor, you've got all these patients here waiting to see you, and I need to finish up and go home to my own problems. Quit worrying."

Brad Cummins was another matter. What would he think if she bailed on the big surgery case tomorrow as co-surgeon? "You can handle the case," she could say. "I hope you understand. My excuse? Well ... out late last night taking care of more of my nightmare."

But then Brad had done the same to her last month: cancelling last-minute as co-surgeon on a major case, the excuse—something about a pulled muscle in his lower back and a sore shoulder from a basketball game at the club. "Shouldn't have blocked that guy on his layup. Shouldn't have been playing with some junior college all-stars home for the weekend," Brad said.

Diana remembered her response: "If I hadn't left the patient's record unsealed, then you wouldn't know what a train wreck case we were up against, then your pain might not be so bad."

"Let me guess," Brad said. "Fifty-eight-year-old male, morbidly obese—yeah, that's right. BMI totaled 42—heavy smoker, asthma, abdominal surgery for colon cancer three years ago and spent two weeks in ICU afterward. Sounds fun. Sure wish I could help." He then stretched his back and shoulders and moaned. His vertebra screamed a cracking, popping sound in support.

Diana neared Phoebe's street as a police a car turned off Ridgewood ahead of her.

Another police cruiser partially blocked Phoebe's driveway. A front tire had left the curb and pressed deep into the manicured Zoysia grass. Ahead stood an ambulance at the curb, both vehicles partially blocking the view of Phoebe's front yard. Thankfully, the neighbor across the street wasn't having a party. Diana stopped behind the cruiser.

"Get that stretcher over here," a man yelled from the other side of the ambulance. "Bring another cylinder of oxygen. We need to make sure she's stable before transport."

Diana shoved past the two uniforms standing at the cruiser. "Officers, what's happened?"

No one seemed to hear her between the continued shouts of the EMTs and chatter from the police radios. Diana worked her way around the corner of the ambulance. Artificial lighting hung from portable, fold-out poles stationed across the front lawn and living room window. Wood and glass littered the shrubbery and lawn below. "That chair only knocked out a pane or two," she said. "This damage is worse. What the hell happened after Brad and I left?"

A tall man in a dark jumpsuit yelled over his shoulder: "I said, I need another oxygen cylinder." He held an oxygen mask in position over Phoebe's nose and mouth. Her hair was tangled in fragments of glass and splintered wood. Blood oozed from a fresh gash high on her forehead, directly below the hair line. Phoebe's right arm was wrapped tightly along her side. A cervical collar was in place.

The rise and fall of her chest was a relief. Diana rushed the stretcher.

"Ma'am, get back." Another EMT, a woman about as tall as the man hovering over Phoebe, threw an arm in Diana's way. The other hand held the replacement oxygen cylinder.

Diana forced control in her voice. "I'm a doctor. Don't you guys think I might can help? Besides, that woman on the stretcher is my aunt."

A man called from inside the house. "Yes, guys, I can confirm that Dr. Bratton is the victim's niece. Let her through, please." Key Martin emerged at the top of the steps. Officer Myers was behind him. "It didn't take you very long to get here, Doc. Better watch that speedometer," Martin said.

"It was easy," Diana said. "I simply got behind the sirens."

"Those godforsaken things can wake the dead. Thank God they turned the freaking things off," Phoebe said under the oxygen mask. Puffs of vapor blew out the sides with each word. She freed her right hand from under the sheet and strap and lifted the mask from her face.

"You need to keep that thing on, Phoebe." Diana reached to reposition the clumsy, plastic mask, before Phoebe jerked it from her face and hurled it to the lawn. A few tangled strands of red hair caught in the clip between the strap and mask, leaving it to dangle from the tubing and swing from the stretcher. Phoebe pushed herself up erect.

"Ma'am, please!" Both EMTs said.

"Aunt Phoebe," Diana said, "let these people take care of you." She looked over in the direction of the broken window. The fragments of brightly painted-white wood and glass littered the lawn and shrubbery near the stretcher and reflected the landscape and front porch lighting. "You shouldn't have been out here at night, trying to clean this mess up. I should have called someone for you before I left."

Martin stepped up behind Diana, startling her. "Doc, that's not what transpired here. Your aunt says she was inside with Mr. Bratton."

"Alex?" Diana turned and backed away for a good look at both Phoebe and Martin. Martin moved to the head of the stretcher. "Alex had already left the house," Diana said.

"Apparently, Mr. Bratton returned," Martin said. "Your aunt defended herself quite well."

"Phoebe, what's he talking about? What does he mean 'defended yourself'? Did that bastard Alex hurt you?"

Deep wrinkles appeared in Phoebe's forehead.

Diana thought back to the time before Alex and she divorced. She was immersed in her surgical residency, not far from completion. In the room down the hall, Kelsey slept in her crib. That was the last time that Alex beat Diana in their bedroom and then forced her to have sex. She and Kelsey left that night, Alex asleep—drunk.

Diana swept the fallen hair from Phoebe's face, the remnants of the day's styling. In the paramedics' temporary lighting, a long red mark rose across Phoebe's neck. A bruise encircled it, easy to see on her fair skin.

Phoebe put her hand to her throat to hide the stain of Alex's belt. "Diana, I …"

"Your aunt defended herself quite well, Dr. Bratton," Martin interrupted. "No need for the personal defense classes at the Y."

"No, she would expect private lessons," Diana said.

Martin said, "Maybe she learned from watching a lot of TV dramas. Anyway, we've got tissue samples from under her nails. And these nice medical people here tell me your aunt should be fine after a couple of stitches. Now, for your ex-husband? We don't know what kind of shape he's in."

"We're going to transport her to Metropolitan now," the male paramedic said. "The ER will check her out first—most likely get a CT. If you want, check with admissions. They'll know whether she was sent to ICU or out to the floor." The paramedics lifted Phoebe on the stretcher and into the back of the van.

"Martin, what went on here?" Diana asked.

The paramedics closed the rear doors, and the ambulance pulled away. The lights atop the van streaked blue across the surrounding houses, splattering the brick boundary walls and mature oak trees before it disappeared around the curve.

Corey Myers stepped forward. "Dr. Bratton, the victim says that your ex-husband, Alex Bratton, attacked her. He tried to strangle her with this belt before she fought back, stumbled, and fell through the window that was already broken. She thinks he may have pushed her. The couple walking their dog … they come along after it was over. We don't know how long your aunt was unconscious."

"I need to call Kelsey. I need to check on her. She's the only one who really …"

"Really cares, Dr. Bratton. Is that what you mean?" Officer Myers asked. "Really cares about your ex-husband?"

Diana dropped her eyes slightly. "Martin, what's this guy from Oxford still doing here?"

"He's not hard of hearing, Diana. Officer Myers and I are still working together on his case."

Diana shook her head and massaged her temples. "I didn't mean to be rude. Maybe I'm not thinking straight," Diana said. "This is a lot, a lot to take in."

"Don't worry about it, Dr. Bratton," Corey said. "Maybe you're in shock."

"Officer, I'm a physician. I know when somebody's in shock."

"This is different, Dr. Bratton," Martin said. "This is about you, or your family."

"OK," Diana said. "OK." The break in her voice surprised her. She needed to talk to Kelsey. Her father would be arrested soon. "Phoebe and my ex-husband have had their differences, but why would Alex attack her, try to kill her? He was supposed to be living here, renting a room of sorts."

Martin answered, "We don't know what he was after."

"Phoebe's not a weak woman, even if playing bridge and supervising house staff is her only exercise. She's definitely *not* a little ol' lady."

"We found this black belt inside the living room, near the shattered window," Corey said.

"Same size as the one we found that day in the pharmacist's condo, Dr. Bratton," Martin said.

Another flashback to one of the last nights in their apartment. She put her hand to the side of her chest. "Alex and his belts."

"Forensics is in the house now," Martin said.

"Forensics?" Diana asked.

"You want to know what else your aunt told us?"

Diana studied Chief Martin, then Corey Myers. "I guess I do, particularly since the paramedics whisked her away before I could get anything out of her."

"She told us that she was talking with Mr. Bratton," Corey said, "and he wrapped something tight around her neck when she turned away, something that smelled like leather. She reached behind her and pushed her hands against his chest, as hard as she could. They both fell against the shelves. She was about to black out and grabbed the first thing she could, a statue of a dog on the shelf."

"A piece of her antique Staffordshire—that would definitely take a chunk out of somebody's head," Diana said.

"Seems so," Martin said. "She blacked out and doesn't remember anything else."

"We found bloody pieces of ceramic all over the place. Forensics will bag it all up," Corey said.

"Alex ... my husband ... ex-husband ... did this?" Diana again surprised herself. Her knees felt weak. "He's an asshole, but I would never have thought he could do this."

"You OK, Doc?" Martin reached toward Diana but she straightened and stepped back.

"I'm fine. But I need to call my daughter. I just don't know what this will do to Kelsey."

"There'll be an investigation," Corey said. "Hopefully, your aunt can explain all this for Chief Martin's people when she's feeling better."

"Yes," Diana said. "I hope. But for now, I need to get home."

Diana could see Kelsey in the kitchen with the English paper: candy and gum wrappers covering the table and floor, two or three, maybe four, empty cans of Coke Zero—or was she back to Diet Coke? What Diana could not see were the local TV news vans gathering in her driveway and in front of her house.

CHAPTER 36

Winston slowed at the hospital receptionist's desk. A miniature placard on a brass easel posted visiting hours and stood partially hidden by a potted plant interlaced with yellow flowers. Winston pushed the plant aside. "Miss?"

The young, light-skinned black female raised her head from the computer monitor. Micro braided hair extensions covered her shoulders, and a cell phone lay face-up next to the keyboard. "Yes, may I help you?"

Winston guessed early twenties. He gestured to the post on the easel. "Looks like I'm just under the wire."

"Nobody pays attention to those visitor times," the receptionist smiled. "Besides, you look like a nice man, not a red flag for security or anything like that. Just be nice and quiet." She resumed work at the keyboard but not before tapping her cell phone a few times and smiling. "Oh, but, sir, overnight visitors have to register with administration," she said without looking up.

Winston was halfway down the hall toward the elevator before she finished talking. From Phoebe's call last night from the ER (A nice nurse had loaned her a cell phone), he already knew the room number. He punched the elevator controls, stepped onto the fifth floor, and found Phoebe's room.

He didn't knock.

"You called me so I guess you wanted to talk," Winston said. He surveyed the sparse, antiseptic area. Pale pink curtains were drawn loosely over half closed blinds. Light peeked through the split between the two drapery panels. "No flowers, no fruit baskets, no teddy bears. Let me call someone and get this place fixed up."

"Don't bother, Winston. I don't plan to stay long," Phoebe said. Winston looked thinner and much older than just a few days ago. The IV tubing taped to her right forearm bounced along the bridge of her nose

THE 5 MANNERS of DEATH

as she brushed more strands of limp hair out of her eyes. This made her sneeze. "I've got to get out of here."

"Anything broken?" Winston asked.

"The doctors said no," Phoebe answered. She shuddered and clutched the bedspread with her fists. "They put me through one of those horrid CT scan things. I never realized I was so damn claustrophobic."

"Sorry you had to endure that damn thing," Winston said. "My late wife hated those tests so. Every time her tumor markers went up, it was another trip to that dark, dismal corner of the hospital—and another bill from radiology."

"You haven't mentioned Trudy to me since her death."

Winston stepped closer and pushed on the button to the overhead light. His eyes traced the curvature of her neck. "I see a few bruises."

"Only a few, where Alex tried to …"

"Strangle you?"

"What the hell, Winston. Cut off that light!" Phoebe jerked her hand to her neck. The IV tubing fell against the bedside tray table and overturned the plastic water dispenser. Liquid ran across the surface to pool against the raised edge. She sat up and moved her extra pillow nearest Winston, as though a barrier.

"I didn't want this to happen," she said. Phoebe ran her fingers across the bruises encircling her neck, sitting more erect. "Alex had slipped out the back when those officers showed up. Then he came back and threatened to tell what he knew. I saw the rage in his eyes that Diana used to talk about when they were married. I told him to go ahead—tell everything he knew to anybody who would listen and maybe see who would believe him."

"That's just it," Winston said. "Alex doesn't know."

"Anyone can see right through your lies. Alex told me that he knew everything … everything about what happened to Rusty. How we took care of …"

"Phoebe!" Winston yelled, then abruptly lowered to a hush. "Don't talk about any of this in such a public place."

"This is my hospital room, not a public place. It's not bugged. There're no security cameras in here." She wrinkled her forehead and checked the ceiling and corners of the room, never really having considered the possibility. "And the nurses always tap on the door before they come in."

"The police are saying you acted in self-defense," Winston said, eyeing the door. "At least that's what the news is saying. We just need to get our story straight."

"How odd, Winston. That's just what Alex said before he wrapped his belt around my neck and told me that playing victim was my ticket out of this mess." She massaged her neck again and with her finger traced the thin suture line barely visible, high on her forehead.

CHAPTER 37

Diana called Brad on the way home from work the next day, and he agreed to meet her. It would be their second driveway rendezvous in as many days. Already home from school, Kelsey was at the kitchen table with the English assignment near completion.

"Martin texted me that there's no sign of Alex, except for fingerprints all over Phoebe's house. She admitted he's been living there."

"How about the impressions on her neck?"

"No fingerprints, only belt marks. Turns out, the tissue under her nails was her own."

"So, sweet Aunt Phoebe made the whole thing up? Tossed herself through a window for attention?"

"I don't know. But for sure, Phoebe won't be charged with a crime. It was her property."

"Your call to come back over was a surprise. I thought that you might need to stay home alone with Kelsey—because of what they're saying about her father," Brad said.

Diana was silent, motionless, staring through the windshield down onto the driveway.

"Well, how did she take it?" he asked.

"I didn't tell her. There wasn't time. Besides, I'm not sure what's true. Kelsey's deep into that big English paper. Her grades suck in that class, worse after all the subs for Mr. Marzel. They finally hired a permanent replacement. And if she doesn't pull that course up to at least a B, she won't qualify for cheerleader tryouts."

Brad lowered his window and stretched his arm across the back of the seat. He turned toward Diana. "Aren't you afraid she'll hear about Alex first on the news or from somebody at school?"

"I don't know," she said without turning to him. "I guess I suck at motherhood."

"You're not a bad mother," Brad said. He pulled his arm back down to his side. "You have a lot of shit eating at you, Diana. Maybe it's starting to affect your judgment."

"My judgment? So you think I'm slipping. Does that opinion extend to the OR?"

"Don't try to change the subject, Diana. You know that's not what I mean."

"Just take me to Phoebe's house," Diana said. "I don't know why. I just need to look around. There's no reason for any more secrecy. Maybe I can put this all together and get some closure."

"Closure? That sounds like dialogue from a Lifetime movie," Brad said. "Besides, won't the police have the place roped off with yellow tape and personnel posted out front to protect the evidence?"

"That's only on TV, I think," Diana said. "Martin told me the investigation is finished. It's Phoebe's word against Alex."

"Ol' Phoeb is playing victim in this whole thing," Brad said.

"She's free to return home anytime she wishes, as soon as she's discharged from the hospital or decides to leave AMA," Diana said. "I'm afraid there may not be much time to snoop around the place, although this time it's through the front door."

Brad stood with Diana at the front door of Phoebe's house, checking up and down the street as she slid her key into the lock. Chief Martin was true to his word: no yellow crime tape, no police cars, no officer posted at the front door. "What do you expect to find here?"

Diana answered, "I'm not sure."

Brad went ahead of her into the foyer. The house was still, silent. "Your aunt have a computer?" he asked. "That's a good place to start."

"She mentioned getting a new one when she moved. I haven't noticed a desktop over here nor in the old house. I doubt she does anything but follow bridge scores posted on line."

They walked past the mess in the formal living room where Phoebe accused Alex of the attack. There were no blood stains. Dark, heavy plastic covered the broken living room window. The upholstered chair lay turned on its side. They checked the library.

Brad said, "No desktop for sure, and I don't see a laptop either ... not even an iPad."

"Let's try the bedroom," Diana said. "Fortunately, I haven't had to make a house call in there."

They headed down the hall opposite the kitchen into the wing of bedrooms. Diana recognized the bedspread. "This is Aunt Phoebe's bedroom," she said. "It's larger than her old one. Some of the same drapery. I don't see a computer."

"What's this?" Brad pushed against the right side of a pair of door high wall panels, no knobs and covered in the same paper as the rest of the bedroom. The door sprung open toward Brad. "A secret room?" he asked.

"Now, who's being melodramatic like an afternoon movie?" Diana said. She pulled open the left side of the entrance way. An overhead light switch was inside to the right. "This is nothing but a large closet—bigger than some bedrooms. It looks like Aunt Phoebe stores her out-of-season wardrobe in here."

"Got to give her credit. The woman's always decked. Even in a hospital room. I'm surprised that she keeps old things around." Brad leaned against the opening.

Diana ran her hand along the shoulders of the fall and winter clothes. She pushed apart several evening gowns with velvet collars, some with rhinestones. "A lot of this stuff is from several seasons back, several years back. Goodwill pick up must not have answered the phone."

Brad pointed. "What's that under the black wool coat?"

"That's not wool, Brad. It's mink." Diana lifted the full-length mink coat from an oversized, clothes hanger covered in quilted pink fabric and held it to her chest. "I've never seen Phoebe wear this," Diana said.

"Looks like she keeps more in here than skin from murdered animals," Brad said. He pushed aside the adjacent hanging garments, all heavy and bulky, exposing an approximate four-foot-wide recessed area fitted with desk and laptop. The desk was typical of an office supply store and was shoved tight against the wall. Several shoe boxes were stacked on either side of the desk and a few underneath. "Who hides an office in a closet, particularly when you live by yourself?"

Diana stepped into the area and traced the power cord to the electric wall outlet. "The laptop's plugged in, all powered up. I guess it's been used recently." She looked past Brad, back into the main area of the large closet. There was an air circulation vent to the side of the recessed ceiling lights. "Maybe she's got wi-fi in here."

Brad opened up the laptop screen. "We're in luck. No password required. Let's see what she's been up to."

"Brad, wait," Diana said and closed the laptop. "Maybe you're right and we shouldn't be here. Maybe you're right that I've been jumping to conclusions. Aunt Phoebe's done nothing to hurt me. I should help her."

"We've come this far. Let's see what your little auntie's been up to in her secret office." He pushed aside the shoeboxes, pulled out the chair, and sat, then tapped a few keys on the laptop. The search engine history popped onto the screen: *bee keeping*.

Diana said, "Stop right there, Brad."

"You didn't know your aunt bottled her own honey?" Brad asked. "Maybe she has more than bridge as a hobby," he said.

"Something tells me that that's not the case," Diana said. She pushed Brad off the chair and took his place at the keyboard. She scrolled through the history of recent Google entries:

bee venom how fast it works
bee venom how fast it kills.

"Kelsey's teacher, Mr. Marzel. He was in college with Phoebe. They found dead him in his backyard bee hive," she said.

Brad reached over her shoulder and tapped a few keys. "Scoot over a little," he said. He brought up the next set of keywords in the search history. "This says: *when do EpiPens expire*. I wonder what that's all about."

A series of websites advertising pre-measured, injectable epinephrine appeared on the screen. Brad began to click through the addresses and scrolled through the information. Another site detailed the mechanism of epinephrine in preventing or halting allergic reactions. "Basic biochem stuff," he said. "When did Aunt Phoebe become such a scientist?"

"Just keep looking," Diana said.

"Here's pay dirt," Brad said and skimmed the ask-the-doctor type website. "This is some pretty basic stuff." The article noted that epinephrine pens should be kept up to date but if stored properly could remain potent for years past the expiration date. "But this guy says that it's not so much the expiration date that's important but the color of the solution in the window on the label. High temperature or direct sunlight for even a few hours will turn the solution from clear to ice-tea color, regardless of the expiration date."

Diana said, "Heat makes it no longer effective." She drew her cell from her pocket and took a photo of the image.

"What are you doing?" Brad asked.

"I think I've heard that before—the thing about ice-tea. She sent the photo to Key Martin then punched in the chief's number.

"Yeah, we found an expired EpiPen next to the dead teacher," Martin said. "I thought I mentioned it to you. Why?"

Diana tapped *SPEAKER*. "Did your investigators think the pen belonged to Mr. Marzel?"

"Why wouldn't we? We found it with the body. The amateur bee keeper got sloppy with his hobby."

"Any fingerprints?" Diana said.

Martin did not answer.

Brad shrugged his shoulders. "Can you go back and check for fingerprints, Chief Martin?" he asked.

More pause from the other end. "Dr. Cummins, so you're with Dr. Bratton. You two together at the office?"

"Martin, it's not important where we are, at least not for now. We want to know if you found any fingerprints on the EpiPen."

"No reason to check, no sign of foul play. Like I said, looked to us like the eccentric English teacher just got careless."

"Any way you can go back and check?" Diana asked. "It's important."

"The EpiPen should still be in the evidence locker," Martin said. "Whose prints are you looking for?"

"My aunt Phoebe's," Diana answered.

"I'm ready to leave now. Will you call me a taxi?" Phoebe asked. The hospital nursing assistant wrapped the blood pressure cuff around Phoebe's arm and pressed the control for a reading.

"Like I told you the last time, that thing is too damn tight. Cuts off my circulation." Phoebe pulled her arm away from the machine. "And if you won't call a taxi, then I'll do it myself. Or maybe one of those Uber things."

"Please, like we discussed yesterday, pulling against the machine throws off the numbers. Your doctor will think your pressure is too high." The assistant pushed the stand closer to ease tension on the controls. "Calling a taxi for you is against the rules. The doctor hasn't even discharged you. Your nurse would've let me know."

"If you're not going to help me, then hand me my cell from the tray. I'll call a car myself."

The nursing assistant unsnapped the blood pressure cuff and returned it to its place on the stand. She found the cell phone and handed it to Phoebe. "Is this what you're looking for?"

"Thank you, and that will be all," Phoebe said.

The assistant stood motionless, a deep frown on her face.

"Doesn't someone down the hall need you?" Phoebe said.

The young woman frowned more deeply and pushed the blood pressure machine toward the door. She jotted a few numbers on a notepad before sliding it back into a compartment on the stand. "Not many like you, ma'am," she said and pulled the door closed behind her.

"Some might say that's a good thing," Phoebe called out after her. Her head ached along the narrow line of sutures across her forehead. She strained for the IV tubing and followed it to the control panel. The on-off button looked simple, a mere tap of the finger on the word, then darkness. "There, that did it. Didn't even need nursing school."

She yanked the main line of tubing free from the infusion unit and followed the shorter plastic segment leading to the tiny catheter in her arm. Bright-red blood filled the tube, mixing with the stagnant IV fluid. "Disgusting. I'll get Diana to take this nasty damn thing out later."

Phoebe grabbed an unfolded napkin from her lunch tray and fashioned a makeshift bandage, wrapping the site where the IV catheter punctured her left wrist. The blood stopped flowing. "That might be a little snug," she said and loosened the knot in the crude bow. The closet was only a few feet from her bed but with unsteady legs seemed much farther. The floor felt frigid and slick without her favorite slippers. Phoebe pulled her hospital gown tighter against her waist and fidgeted with the metal snaps. "Jesus, my legs are nearly as swollen as my feet."

She made it to the handle on the closet door, meeting little resistance to her tug and managing not to fall. Except for the slacks and blouse worn the day Alex attacked her, the closet was empty. The wrinkled outfit on wire hangers was marred with grass and oil stains and dried, smeared blood—her blood.

"Dammit, nobody brought me clean clothes," Phoebe said. "I can't be seen out in these horrid things. But I've no choice." She grabbed the hangers and clothes. "I better hurry before that nurse aide bitch bothers me again."

Next, she reached into her purse for a hair brush and struggled to the bathroom to dress. Her legs felt like limp pasta. Shutting the door behind her, she snagged the sleeve of the blouse on the IV catheter—but she still managed to put it on. The dirty slacks came next, and she shook her head at the mess.

"I shouldn't have made this so convincing," she said.

Phoebe leaned against the door for support, taking each leg slowly, then buttoned the waist and smoothed the fabric to freshen the old creases the best she could. Someone, she assumed Diana, had brought her purse to the hospital, or maybe she'd asked the ambulance people to get it for her that night. The side pocket contained a travel size kit of blush and lipstick—not an ideal shade, but would have to do. She stared at her face and shoulders in the mirror and fluffed the collar to conceal the marks on her neck.

"Not so bad after all."

Phoebe left the bathroom door ajar and rechecked her purse for keys and wallet. "I'm surprised they don't keep personals like this locked up at the nurses' desk, like at the jail. Thank God I don't have to beg that bitch nurse's aide." Phoebe looked up from inside her purse at the closed door out to the hallway. She remembered the gurney and the sound of the ambulance doors shutting behind her. The BMW was at home in the garage or should be. "No need for my car keys. At least I have money for a taxi."

"I'm one step ahead of you two docs," Martin said. "I had forensics take a look at that late yesterday. Our late teacher's prints popped up— seems like he landed a DUI a few years back."

"Anything else?" Diana asked.

"The FBI maintains the IAFIS, which includes civil prints as well as those submitted by law enforcement agencies, but nothing matched the other three partials on the EpiPen," Martin said.

"Same individual?" Brad moved closer to ask.

"So says the guys in forensics," Martin said. "Prints probably female, looks like the individual handled the pen loosely, trying not to leave a trace. Most professionals would have worn gloves."

"I was fingerprinted once at a bank, years ago, just my thumb, to cash a check," Diana said. "I guess that's what you meant about civil."

Brad was silent, but backed away from the phone a bit. He hit the mute button and said, "If you think your aunt had something to do with that guy's death, then you need to ask her and make sure she has a lawyer. Stop sneaking around."

"Dr. Bratton? You and Dr. Cummins still there?"

Brad whispered, then remembered the mute. "What do you want to do, Diana? Pull a prank to get Phoebe's prints like on some lame detective TV show?"

"Why not get Phoebe to drink from a glass and collect her prints for the police?" she asked.

More from the speaker phone: "Dr. Bratton … Dr. Cummins?"

Diana killed the mute. "Sorry, Chief Martin. I'm tired of skirting around this. I need to know if my aunt is mixed up in any of mess."

Martin said, "Since she didn't show up in the data base, get me a set of prints. Just invite her over for a drink."

Brad nodded. "Whatever."

CHAPTER 38

Phoebe turned the knob to her hospital room and cracked open the door. She worked her fingers through the several-inch space and eased it fully open, checking both ways down the hall. A middle-aged man in white scrubs passed by slowly and smiled. Phoebe lowered her head to hide her face.

"Can I help you with something, ma'am? You need somethin'?"

"No, I'm just visiting the lady in here." Phoebe stepped into the hall and pulled the door closed. "She wants me … to pick up something for her … at the mall … in a hurry. I need to find the nearest exit."

Despite her admissions to the hospital, Phoebe remained clueless to the building's layout. Had she obeyed the nursing assistant's order to "walk in the hall for blood circulation," after her transport by gurney from the ER, she might have known her way around a bit.

"Well, lady," he gestured to his scrubs and cheap tennis shoes and the uneven haircut, "you might see that I'm not much of a shopper—don't frequent the stores and the malls around here much. So you better ask the visitor information desk on the first floor."

Phoebe raised her eyebrows. "What I need are directions to the first floor—to the exit. I have been visiting my sick friend, and I'm ready to leave." She nodded at the closed door to the hospital room.

"No problem, ma'am." He pointed. "The elevators are around the corner to the right. You can't miss. Just push the lobby button."

Without a thank you, Phoebe shuffled toward the elevators. The door opened as she approached.

Winston Ivy stepped from the elevator. "Phoebe, I came to visit the sick. Looks like you're already well."

"Get back inside. I'm getting out of this place—well or not." She pushed inside the elevator, touched LOBBY, and reached for Winston. The segment of remaining IV tubing dangled from her arm and out the end of her blouse to brush against his jacket sleeve.

"Hey, be careful. This is Italian." The elevator started to descend.

"You won't be wearing anything but polyester orange and stripes if we don't do something about what's going on," Phoebe said. "I need a ride home, so your visit was timed perfectly."

Winston straightened his sleeve and the rest of his jacket. "My visit was not just to wish you a speedy recovery. I've got an ulterior motive."

"Ulterior motive?" The elevator opened into the lobby. The same nurse aide stood waiting to push an obese elderly man in an oversized wheelchair into the elevator. Phoebe melted into a corner and bowed her head. She put her forefinger to her lips and shook her head at Winston. *Be quiet.*

He shrugged in question.

She turned and slipped out of the elevator, then Winston followed. The aide was too engrossed with the tangled tubing connected to the man's IV bag and oxygen canister to look in their direction. The patient breathed heavily as he and the nurse replaced Phoebe and Winston in the elevator, a cloud of stale cigarette smoke and the reek of perspiration in his wake.

Once inside the lobby, Winston whispered. "Like I said, I didn't drop by to check on your medical progress. I came by to warn you."

Phoebe looked over her shoulder, noting the elevator doors closed and the nursing aide gone. "Warn me about what, Winston?"

A large potted palm grew near the row of windows across the lobby. Just after Winston had entered the hospital, sheets of rain drenched the landscaped hospital grounds. The brief rainstorm had passed. Drops of water gleamed from the blades of grass and dripped from tree and shrub branches like prisms or melting stalactites. Winston ushered her to the seclusion and quiet of the upholstered chairs along the windows, away from the people milling about the room's center flower arrangement, although a woman and her toddler meandered toward them.

Winston said, hushed, "I wasn't sure how long you would be hospitalized. I started thinking about your nosey niece and her doctor friend and her access to your place. I rode by your house and a car was parked out front. It wasn't yours."

"No, my BMW should be in the garage."

"It was a much cheaper vehicle than that, not sure which model," Winston said.

"I bet it was Diana's car," Phoebe said. "She has a key to my house."

"How could you be so freaking careless?" The mounting frustration in Winston's voice becoming almost a growl. "You should have had the locks changed after that thing with Alex."

Phoebe pushed closer to Winston, raising herself on tiptoes. Her eyes almost met his. "I've been in the hospital, you ass. When would I have called a locksmith?"

The woman with the toddler looked disapprovingly at them as she reached into a padded cloth bag embroidered with the picture of a rabbit. She withdrew a Sippy cup with Mickey-mouse ears and pried it into the child's mouth.

Winston seemed to notice that the rain had stopped. "What were Diana and that other doctor doing in your house?"

"How would I know? Maybe they were just hooking up." Phoebe backed away.

He grabbed her by the arm, just missing the IV. "They were definitely looking for something. One of my agents showing a property downtown saw your niece leaving JPD headquarters a day or two ago. That other doctor was with her, the male. They must be working with the police."

"Let's get away from here, Winston. I'm still supposed to be upstairs, hooked to one of those damn IV poles." She motioned to one of the other patients, stooped and dragging a pole behind him across the lobby toward the exit. His other hand clutched a pack of cigarettes.

Winston still had her arm and escorted her to the front door. "Other than maybe screwing, what do you think they were doing in your house, Phoebe?" he asked. "What were they looking for?"

"There's nothing there. Alex never left anything lying around. I don't leave sticky notes. I don't have a diary."

"Or a computer?" Winston asked.

"Oh, my God!" Phoebe halted in the doorway and yelled. Winston's size 11 leather shoes pounded her heel at the rear of the hospital issue loafers. (Her shoes did not make the ambulance ride.) "My computer, they may have found my computer."

"You do have a computer? I didn't know you knew anything about that stuff."

"Yes, a very small one—a laptop. I keep it …"

"My guess is that a prima donna with a computer would have the maid handle everything: the Internet, the passwords, your social media." Winston said. The parking lot of Jackson Metropolitan Hospital was nearly full, lots of arrivals and few departures since Winston had parked, and he was uncertain where he had left his vehicle—in too much of a hurry to remember landmarks. He reached into his pants pocket for his keys and pressed the keyless entry. A thud and a click directed them to his car a few rows over.

"I'm not as dumb as you think, Winston."

"Nowadays they call it *clueless*, Phoebe." He nudged her shoulder in the direction of the car.

"I've never been that either," Phoebe said. "However, I'm worried about how far Diana will take this."

"Keep moving, Phoebe." He pushed this time. "That's the reason we need to get over to your house." Winston opened his door and slid into the driver's seat.

"You used to open mine for me," Phoebe said.

"That was a long time ago. A lot has happened since then."

CHAPTER 39

Diana and Brad approached the hospital. "Ok, Ok, Diana. Why come here to get Phoebe's fingerprints?" Brad asked. "Her prints would be all over her house."

"Just take the back entrance," Diana said.

"Park next to the dumpster?" Brad asked, but followed the directive and made the turn. "Not sure hospital security makes rounds back here, but maybe the security camera will pick it up if somebody rips off my F-150."

"Phoebe's room is in the south wing. I know because I brought her purse to her while she was sleeping. We can take the service elevator. It's closer."

"What do you know about the service elevator?"

"I use it a lot—less congested—less likely to run across patients or families and have to chitchat," Diana answered. "That will be the quickest way up."

When in a hurry, Brad sometimes jumped past the running board of his pickup to the ground or pavement. This time he used the step. Diana was already at the hospital rear entrance. He jogged to reach her.

Before waving her security badge over the electronic sensor, she turned to Brad. "I'm going to follow through with this even if you disagree or think I'm being foolish. I don't want any question about whose prints are whose. I need Phoebe's fingerprints."

"You know it won't be official," Brad said. "What you're doing here—there's no chain of evidence, or whatever the police call it."

"That doesn't matter. Martin will run the prints for me off the record. I need to know."

The sensor emitted a weak beeping sound and the door unlocked. Diana opened it. Brad shook his head and followed. Without turning back around to face him, Diana said, "I saw that."

She ran left to the stairs, skipping the service elevator, and Brad picked

233

up speed behind her. In seconds they were at the nurses' station, both out of breath.

"Dr. Bratton?" an older female nurse stood at a computer mounted on a rolling stand in the hall. She looked up without slowing her typing at the keyboard. "Can I help you with something? I don't think you have any patients on this floor."

Diana continued toward Phoebe's room and Brad followed. "This time I'm just visiting. My aunt … she's in this room a few doors down."

"If you're talking about 306, the charge nurse assigned her to me. I haven't made my initial rounds, but the patient should be in the room."

Diana pushed open the door, greeted by the loud beeping of the abandoned IV pump. Plastic tubing dangled from the machine.

The nurse was behind Brad and moved around him into the room. "I need to silence that IV pump, please."

Diana was already checking the empty closet. A hospital gown lay twisted on the floor of the bathroom, the hospital grade toothbrush left dropped in the sink, the miniature tube of toothpaste opened to a trail of bluish-green goo. "Don't bother," Diana said. "I'll take care of it."

She stepped over to the pump and slammed the off control.

"I guess she left AMA," Brad said.

"And it looks like she left in a hurry," Diana said. "She doesn't have her car. I guess she took a taxi. I don't think she knows about Uber."

Brad said, "We might have run up on Phoebe if …"

"Don't say it, Brad," Diana interrupted. "I know. If we had come through the front lobby, we might have seen her. But why would she sneak out of the hospital?"

"Maybe she didn't sneak out," he said. "Maybe she walked out the front door."

"Excuse me, Dr. Bratton. I'm going to have to report this to the nursing supervisor. This may be a patient safety issue."

"Nurse, please, go ahead and do your job. In the meantime, I'm going to track down my aunt. Tell the business office to bill her. She can afford it."

This time Brad led the way.

"Come on, Diana," he said. "Let's head back to Phoebe's house."

"Maybe you should just drop me off, Winston," Phoebe said, opening the car door. "Your car shouldn't be seen here."

"What difference does it make? I think your niece has this already figured out." Winston stepped onto the driveway.

"I'm not sure what's going through Diana's mind," Phoebe answered, "not sure at all."

Still in the passenger seat, Phoebe fumbled in her purse for her house key. "She was around for me when they shoved me into the back of that ambulance and forced me into the hospital. Wasn't that kind?" She checked the remaining pocket of the Kate Spade handbag and withdrew the keys. "I always drop my keys back into my purse. They have to be in here somewhere."

Winston reached back into the car and grabbed the keys from her. "Come on, Phoebe. I need to know what your niece might have found on your computer. Forget the sight of me in orange; we'll see how thoughtful she is visiting you in the penitentiary or at your gravesite if they execute you."

"Nothing's there, Winston. I don't use my computer all that much." She followed him up the flagstone path from the driveway to the front steps.

"That's even worse. Fewer files on your computer means Dr. Diana Bratton wouldn't have to search very hard."

The house alarm tripped when Winston unlocked the front door. Phoebe shut the door behind them and reached the wall control to enter the deactivating code. "Obviously, I didn't set the alarm before they hauled me away. And the maid hasn't been here. She's had the week off."

"So somebody's been in this house," Winston said.

Phoebe motioned to the broken window covered in black plastic. "Of course, someone's been here. The contractors came by to work up a repair estimate."

"I'm not sure why you continue to cover for your niece. She's been here and activated the alarm when she left. Now, where's that computer? The den? Or did you say your bedroom?"

"The bedroom."

Winston didn't wait for her to follow. He called from inside the bedroom. "I don't see any computer."

Phoebe ambled slowly after him. She was still sore. "Not so loud. It's in my closet," she said from behind him. "It's just a laptop, remember?"

He walked into the center of the closet and surveyed the rows of shelving stuffed with hat boxes and expensive-looking shoes. Hooks draped with scarves—multiple colors—mostly muted—jutted from the corners. "Phoebe, my agent found you a place with a very generous master closet, much larger than average."

"No one's ever associated me with average, Winston, particularly not you."

"So, where is the laptop?"

Phoebe went to the rack of coats banked by a line of blouses, mostly silk. Her full-length mink, the one that needed to go back into storage along with the stroller, hung among them as did her long black wool coat, the one with the zippered lining. Then there were the Waffle-Pique knit blazer and the down parka with genuine coyote fur trim that she had never worn. The garments no longer hung evenly spaced; they had been disturbed.

She plunged her forearms into the center of the rack and pushed the clothes apart. The dark monitor and keyboard waited on the desk. Phoebe jingled the mouse, and the screen lit up.

"Well, go ahead and enter your password."

"I don't have a password."

"No password? You think you don't have any secrets?" Winston grabbed the chair and sat at the desk. Phoebe looked over his shoulder. The Internet sites concerning bee-keeping, venom allergies, and EpiPens jumped at him. "When did you last look at this stuff?"

She looked down at the screen, puzzled. "I don't remember."

Winston noted the dates and times recorded for the log in to each site, methodically tracking the search engine history. "Well, someone's been at it more recently, and any first grader would know that it was your Internet research they were interested in. Your brilliant surgeon niece and her friend, they are your spies."

Phoebe stepped over to her hat boxes. She had not worn a hat in years. "I ready should give all of this old stuff to Goodwill."

"I would have considered you smarter than to leave this computer trail, Phoeb. Did you actually read through all of this stuff?"

"Why would I be interested in any of that, Winston? I shop Saks and Bloomingdale's on that thing, not EpiPens." She lifted the top of one of the hat boxes. Inside was an elaborate collection of silk and feathers that had belonged to her mother. A heavily jeweled hat pin of costume stones speared the center of the accessory. Phoebe ran her fingernails across the colored glass, sliding her smooth, polished tips into the crevices between the glistening pieces.

"I didn't know that someone our age, even you, could be such a whiz with electronic gadgets, Winston," she said. "You truly amaze me, always have."

"This information about allergies to bee venom," Winston asked, "and these photographs of victims. Some are quite gruesome, wouldn't you say?" He scrutinized the contorted bodies with pale, swollen skin. "Your inspiration, perhaps?"

Phoebe loosened the hat pin. A few barbs from one of the feathers floated to the carpet. "You want someone to be guilty. I guess you think that someone like me would need to be prepared, to know what it would look like. But still ..."

Winston clicked onto another page. It was a pictorial of anti-venom products and explained the significance of medication expiration dates. "So, this one company in Mexico—they offer discounted EpiPens near expiration. Unless it appears discolored, the medication is still effective. Heat will discolor it."

Phoebe pulled the pin free of the hat, the shaft much longer and stronger than she remembered, but just as sharp. "The one that Dewey had, the one they would have found with him. It was discolored then. Do you think I heated it under a lamp—or maybe used the kitchen stove?"

Winston continued at the laptop, mesmerized but shaking his head. "Your research was thorough, Phoebe."

She stood behind Winston, holding the hat pin by the head. "Thorough?"

"You unearthed the answer, figured out exactly what would do the trick," he said. "Where's the purchase invoice for the EpiPen."

"The invoice?" She stepped closer. Winston did not look up from the keyboard.

"Here it is." He pulled up the document and studied it. "This invoice proves you purchased that special EpiPen. I wonder if your dear niece, Dr. Bratton, found this little piece of evidence."

"Special? Phoebe asked.

"Definitely special ... and its ineffectiveness a terrible surprise for Marzel."

Phoebe raised the hairpin.

"Aunt Phoebe, stop! What are you doing?"

In one motion Brad rushed past Diana and her scream, grabbing and twisting Phoebe's forearm, knocking the hairpin to the floor.

Winston came off the chair and whirled around. "Yes, dear Phoebe," he said short of breath, "what are you doing?"

Phoebe squirmed lose from Brad's hold and sank into the corner of the closet, massaging her sore arm. "I wanted to stop you, Winston," she said, "stop you from hurting Diana."

"From hurting me?" Diana's voice shook. She turned from Phoebe to Winston. "Mr. Ivy, why so interested in that computer?"

"I might ask you the same thing, Dr. Bratton. What were you doing at this computer?"

"I ... uhh ... I haven't been doing ..."

Winston interrupted, "Someone was searching through Phoebe's archived websites, checking out her research into beekeeping. Was it you, Dr. Bratton? According to Phoebe, you're the only one else with a key to this house."

Brad said, "I think we need to turn this shit over to the police, Diana. Go ahead and call your buddy at JPD."

"Let's not do that, Dr. Bratton, regardless of what this gentleman says." Winston slid a Glock 30S from inside his navy blazer and pointed it at Brad. "You're the Dr. Cummins I've heard so much about."

Phoebe said, "Why didn't you let me cut him while I had the chance?"

Winston directed the gun at Phoebe, then waved it between Diana and Brad.

Brad clinched his fists and stepped toward Winston.

"Brad, don't," Diana said, her hands trembling.

"Yes, Dr. Bratton," Winston said. "We all need to remain calm here. By the way, how well do you know your aunt?"

"Shut the fuck up, Winston."

"*Shut the fuck up?* Phoebe, I haven't heard such language out of you since our college days, like that day I caught you and Rusty together. Now they call it *hooking up.*"

"Winston, that's a lie."

Winston continued to wave the gun around. "Are you surprised about your aunt, Dr. Bratton? She's only a façade of a true lady, really just a stuck-up, trashy bitch from the sixties. Fortunately for you, you're not a blood relative to this terrible woman."

"I don't know what you're talking about, Mr. Ivy." Diana looked at Brad.

He returned her stare with a question. *Isn't that what you've been driving at? Isn't that why we've been snooping around after Phoebe?*

"And Miss Phoebe's quite the actress. Isn't she?" Winston continued. "So convincing when you interrupted our little tea party in her new living room that afternoon, making the case that she barely remembered me from Ole Miss."

Brad took another step closer. "OK, Ivy, what's the game here? Why don't we call the police and let them sort all this crap out?"

"I doubt that Phoebe would want the police in on this. She didn't before, so why now?"

"Phoebe, it you need a lawyer, then we better call ..."

"Diana," Phoebe interrupted, "please, just be quiet."

"Doctors, I'm not the enemy here." Winston settled the weapon on Phoebe. "I've been trying to help you with your little secret," he said and moved closer. "Your problem is that you're so damn headstrong, Phoebe, always taking things into your own hands. Now I feel the need to protect myself."

Winston stepped even closer to Phoebe, turning slightly away from Brad. Brad moved slowly behind Winston as Diana watched. She wanted to shake her head "No" but thought Winston would see. Brad lunged, hitting him hard against the back of his legs. Winston tumbled into the shelving to the right of the computer desk, boxes falling. The gun fired as it flew from his hand, piercing the plumbing in the wall. Brad and Winston groped for the Glock.

Water spewed in every direction, drenching Phoebe's wardrobe and spraying the two men. Brad reached the weapon first, but Winston came down across his back loosening the grip. The gun dropped to the carpet, landing at Phoebe's feet. Brad's hard fist against Winston's jaw was answered with a knee to the crotch.

Phoebe retrieved the gun. "Put that thing down," Diana screamed.

Phoebe pushed closer to the fight, following Winston's temple with the tip of the barrel, the gun unsteady.

Winston yanked free of Brad's right arm and hooked it around his neck, pulling Brad against his chest. The sudden movement startled Phoebe, and Winston's strength surprised them all. Phoebe stumbled toward Brad and Winston, tripping over a purse. The gun fired into Winston's head. Blood and grey matter splattered the white mink hanging from its padded silk clothes hanger and already wet from the plumbing.

Out of breath, Brad backed away on his knees, unable to stand. His neck and trachea ached from Winston's squeeze. Putting his hand to his neck, he struggled to speak. "Diana … Diana, get … get that gun away from her."

Blood oozed from Winston's body, a thick red pool spreading across the carpet from underneath his head. "That old guy," Brad managed to say between coughing spells, almost choking. "Unbelievable strength. He must be seventy."

"Close," Phoebe said and dropped the gun.

Diana reached for the hat pin. She yanked it from where it had pierced the carpet near Phoebe's shoe. Almost in reflex, she wiped the head and blade clean of Phoebe's prints with her blouse and stuck the pin inside an open hat box spared by the water. Several small blue feathers and beads flew loose from the hat.

CHAPTER 40

Key Martin joined the team responding to Diana's call. Standard directive with the dispatcher alerted him to anything related to Dr. Diana Bratton and Phoebe's address on Lacewood Drive. Martin walked past the small gathering in Phoebe's living room for the closet and the work of the forensics team. Then he returned to the living room.

"I'm surprised you didn't call me directly, Dr. Bratton," he said, interrupting the female police officer interviewing Phoebe, Diana, and Brad. The three sat on the sofa while the officer stood. Phoebe sobbed, sitting in the center. Diana, nearest the officer, was about to answer a question but turned toward Martin. Brad held an ice pack to his jaw.

"I planned to go through proper channels this time," Diana responded.

"JPD is going to have to create a separate division just to handle you and your family," Martin said. He turned his head to acknowledge Brad. "Including your extended family, of course."

Everyone's attention was directed at Martin, including the female officer first on the scene. Phoebe regained composure and reached for a fresh handkerchief from the drawer of the antique chest.

"Winston, my dear, dear friend from college, pulled a gun on us," she said, wiping her eyes with the silk. "I just couldn't help him anymore."

Diana's expression was cold, blank. She had taken the lead in answering the officer's questions, and this was Phoebe's first statement. Diana darted her eyes at Brad not to disagree.

"Mind if I take a seat in this nice chair over here?" Martin asked, righting the living room piece left overturned next to the window. He eased into the chair and the soft fabric.

"I'm sure it's expensive furniture, but my suit is clean, just back from the cleaners."

He kept his eyes on Phoebe and motioned the officer to take the remaining chair and continue her note taking.

"The investigative team … in your closet … has identified the deceased as Mr. Winston Ivy," Martin said. "You said something about trying to help Mr. Ivy?"

"I hadn't seen or heard from Winston since college. It was a coincidence that my real estate agent was associated with his firm."

Diana spoke. "Phoebe, maybe we … you … should hold off on this a bit. Maybe we need to call an attorney first, somebody over at Stephen Kruger's office, if they handle this sort of thing."

"You all can certainly call in legal counsel. It's your right. Except for right now, we're just having a friendly little conversation, a little chat, like you might have down at the bridge club. You play a lot of bridge, don't you?"

"Yes, I do, officer," Phoebe answered. "There's a tournament down at the bridge hut tomorrow afternoon, but that doesn't have …"

"It's Chief," Diana interrupted. "And you're right. Your playing cards has nothing to do with this."

"Winston was worried, worried about something he had seen in the papers," Phoebe said. She dabbed her eyes again. The tears were a dead ringer for genuine. "Some construction worker at Ole Miss unearthed some remains."

"Oh, yes, we've discussed this before, the Rusty Reynolds case. I should have brought Officer Myers with me, but he's back in Oxford. He would find this discussion of interest."

"Phoebe, stop talking. I'm going to call Kruger."

"No, Diana, I haven't done anything wrong, not at all. I want to go ahead and set the record straight, right here and now."

"You go right ahead," Martin said. "No one is being arrested." He reminded the officer to continue her notes, pointing and waving his right finger as though writing cursive.

"There was a boy we all knew in college," she said. "Yes, his name was Rusty Reynolds."

"Everyone knew Mr. Reynolds?" Martin asked. "Even the deceased in your bedroom closet?"

Phoebe ignored Diana's shake of the head and her visual plea to Brad for support in stopping the conversation. Instead, she answered Martin without hesitation. "That's right. They all played cards. Rusty started to win a lot, or so I heard. We were all great friends."

"When did you last see Mr. Reynolds?"

Phoebe laughed. "I hadn't seen Rusty since college. He was a little younger."

Diana said, "This is enough, Martin."

"Now, now, Dr. Bratton. Like I said, we're just chatting—just talking things over. Your aunt's been through a lot in the last couple of days. She needs to unwind."

Phoebe straightened against the sofa cushions. Brad checked his phone for messages.

"To review what has happened over the last few weeks," Martin said, "Mr. Reynolds' sister visited Officer Myers in Oxford. She explained that her big brother sort of disappeared when she was a little girl. Her parents told her that he dropped out of Ole Miss and ran off with some girlfriend. Was that girl you?"

"Certainly not. Rusty definitely had a crush on me, a big one—sure he did. A lot of boys did."

"I bet that's right," Brad said, while still massaging his jaw. He held his phone in the left hand and scrolled through messages with his thumb.

"Phoebe, who was the girlfriend?" Diana asked. "Maybe she's responsible."

"How would I know that? He was only a freshman; we were juniors."

"When I think about my college days … well, junior college … before police academy, we all kept up with who all was dating who. You know, even boys liked to gossip about those things … talked about more than just holding hands." Martin looked at his officer. She was still taking notes.

"You ever hold hands with Rusty Reynolds?"

"I think I know what you mean, officer, and I won't take offense. But I assure you, I was never intimate with Rusty Reynolds, even if he did come into lots of money," Phoebe said. "It wasn't family money. Rusty started to win at cards."

"You're not talking anymore about bridge. Are you Phoebe?"

"No, Diana. I don't think so," Brad interrupted. "And in case anyone is interested, I might need an x-ray of my jaw."

"Winston's father sent him a check every two weeks, a big one," Phoebe continued. "But even if you're rich, you don't like losing your money. Don't you agree, officers?"

While Chief Martin did not respond, the woman officer glanced up briefly, letting a smile slip before returning her pen to the notepad.

"I would tell Winston over and over, try to reassure him that Rusty meant nothing to me," Phoebe said. "Not one thing."

The paramedics rolled a stretcher through the front foyer with Winston's body draped. The female officer walked over to hold the door open for them.

"So jealousy was brewing?" Martin asked. "I'm sure you were a looker back then. Still are."

Diana said, "Come on, Martin. This really is enough."

Phoebe held up her hands. "No, it's all right, Diana. We need to get this out in the open. Winston was jealous of Rusty's looks. He was jealous of Rusty's winnings at poker. They guy was taking all of our money—I mean their money."

Brad moaned and left for the kitchen and more ice.

"Winston saw Rusty smile at me more than once. I think that put him over the edge."

"What are you trying to tell Chief Martin, Aunt Phoebe?"

"I knew that Rusty wasn't around campus anymore. But I didn't ask any questions. I should have." Phoebe wiped her eyes on her blouse. "I thought Winston was responsible, but I didn't understand what he was truly capable of."

"Capable of what?" Martin asked.

Diana said, "Phoebe, I think we should stop this now."

"Winston told me that afternoon, that afternoon that he was over for tea, that he had killed Rusty and buried him in the woods on the edge of campus. He said that until they found the body, he understood everything was taken care of. He said others would also know what happened."

Diana could see the college yearbook and the photographs from the mid-sixties and Phoebe's letter from Rusty. "Winston ... Mr. Ivy ... he suspected that Carvel Eaves and Mr. Marzel would tell what had happened to Rusty," Diana said. "Is that right?"

"I wasn't sure at first," Phoebe answered. "Believed it was just a coincidence. Then Winston started talking about this crazy professor we had at Ole Miss, a writing class. The guy was tall, with wiry, grey hair."

"How does the 'Back to the Future' professor play into all of this?" Brad asked, returning from the kitchen with a fresh ice pack.

Martin removed a fingernail clipper from his pants pocket and began to check his nails. He started with the middle finger of his left hand.

"There was a series of lessons on mystery writing and a whole week about murder mysteries. How someone could make that subject boring, I'll never understand. The class seemed like it would never end. The teacher went on and on talking about the five ways to die."

"That list that Mr. Eaves found near your old house, with the heading: *Five Manners of Death*," Diana said.

"Yes, something like that. Winston became fascinated with the whole thing." Phoebe stood and began to pace the room. She stopped to examine the initial efforts at carpentry repair of the front window, covered in black plastic safety covering. She began to trace the edging of the millwork.

Martin called from across the room. "Looks like a nice match from here, but tell us more about your co-ed years with Reynolds. Unfortunately, ma'am, police don't get paid by the hour."

Phoebe stroked the drapery to the sides and smoothed out the wrinkles. "Thank God this precious fabric escaped unscathed when I was attacked. Anyway, Winston would stay after class and talk to the compositions teacher about the five ways to die. I think he managed an *A*+. I got a *C*, I think, maybe a *D*. At least I passed."

"Great trip down memory lane, ma'am. You know, Dr. Bratton has also been fascinated about putting those classifications to use, retroactive, of course." Finished with the nail grooming, Martin ignored the mess made by the clippings on the rug.

"I think Winston used that list as a recipe to do …"

"To do what?" Brad asked. He had joined Phoebe in walking around the room—his ice pack firmly in place, his phone put away—stopping every few seconds to arch his back and massage the lower lumbar area.

"A recipe to get rid of all of our friends from that era. Anyone who might have put him and Rusty together before his death."

"Dr. Bratton." Martin inspected his manicure one last time. "That collection of photographs cut out of the yearbook, those are the friends that your aunt is talking about. Right?"

Phoebe said, "Diana, you denied taking my yearbook. Were you lying to me and what collection of pictures is he talking about?" She returned to the sofa, arms folded. "By the way, Officer Martin, you've littered the rug, and that irritating clip-clip-clip sound has driven me insane."

Martin glanced a look of warning at Diana before she could say, *"But, Phoebe, you went over to the rental cottage. The owner told us. You knew all about the yearbook pictures."*

"I did find your yearbook from your senior year at Ole Miss," Diana answered. "It was in a box when you were moving—pictures of you, Ivy, Mr. Marzel, Carvel Eaves, and Rusty Reynolds. All these people have died, all except you."

"Yes, Diana. Like I said, Winston was afraid we would reveal his secret. He was killing us all one by one."

"One by one," Martin said staring at his shoes. The nail clipper remained in his right hand.

"And I was next. That's what you saw today." Phoebe wiped a tear away with a finger. "Thank God all of you showed up. It would have been me on that stretcher for the final time—covered in blood."

Chapter 40

Chief Martin stood up. A few stray fingernail clippings scattered to the floor from his slacks. Phoebe renewed the look of disgust. Diana realized that Martin was trying to unnerve Phoebe. "I don't think we need anything else for right now," he said, and motioned for the woman officer to follow. "We'll write up a report. More questions will follow. You can count on it. The DA has to look over everything."

He walked to the door and tipped his hat to Diana. "The pictures we've been studying, the ones posted on my investigation board, I guess it's time they came down. The place is looking kinda cluttered. My secretary will file them away."

"I'm sure you have other cases, Chief Martin," Diana said.

"I liked it better when you called me Key. But you're right. The criminals keep us busy—always lots going on in the department—just like on TV. Lots of major and minor stuff, but it will be nice to clean things up a bit."

CHAPTER 41

The restaurant in the Fondren area of Jackson was busy. Part of a brick building once used as a public school, this section had served as the cafeteria. It was a Friday night, and without high school football games to compete, the place was filled with teenagers and young parents with kids. Video footage of *I Love Lucy* illuminated a corridor to the restrooms. Ventilation ductwork hung suspended from the ceiling and distressed concrete flooring added to the casual atmosphere. Diana and Brad took a raised table immediately inside the bar area, which led from the main entrance and dining section.

Brad consumed most of the fresh guacamole dip appetizer made tableside, then followed with the specialty hamburger.

Diana held to three fish tacos after only a taste of the dip. "You didn't say much during Martin's questioning," she said, adjusting her hold of the menu to see better in the scattered drop-down lighting. The chocolate cake called her.

"No need to fret, Diana," Brad said. "I'll order that cake." He smiled at the waiter and put his hand to his chin. "I was busy nursing my wounds during Phoebe's interrogation. It's still sore when I yawn or chew really hard. That old guy's strength still amazes me."

"I'm still amazed by Aunt Phoebe's performance to Key Martin. Quite the actress she is."

"Performance?"

The server was quick with the chocolate cake and two fresh forks. Brad asked for coffee. Diana wanted decaf.

"Phoebe has heard me talk about Kelsey's teacher. She played bridge with Carvel Eaves. Then there's Ivy. She never mentioned any of them as college classmates, appeared surprised as though she had forgotten all the connections. She knew I had seen the yearbook. Strange, don't you think?" Diana took her fork, sampled the cake, and washed it down with the coffee.

"I think your aunt was a real snob in college, seems the type."

"That's not it. I think she wanted to forget that part of her life. She was trying to hide it. That's why she wanted to see Rusty's sister."

"And Rusty's sister is also dead." Phoebe's voice came from behind her, and Diana choked on her second bite of cake.

Brad froze in the last bite of his burger. "Phoebe? Uhh, why don't you join us?" he asked, his mouth full.

"This is no coincidence, you two." Phoebe remained standing. "You're not the only one in the family who can play detective. I followed you here. We need to talk."

"We're … just about finished. We can leave and meet you back at my house or at your place." Diana began to look around for her purse. She eyed Brad to ask for the check. "Have you been here long?" she asked.

"I waited in the car. Wasn't really sure what to do. Why don't we go ahead and hash things out here?" Phoebe spotted a fresh napkin on the table and wiped the stool. Her heels tangled in the legs. She rested her purse on the floor under her feet.

Despite the laughter, the room conversation at wide-ranging pitches, and tinkling of tableware, an awkward silence covered the table. Diana broke the impasse. "What is it you want to say?"

"Winston got nervous when Sylvia DeLoach started asking questions," Phoebe answered, "particularly when she went up to Oxford."

"Winston Ivy told you that he was nervous?" Brad asked.

Phoebe considered Brad for a few seconds then redirected her attention to Diana. "I think he sent Alex after DeLoach. The next thing in the news, a body is floating in a pond on the Ole Miss campus, and Rusty's sister doesn't come home."

Concerned that someone would overhear, Diana surveyed the tables around them and leaned closer to Phoebe. "You think Alex murdered that woman?"

"We all know that Alex Bratton was up to no good. You saw what he tried to do to me." She massaged her neck. "He thought I was going to spill the beans," Phoebe said.

The conversation stopped when the waiter returned, a college-age guy with a short, dark beard and ponytail. Brad handed him the credit card linked to the surgery clinic expense account.

"Ma'am, can I get you anything?" the waiter asked. Phoebe waved him off.

"But you handled Diana's ex pretty well, didn't you, Phoebe?" Brad asked. "Too bad that woman who died in Oxford couldn't put Alex down."

"I don't have any idea about that, Dr. Cummins. I wasn't there." Another lull followed.

The waiter returned with the receipt inside a black padded-leather folder and handed Brad a pen for signature.

"Thank you, sir, and we hope you'll come back to see us again at Babalu."

Once the waiter was out of earshot, Brad said, "Phoebe, since you're here, I need to ask you something."

"Brad?" Diana said.

"You wanna know this too, Diana," he answered. "How long have you been interested in bee keeping and EpiPens?"

Both women were silent.

"Well, Phoebe?" he asked.

"I haven't a clue what you're talking about."

"Diana and I had already checked the server of your laptop, the one hidden in the closet."

Phoebe looked away. "Winston was right," she mumbled.

"What was that?" Diana asked. "Winston was right about what?"

Phoebe inhaled deeply. She frowned and studied the wall as though to admire its piece of local art. The canvas was a collage of spattered red, orange, and black. "He told me that the two of you might be snooping around my house."

She grabbed her purse from the floor and stood, pushing the stool away from her.

"Wait, wait, don't leave!" Diana's voice carried halfway across the bar area despite the swarm of patrons sipping wine or longneck beer. The people nearest turned toward her for a few seconds, and then lost interest. Diana waved them off. *Sorry.*

"Sit back down, Aunt Phoebe, please. When did Winston Ivy tell you that?"

Phoebe held her purse firmly to her chest and remained standing.

Brad had continued his beer but stopped before the last of it. "Another thing—why did you leave the hospital the last time before the doctors released you?" he asked.

"Winston made me look up all that stuff for him on the computer. I had no idea what he was going to do with it." She stepped away from the table and almost backed into the one adjacent. The man seated closest turned annoyed and moved his chair. Phoebe looked in the direction of the door.

"I want to believe all of this, Aunt Phoebe, all of what you're telling us now," Diana said.

"Well, why don't you, Diana? Is it Dr. Cummins here who's putting all these questions in your head?"

Brad threw a *Who me?* expression at Diana.

Diana moved closer and whispered over the restaurant hum. "I found a letter, a letter written to you from Rusty Reynolds. It was in your basement inside one of the yearbooks."

"My, my. You really have been snooping around, Diana. I told you that Winston was jealous of Rusty. And what's more, it seems that he was correct about you. I can't even trust my own niece."

"Of course, you can trust me." Diana motioned to Brad. "And you can trust Brad ... completely."

The waiter returned. "Have y'all decided to stay for another round of drinks or more dessert?"

"No, we haven't, young man, and I still don't want anything," Phoebe said. "So why don't you pester someone else." The guy turned red in the face, shrugged, and walked off. He snapped his leather folder closed.

"Diana and Dr. Cummins, your policeman friend says he has his answers or his culprit, as they say. He's satisfied, and if he's satisfied that Winston killed Rusty and Marzel and that Alex had some hand in all of this, then you should be too." Phoebe turned and almost collided with the waiter, armed with a tray of small plates of chicken barbeque and glasses of wine.

"Damn you!" Phoebe scolded and pushed past him.

Brad and Diana watched her parade past the reception area and exit without looking back. "Diana, your mouth—close it," Brad said. "It's hanging wide open."

"Yours too," she said.

Several tables for two stood along the wall of windows at the far end of the bar where a male in a hooded parka sat with his back turned to Diana and Brad. He picked up his glass of Maker's and slid off his stool to maneuver through the drinkers, crowded tables, and busy servers, making his way toward Diana and Brad. Still mesmerized in the wake of Phoebe's drama, neither saw him approach.

"Mind if I take Phoebe's seat?" he asked. Alex Bratton's speech was not slurred or garbled, though his breath was stout with whiskey.

Brad said, "What's going on here, Bratton? Aren't you supposed to be ..."

"In South America, somewhere?" Alex answered. "Or maybe Canada? That's what Phoebe thinks and that's what you had to think."

Diana started to speak, but Alex put a finger to her lips.

"No, no, Diana, don't feel guilty for not telling our daughter that her dad might be dead since Phoebe claimed she stabbed me and I escaped to die somewhere." Alex sipped his drink. "And I guess I also should thank you for not telling Kelsey that her dad might have survived and be wanted for murder. You see, I called Kelsey after the scuffle and told her not to worry. I guess she doesn't tell her mom everything."

"Alex, of course, I'm relieved that you're OK … for Kelsey's sake … but I don't understand."

"Diana, go ahead and call Key Martin. He'll want to pick up this dirt bag."

"Sorry to disappoint you that I'm still around, Dr. Cummins," Alex said. "I can leave now or I can help you understand this. Which way is it, Diana?"

Diana rubbed her temples. "Go ahead, Alex. Talk."

"Winston was trying to protect Phoebe," he said. "Shit, I was trying to protect her. The woman couldn't keep her lies straight. She paid me to fake the attack on her."

"You know Winston Ivy?" Diana said.

"I think Winston really cared for your not-so-innocent aunt, the one you always considered so sweet and helpful. He always suspected that Rusty Reynolds had met with foul play but was sure when the body turned up." Another taste of his Maker's. "He assumed Phoebe responsible but wanted either to prove himself wrong, or if she did it let her expose herself. I was caught in the middle."

"That fight you had at Phoebe's … she said you attacked her," Diana said.

"Just part of the plan—her plan. I went against Winston on that, and I've already gone to the police."

"So that's what you meant with the line, *caught in the middle?*" Brad asked.

Alex directed his answer to Diana. "Phoebe wanted to play the victim—get the police off her back. She paid me to fake the attack and then leave town. It was supposed to be some random break-in. I didn't want to do it, but as you know already, Diana, I needed the money."

"When the police and paramedics arrived, Phoebe named you," Diana said. The waiter rebuked by Phoebe walked by, and Diana signaled for another glass of wine. "No, better make that a scotch."

"Answer me this, Bratton. When were you gonna fill Diana in on all of this?" Brad asked.

"That's what I meant earlier. Winston was pushing for the truth, and I could definitely see his side of things. He thought that the two of you were blindsided by loyalty to Phoebe."

Diana and Brad raised their eyes to each other: a flashback to the laptop in the closet and Phoebe with the hatpin over the unsuspecting Winston.

"Diana, I hate to go along with this jerk, but you were beginning to suspect Phoebe," Brad said.

Diana frowned. "I still cannot believe that she would hurt anybody … physically, much less murder someone."

Alex said, "Martin's got her fingerprints on the EpiPen and JPD has her laptop."

Brad shook his head. "Then Martin was just playing cat-and-mouse yesterday when Ivy was shot. He already had Phoebe's number."

The waiter arrived with Diana's scotch. She glanced up at him, her eyes watering. She smiled embarrassed and he left. "You two are playing this like some corny detective drama, like something from the thirties."

Diana took a long drink.

"Come on, Diana, play fair," Brad said. "Don't put me in the same sentence with this guy. You've suspected all along that something was up with Phoebe."

Diana ignored the clean cocktail napkin under her scotch, now half gone, and wiped her eyes with her sleeve. "I guess I didn't want to accept it. Besides Kelsey, Phoebe's the only thing left of family."

"There's hope for you yet," Alex said. "You and Pretty Boy Surgeon here look good together. Y'all outta mix it up and make it count—go ahead and spit out a couple of kids."

A flicker of blue light from Duling Avenue broke through at an angle, piercing the entrance windows. All three looked that way. "I guess they called in reinforcements," Alex said. "No surprise if your auntie put up an argument, a big one."

Diana took a fleeting look at Brad for support, for answers. Her antipathy for Alex Bratton, the father of her child, resurfaced whenever she heard his name, saw him in the flesh, or simply saw his picture or remembered anything about him. She wanted to know more of the young pharmacist and his true feelings for deceased wife Blythe, but unearthing an ounce of sincerity in Alex Bratton was hopeless.

Alex continued, "Martin asked me for a head's up if I ran across Phoebe—or you, Diana, for that matter. He figured that you and Phoebe would be in close proximity. I texted him the minute she showed up at Babalu."

The police lights had spread outside the windows. The diners closest stopped to look away from their meals, and several older elementary-aged children ran to the windows in excitement. The table conversations were easy to imagine.

"What's in this for you, Bratton?" Brad asked. The gruffness in his voice matched Diana's feelings. She wanted someone to hold her, comfort her, someone to tell her that the last several weeks had only been fiction.

"You must look for an angle in everything, Dr. Cummins, and maybe you're on target this time. It's no secret with Diana that my legal practice has stalled over the last few years. I'm sure she's shared that tidbit with you."

"Here it comes," Brad muttered to Diana, loud enough for Alex to hear.

"Martin has promised to give me an edge with the DA's office and the county prosecutor as court-appointed defender," Alex said. "All the slime bags moving through the system will guarantee a steady income."

"You're a leach, Alex, and a slime bag yourself," Diana said. "You've always been. And you're still drinking too much. I need to go outside and see what this is all about."

The waiter was back. "Sir, here's the tab you asked to be transferred from the bar to this table. Will you also be dining with us tonight?" he asked.

Alex produced a wallet and opened it. It was empty.

"You never can tell what this joker will be doing," Brad said to the waiter, then stood after Diana. "Here's a couple of Benjamins to cover everybody's tab, including the deadbeat's. This little group has been a handful for you tonight."

Outside the restaurant, the scene was not the chaos Diana anticipated: only one squad car parked in the undeveloped lot adjacent to the restaurant and the revolving lights extinguished. Key Martin spotted Diana and Brad and walked toward them. "We've got your aunt inside," he said. He cocked his head toward the police sedan. "We stopped her just as she was getting into her vehicle."

"Stopped her?" Diana asked. "Has she been arrested?"

"Looks like she was ready to skip town—several suitcases packed in the trunk and a rack of clothes in the back seat. A box labeled *FINE CHINA* is on the floorboard of her car. She says she's got several thousand cash in her purse."

"Your drunken buddy inside told Diana and me that he was cooperating with police," Brad said. "One drink more and he wouldn't have been able to text you. A real opportunist you've got there, Martin. He sure sunk Phoebe."

Diana's eyes watered more. She fought sobbing, grateful for the darkness. No one could see her tears, much less recognize her. "Can I see her, talk to her?"

"My detective is keeping her company," Martin answered. "She doesn't want to talk to anyone—gotta respect her for that."

"So we'll just have to visit Phoebe in jail, I guess," Brad said, "if we want answers."

"Brad! Please!" Diana slapped him on the upper chest with the back of her hand. "This can't be happening."

"I'm afraid it is," Martin said. "But there's more."

Brad took Diana's hand, the one that hit him. "Be honest with yourself. We didn't want this, but you've had your questions all along."

Diana was crying now. One part of her wanted Phoebe to hear her—to know how upset she was—the other part never wanted to see her again.

Alex slipped away from the waiter while the young man handled Brad's money. He exited through the main door and around the outdoor patio area toward the street, then called an Uber from his cell. He still had one of Phoebe's credit cards on file and figured it would still be good, at least for now. Incarceration for her crime was no reason to freeze assets. It wasn't narcotics nor tax evasion nor espionage. She was going down for murder.

Where is that fucking driver? Alex checked the Uber app again and the miniature pictures of a Middle Eastern-looking guy and a Ford Focus. *I should have upgraded.*

Couples and singles left the restaurant for their own vehicles—laughing, talking, happy—walking briskly past Alex. Happy was something he had missed for a very long time. He meant what he said about Diana and Brad Cummins. They made a hot-looking couple and would get on with their relationship with all this Phoebe shit behind them.

His back to the police car parked at a distance across the vacant lot, Alex smiled at the thought of Phoebe, the actress. She played her part all the way to the Academy Awards—believable, dramatic, and endearing at times. No movie director could have hoped for better. Phoebe's own search for answers into the deaths of her cronies at Ole Miss and her paranoia over what Diana may or may not have known damned her to hell.

Sooner or later Diana would quit worrying about Phoebe. She was too upper crust to be executed—too attractive, too refined, too white. Parchman Penitentiary was only a couple of hours north in the Delta, not far from where Phoebe grew-up and not too far away to visit. After a few months, maybe a year or so, Diana's obligation would lessen.

If not for his boring law professor at Ole Miss, he might be the one going to jail. "But I would have taken the needle for sure," Alex said.

"Excuse me?" A girl asked as she walked by. She pulled a cigarette from her handbag, and Alex waved her off. He lit his own cigarette, unaware that another squad car, this one from Lafayette County, had pulled in beside Martin.

Alex checked up and down Duling Avenue for the Uber and looked across to the grocery store parking lot. The app indicated that Omar, his driver, was still ten minutes away. He blew another cloud of smoke and thought more about that law professor. The guy spent a week of lecture dissecting a seventies hate crime. The victim had been gay.

During that era, law enforcement relied heavily on finger print analysis. The professor dodged detailed questions and discussion of that aspect of physical evidence presented at trial. His weakness in forensic science was glaring and an easy target for one-upmanship, particularly by a well-prepared, inquisitive student. Alex seized the opportunity and immersed himself in the study of fingerprint technology. The time spent on his own research, time better spent on assigned reading in other courses, earned a *4.0* in that class and near ruin for the rest of the semester's curriculum.

Regardless, he received a law degree, and Alex no longer regretted his mastering the art of lifting and transferring fingerprints. He decided it had been a good investment, a great investment.

Planting the EpiPen and linking it to Phoebe had been simple. With a key to her house and plenty of time, he collected Phoebe's prints from a kitchen drinking glass. The trick was transferring the impressions to the EpiPen. When Chief Martin finally utilized that evidence to link her to the death of Dewey Marzel, Alex was sure of his accuracy and took additional pleasure in duping the police.

What a score.

Near unlimited access to Phoebe's unsecured, personal laptop at her secret desk allowed him to set her up. He created an incriminating trail in the search engine—articles and more articles about bees and injectable pens containing the chemical epinephrine. The most damning post was one from four years ago, detailing the plight of a longtime beekeeper allergic to bee venom and caught with an expired pen. The short, slender man died in minutes. The article even included a photograph of the discolored fluid in the expired device matching that found with the body of Dewey Marzel.

Alex interspersed articles into Phoebe's computer search engine history about mixing bee venom into food—information gathered for his trial run at killing Dewey Marzel at the gym. Disguised in a black knit hat, sunglasses, and gym shorts, Alex watched from a plastic chair in the lobby with other students as Marzel enjoyed one of his peanut butter-bee venom cookies. Diana just missed him when he exited the front before class started.

Of course, the downside was Winston's death. That wasn't supposed to happen, but didn't cost him. He and Winston had a verbal agreement: fifty thousand cash paid in advance to frame Phoebe for the murder of Rusty Reynolds and another fifty each for the murders of that English teacher and Phoebe's neighbor—all could have incriminated Winston. When Carvel Eaves died of natural causes, the 50 grand was redirected to taking care of Reynold's sister even though Winston showed up in Oxford to assist.

There was no money earned for the pharmacist. That one was on him, and he wouldn't have done it if he had known Blythe was going to die. It was easy to fake that girl's suicide in her condo. She was stealing the pills anyway and was going to get caught sooner or later. *They never suspect the squeaky-clean ones, particularly the ones with good grades.*

In exchange for his cooperation in nabbing Phoebe, Martin had shared the official police report with him, detailing the struggle in Phoebe's closet when Winston was killed. There was no mention of a confession on Winston's part for the murder of Rusty Reynolds nor did he implicate Alex in the cover-up more than a half century later.

Alex never quite accepted Winton's motive for the murder of Rusty Reynolds in the fall of 1965. It was not, as he accused Winston, jealous rage over competing for Phoebe's affections. Winston stuck to the story of revenge against Reynolds for swindling him in a series of heated, crooked poker games. Eaves and Marzel were certain of stacked decks on more than one occasion and assisted Winston after he attacked and strangled Rusty in the student union. The night of the murder, the three smuggled the body stashed in the janitor's closet into the trunk of Winston's car and drove it to the wooded area at the west end of campus.

Winston slid his tight, dark leather face mask over Reynolds' head and each lit their cigarette lighter to torch Reynolds' jacket and leather pants. Winston admitted that all three gagged at the stench of the burning blond hair and light skin. Out of fear of attracting the University or Oxford Police with the smoke, they smothered the fire in the dry soil.

Their surprise years later: the flames burned long enough to sear and retract the skin against Rusty's lean muscle and bone, mummifying and preserving sections of the skeleton.

"Before long, they'll also pin Rusty Reynolds' murder on Phoebe,"

Alex said aloud to himself as the Uber drove up. "But no need to make waves." His phone indicated a change in the driver's vehicle. Instead of the Taurus, Omar arrived in a late model, light-colored Chevrolet Z-71 pick-up, shiny even in the dim street lights. Alex opened the door and matched the appearance of the driver to that shone on the app. "Proving Phoebe killed Reynolds is next on the list for that shithead Martin."

"You say something?" Omar asked.

"Nice wheels," Alex answered. "I should be able to afford one of these soon, once Uncle Winston's will clears probate. He left me everything."

Diana never met Winston Ivy at their wedding. Her own family was dwindling in numbers, and she didn't pay much attention to Alex's. If Uncle Winston had shown up to the reception on time, she might have gotten to know him and recognized him years later. Winston would have been more than Phoebe's mysterious college tryst. Things might have played out differently.

Alex double checked the screen ID. It was still a match. "How long you been driving this truck, Omar?"

"Only a couple of months. Doesn't take long for transplants to the South to want to drive trucks."

Alex tossed his cigarette to the pavement and stepped onto the running board. He lifted himself into the front passenger seat and ran his hand across the leather upholstery and the drink holders. He admired the carpeting and instrument panel, including the music system. He surveyed the rear seating area and strained to see the depth of the payload rear storage outside. "I'll have to get me one of these things," he said.

"New models coming out soon," Omar said and motioned for Alex to shut his door. "But price goes up every year. That's America."

"I should be able to handle it," Alex said. "I'm my uncle's only heir. I should be able to handle a lot of things."

"Handle this." A male voice pulled against Alex's door before it closed. The voice belonged to a black police officer pointing a gun at him.

"That's America," Omar repeated.

"Alex Bratton? Officer Corey Myers of the Oxford Police Department. Exit the vehicle. You're under arrest for the murder of Sylvia DeLoach."

Martin and Diana stood behind Corey. Brad was only a few steps back.

"Chief Martin just told me that they did find foreign DNA under Phoebe's fingernails," Diana said, "and it belongs to you. I guess you faked the struggle a little too well."

"So what? I explained that fight. She wanted it … to throw off suspicion," Alex said, staring into the barrel of the weapon.

"What is this going to do to Kelsey, Alex? Her father—a murderer."

Martin said, "The department played along with the aunt's involvement in the other crimes, Mr. Bratton, but new evidence implicating you in Oxford will put all that in question."

"Phoebe sure was playing the guilty part," Brad said, still at the rear.

"I told you guys what went down," Alex said, sliding out of the truck onto the pavement, hands raised. "I admitted the struggle with Phoebe; it was staged. You don't have anything."

"Your DNA is a match to that found under the nails of the murdered victim in Oxford," Corey answered. "Alex Bratton, turn around with your hands to the back."

"Officer Myers, let me do the honors with the handcuffs," Martin said. "Or would you like to give it a try, Dr. Bratton? You're good with instruments."

Also Available From:

WordCrafts Press

When Kings Clash
by J.E. Lowder

The Scavengers
by Mike Parker

Odd Man Outlaw
by K.M. Zahrt

Maggie's Refrain
by Marcia Ware

The Awakening of Leeowyn Blake
by Mary Parker

End of Summer
by Michael Potts

www.wordcrafts.net

CPSIA information can be obtained
at www.ICGtesting.com
Printed in the USA
FFOW04n0800270617
37179FF